PENGUIN BOOKS
Stand By Me

'This is the most complete – and the most powerful – vision of any American writer in my time. The stories of the Port William Membership are a delight, a goad, and a testament less to what was, than to what could be. They will leave no reader unmoved and unchanged' Bill McKibben

'The farmer-environmentalist's precisely drawn tales about family loyalties span a century of rural life . . . after reading *Stand By Me*, I get it' Jane Smiley, *Guardian*

'In a series of eighteen linked stories, Berry describes everyday life in Port William, and the gradual erosion of its farming community' John Burnside, *Spectator*

'Like Denis Johnson, Marilynne Robinson or Seamus Heaney, Wendell Berry shows us that sometimes looking deeply into one world can become a profound way of looking at the whole world' Barney Norris, author of *Five Rivers Met on a Wooded Plain*

'What unites [these stories] is a deep humanity, compassion and a sense of recognition that our modern lives unfolded at some point on Earth from stories such as these' *Seattle Times*

'A masterpiece . . . Like Isaac Bashevis Singer, Berry has been expanding by contraction, husbanding by close focus – in Berry's case, on the familiar demesne of Port William, Kentucky . . . Berry moves way beyond nostalgia toward an immersion in other lives that expresses itself as a sense of intimate apartness; a willingness to follow his characters, but not necessarily to change them. Poetry nestled inside prose: startlingly and classically moving' *Kirkus Reviews*

'Berry is the master of earthy country living seen through the eyes of laconic farmers ... . He makes his stories shine with meaning and warmth' *Christian Science Monitor*

'No writer has written of a place better or more completely than Wendell Berry has written of Port William' *Arkansas Democrat Gazette*

'Wendell Berry writes with a good husbandman's care and economy . . . His stories are filled with gentle humour'
The New York Times Book Review

'Wendell Berry gives us an intimate portrayal of the mind and heart of rural America. His graceful prose is truthful and eloquent. His tone is reliable and steady, like a good rain, sober and serious – all this and at times he is so funny you have to stop and roll on the floor' Bobbie Ann Mason

'Berry is a thought-provoking writer who uses humour and sorrow to evoke memorable characters, atmosphere and setting' Brian Maye, *Irish Times*

'The stories express a biblical reverence for life and community, yet they're funny, too, and so beautiful' *Booklist*

'Quite simply, Wendell Berry is one of the greatest writers of our times. Somehow he manages to spin out a universe from the most intricate dust. His work is a marvel of feeling and thought' Colum McCann

ABOUT THE AUTHOR

'A farmer of sorts and an artist of sorts,' Wendell Berry is the author of more than fifty books of poetry, fiction and essays. He has received fellowships from the Guggenheim, Lannan, and Rockefeller foundations and from the National Endowment for the Arts, and also the Dayton Literary Peace Prize, the Cleanth Brooks Medal for Lifetime Achievement, and the National Humanities Medal. For more than forty years, he has lived and farmed in his native Henry County, Kentucky, with his wife, Tanya, and their children and grandchildren.

Stand By Me

WENDELL BERRY

PENGUIN BOOKS

PENGUIN BOOKS

UK | USA | Canada | Ireland | Australia
India | New Zealand | South Africa

Penguin Books is part of the Penguin Random House group of companies
whose addresses can be found at global.penguinrandomhouse.com

First published by Allen Lane 2019
Published in Penguin Books 2020

004

This collection copyright © Wendell Berry, 2019
The acknowledgements on p. 387 constitute an extension of this copyright page

Typeset by Jouve (UK), Milton Keynes
Printed and bound in Great Britain by Clays Ltd, Elcograf S.p.A.

A CIP catalogue record for this book is available from the British Library

ISBN: 978–0–141–99024–8

www.greenpenguin.co.uk

MIX
Paper from
responsible sources
FSC® C018179

Penguin Random House is committed to a
sustainable future for our business, our readers
and our planet. This book is made from Forest
Stewardship Council® certified paper.

Contents

Contents

The Hurt Man
(1888)

When he was five Mat Feltner, like every other five-year-old who had lived in Port William until then, was still wearing dresses. In his own thoughts he was not yet sure whether he would turn out to be a girl or a boy, though instinct by then had prompted him to take his place near the tail end of the procession of Port William boys. His nearest predecessors in that so far immortal straggle had already taught him the small art of smoking cigars, along with the corollary small art of chewing coffee beans to take the smoke smell off his breath. And so in a rudimentary way he was an outlaw, though he did not know it, for none of his grown-ups had yet thought to forbid him to smoke.

His outgrown dresses he saw worn daily by a pretty neighbor named Margaret Finley, who to him might as well have been another boy too little to be of interest, or maybe even a girl, though it hardly mattered – and though, because of a different instinct, she would begin to matter to him a great deal in a dozen years, and after that she would matter to him all his life.

The town of Port William consisted of two rows of casually maintained dwellings and other buildings scattered along a thoroughfare that nobody had ever dignified by calling it a street; in wet times it hardly deserved to be called a road. Between the town's two ends the road was unevenly rocked, but otherwise had not much distinguished itself from the buffalo trace it once had been. At one end of the town was the school, at the other the graveyard. In the center there were several stores, two saloons, a church, a bank, a hotel, and a blacksmith shop. The town was the product of its own becoming, which, if not accidental exactly, had also been unplanned. It had no formal government or formal history. It was without pretense or ambition, for it was the sort of place that pretentious or ambitious people were inclined to leave. It had never declared an aspiration to become anything it was not. It did not thrive so much as it merely lived, doing the things it needed to do to stay alive. This tracked and rubbed little settlement had been built in a place of great natural abundance and beauty, which it had never valued highly enough or used well enough, had damaged, and yet had not destroyed. The town's several buildings, shaped less by art than by need and use, had suffered tellingly and even becomingly a hundred years of wear.

Though Port William sat on a ridge of the upland, still it was a river town; its economy and its thoughts turned toward the river. Distance impinged on it from the river, whose waters flowed from the eastward mountains ultimately, as the town always was more or less aware, to the sea, to the world. Its horizon, narrow enough though it reached across the valley to the ridgeland fields and farmsteads on the other side, was pierced by the river, which for the next forty years would still be its main thoroughfare. Commercial people, medicine showmen, evangelists, and other river travelers came up the hill from Dawes Landing to stay at the hotel in Port William, which in its way cherished these transients, learned all it could about them, and talked of what it learned.

Mat would remember the town's then-oldest man, Uncle Bishop Bower, who would confront any stranger, rap on the ground with his long staff, and demand, 'Sir! What might your name be?'

And Herman Goslin, no genius, made his scant living by meeting the steamboats and transporting the disembarking passengers, if any, up to the hotel in a gimpy buckboard. One evening as he approached the hotel with a small trunk on his shoulder, followed by a large woman with a parasol, one of the boys playing marbles in the road said, 'Here comes Herman Goslin with a fat lady's trunk.'

'You boys can kiss that fat lady's ass,' said Herman Goslin. 'Ain't that tellin 'em, fat lady?'

The town was not built nearer the river perhaps because there was no room for it at the foot of the hill, or perhaps because, as the town loved to reply to the inevitable question from travelers resting on the hotel porch, nobody knew where the river was going to run when they built Port William.

And Port William did look as though it had been itself forever. To Mat at the age of five, as he later would suppose, remembering himself, it must have seemed eternal, like the sky.

However eternal it might have been, the town was also as temporal, lively, and mortal as it possibly could be. It stirred and hummed from early to late with its own life and with the life it drew into itself from the countryside. It was a center, and especially on Saturdays and election days its stores and saloons and the road itself would be crowded with people standing, sitting, talking, whittling, trading, and milling about. This crowd was entirely familiar to itself; it remembered all its history of allegiances, offenses, and resentments, going back from the previous Saturday to the Civil War and long before that. Like every place, it had its angers, and its angers as always, as everywhere, found justifications. And in Port William, a dozen miles by river from the courthouse and the rule of law, anger had a license that it might not have had in another place.

Sometimes violence would break out in one of the saloons or in the road. Then proof of mortality would be given in blood.

And the mortality lived and suffered daily in the town was attested with hopes of immortality by the headstones up in the graveyard, which was even then more populous than the town. Mat knew – at the age of five he had already forgotten when he had found out – that he had a brother and two sisters up there, with carved lambs resting on the tops of their small monuments, their brief lives dated beneath. In all the time he had known her, his mother had worn black.

But to him, when he was five, those deaths were stories told. Nothing in Port William seemed to him to be in passage from any beginning to any end. The living had always been alive, the dead always dead. The world, as he knew it then, simply existed, familiar even in its changes: the town, the farms, the slopes and ridges, the woods, the river, and the sky over it all. He had not yet gone farther from Port William than to Dawes Landing on the river and to his Uncle Jack Beecham's place out on the Bird's Branch Road, the place his mother spoke of as 'out home'. He had seen the steamboats on the river and had looked out from the higher ridgetops, and so he understood that the world went on into the distance, but he did not know how much more of it there might be.

Mat had come late into the lives of Nancy and Ben Feltner, after the deaths of their other children, and he had come unexpectedly, 'a blessing'. They prized him accordingly. For the first four or so years of his life he was closely watched, by his parents and also by Cass and Smoke, Cass's husband, who had been slaves. But now he was five, and it was a household always busy with the work of the place, and often full of company. There had come to be times, because his grown-ups were occupied and he was curious and active, when he would be out of their sight. He would stray off to where something was happening, to the farm buildings behind the house, to the blacksmith shop, to one of the saloons, to wherever the other boys were. He was beginning his long study of the town and its place in the world, gathering up the stories that in years still far off he would hand on to his grandson Andy Catlett, who in his turn would be trying to master the thought of time: that there were times before his time, and would be times after. At the age of five Mat was beginning to prepare himself to help in educating his grandson, though he did not know it.

His grown-ups, more or less willingly, were letting him go. The town had its dangers. There were always horses in the road, and sometimes droves of cattle or sheep or hogs or mules. There were in fact uncountable ways for a boy to get hurt, or worse. But in spite of her losses, Nancy Beechum Feltner was not a frightened woman, as her son would learn. He would learn also that, though she maintained her sorrows with a certain loyalty, wearing her black, she was a woman of practical good sense and strong cheerfulness. She knew that the world was risky and that she must risk her surviving child to it as she had risked the others, and when the time came she straightforwardly did so.

But she knew also that the town had its ways of looking after its own. Where its worst dangers were, grown-ups were apt to be. When Mat was out of the sight of her or his father or Cass or Smoke, he was most likely in the sight of somebody else who would watch him. He would thus be corrected, consciously ignored, snatched out of danger, cursed, teased, hugged, instructed, spanked, or sent home by any grown-up into whose sight he may have strayed. Within that watchfulness he was free – and almost totally free when, later, he had learned to escape it and thus had earned his freedom. This was a *free* country when I was a boy,' he would sometimes say to Andy, his grandson.

When he was five and for some while afterward, his mother drew the line unalterably only between him and the crowds that filled the town on Saturday afternoons and election days when there would be too much drinking, with consequences that were too probable. She would not leave him alone then. She would not let him go into the town, and she would not trust him to go anywhere else, for fear that he would escape into the town from wherever else she let him go. She kept him in sight.

That was why they were sitting together on the front porch for the sake of the breeze there on a hot Saturday afternoon in the late summer of 1888. Mat was sitting close to his mother on the wicker settee, watching her work. She had brought out her sewing basket and was darning socks, stretching the worn-through heels or toes over her darning egg and weaving them whole again with her needle and thread. At such work her fingers moved with a quickness and assurance that fascinated Mat, and he loved to watch her. She would have been telling him a story. She was full of stories. Aside from the small movements of her hands and the sound of her voice, they were quiet with a quietness that seemed to have increased as it had grown upon them. Cass had gone home after the dinner dishes were done. The afternoon had half gone by.

From where they sat they could see down into the town where the Saturday crowd was, and they could hear it. Doors slammed, now and then a horse nickered, the talking of the people was a sustained murmur from which now and then a few intelligible words escaped: a greeting, some bit of raillery, a reprimand to a horse, an oath. It was a large crowd in a small place, a situation in which a small disagreement could become dangerous in a hurry. Such things had happened often enough. That was why Mat was under watch.

And so when a part of the crowd intensified into a knot, voices were raised, and there was a scuffle, Mat and his mother were not surprised. They were not surprised even when a bloodied man broke out of the crowd and began running fast up the street toward them, followed by other running men whose boot heels pounded on the road.

The hurt man ran toward them where they were sitting on the porch. He was hatless. His hair, face, and shirt were bloody, and his blood dripped on the road. Mat felt no intimation of threat or danger. He simply watched, transfixed. He did not see his mother stand and put down her work. When she caught him by the back of his dress and fairly poked him through the front door – 'Here! Get inside!' – he still was only alert, unsurprised.

He expected her to come into the house with him. What finally surprised him was that she did not do so. Leaving him alone in the wide hall, she remained outside the door, holding it open for the hurt man. Mat ran halfway up the stairs then and turned and sat down on a step. He was surprised now but not afraid.

When the hurt man ran in through the door, instead of following him in, Nancy Feltner shut the door and stood in front of it. Mat could see her through the door glass, standing with her hand on the knob as the clutch of booted and hatted pursuers came up the porch steps. They bunched at the top of the steps, utterly stopped by the slender woman dressed in mourning, holding the door shut.

And then one of them, snatching off his hat, said, 'It's all right, Mrs Feltner. We're his friends.'

She hesitated a moment, studying them, and then she opened the door to them also and turned and came in ahead of them.

The hurt man had run the length of the hall and through the door at the end of it and out onto the back porch. Nancy, with the bunch of men behind her, followed where he had gone, the men almost with delicacy, as it seemed to Mat, avoiding the line of blood drops along the hall floor. And Mat hurried back down the stairs and came along in his usual place at the tail end, trying to see, among the booted legs and carried hats, what had become of the hurt man.

Mat's memory of that day would always be partly incomplete. He never knew who the hurt man was. He knew some of the others. The hurt man had sat down or dropped onto a slatted green bench on the porch. He might have remained nameless to Mat because of the entire strangeness of the look of him. He had shed the look of a man and assumed somehow the look of all things badly hurt. Now that he had stopped running, he looked used up. He was pallid beneath the streaked bright blood, breathing in gasps, his eyes too widely open. He looked as though he had just come up from almost too deep a dive.

Nancy went straight to him, the men, the friends, clustered behind her, deferring, no longer to her authority as the woman of the house, as when she had stopped them at the front door, but now to her unhesitating, unthinking acceptance of that authority.

Looking at the hurt man, whose blood was dripping onto the bench and the porch floor, she said quietly, perhaps only to herself, 'Oh my!' It was as though she knew him without ever having known him before.

She leaned and picked up one of his hands. 'Listen!' she said, and the man brought his gaze it seemed from nowhere and looked up at her. 'You're at Ben Feltner's house,' she said. 'Your friends are here. You're going to be all right.'

She looked around at the rest of them who were standing back, watching her. 'Jessie, you and Tom go see if you can find the doctor, if he's findable.' She glanced at the water bucket on the shelf over the wash table by the kitchen door, remembering that it was nearly empty. 'Les, go bring a fresh bucket of water.' To the remaining two she said, 'Get his shirt off. Cut it off. Don't try to drag it over his head. So we can see where he's hurt.'

She stepped through the kitchen door, and they could hear her going about inside. Presently she came back with a kettle of water still warm from the noon fire and a bundle of clean rags.

'Look up here,' she said to the hurt man, and he looked up.

She began gently to wash his face. Wherever he was bleeding, she washed away the blood: first his face, and then his arms, and then his chest and sides. As she washed, exposing the man's wounds, she said softly only to herself, 'Oh!' or 'Oh my!' She folded the white rags into pads and instructed the hurt man and his friends to press them onto his cuts to stop the bleeding. She said, 'It's the Lord's own mercy we've got so many hands,' for the man had many wounds. He had begun to tremble. She kept saying to him, as she would have spoken to a child, 'You're going to be all right.'

Mat had been surprised when she did not follow him into the house, when she waited on the porch and opened the door to the hurt man and then to his friends. But she had not surprised him after that. He saw her as he had known her: a woman who did what the world put before her to do.

At first he stayed well back, for he did not want to be told to get out of the way. But as his mother made order, he grew bolder and drew gradually closer until he was almost at her side. And then he was again surprised, for then he saw her face.

What he saw in her face would remain with him forever. It was pity, but it was more than that. It was a hurt love that seemed to include entirely the hurt man. It included him and disregarded everything else. It disregarded the aura of whiskey that ordinarily she would have resented; it disregarded the blood puddled on the porch floor and the trail of blood through the hall.

Mat was familiar with her tenderness and had thought nothing of it. But now he recognized it in her face and in her hands as they went out to the hurt man's wounds. To him, then, it was as though she leaned in the black of her mourning over the whole hurt world itself, touching its wounds with her tenderness, in her sorrow.

Loss came into his mind then, and he knew what he was years away from telling, even from thinking: that his mother's grief was real; that her children in their graves once had been alive; that everybody lying under the grass up in the graveyard once had been alive and had walked in daylight in Port William. And this was a part, and belonged to the deliverance, of the town's hard history of love.

The hurt man, Mat thought, was not going to die, but he knew from his mother's face that the man *could* die and someday would. She leaned over him, touching his bleeding wounds that she bathed and stanched and bound, and her touch had in it the promise of healing, some profound encouragement.

It was the knowledge of that encouragement, of what it had cost her, of what it would cost her and would cost him, that then finally came to Mat, and he fled away and wept.

What did he learn from his mother that day? He learned it all his life. There are few words for it, perhaps none. After that, her losses would be his. The losses would come. They would come to him and his mother. They would come to him and Margaret, his wife, who as a child had worn his cast-off dresses. They would come, even as Mat watched, growing old, to his grandson, Andy, who would remember his stories and write them down.

But from that day, whatever happened, there was a knowledge in Mat that was unsurprised and at last comforted, until he was old, until he was gone.

Fly Away, Breath
(1907)

Andy Catlett keeps in his mind a map of the country around Port William as he has known it all his life and as he has been told about it all his life from times and lives before his. There are moments, now that he is getting old, when he seems to reside in that country in his mind even as his mind still resides in the country.

This is the country of his own life and history, fragmentary as they necessarily have been. It is his known country. And perhaps it differs also from the actual, momentary country insofar as time is one of its dimensions, as reckonable in thought as length and breadth, as air and light. His thought can travel like a breeze over water back and forth upon the face of it, and also back and forth in time along its streams and roads.

As in thought he passes backward into time, the country becomes quieter, and it seems to grow larger. The sounds of engines become less frequent and farther apart until finally they cease altogether. As the roads get poorer or disappear, the distances between places seem to grow longer. Distances that he can now travel in minutes in an automobile once would have taken hours and much effort.

But it is possible, even so, to look back with a certain fondness to a time when the sounds of engines were not almost constant in the sky, on the roads, and in the fields. Our descendants may know such a time again when the petroleum all is burnt. How they will fare then will depend on the neighborly wisdom, the love for the place and its genius, and the skills that they may manage to revive between now and then.

The country in Andy Catlett's mind has assuredly a past, which exists in relics and scraps of memory more or less subject to proof. It has presumably a future that will verify itself only by becoming the past. Its present is somewhat conjectural, for old Andy Catlett, like everybody else, cannot be conscious of the present while he is thinking of the past. And most of us, most of the time, think mostly of the past. Even when we say, 'We are living now', we can mean only that we were living a moment ago.

Nevertheless, in this sometimes horrifying, sometimes satisfying, never-sufficiently-noticed present, between a past mostly forgotten and a future that we deserve to fear but cannot predict, some few things can be recalled.

In all the country from Port William to the river, one light shines. It is from a flame on the wick of an oil lamp, turned low, on a little stand table at the bedside of Maximilla Dawe in a large unpainted house facing the river in Glenn's Bottom between Catlett's Fork and Bird's Branch. The old lady lies somewhat formally upon the bed, seemingly asleep, in a long-sleeved flannel nightgown, clean but not new, the covers laid neatly over her. Her arms lie at her sides, the veined and gnarled old hands at rest. She is propped, in the appearance at least of comfort, on several pillows, for she is so bent by age and work that she could not lie flat.

She has been old a long time. Though 'Maximilla' was inscribed in her father's will, by which he left her the farm in the river bottom, the family of 'the slave woman known as Cat', and his stopped gold watch, and though it was signed in her own hand at the end of two or three legal documents, she was never well known even to herself by that name. Once upon a time she was 'Maxie' – 'Miss Maxie' to the Negroes and some whites. For at least as long, to herself as to all the neighborhood of Port William, she has been 'Aunt Maxie'. To her granddaughter, who was Andy Catlett's grandmother, she had always been 'Granny Dawe', as to Andy she still is known.

Andy's grandmother, born Margaret Finley, now Margaret Feltner, sits by the bedside of Granny Dawe in that room in the dim lamplight in the broad darkness of the river valley in the fall of 1907, a hundred years ago. Margaret Feltner is a pretty woman – or girl, as the older women still would have called her – with a peculiar air of modesty, for she knows she is pretty but would prefer not to be caught knowing it. She is slenderly formed and neatly dressed, even prettily dressed, for her modesty must contend also with her knowledge that her looks are pleasing to Mat Feltner, her young husband.

With her are three other young women, also granddaughters of the old woman on the bed. They are Bernice Gibbs, and Oma and Callie Knole. Kinswomen who know one another well, they sit close together, leaving a sort of aisle between their chairs and the bed.

Their voices are low, and their conversation has become more and more intermittent as the night has gone on. The ancient woman on the bed breathes audibly, but slowly too and tentatively, so that they who listen even as they talk are aware that at any moment there may be one more breath, and then no more.

But she is dying in no haste, this Aunt Maxie, this Granny Dawe, who lived and worked so long before she began to die that she was the only one alive who still knew what she had known. She was born in 1814 in the log house that long ago was replaced by the one in which she now is dying. At the time of her birth, the Port William neighborhood was still in its dream of itself as a frontier, 'the West', a new land. The chief artery of trade and transportation for that part of the country then was the river, as it would be for the next hundred years. When the time came, she bestowed her land, her slaves, and herself upon a man named James John Dawe, whose worldly fortune consisted of a singular knack for trade and the store and landing, the port of Port William, known as Dawe's Landing. He left the care of the farm to her. With the strength and the will and the determined good sense that have kept the farm and household in her own hands until now, she ruled and she served through times that were mostly hard.

The Civil War had its official realization in movements of armies and great battles in certain places, but in places such as Port William it released and licensed an unofficial violence also terrible, and more lasting. At its outset, Galen Dawe, on his way to join the Confederate army, was shot from his horse and left dead in the road, no farther on his way than Port William, by a neighbor, a Union sympathizer, with whom he had quarreled. And Maxie Dawe, with the help of a slave man named Punkin, loaded the dead boy onto a sled drawn by a team of mules. Looking neither right nor left at those who watched, she brought home the mortal body of her one son, which she washed and dressed herself, and herself read the great psalm over him as he lay in his grave.

The rest of her children were daughters, four of them. Her grief and her bearing in her grief gave her a sort of headship over daughters and husband that they granted without her ever requiring it. When a certain superiority to suffering, a certain indomitability, was required, she was the one who had it. Later, when a band of self-denominated 'Rebel' cavalry hung about the neighborhood, she saved her husband, the capable merchant James John, from forcible recruitment or murder, they never knew which, by hiding him three weeks in a succession of corn shocks, carrying food and water to him after dark. By her cunning and sometimes her desperate bravery, she brought her surviving family, her slaves, and even a few head of livestock through the official and the unofficial wars, only to bury her husband, dead of a fever, at the end of the official one.

When the slaves were freed in Kentucky, when at last she had heard, she gathered those who had been her own into the kitchen. She told them: 'Slavery is no more, and you are free. If you wish to stay and share our fate, you are free to stay, and I will divide with you as I can. If you wish to go, you are free to go.'

There were six of them, the remaining family of the woman known as Cat, and they left the next morning, taking, each of them, what could be carried bundled in one hand, all of them invested with an official permission that had made them strange to everything that had gone before. They left, perhaps, from no antipathy to staying, for they arrived in Hargrave and lived there under the name of Dawe – but how could they have known they were free to go if they had not gone? Or so, later, Maxie Dawe would explain it, and she would add, 'And so would I have, had it been me.'

She and her place never recovered from the war. Unable to manage it herself, and needing money, she sold the landing. She hired what help she could afford. She rented her croplands on the shares. After her daughters married and went away, she stayed on alone. To her young granddaughters, and probably to herself as well, the world of the first half of her life was another world.

No more would she be 'Maxie' to anybody. Increasingly she

would be 'Aunt Maxie'. She was respected. By those who lacked the sense to respect her she was feared. She held herself strictly answerable to her necessities. She worked in the fields as in the house. Strange and doubtful stories were told about her, all of them perhaps true. She was said to have shot off a man's ear, only his ear, so he would live to tell it.

And now her long life, so strongly determined or so determinedly accepted by her, has at last submitted. It is declining gently, perhaps willingly, toward its end. It has been nearly a day and now most of a night since she uttered a word or opened her eyes. A younger person so suddenly moribund as she would have been dead long ago. But she seems only asleep, her aspect that of a dreamer enthralled. The two vertical creases between her brows suggest that she is raptly attentive to her dream.

That she is dying, she herself knows, or knew, for early in the morning of the previous day, not long before she fell into her present sleep, her voice, to those who bent to listen, seeming to float above the absolute stillness of her body, and with the tone perhaps of a small exasperation, she said, 'Well, if this is dying, I've seen living that was worse.'

The night began cloudy, and the clouds have deepened over the valley and the old house with its one light. The first frosts have come, hushing the crickets and the katydids. The country seems to be waiting. At about dawn a season-changing rain will begin so quietly that at first nobody will notice, and it will fall without letup for two days.

When midnight passes through the room, nobody knows, neither the old woman on the bed nor the young ones who watch beside it. The room would seem poor, so meager and worn are its furnishings, except that its high ceiling and fine proportions give it a dignity that in the circumstances is austere. Though the night is not quite chilly, the sternness of the room and the presence of death in it seemed to call for additional warmth, and the young wives have kindled a little fire. From time to time, one or another has risen to take from the stone hearth a stick of wood and lay it on the coals. From time to time, one or another has risen to smooth the bedclothes that need no smoothing, or to lay a hand upon the old woman's forehead, or to touch lightly the pulse fluttering at her wrist.

After midnight, stillness grows upon them all. The talk has stopped, the fire subsided to a glow, when Bernice Gibbs raises her hand and the others look at her. Bernice is the oldest of the four. The others have granted her an authority which, like their grandmother perhaps, she has accepted merely because she has it and the others don't. She looks at each of them and looks away, listening.

They listen, and they hear not a sound. They hear instead a silence that reaches into every room and into the expectant night beyond. They rise from their chairs, first Bernice, and then, hesitantly, the others. They tiptoe to the bed, two to a side, and lean, listening, at that edge which they and all their children too have now passed beyond. The silence grows palpable around them, a weight.

Now, as Andy Catlett imagines his way into this memory that is his own only because he has imagined it, he is never quite prepared for what he knows to have happened next. Always it comes to him somewhat by surprise, as it came to those who remembered it from the actual room and the actual night.

In silence that seems to them utterly conclusive, the young women lean above the body of the old woman, the mold in which their own flesh was cast, and they listen. And then, just when one of them might have been ready to say, 'She's gone,' the old woman releases with a sigh her held breath: 'Hooo!'

They startle backward from the bedside, each seeing in the wide-opened mouths and eyes of the others her own fright. Oma Knole, who is clumsy, strikes the lamp and it totters until Bernice catches and steadies it.

They stand now and look at one another. The silence has changed. The dying woman's utterance, brief as it was, spoke of a great weariness. It was the sigh of one who has been kept waiting. The sound hangs in the air as if visible, as if the lamp flame had flown upward from the wick. It stays, nothing moves, until some lattice of the air lets pass the single distant cry of an owl – 'Hoo!' – as if in answer.

Callie Knole turns away, bends forward, and emits what, so hard suppressed, might have been a sob, but it is a laugh.

And then they all laugh, at themselves, at one another, and they cannot stop. Their sense of the impropriety of their laughter renews their laughter. Looking at each other, flushed and wet-eyed with laughter, makes them laugh. They laugh because they are young and they are alive, and life has revealed itself to them, as it often had and often would, by surprise.

Margaret Feltner, when she had become an old woman, 'Granny' in her turn, told Andy of this a long time ago. 'Oh, it was awful!' she said, again laughing. 'But the harder we tried to stop, the funnier it was.'

And Andy, a hundred years later, can hear their laughter. He hears also the silence in which they laugh: the ancient silence filling the dark river valley on that night, uninterrupted in his imagination still by the noise of engines, the great quiet into which they all have gone.

*

The laughter, which threatened to be endless, finally ends and is gathered into the darkness, into the past. The night resumes its solemn immensity, and again in the silence the old woman audibly breathes. But now her breaths come at longer intervals, until the definitive quiet settles upon her at last. They who have watched all night then fold her hands. Her mouth has fallen open, and Bernice thinks to bind it shut. They draw the counterpane over her face. Day whitens again over the old house and its clutch of old buildings. As they sit on in determined noiselessness, it comes to the young women that for some time they have been hearing the rain.

A Consent
(1908)
For my friends at Monterey, Kentucky

Ptolemy Proudfoot was nothing if not a farmer. His work was farming, his study and passion were farming, his pleasures and his social life occurred in the intervals between farm jobs and in the jobs themselves. He was not an ambitious farmer – he did not propose to own a large acreage or to become rich – but merely a good and a gifted one. By the time he was twenty-five, he had managed, in spite of the hard times of the 1890s, to make a down payment on the little farm that he husbanded and improved all his life. It was a farm of ninety-eight acres, and Tol never longed even for the two more that would have made it a hundred.

Of pleasures and social life, he had a plenty. The Proudfoots were a large, exuberant clan of large people, though by my time Tol was the last one of them in the Port William neighborhood, and Tol was childless. The Proudfoots were not, if they could help it, solitary workers. They swapped work among themselves and with their neighbors, and their workdays involved a mighty dinner at noontime, much talk and laughter, and much incidental sport.

As an after-dinner amusement and aid to digestion, the Proudfoot big boys and young men would often outline a square or a circle on the ground, and get into it and wrestle. Everybody wrestled with everybody, for the object was to see who would be the last one in the ring. The manpower involved might better have been rated as horsepower, and great feats of strength were accomplished. Now and again great physical damage was accomplished, as when, for example, one Proudfoot would endeavor to throw another Proudfoot out of the ring through the trunk of a large tree. Sometimes, after failing to make headway through a tree trunk or barn door, a Proudfoot would lie very still on the ground for several minutes before he could get up. Sometimes, one Proudfoot or another would be unable to go back to work in the afternoon. These contests would be accompanied by much grunting, and by more laughter, as the Proudfoots were hard to anger. For a Proudfoot boy to become big enough and brave enough finally to set foot in that ring was a rite of passage. For a Proudfoot to stand alone in that ring – as Tol did finally, and then often did – was to know a kind of triumph and a kind of glory. Tol was big even for a Proudfoot, and the others could seldom take him off his feet. He tumbled them out, ass over elbows, one by one, in a manner more workmanly than violent, laughing all the time.

Tol was overabundant in both size and strength. And perhaps because animate creatures tended to get out of his way, he paid not much attention to himself. He damaged his clothes just by being in them, as though surprising them by an assortment of stresses and strains for which they had not been adequately prepared. The people around Port William respected Tol as a farmer; they loved to tell and retell and hear and hear again the tales of his great strength; they were amused by the looks of him, by his good humor, and by his outsized fumblings and foibles. But never, for a long time, would any of them have suspected that his great bulk might embody tender feelings.

But Tol did embody tender feelings, and very powerful tender feelings they were. For Tol, through many years, had maintained somewhere about the center of himself a most noble and humble and never-mentioned admiration for Miss Minnie Quinch. Miss Minnie was as small and quick as Tol was big and lumbering. Like him, she was a Port Williamite. She had taught for many years at Goforth School, grades one through eight, which served the neighborhood of Katy's Branch and Cotman Ridge in which Tol's farm lay. When she was hardly more than a girl, Miss Minnie had gone away to a teacher's college and prepared herself to teach by learning many cunning methods that she never afterward used. For Miss Minnie loved children and she loved books, and she taught merely by introducing the one to the other. When she had trouble with one of the rougher big boys, she went straight to that boy's father and required that measures be taken. And measures usually were taken, so surprisingly direct and demanding was that lady's gaze.

For as many years as Miss Minnie had taught at Goforth School, Tol had admired her from a distance, and without ever looking directly at her when she might have been about to look directly at him. He thought she was the finest, prettiest, nicest little woman he had ever seen. He praised her to himself by saying, 'She's just a pocket-size pretty little thing.' But he was sure that she would never want to be around a big, rough, unschooled fellow like himself.

Miss Minnie did, from time to time, look directly at Tol, but not ever when he might have been about to look directly at her. More than once she thought rather wistfully that so large and strong a man as Tol ought to be some woman's knight and protector. She was, in fact, somewhat concerned about him, for he was thirty-six, well past the age when men usually got married. That she herself was thirty-four and unmarried was something she also thought from time to time, but always in a different thought. She kept her concern about Tol limited very strictly to concern, for she was conscious of being a small person unable even to hope to arrest the gaze of so splendid a man.

For years, because of mutual avoidance of each other's direct gaze, their paths did not cross. Although they met and passed, they did not do so in a way that required more than a polite nod, which they both accomplished with a seriousness amounting almost to solemnity. And then one morning in Port William, Tol came out of Beater Chatham's store directly face-to-face with Miss Minnie who was coming in, and who smiled at him before she could think and said, 'Well, good morning, Mr Proudfoot!'

Tol's mouth opened, but nothing came out of it. Nothing at all. This was unusual, for Tol, when he felt like it, was a talkative man. He kept walking because he was already walking, but for several yards he got along without any assistance from his faculties. Sight and sense did not return to him until he had walked with some force into the tailgate of his wagon.

All the rest of that day he went about his work in a somewhat visionary state, saying to himself, and to the surprise of his horses and his dog, 'Good morning, mam!' and 'How do you do, Miss Minnie?' Once he even brought himself to say, bowing slightly and removing his hat, 'And a good morning to you, little lady.'

And soon, as if they had at last come into each other's orbit, they met face-to-face again. It was a fine fall afternoon, and Tol happened to be driving down past Goforth School, slowing his team, of course, so as not to disturb the concentration of the scholars inside. Miss Minnie was standing by the pump in front of the schoolhouse, her figure making a neat blue silhouette against the dingy weatherboarding.

Again she smiled at him. She said, 'How do you do, Mr Proudfoot?'

And Tol startled at the sound of her voice as if he had not seen her there at all. He could not remember one of the pleasantries he had invented to say to her. He looked intently into the sky ahead of him and said quickly as if he had received a threat, 'Why, howdy!'

The conversation thus established was a poor thing, Tol knew, so far as his own participation in it went, but it was something to go on. It gave him hope. And now I want to tell you how this courtship, conducted for so long in secret in Tol's mind alone, became public. This is the story of Miss Minnie's first consent, the beginning of their story together, which is one of the dear possessions of the history of Port William.

That fall, Miss Minnie and her students had worked hard in preparation for the annual Harvest Festival at the school. The Harvest Festival was Miss Minnie's occasion; she had thought it up herself. It might have been a Halloween party, except that Halloween in that vicinity got enough out of hand as it was without some public function to bring all the boys together in one place. And so she had thought of the Harvest Festival, which always took place two weeks before Halloween. It was a popular social event, consisting of much visiting, a display of the students' work, recitations by the students, an auction of pies and cakes to raise money for books and supplies, and abundant refreshments provided by the mothers of the students.

Ptolemy Proudfoot had never been to the Harvest Festival. He had no children, he told himself, and so did not belong there. But in fact he had always longed to go, had always been afraid to intrude himself without excuse into Miss Minnie's world, and had always, as a result, spent an unhappy night at home. But this year, now that he and Miss Minnie were in a manner of becoming friends, he determined that he would go.

Tol had got along as bachelors must. He had even become a fair cook. From the outside, his house was one of the prettiest and best kept in the neighborhood. It was a small house with steep, gingerbreaded gables, and it stood under two white oaks in the bend of the road, just where the road branched off to go down into the Katy's Branch valley where Goforth and its school were. Tol kept the house painted and the yard neat, and he liked to turn in off the road and say to himself, 'Well, now, I wonder who lives in such a nice place!' But what he had thought up to do to the inside of the house was not a great deal above what he had thought up to do to the inside of his barn. Like the barn, the house was clean and orderly, but when he went into it, it did not seem to be expecting him, as it did after Miss Minnie came there to live.

On the day of the festival, Tol cut and shocked corn all day but he thought all day of the festival, too, and he quit early. He did his chores, fixed his supper and ate it, and then, just as he had planned in great detail to do, he began to get ready. He brought his Sunday clothes to the kitchen and laid them out on a chair. He hunted up his Sunday shoes and polished them. He set a large washtub on the floor in front of the stove, dipped hot water into it from the water well at the end of the stove, cooled the hot water with water from the water bucket on the shelf by the door, put soap and washrag and towel on the floor beside the tub. And then he undressed and sat in the tub with his feet outside it on the floor, and scrubbed himself thoroughly from top to toe. He dried himself and put on his pants. Gazing into the mirror over the little wash table by the back door, he shaved so carefully that he cut himself in several places. He put on his shirt, and after several tries buttoned the collar. He put on his tie, tying a knot in it that would have broken the neck of a lesser man and that left even him so nearly strangled that he supposed he must look extremely handsome. He wet his hair and combed it so that when it dried it stuck up stiffly in the air as Proudfoot hair was inclined to do. He put on his suspenders, his gleaming shoes, and his Sunday hat. And then he sat in a chair and sweated and rubbed his hands together until it was time to hitch old Ike to the buggy and drive down to the school.

Before he got to the schoolhouse, he could hear voices, an uninterrupted babble like the sound of Katy's Branch in the spring, and then he could see a glow. When he got to the bottom of the hill and saw, among the trunks of the big walnuts and water maples and sycamores that stood there, the schoolhouse windows gleaming and the school yard strung with paper lanterns, lighting the bare-worn ground and throwing the shadows of the trees out in all directions like the spokes of a wheel, he said, 'Whoa, Ike.' The light around the old schoolhouse and within it seemed to him a radiance that emanated from the person of Miss Minnie herself. And Tol's big heart quaked within him. He had to sit there in the road behind his stopped horse and think a good while before he could decide not to go on by, pretending to have an errand elsewhere.

Now that he had stopped, it became quiet where he was; he could hear the crickets singing, and he was aware of Willow Hole on Katy's Branch, a little beyond the school, carrying on its accustomed business in the dark. As he sat and thought – thought hard about nothing that he could fix in a thought – Tol slid his fingers up beneath his hat from time to time and scratched, and then jerked the hat down firmly onto his head again, and each time he did this he rotated the front of his hat a little further toward his right ear. Presently the sound of another buggy coming down the hill behind him recalled him to himself; he clucked to Ike and drove on, and found a hitching place among the other buggies and the wagons and the saddled horses at the edge of the school yard.

There was a perimeter of voices out on the very edge of the light, where the boys had started a game of tag, unwilling to come nearer the schoolhouse than they had to. Near the building the men were gathered in groups, smoking or chewing, talking, as they always talked, of crops, livestock, weather, work, prices, hunting, and fishing, in that year and the years before.

Tol, usually a sociable man, had nothing to say. He did not dare to say anything. He went past the men, merely nodding in response to their greetings, and since he did not want to talk and so could not stop, and was headed in that direction, he went on into the schoolhouse, and immediately he realized his mistake. For there were only women and girls in there, and not one man, not a single one. Beyond the boys' voices out on the edge of the dark and the men's voices in the school yard was this bright, warm nucleus of women's voices, and of women themselves and of women's eyes turned to see who had burst through the door with so much force.

Those women would always remember the way Tol looked when he came in that night. After all his waiting and anxiety, his clothes were damp and wrinkled, his shirt-tail was out, there was horse manure on one of his shoes. His hat sat athwart his head as though left there by somebody else. When, recognizing the multiflorous female presence he was in, he snatched his hat off, his hair stuck up and out and every which way. He came in wide-eyed, purposeful, and alarmed. He looked as if only his suspenders were holding him back – as if, had it not been for that restraint upon his shoulders, he might have charged straight across the room and out through the back wall.

He had made, he thought, a serious mistake, and he was embarrassed. He was embarrassed, too, to show that he knew he had made a mistake. He did not want to stay, and he could not go. Struck dumb, his head as empty of anything sayable as a clapperless bell, he stood in one place and then another, smiling and blushing, an anxious, unhappy look in his eyes.

Finally, a voice began to speak in his mind. It was his own voice. It said, 'I would give forty dollars to get out of here. I would give forty-five dollars to get out of here.' It consoled him somewhat to rate his misery at so high a price. But he could see nobody to whom he could pay the forty dollars, or the forty-five either. The women had gone back to talking, and the girls to whispering.

But Tol's difficulty and his discomfort had not altogether failed of a compassionate witness. His unexpected presence had not failed to cause a small flutter in the bosom of Miss Minnie and a small change in the color of her face. As soon as she decently could, Miss Minnie excused herself from the circle of women with whom she had been talking. She took the bell from her desk and went to the door and rang it.

Presently the men and boys began to come inside. Tol, though he did not become inconspicuous, began at least to feel inconspicuous, and as his pain decreased, he was able to take intelligent notice of his whereabouts. He saw how prettily the room was done up with streamers and many candles and pictures drawn by the students and bouquets of autumn leaves. And at the head of the room on a large table were the cakes and pies that were to be auctioned off at the end of the evening.

In the very center of the table, on a tall stand, was a cake that Tol knew, even before he heard, was the work of Miss Minnie. It was an angel food cake with an icing as white and light and swirly as a summer cloud. It was as white as a bride. The sight of it fairly took his breath – it was the most delicate and wondrous thing that he had ever seen. It looked so beautiful and vulnerable there all alone among the others that he wanted to defend it with his life. It was lucky, he thought, that nobody said anything bad about it – and he just wished somebody would. He took a position in a corner in the front of the room as near the cake as he dared to be, and watched over it defensively, angry at the thought of the possibility that somebody *might* say something bad about it.

'Children, please take your seats!' Miss Minnie said.

The students all dutifully sat down at their desks, leaving the grown-ups to sit or stand around the walls. There was some confusion and much shuffling of feet as everybody found a place. And then a silence, variously expectant and nervous, fell upon the room. Miss Minnie stepped to the side of her desk. She stood, her posture very correct, regarding her students and her guests in silence a moment, and then she welcomed them one and all to the annual Harvest Festival of Goforth School. She told the grown-ups how pleased she was to see them there so cherishingly gathered around their children. She gave them her heartfelt thanks for their support. She asked Brother Overhold if he would pronounce the invocation.

Brother Overhold called down the blessings of Heaven upon each and every one there assembled, and upon every family there represented; upon Goforth School and Miss Minnie, its beloved teacher; upon the neighborhood of Katy's Branch and Cotman Ridge; upon the town of Port William and all the countryside around it; upon the county, the state, the nation, the world, and the great universe, at the very center of which they were met together that night at Goforth School.

And then Miss Minnie introduced the pupils of the first grade, who were to read a story in unison. The first grade pupils thereupon sat up straight, giving their brains the full support of their erect spinal columns, held their primers upright in front of them, and intoned loudly together:

'Once – there – were – three – *bears*. The – big – bear – was – the – *pop*pa – bear. The – middle – bear – was – the – *mom*ma bear. The – little – bear – was – the – *ba*by bear' – and so on to the discovery of Goldlilocks and the conclusion, which produced much applause.

And then, one by one, the older children came forward to stand at the side of the desk, as Miss Minnie had stood, to recite poems or Bible verses or bits of famous oratory.

A small boy, Billy Braymer, recited from Sir Walter Scott:

> *Breathes there the man with soul so dead*
> *Who never to himself hath said:*
> *'This is my own, my native land'?*

– and on for thirteen more lines, and said 'Whew!' and sat down to enthusiastic applause. Thelma Settle of the sixth grade, one of the stars of the school, made her way through 'Thanatopsis' without fault to the very end. The audience listened to 'A Psalm of Life', the First, the Twenty-third, and the Hundredth Psalms, 'The Fool's Prayer', 'To a Waterfowl', 'To Daffodils', 'Concord Hymn', 'The Choir Invisible', 'Wolsey's Farewell to His Greatness', Hamlet's Soliloquy, 'The Epitaph' from Gray's 'Elegy Written in a Country Church-Yard', and other pieces. Hibernia Hopple of the eighth grade declared with a steadily deepening blush and in furious haste that she loved to the depth and breadth and height her soul could reach. Walter Crow said in a squeaky voice and with bold gestures that he was the master of his fate and the captain of his soul. Buster Niblett implored that he be given liberty or death.

And then Miss Minnie called the name of Burley Coulter, and a large boy stood up in the back of the room and, blushing, made his way to the desk as he would have walked, perhaps, to the gallows. He turned and faced the audience. He shut his eyes tightly, opened them only to find the audience still present, and swallowed. Miss Minnie watched him with her fingers laced at her throat and her eyes moist. He was such a good-looking boy, and – she had no doubt – was smart. Against overpowering evidence she had imagined a triumph for him. She had chosen a poem for him that was masculine, robust, locally applicable, seasonally appropriate, high spirited, and amusing. If he recited it well, she would be so pleased! She had the poem in front of her, just in case.

He stood in silence, as if studying to be as little present as possible, and then announced in an almost inaudible voice, ' "When the Frost Is on the Punkin" by James Whitcomb Riley'.

He hung his hands at his sides, and then clasped them behind him, and then clasped them in front of him, and then put them into his pockets. He swallowed a dry-mouthed swallow that in the silence was clearly audible, and began:

'When the frost is on the punkin and the fodder's in the shock,
    And you hear the kyouck and gobble of the struttin' turkey-cock,
    And the clackin' of the – of the, uh – the clackin' of the –'

'Guineys!' Miss Minnie whispered.
'Aw, yeah, guineys,' he said:

'And the clackin' of the guineys, and the cluckin' of the hens,
And the rooster's hallylooyer as he tiptoes on the fence
– uh, let's see –'

'Oh, it's then's . . .'

'Oh, it's then's the time's a feller' is a-feelin' at his best,
With the risin' sun to greet him from a night of peaceful rest,
When he – uh –'

'As he leaves . . .'

'As he leaves the house, bare-headed, and goes out to feed the stock,
When the frost is on the punkin and the fodder's in the shock.'

He looked at his feet, he scratched his head, his lips moved
soundlessly.
'They's something . . .'
'Aw, yeah.

'They's something kindo' harty-like about the atmusfere
When the heat of summer's over – uh – kindo' lonesome-like,
but still – uh –

'When, let's see. Uh –

'Then your apples – Then your apples all –'

Miss Minnie was reading desperately, trying to piece the
poem together as he dismembered it, but he had left her behind
and now he was stalled. She looked up to see an expression on

his face that she knew too well. The blush was gone; he was grinning; the light of inspiration was in his eyes.

'Well, drot it, folks,' he said, 'I forgot her. But I'll tell you one I *heard*.'

Miss Minnie rose, smiling, and said in a tone of utter gratification, '*Thank* you, Burley! Now you may be seated.'

She then called upon Kate Helen Branch, who came to the front and sang 'In the Gloaming' in a voice that was not strong but was clear and true.

That brought the recitations to an appropriate conclusion. There was prolonged applause, after which Miss Minnie again arose. 'Mr Willis Bagby', she said, 'will now conduct our auction of pies and cakes.'

Mr Bagby took his place behind the table of pies and cakes.

'Folks,' he said, 'this here is for the good of the school, and to help out this little teacher here that's doing such a good job a-teaching our children. For what would tomorrow be without the young people of today? And what would our young people be without a fine teacher to teach them to figger and read and write, and to make them do all the fine things we seen them do here on this fine occasion this evening? So now, folks, open up your hearts and let out your pocketbooks. What am I bid for this fine cherry pie?' And he tilted the pie toward the crowd so that all could see the lovely crisscrossing of the top crust.

Tol had stood and watched and listened in a state of anxiety that prevented him from benefiting at all from the program. He had never seen in his life, he thought, such a woman as Miss Minnie – she was so smart and pretty, and so knowing in how to stand and speak. And when she stopped that Burley Coulter and set him down, Tol felt his heart swerve like a flying swift. She was as quick on her feet, he thought, as a good hind-catcher.

And yet the more he looked upon her, the higher above him she shone, and the farther he felt beneath her notice.

Now there was old Willis Bagby auctioning off the pies and cakes, which were bringing more or less than fifty cents, depending on what they looked like and who had made them. And Tol was sweating and quaking like a man afraid. For what if her cake brought less than fifty cents? What if – and he felt his heart swerve again – nobody bid on it? He would bid on it himself – but how could he dare to? People would think he was trying to show off. Maybe *she* would think he was trying to show off.

Tol backed into his corner as far as he could, trying to be small, wishing he had not come. But now Willis Bagby put his hands under the beautiful white cake and lifted it gleaming on its stand.

'*Now* look a-here, folks,' he said. 'For last, we got this fine cake made by this mighty nice lady, our schoolteacher. What am I bid for it?'

'One dollar,' said Gilead Hopple, who with his wife, Ag, was standing not far in front of Tol Proudfoot. Gil Hopple was the local magistrate, who now proposed for himself the political gallantry of offering the highest bid for the teacher's cake. After his bid, he uttered a small cough.

'Dollar bid! I've got a dollar bid,' said Willis Bagby. 'Now, anywhere a half?'

Nobody said anything. Nobody said anything for a time that got longer and longer, while Gil Hopple stood there with his ears sticking out and his white bald head sticking up through its official fringe of red hair.

And Tol Proudfoot was astonished to hear himself say right out and in a voice far too loud, '*Two dollars!*'

Gil Hopple coughed his small cough again and said, his voice slightly higher in pitch than before, 'Two and a quarter.'

It seemed to Tol that Gil Hopple had defiled that priceless

cake with his quarter bid. Gil Hopple happened to be Tol's neighbor, and they had always got along and been friends. But at that moment Tol hated Gil Hopple with a clear, joyful hatred. He said, '*Three* dollars!'

Gil Hopple did not wish to turn all the way around, but he looked first to the right and then to the left. His ears stuck out farther, and the top of his head had turned pink. It had been a dry year. He looked as if the room smelled of an insufficient respect for hard cash. 'Three and a quarter,' he said in a tone of great weariness.

Willis Bagby was looking uncomfortable himself now. Things obviously were getting out of hand, but it was not up to him to stop it.

Tol said, 'Four!'

At that point a revelation came to Miss Minnie. It seemed to her beyond a doubt that Tol Proudfoot, that large, strong man whom she had thought ought to be some woman's knight and protector, was bidding to be *her* knight and protector. It made her dizzy. She managed to keep her composure: she did not blush much, the tears hardly showed in her eyes, by great effort she did not breathe much too fast. But her heart was staggering within her like a drunk person, and she was saying over and over to herself, 'Oh, you magnificent man!'

'Four and a quarter,' said Gil Hopple.

'*Five!*' said Tol Proudfoot.

'Five and a quarter,' said Gil Hopple.

'*Ten!*' shouted Tol Proudfoot.

And at that moment another voice – Ag Hopple's – was raised above the murmuring of the crowd: 'Good *lord*, Gil! I'll *make* you a cake!'

Willis Bagby, gratefully seeing his duty, said, 'Sold! To Tol Proudfoot yonder in the corner.'

Tol could no more move than if he had been turned by his audacity into a statue. He stood in his corner with sweat running down his face, unable to lift his hand to wipe it off, frightened to think how he had showed off right there in front of everybody for her to see.

And then he saw that Miss Minnie was coming to where he was, and his knees shook. She was coming through the crowd, looking straight at him, and smiling. She reached out with her little hand and put it into one of his great ones, which rose of its own accord to receive it. 'Mr Proudfoot,' she said, 'that was more than kind.'

Tol was standing there full in public view, in the midst of a story that Port William would never forget, and as far as he now knew not a soul was present but Miss Minnie and himself.

'Yes, mam – uh, mam – uh, miss – uh, little lady,' he said. 'Excuse me, mam, but I believe it was worth every cent of it, if you don't mind. And I ain't trying to act smart or anything, and if I do, excuse me, but might I see you home?'

'Oh, Mr Proudfoot!' Miss Minnie said. 'Certainly you may!'

Pray Without Ceasing
(1912)

Mat Feltner was my grandfather on my mother's side. Saying it thus, I force myself to reckon again with the strangeness of that verb *was*. The man of whom I once was pleased to say, 'He is my grandfather,' has become the dead man who was my grandfather. He was, and is no more. And this is a part of the great mystery we call time.

But the past is present also. And this, I think, is a part of the greater mystery we call eternity. Though Mat Feltner has been dead for twenty-five years, and I am now older than he was when I was born and have grandchildren of my own, I know his hands, their way of holding a hammer or a hoe or a set of checklines, as well as I know my own. I know his way of talking, his way of cocking his head when he began a story, the smoking pipe stem held an inch from his lips. I have in my mind, not just as a memory but as a consolation, his welcome to me when I returned home from the university and, later, from jobs in distant cities. When I sat down beside him, his hand would clap lightly onto my leg above the knee; my absence might have lasted many months, but he would say as though we had been together the day before, 'Hello, Andy.' The shape of his hand is printed on the flesh of my thigh as vividly as a birthmark. This man who was my grandfather is present in me, as I felt always his father to be present in him. His father was Ben. My own live knowledge of the Feltners in Port William begins with Ben, whom I know from my grandparents' stories. That is the known history. The names go back to Ben's father and grandfather.

But even the unknown past is present in us, its silence as persistent as a ringing in the ears. When I stand in the road that passes through Port William, I am standing on the strata of my history that go down through the known past into the unknown: the blacktop rests on state gravel, which rests on county gravel, which rests on the creek rock and cinders laid down by the town when it was still mostly beyond the reach of the county; and under the creek rock and cinders is the dirt track of the town's beginning, the buffalo trace that was the way we came. You work your way into the interior of the present, until finally you come to that beginning in which all things, the world and the light itself, at a Word welled up into being out of their absence. And nothing is here that we are beyond the reach of merely because we do not know about it. It is always the first morning of Creation and always the last day, always the now that is in time and the Now that is not, that has filled time with reminders of Itself.

When my grandfather was dying, I was not thinking about the past. My grandfather was still a man I knew, but as he sub-sided day by day he was ceasing to be the man I had known. I was experiencing consciously for the first time that trans-formation in which the living, by dying, pass into the living, and I was full of grief and love and wonder.

And so when I came out of the house one morning after breakfast and found Braymer Hardy sitting in his pickup truck in front of my barn, I wasn't expecting any news. Braymer was an old friend of my father's; he was curious to see what Flora and I would do with the long-abandoned Harford Place that we had bought and were fixing up, and sometimes he visited.

His way was not to go to the door and knock. He just drove in and stopped his old truck at the barn and sat looking around until somebody showed up.

'Well, you ain't much of a Catlett,' he said, in perfect good humor. 'Marce Catlett would have been out and gone two hours ago.'

'I do my chores *before* breakfast,' I said, embarrassed by the lack of evidence. My grandfather Catlett would, in fact, have been out and gone two hours ago.

'But,' Braymer said in an explanatory tone, as if talking to himself, 'I reckon your daddy is a late sleeper, being as he's an office man. But that Wheeler was always a shotgun once he *got* out,' he went on, clearly implying, and still in excellent humor, that the family line had reached its nadir in me. 'But maybe you're a right smart occupied of a night, I don't know.' He raked a large cud of tobacco out of his cheek with his forefinger and spat.

He looked around with the air of a man completing an inspection, which is exactly what he was doing. 'Well, it looks like you're making a little headway. You got it looking some better. Here,' he said, pawing among a litter of paper, tools, and other odds and ends on top of the dashboard and then on the seat beside him, 'I brought you something.' He eventually forceped forth an old newspaper page folded into a tight rectangle the size of a wallet and handed it through the truck window. 'You ought to have it. It ain't no good to me. The madam, you know, is hell for an antique. She bought an old desk at a sale, and that was in one of the drawers.'

I unfolded the paper and read the headline: BEN FELTNER, FRIEND TO ALL, SHOT DEAD IN PORT WILLIAM.

'Ben Feltner was your great-granddaddy.'

'Yes. I know.'

'I remember him. They never made 'em no finer. The last man on earth you'd a thought would get shot.'

'So I've heard.'

'Thad Coulter was a good kind of feller, too, far as that goes. I don't reckon he was the kind you'd a thought would shoot somebody, either.'

He pushed his hat back and scratched his forehead. 'One of them things,' he said. 'They happen.'

He scratched his head some more and propped his wrist on top of the steering wheel, letting the hand dangle. 'Tell you,' he said, 'there ain't a way in this world to know what a human creature is going to do next. I loaned a feller five hundred dollars once. He was a good feller, too, wasn't a thing wrong with him far as I knew, I liked him. And dogged if he didn't kill himself fore it was a week.'

'Killed himself?' I said.

'*Killed* himself,' Braymer said. He meditated a moment, looking off at his memory of the fellow and wiggling two of the fingers that hung over the steering wheel. 'Don't you know,' he said, 'not wishing him no bad luck, but I wished he'd a done it a week or two sooner.'

I laughed.

'Well,' he said, 'I know you want to be at work. I'll get out of your way.'

I said, 'Don't be in a hurry,' but he was starting the truck and didn't hear me. I called, 'Thanks!' as he backed around. He raised his hand, not looking at me, and drove away, steering with both hands, with large deliberate motions, as if the truck were the size of a towboat.

There was an upturned feed bucket just inside the barn door. I sat down on it and unfolded the paper again. It was the front page of the Hargrave *Weekly Express,* flimsy and yellow, nearly illegible in some of the creases. It told how, on a Saturday morning in the July of 1912, Ben Feltner, who so far as was known had had no enemies, had been killed by a single shot to the head from a .22 caliber revolver. His assailant, Thad Coulter, had said, upon turning himself in to the sheriff at Hargrave soon after the incident, 'I've killed the best friend I ever had.' It was not a long article. It told about the interment of Ben Feltner and named his survivors. It told nothing that I did not know, and I knew little more than it told. I knew that Thad Coulter had killed himself in jail, shortly after the murder. And I knew that he was my grandfather Catlett's first cousin.

I had learned that much, not from anyone's attempt, ever, to tell me the story, but from bits and pieces dropped out of conversations among my elders, in and out of the family. Once, for instance, I heard my mother say to my father that she had always been troubled by the thought of Thad Coulter's lonely anguish as he prepared to kill himself in the Hargrave jail. I had learned what I knew, the bare outline of the event, without asking questions, both fearing the pain that I knew surrounded the story and honoring the silence that surrounded the pain.

But sitting in the barn that morning, looking at the old page opened on my knees, I saw how incomplete the story was as the article told it and as I knew it. And seeing it so, I felt incomplete myself. I suddenly wanted to go and see my grandfather. I did not intend to question him. I had never heard him speak so much as a word about his father's death, and I could not have imagined breaking his silence. I only wanted to be in his presence, as if in his presence I could somehow enter into the presence of an agony that I knew had shaped us all.

With the paper folded again in my shirt pocket, I drove to Port William and turned in under the old maples beside the house.

When I let myself in, the house was quiet, and I went as quietly as I could to my grandfather's room, thinking he might be asleep. But he was awake, his fingers laced together on top of the bedclothes. He had seen me drive in and was watching the door when I entered the room.

'Morning,' I said.

He said, 'Morning, son,' and lifted one of his hands.

'How're you feeling?'

'Still feeling.'

I sat down in the rocker by the bed and told him, in Braymer's words, the story of the too-late suicide.

My grandfather laughed. 'I expect that grieved Braymer.'

'Is Braymer pretty tight?' I asked, knowing he was.

'I wouldn't say "tight", but he'd know the history of every dollar he ever made. Braymer's done a lot of hard work.'

My grandmother had heard us talking, and now she called me. 'Oh, Andy!'

'I'll be back,' I said, and went to see what she wanted.

She was sitting in the small bedroom by the kitchen where she had always done her sewing and where she slept now that my grandfather was ill. She was sitting by the window in the small cane-bottomed rocking chair that was her favorite. Her hands were lying on her lap and she was not rocking. I knew that her arthritis was hurting her; otherwise, at that time of day, she would have been busy at something. She had medicine for the arthritis, but it made her feel unlike herself; up to a certain point of endurability, she preferred the pain. She sat still and let the pain go its way and occupied her mind with thoughts. Or that is what she said she did. I believed, and I was as sure as if she had told me, that when she sat alone that way, hurting or not, she was praying. Though I never heard her pray aloud in my life, it seems to me now that I can reproduce in my mind the very voice of her prayers.

She had called me in to find out things, which was her way. I sat down on the stool in front of her and submitted to examination. She wanted to know what Flora was doing, and what the children were doing, and when I had seen my mother, and what she had been doing. She asked exacting questions that called for much detail in the answers, watching me intently to see that I withheld nothing. She did not tolerate secrets, even the most considerate ones. She had learned that we sometimes omitted or rearranged facts to keep her from worrying, but her objection to that was both principled and passionate. If we were worried, she wanted to worry with us; it was her place, she said.

After a while, she quit asking questions but continued to look at me. And then she said, 'You're thinking about something you're not saying. What is it? Tell Granny.'

She had said that to me many times in the thirty years I had known her. By then, I thought it was funny. But if I was no longer intimidated, I was still compelled. In thirty years I had never been able to deceive her when she was looking straight at me. I could have lied, but she would have known it and then would have supposed that somebody was sick. I laughed and handed her the paper out of my pocket.

'Braymer Hardy brought that to me this morning.'

She unfolded it, read a little of the article but not all, and folded it back up. Her hands lay quiet in her lap again, and she looked out the window, though obviously not seeing what was out there that morning. Another morning had come to her, and she was seeing it again through the interval of fifty-three years.

'It's a wonder,' she said, 'that Mat didn't kill Thad Coulter that morning.'

I said, 'Granddad?'

And then she told me the story. She told it quietly, looking through the window into that July morning in 1912. Her hands lay in her lap and never moved. The only effect her telling had on her was a glistening that appeared from time to time in her eyes. She told the story well, giving many details. She had a good memory, and she had lived many years with her mother-in-law, who also had a good one. I have the impression that they, but not my grandfather, had pondered together over the event many times. She spoke as if she were seeing it all happen, even the parts of it that she had in fact not seen.

'If it hadn't been for Jack Beechum, Mat *would* have killed him,' my grandmother said.

That was the point. Or it was one of the points – the one, perhaps, that she most wanted me to see. But it was not the beginning of the story. Adam and Eve and then Cain and Abel began it, as my grandmother depended on me to know. Even in Thad Coulter's part of the story, the beginning was some years earlier than the July of 1912.

Abner Coulter, Thad's only son, had hired himself out to a grocer in Hargrave. After a few years, when he had (in his own estimation) learned the trade, he undertook to go into business for himself in competition with his former employer. He rented a building right on the courthouse square. He was enabled to do this by a sizable sum of money borrowed from the Hargrave bank on a note secured by a mortgage on his father's farm.

And here Thad's character enters into the story. For Thad not only secured his son's note with the farm that was all he had in the world and that he had only recently finished paying for, but he further committed himself by bragging in Port William of his son's new status as a merchant in the county seat.

'Thad Coulter was not a bad man,' my grandmother said. 'I believed then, and I believe now, that he was not a bad man. But we are all as little children. Some know it and some don't.'

She looked at me to see if I was one who knew it, and I nodded, but I was thirty then and did not know it yet.

'He was as a little child,' she said, 'and he was in serious trouble.'

He had in effect given his life and its entire effort as hostage to the possibility that Abner, his only son, could be made a merchant in a better place than Port William.

Before two years were out, Abner repaid his father's confidence by converting many small private fritterings and derelictions into an undisguisable public failure and thereupon by riding off to somewhere unknown on the back of a bay gelding borrowed ostensibly for an overnight trip to Port William. And so Thad's fate was passed from the reckless care of his son to the small mercy of the law. Without more help than he could confidently expect, he was going to lose his farm. Even with help, he was going to have to pay for it again, and he was close to sixty years old.

As he rode home from his interview with the Hargrave banker, in which the writing on the wall had been made plain to him, he was gouging his heel urgently into his mule's flank. Since he had got up out of the chair in the banker's office, he had been full of a desire as compelling as thirst to get home, to get low to the ground, as if to prevent himself from falling off the world. For the country that he had known all his life and had depended on, at least in dry weather, to be solid and steady underfoot had suddenly risen under him like a wave.

Needing help as he did, he could not at first bring himself to ask for it. Instead, he spent most of two days propped against a post in his barn, drinking heavily and talking aloud to himself about betrayal, ruin, the cold-heartedness of the Hargrave bankers, and the poor doings of damned fools, meaning both Abner and himself. And he recalled, with shocks of bitterness that only the whiskey could assuage, his confident words in Port William about Abner and his prospects.

'I worked for it, and I come to own it,' he said over and over again. 'Now them will own it that never worked for it. And him that stood on it to mount up into the world done run to perdition without a patch, damn him, to cover his ass or a rag to hide his face.'

When his wife and daughter begged him to come into the house, he said that a man without the sense to keep a house did not deserve to be in one. He said he would shelter with the dogs and hogs, where he belonged.

The logical source of help was Ben Feltner. Ben had helped Thad to buy his farm – had signed his note and stood behind him. Ben was his friend, and friendship mattered to Ben; it may have mattered to him above all. But Thad did not go to Ben until after his second night in the barn. He walked to Ben's house in Port William early in the morning, drunk and unsteady, his mind tattered and raw from repeated plunges through the thorns and thistles of his ruin.

Ben was astonished by the look of him. Thad had always been a man who used himself hard, and he had grown gaunt and stooped, his mouth slowly caving in as he lost his teeth. But that morning he was also soiled, sagging, unshaved and uncombed, his eyes bloodshot and glary. But Ben said, 'Come in, Thad. Come in and sit down.' And he took him by the arm, led him in to a chair, and sat down facing him.

'They got me, Ben,' Thad said, the flesh twitching around his eyes. 'They done got me to where I can't get loose.' His eyes glazed by tears that never fell, he made as much sense of his calamity as he was able to make: 'A poor man don't stand no show.' And then, his mind lurching on, unable to stop, he fell to cursing, first Abner, and then the Hargrave bank, and then the ways of the world that afforded no show to a poor man.

Ben listened to it all, sitting with his elbow on the chair arm and his forefinger pointed against his cheek. Thad's language and his ranting in that place would not have been excusable had he been sober. But insofar as Thad was drunk, Ben was patient. He listened attentively, his eyes on Thad's face, except that from time to time he looked down at his beard as if to give Thad an opportunity to see that he should stop.

Finally Ben stopped him. 'Thad, I'll tell you what. I don't believe I can talk with you anymore this morning. Go home, now, and get sober and come back. And then we'll see.'

Thad did not have to take Ben's words as an insult. But in his circumstances and condition, it was perhaps inevitable that he would. That Ben was his friend made the offense worse – far worse. In refusing to talk to him as he was, Ben, it seemed to Thad, had exiled him from friendship and so withdrawn the last vestige of a possibility that he might find anywhere a redemption for himself, much less for his forfeited land. For Thad was not able then to distinguish between himself as he was and himself as he might be sober. He saw himself already as a proven fool, fit only for the company of dogs and hogs. If he could have accepted this judgment of himself, then his story would at least have been different and would perhaps have been better. But while he felt the force and truth of his own judgment, he raged against it. He had fled to Ben, hoping that somehow, by some means that he could not imagine, Ben could release him from the solitary cage of his self-condemnation. And now Ben had shut the door.

Thad's whole face began to twitch and his hands to move aimlessly, as if his body were being manipulated from the inside by some intention that he could not control. Patches of white appeared under his whiskers. He said, 'I cuss you to your damned face, Ben Feltner, for I have come to you with my hat in my hand and you have spit in it. You have throwed in your lot with them sons of bitches against me.'

At that Ben reached his limit. Yet even then he did not become angry. He was a large, unfearful man, and his self-defense had something of merriment in it. He stood up. 'Now, Thad, my friend,' he said, 'you must go.' And he helped him to the door. He did not do so violently or with an excess of force. But though he was seventy-two years old, Ben was still in hearty strength, and he helped Thad to the door in such a way that Thad had no choice but to go.

But Thad did not go home. He stayed, hovering about the front of the house, for an hour or more.

'It seemed like hours and hours that he stayed out there,' my grandmother said. She and my great-grandmother, Nancy, and old Aunt Cass, the cook, had overheard the conversation between Ben and Thad, or had overheard at least Thad's part of it, and afterward they watched him from the windows, for his fury had left an influence. The house was filled with a quiet that seemed to remember with sorrow the quiet that had been in it before Thad had come.

The morning was bright and still, and it was getting hot, but Thad seemed unable to distinguish between sun and shade. There had got to be something fluttery or mothlike about him now, so erratic and unsteady and unceasing were his movements. He was talking to himself, nodding or shaking his head, his hands making sudden strange motions without apparent reference to whatever he might have been saying. Now and again he started resolutely toward the house and then swerved away.

All the while the women watched. To my grandmother, remembering, it seemed that they were surrounded by signs that had not yet revealed their significance. Aunt Cass told her afterward, 'I dreamed of the dark, Miss Margaret, all full of the sound of crying, and I knowed it was something bad.' And it seemed to my grandmother, as she remembered, that she too had felt the house and town and the bright day itself all enclosed in that dreamed darkness full of the sounds of crying.

Finally, looking out to where the road from upriver came over the rise into town, they saw a team and wagon coming. Presently they recognized Thad Coulter's team, a pair of mare mules, one black and the other once gray and now faded to white. They were driven by Thad's daughter, wearing a sun-bonnet, a sun-bleached blue cotton dress, and an apron.

'It's Martha Elizabeth,' Nancy said.

And Aunt Cass said, 'Poor child.'

'Well,' Nancy said, relieved, 'she'll take him home.'

When Martha Elizabeth came to where Thad was, she stopped the mules and got down. So far as they could see from the house, she did not plead with him. She did not say anything at all. She took hold of him, turned him toward the wagon, and led him to it. She held onto him as he climbed unsteadily up into the wagon and sat down on the spring seat, and then, gathering her skirts in one hand, she climbed up and sat beside him. And all the while she was gentle with him. Afterward and always, my grandmother remembered how gentle Martha Elizabeth had been with him.

Martha Elizabeth turned the team around, and the Feltner

women watched the wagon with its troubled burden go slowly away.

Ben, who had meant to go to the field where his hands were at work, did not leave the house as long as Thad was waiting about outside. He saw no point in antagonizing Thad when he did not have to, and so he sat down with a newspaper.

When he knew that Thad was gone and had had time to be out of sight, Ben got up and put on his hat and went out. He was worried about the state both of Thad's economy and of his mind. He thought he might find some of the other Coulters in town. He didn't know that he would, but it was Saturday, and he probably would.

The Feltner house stood, as it still does, in the overlap of the northeast corner of the town and the southwest corner of Ben's farm, which spread away from the house and farmstead over the ridges and hollows and down the side of the valley to the river. There was a farmstead at each of the town's four corners. There was, as there still is, only the one road, which climbed out of the river valley, crossed a mile of ridge, passed through the town, and, after staying on the ridge another half mile or so, went back down into the valley again. For most of its extent, at that time, it was little more than a wagon track. Most of the goods that reached the Port William merchants still came to Dawes Landing by steamboat and then up the hill by team and wagon. The town itself consisted of perhaps two dozen houses, a church, a blacksmith shop, a bank, a barber shop, a doctor's office, a hotel, two saloons, and four stores that sold a variety of merchandise from groceries to dry goods to hardware to harness. The road that passed through town was there only as a casual and hardly foreseen result of the comings and goings of the inhabitants. An extemporaneous town government had from time to time caused a few loads of creek rock to be hauled and knapped and spread over it, and the townspeople had flung their ashes into it, but that was all.

Though the houses and shops had been connected for some time by telephone lines carried overhead on peeled and white-washed locust poles, there was as yet not an automobile in the town. There were times in any year still when Port William could not have been reached by an automobile that was not accompanied by a team of mules to pull it across the creeks and out of the mud holes.

Except for the telephone lines, the town, as it looked to Ben Feltner on that July morning seventy-eight years ago, might have been unchanged for many more years than it had existed. It looked older than its history. And yet in Port William, as everywhere else, it was already the second decade of the twentieth century. And in some of the people of the town and the community surrounding it, one of the characteristic diseases of the twentieth century was making its way: the suspicion that they would be greatly improved if they were someplace else. This disease had entered into Thad Coulter and into Abner. In Thad it was fast coming to crisis. If Port William could not save him, then surely there was another place that could. But Thad could not just leave, as Abner had; Port William had been too much his life for that. And he was held also by his friendship for Ben Feltner, and for himself as a man whom Ben Feltner had befriended – a friendship that Ben Feltner seemed now to have repudiated and made hateful. Port William was a stumbling block to Thad, and he must rid himself of it somehow.

Ben, innocent of the disease that afflicted his friend yet mortally implicated in it and not knowing it, made his way down into the town, looking about in order to gauge its mood, for Port William had its moods, and they needed watching. More energy was generated in the community than the work of the community could consume, and the surplus energy often went into fighting. There had been cuttings and shootings enough. But usually the fighting was more primitive, and the combatants simply threw whatever projectiles came to hand: corncobs, snowballs, green walnuts, or rocks. In the previous winter, a young Coulter by the name of Burley had claimed that he had had an eye blackened by a frozen horse turd thrown, so far as he could determine, by a Power of the Air. But the place that morning was quiet. Most of the crops had been laid by and many of the farmers were already in town, feeling at ease and inclined to rest now that their annual battle with the weeds had ended. They were sitting on benches and kegs or squatting on their heels under the shade trees in front of the stores, or standing in pairs or small groups among the hitched horses along the sides of the road. Ben passed among them, greeting them and pausing to talk, enjoying himself, and all the while on the lookout for one or another of the Coulters.

Martha Elizabeth was Thad's youngest, the last at home. She had, he thought, the levelest head of any of his children and was the best. Assuming the authority that his partiality granted her, she had at fifteen taken charge of the household, supplanting her mother, who was sickly, and her three older sisters, who had married and gone. At seventeen, she was responsible beyond her years. She was a tall, raw-boned girl, with large hands and feet, a red complexion, and hair so red that, in the sun, it appeared to be on fire.

'Everybody loved Martha Elizabeth,' my grandmother said. 'She was as good as gold.'

To Thad it was a relief to obey her, to climb into the wagon under the pressure of her hand on his arm and to sit beside her as she drove the team homeward through the rising heat of the morning. Her concern for him gave him shelter. Holding to the back of the seat, he kept himself upright and, for the moment, rested in being with her.

But when they turned off the ridge onto the narrower road that led down into the little valley called Cattle Pen and came in sight of their place, she could no longer shelter him. It had long been, to Thad's eye, a pretty farm – a hundred or so acres of slope and ridge on the west side of the valley, the lower, gentler slopes divided from the ridge land by a ledgy bluff that was wooded, the log house and other buildings occupying a shelf above the creek bottom. Through all his years of paying for it, he had aspired toward it as toward a Promised Land. To have it, he had worked hard and long and deprived himself, and Rachel, his wife, had deprived herself. He had worked alone more often than not. Abner, as he grew able, had helped, as the girls had, also. But Abner had been reserved for something better. Abner was smart – too smart, as Thad and Rachel agreed, without ever much talking about it, to spend his life farming a hillside. Something would have to be done to start him on his way to something better, a Promised Land yet more distant.

Although he had thought the farm not good enough for Abner, Thad was divided in his mind; for himself he loved it. It was what he had transformed his life into. And now, even in the morning light, it lay under the shadow of his failure, and he could not bear to look at it. It was his life, and he was no longer in it. Somebody else, some other thing that did not even know it, stood ready to take possession of it. He was ashamed in its presence. To look directly at it would be like looking

Martha Elizabeth full in the eyes, which he could not do either. And his shame raged in him.

When she stopped in the lot in front of the barn and helped him down, he started unhitching the team. But she took hold of his arm and drew him away gently toward the house.

'Come on, now,' she said. 'You've got to have you something to eat and some rest.'

But he jerked away from her. 'Go see to your mammy!'

'No,' she said. 'Come on.' And she attempted again to move him toward the house.

He pushed her away, and she fell. He could have cut off his hand for so misusing her, and yet his rage at himself included her. He reached into the wagon box and took out a short hickory stock with a braid of rawhide knotted to it. He shook it at her.

'Get up,' he said. 'Get yonder to that house 'fore I wear you out.'

He had never spoken to her in such a way, had never imagined himself doing so. He hated what he had done, and he could not undo it.

The heat of the day had established itself now. There was not a breeze anywhere, not a breath. A still haze filled the valley and redoubled the light. Within that blinding glare he occupied a darkness that was loud with accusing cries.

Martha Elizabeth stood at the kitchen door a moment, looking back at him, and then she went inside. Thad turned back to the team then, unhitched them, did up the lines, and led the mules to their stalls in the barn. He moved as if dreaming through these familiar motions that had now estranged themselves from him. The closer he had come to home, the more the force of his failure had gathered there to exclude him.

And it was Ben Feltner who had barred the door and left

him without a friend. Ben Feltner, who owed nothing, had turned his back on his friend, who now owed everything.

He said aloud, 'Yes, I'll come back sober, God damn you to Hell!'

He lifted the jug out of the white mule's manger, pulled the cob from its mouth, and drank. When he lowered it, it was empty. It had lasted him three days, and now it was empty. He cocked his wrist and broke the jug against an upright.

'Well, that does for you, old holler-head.'

He stood, letting the whiskey seek its level in him, and felt himself slowly come into purpose; now he had his anger full and clear. Now he was summoned by an almost visible joy.

He went to the house, drank from the water bucket on the back porch, and stepped through the kitchen door. Rachel and Martha Elizabeth were standing together by the cookstove, facing him.

'Thad, honey, I done fixed dinner,' Rachel said. 'Set down and eat.'

He opened the stairway door, stepped up, and took down his pistol from the little shelf over the door frame.

'No, now,' Martha Elizabeth said. 'Put that away. You ain't got a use in this world for that.'

'Don't contrary me,' Thad said. 'Don't you say another damned word.'

He put the pistol in his hip pocket with the barrel sticking up and turned to the door.

'Wait, Thad,' Rachel said. 'Eat a little before you go.' But she was already so far behind him that he hardly heard her.

He walked to the barn, steadying himself by every upright thing he came to, so that he proceeded by a series of handholds on doorjamb and porch post and gatepost and tree. He could no longer see the place but walked in a shifting aisle of blinding light through a cloud of darkness. Behind him now was almost nothing. And ahead of him was the singular joy to which his heart now beat in answer.

He went into the white mule's stall, unbuckled hame strap and belly-band, and shoved the harness off her back, letting it fall. He unbuckled the collar and let it fall. Again his rage swelled within him, seeming to tighten the skin of his throat, as though his body might fail to contain it, for he had never before in his life allowed a mule's harness to touch the ground if he could help it. But he was not in his life now, and his rage pleased him.

He hooked his finger in the bit ring and led the mule to the drinking trough by the well in front of the barn. The trough was half an oak barrel, nearly full of water. The mule wanted to drink, but he jerked her head up and drew her forward until she stood beside the trough. The shorn stubble of her mane under his hand, he stepped up onto the rim. Springing, he cast himself across the mule's back, straddled her, and sat upright as darkness swung around him. He jerked hard at the left rein.

'Get up, Beck,' he said.

The mule was as principled as a martyr. She would have died before she would have trotted a step, and yet he urged her forward with his heel. Even as the hind feet of the mule lifted from their tracks, the thought of Martha Elizabeth formed itself within the world's ruin. She seemed to rise up out of its shambles, like a ghost or an influence. She would follow him. He needed to hurry.

On the fringe of the Saturday bustle in front of the business houses, Ben met Early Rowanberry and his little boy, Arthur. Early was carrying a big sack, and Art a small one. They had started out not long after breakfast; from the log house on the ridgetop where the Rowanberrys had settled before Kentucky was a state, they had gone down the hill, forded the creek known as Sand Ripple, and then walked up the Shade Branch hollow through the Feltner Place and on to town. Early had done his buying and a little talking, had bought a penny's worth of candy for Art, and now they were starting the long walk back. Ben knew that they had made the trip on foot to spare their mules, though the sacks would weigh sorely on their shoulders before they made it home.

'Well, Early,' Ben said, 'you've got a good hand with you today, I see.'

'He's tol'ble good company, Ben, and he packs a little load,' Early said.

Ben liked all the Rowanberrys, who had been good neighbors to him all his life, and Early was a better-than-average Rowanberry – a quiet man with a steady gaze and a sort of local fame for his endurance at hard work.

Ben then offered his hand to Art, who shyly held out his own. Ben said, 'My boy, are you going to grow up to be a wheelhorse like your pap?' and Art answered without hesitation, 'Yes, sir.'

'Ah, that's right,' Ben said. And he placed his hand on the boy's unladen shoulder.

The two Rowanberrys then resumed their homeward journey, and Ben walked on down the edge of the dusty road into town.

Ben was in no hurry. He had his mission in mind and was somewhat anxious about it, but he gave it its due place in the order of things. Thad's difficulty was not simple; whatever it was possible to do for him could not be done in a hurry. Ben passed slowly through the talk of the place and time, partaking of it. He liked the way the neighborhood gathered into itself on such days. Now and then, in the midst of the more casual conversation, a little trade talk would rouse up over a milk cow or a pocketknife or a saddle or a horse or mule. Or there would be a joke or a story or a bit of news, uprisings of the town's interest in itself that would pass through it and die away like scurries of wind. It was close to noon. It was hot even in the shade now and the smells of horse sweat and horse manure had grown strong. On the benches and kegs along the storefronts, pocketknives were busy. Profound meditations were coming to bear upon long scrolls of cedar or poplar curling backward over thumbs and wrists and piling over shoetops.

Somebody said, 'Well, I can see the heat waves a-rising.'

Somebody else said, 'Ain't nobody but a lazy man can see them heat waves.'

And then Ben saw Thad's cousin, Dave Coulter, and Dave's son, Burley, coming out of one of the stores, Dave with a sack of flour on his shoulder and Burley with a sack of meal on his. Except for his boyish face and grin, Burley was a grown man. He was seventeen, a square-handed, muscular fellow already known for the funny things he said, though his elders knew of them only by hearsay. He and his father turned down the street toward their wagon, and Ben followed them.

When they had hunched the sacks off their shoulders into the wagon, Ben said, 'Dave?'

Dave turned to him and stuck out his hand. 'Why howdy, Ben.'

'How are you, Dave?'

''Bout all right, I reckon.'

'And how are you, Burley?'

Dave turned to his boy to see that he would answer properly; Burley, grinning, said, 'Doing about all right, thank you, sir,' and Dave turned back to Ben.

'Had to lay in a little belly timber,' he said, ' 'gainst we run plumb out. And the boy here, he wanted to come see the sights.'

'Well, my boy,' Ben said, 'have you learned anything worthwhile?'

Burley grinned again, gave a quick nod, and said, 'Yessir.'

'Oh, hit's an educational place,' Dave said. 'We hung into one of them educational conversations yonder in the store. That's why we ain't hardly going to make it home by dinnertime.'

'Well, I won't hold you up for long,' Ben said. And he told Dave as much as he had understood of Thad's trouble. They were leaning against the wagon box, facing away from the road. Burley, who had gone to untie the mules, was still standing at their heads.

'Well,' Dave said, 'hit's been norated around that Abner weren't doing just the way he ought to. Tell you the truth, I been juberous about that loan proposition ever since Thad put his name to it. Put his whole foothold in that damned boy's pocket is what he done. And now you say it's all gone up the spout.'

'He's in a serious fix, no question about it.'

'Well, is there anything a feller can do for him?'

'Well, there's one thing for certain. He was drunk when he came to see me. He was cussing and raring. If you, or some of you, could get him sober, it would help. And then we could see if we can help him out of his scrape.'

'Talking rough, was he?'

'Rough enough.'

'I'm sorry, Ben. Thad don't often drink, but when he does he drinks like the Lord appointed him to get rid of it all.'

Somebody cried, 'Look out!'

They turned to see Thad and the white mule almost abreast of them. Thad was holding the pistol.

'They said he just looked awful,' my grandmother said. 'He looked like death warmed over.'

Ben said, without raising his voice, in the same reasonable tone in which he had been speaking to Dave, 'Hold on, Thad.'

And Thad fired.

Dave saw a small round red spot appear in the center of Ben's forehead. A perplexed look came to his face, as if he had been intending to say something more and had forgot what it was. For a moment, he remained standing just as he had been, one hand on the rim of the wagon box. And then he fell. As he went down, his shoulder struck the hub of the wagon wheel so that he fell onto his side, his hat rolling underneath the wagon.

Thad put the pistol back into his pocket. The mule had stood as still after he had halted her as if she were not there at all but at home under a tree in the pasture. When Thad kicked her, she went on again.

Ben Feltner never had believed in working on Sunday, and he did not believe in not working on workdays. Those two principles had shaped all his weeks. He liked to make his hay cuttings and begin other large, urgent jobs as early in the week as possible in order to have them finished before Sunday. On Saturdays, he and Mat and the hands worked in the crops if necessary; otherwise, that day was given to the small jobs of maintenance that the farm constantly required and to preparations for Sunday, when they would do nothing except milk and feed. When the work was caught up and the farm in order, Ben liked to have everybody quit early on Saturday afternoon. He liked the quiet that descended over the place then, with the day of rest ahead.

On that Saturday morning he had sent Old Smoke, Aunt Cass's husband, and their son, Samp, and Samp's boy, Joe, to mend a fence back on the river bluff. Mat he sent to the blacksmith shop to have the shoes reset on Governor, his buggy horse. They would not need Governor to go to church; they walked to church. But when they had no company on Sunday afternoon and the day was fair, Ben and Nancy liked to drive around the neighborhood, looking at the crops and stopping at various households to visit. They liked especially to visit Nancy's brother, Jack Beechum, and his wife, Ruth, who lived on the Beechum place, the place that Nancy always spoke of as 'out home'.

And so Mat that morning, after his chores were done, had slipped a halter on Governor and led him down through town to the blacksmith's. He had to wait – there were several horses and mules already in line – and so he tied Governor to the rail in front of the shop and went in among the others who were waiting and talking, figuring that he would be late for dinner.

It was a good place. The shop stood well back from the street, leaving in front of it a tree-shaded, cinder-covered yard, which made room for the hitch rail and for the wagons, sleds, and other implements waiting to be repaired. The shop itself was a single large, dirt-floored room, meticulously clean – every surface swept and every tool in place. Workbenches went around three walls. Near the large open doorway were the forge and anvil.

The blacksmith – a low, broad, grizzled man by the name of Elder Johnson – was the best within many miles, a fact well known to himself, which sometimes made him difficult. He also remembered precisely every horse or mule he had ever nailed a shoe on, and so he was one of the keepers of the town's memory.

Elder was shoeing a colt that was nervous and was giving him trouble. He was working fast so as to cause the colt as little discomfort as he could. He picked up the left hind hoof, caught it between his aproned knees, and laid the shoe on it. The shoe was too wide at the heel, and he let the colt's foot go back to the floor. A small sharp-faced man smoking a cob pipe was waiting, holding out a broken singletree for Elder's inspection as he passed on his way back to the forge.

Elder looked as if the broken tree were not the sort of thing that could concern him.

'Could I get this done by this evening?' the man asked. His name was Skeets Willard, and his work was always in some state of emergency. 'I can't turn a wheel,' he said, 'till I get that fixed.'

Elder let fall the merest glance at the two pieces of the single tree, and then looked point-blank at the man himself as if surprised not only by his presence but by his existence. 'What the hell do you think I am? A hammer with a brain? Do you see all them horses and mules tied up out there? If you want that fixed, I'll fix it when I can. If you don't, take it home.'

Skeets Willard elected to lay the pieces down in a conspicuous place by the forge. And Elder, whose outburst had not interrupted the flow of talk among the bystanders, caught the shoe in his tongs and shoved it in among the coals of the forge. He cranked the bellows and made small flames spike up out of the coals. As he turned the handle, he stared in a kind of trance at the light of the open doorway, and the light shone in his eyes, and his face and his arms were shining with sweat. Presently he drew the shoe, glowing, out of the coals and, laying it on the horn of the anvil, turned in the heel. He then plunged the shoe into the slack tub from which it raised a brief shriek of steam.

Somebody turned out of the conversation and said, 'Say, Elder, do you remember that little red mule come in here with a bunch of yearlings Marce Catlett bought up around Lexington? Ned, I think they called him.'

'Newt,' Elder said in so even a voice that Skeets Willard might never have been there. 'You bet I remember him.'

He took the cooled shoe from the slack tub and, picking up the colt's foot and straddling it again, quickly nailed one nail in each side, raking the points over with the claws of his hammer. He let the colt stand on his foot again to see how the shoe set. 'You bet I remember him,' he said. 'That mule could kick the lard out of a biscuit.'

And then they heard the single voice raised in warning out in the road, followed immediately by the shot and by a rising murmur of excited, indistinguishable voices as the whole Saturday crowd turned its attention to the one thing.

Mat hurried out with the others and saw the crowd wedged in between the storefronts and Dave Coulter's wagon. He only began to realize that the occasion concerned him when the crowd began to make way for him as he approached.

'Let him through! Let him through!' the crowd said.

The crowd opened to let him through, turning its faces to him, falling silent as it saw who he was. And then he saw what was left of the man who had been his father lying against the wagon wheel. Those nearest him heard him say, 'Oh!' and it did not sound like him at all. He stepped forward and knelt and took his father's wrist in his hand to feel for the pulse that he did not expect, having seen the wound and the fixed unsighted eyes. The crowd now was as quiet around him as the still treetops along the road. For what seemed a long time Mat knelt there with his father's dead wrist in his hand, while his mind arrived and arrived and yet arrived at that place and time and that body lying still on the soiled and bloodied stones.

When he looked up again, he did not look like the man they had known at all.

'Who did this?' he said.

And the crowd answered, 'Thad Coulter, he done it.'

'Where'd he go?'

'He taken down the road yonder toward Hargrave. He was on that old white mule, old May.'

When Mat stood up again from his father's side, he was a man new-created by rage. All that he had been and thought and done gave way to his one desire to kill the man who had killed his father. He ached, mind and body, with the elation of that one thought. He was not armed, but he never thought of that. He would go for the horse he had left tied at the blacksmith's. He would ride Thad Coulter down. He would come up beside him and club him off the mule. He would beat him down out of the air. And in that thought, which lived more in his right arm than in his head, both he and his enemy were as clear of history as if newborn.

By the time Mat was free of the crowd, he was running.

Jack Beechum had sold a team of mules the day before, and so he had a check to carry to the bank. He also had a list of things that Ruth wanted from town, and now that he had money ahead he wanted to settle his account at Chatham's store. His plan was to do his errands in town and get back home by dinner; that afternoon, he wanted to mow a field of hay, hoping it would cure by Monday. He rode to town on a good black gelding, called Socks for his four white pasterns.

He tied the horse some distance from the center of town in a place of better shade and fewer flies. He went to the bank first and then went about gathering the things that Ruth needed, ending up at Chatham's. He was sitting by Beater Chatham's desk in the back, watching Beater total up his account, when they heard the shot out in the street.

'Sounds like they're getting Saturday started out there,' Jack said.

'I reckon,' Beater said, checking his figures.

'They're going to keep on until they shoot somebody who don't deserve it.'

Beater looked at him then over the tops of his glasses. 'Well, I reckon they'll have to look hard to find him.' He filled out a check for the amount of the bill and handed the check to Jack for him to sign.

And then somebody who had just stepped out of the store stepped back in again and said, 'Jack, you'd better come. They've shot Ben Feltner.'

Jack never signed the check that day or for several days. He ran to the door. When he was outside, he saw first the crowd and then Mat running toward him out of it. Without breaking his own stride, he caught Mat and held him.

They were both moving at some speed, and the crowd heard the shock of the impact as the two men came together. Jack could hardly have known what he was doing. He had had no time to think. He may have been moved by an impulse simply to stop things until he *could* think. At any rate, as soon as Jack had taken hold of Mat, he understood that he *had* to hold him. And he knew that he had never taken hold of any such thing before. He had caught Mat in a sideways hug that clamped his arms to his sides. Jack's sole task was to keep Mat from freeing his arms. But Mat was little more than half Jack's age; he was in the prime of his strength. And now he twisted and strained with the concentration of fury, uttering cries that could have been either grunts or sobs, forcing Jack both to hold him and to hold him up. They strove there a long time, heaving and staggering, and the dust rose up around them. Jack felt that his arms would pull apart at the joints. He ached afterward. Something went out of him that day, and he was not the same again.

And what went out of Jack came into Mat. Or so it seemed, for in that desperate embrace he became a stronger man than he had been. A strength came into him that held his grief and his anger as Jack had held him. And Jack knew of the coming of this strength, not because it enabled Mat to break free but because it enabled Jack to turn him loose. He stepped away, allowing himself to be recognized, and Mat stood still. To Jack, it was as though he had caught one man and let another go.

But he put his eye on Mat, not willing yet to trust him entirely to himself, and waited.

They both were winded, wet with sweat, and for a moment they only breathed, watched by the crowd, Jack watching Mat, Mat looking at nothing.

As they stood so, the girl, Martha Elizabeth, walked by in the road. She did not look at them or at the wagon or at the body crumpled on the ground. She walked past it all, looking ahead, as if she already saw what she was walking toward.

Coming aware that Jack was waiting on him, Mat looked up; he met Jack's gaze. He said, 'Pa's dead. Thad Coulter has shot him.'

They waited, looking at each other still, while the earth shook under them.

Mat said, 'I'll go tell Ma. You bring Pa, but give me a little time.'

Dinner was ready, and the men were late.

'It wasn't usual for them to be late,' my grandmother said,

'but we didn't think yet that anything was wrong. Your mother was just a little girl then, and she was telling us a story about a girl and a dog and a horse.'

Aunt Cass stood by the stove, keeping an eye on the griddle. Nancy was sweeping the floor under the firebox of the stove; she was a woman who was always doing. Margaret, having set the table, had turned one of the chairs out into the floor and sat down. All three were listening to Bess, who presently stopped her story, rolled her eyes, and said, 'I hear my innards a-growling. I reckon I must be hungry.'

They laughed.

'I spect so, I spect so,' Aunt Cass said. 'Well, you'll eat fore long.'

When she heard Mat at the kitchen door, Aunt Cass said, 'Miss Nancy, you want to take the hoecake up?' And then seeing the change in Mat's face, which was new to it but old to the world, she hushed and stood still. Nancy, seeing the expression on Cass's face, turned to look at Mat.

Bess said, 'Goody! Now we can eat!'

Mat looked at his mother and then down at Bess and smiled. 'You can eat directly,' he said.

And then he said, 'Margaret, take Bess and go upstairs. I think she's got a book up there she wants you to read to her.'

'I knew what it was then,' my grandmother said. 'Oh, I felt it go all over me before I knew it in my mind. I just wanted to crawl away. But I had your mother to think about. You always have somebody to think about, and it's a blessing.'

She said, 'Come on, Bess, let's go read a story. We'll eat in a little bit.'

As soon as he heard their footsteps going up the stairs, Mat looked at his mother again. As the silence gathered against him, he said, 'Ma, I'm sorry. Pa's dead.'

She was already wearing black. She had borne four children and raised one. Two of her children she had buried in the same week of a diphtheria epidemic, of which she had nearly died herself. After the third child had died, she never wore colors again. It was not that she chose to be ostentatiously bereaved. She could not have chosen to be ostentatious about anything. She was, in fact, a woman possessed of a strong native cheerfulness. And yet she had accepted a certain darkness that she had lived in too intimately to deny.

She stood, looking at Mat, while she steadied herself and steadied the room around her, in the quiet that, having suddenly begun there, would not end for a long time. And then she said to Mat, 'Sit down.'

She said, 'Cass, sit down.'

They turned chairs away from the table and sat down, and then she did.

'Now,' she said, 'I want to know what happened.'

In the quiet Mat told as much, as little, as he knew.

As if to exert herself against the silence that too quickly filled the room, Nancy stood again. She laid her hand on the shoulder of Mat's wet shirt and patted it once.

'Cass,' she said, 'we mustn't cry,' though there were tears on her own face.

'Mat,' she said, 'go get Smoke and Samp and Joe. Tell them, and tell them to come here.'

To Aunt Cass again, she said, 'We must fix the bed. They'll need a place to lay him.'

And then they heard the burdened footsteps at the door.

In his cresting anger in the minutes before he stopped the mule in the road in Port William and fired the one shot that he ever fired in anger in his life, Thad Coulter knew a fierce, fulfilling joy. He saw the shot home to the mark, saw Ben Feltner stand a moment and go down, and then he kicked the mule hard in the side and rode on. He went on because all behind him that he might once have turned back to was gone from his mind, and perhaps even in his joy he knew that from that time there was to be no going back.

Even before the town was out of sight behind him, his anger and his joy began to leave him. It was as if his life's blood were running out of him, and he tried to stanch the flow by muttering aloud the curses of his rage. But they had no force, and his depletion continued.

His first thought beyond his anger was of the mule. She was thirsty, he knew, and he had denied her a drink.

'When we get to the creek,' he said.

The mule followed the windings of the road down off the upland. Below the cleared ridges, they passed through woods. On the gentler open slopes below, they came into the blank sunlight again, and he could see the river winding between its wooded banks toward its meeting with the Ohio at Hargrave.

At the foot of the hill, the road dipped under trees again and forded a creek. Thad rode the mule into the pool above the ford, loosened the rein, and let her drink. It was a quiet, deeply shaded place, the water unrippled until the mule stepped into it. For the first time in three days Thad could hear the quiet, and a bottomless sorrow opened in him, causing him suddenly to clutch his belly and groan aloud.

When the mule had finished drinking, he rode her out of the pool, dismounted, and, unbuckling one end of the rein from the bit, led her into a clump of bushes and tall weeds and tied her there. For now the thought of pursuit had come to him, and he knew he would have to go the rest of the way on foot. The mule could not be hurried, and she would be difficult to hide.

He went back to the pool and knelt at the edge of it and drank, and then he washed his hands and in his cupped hands lifted the clear water to his face.

Presently, he became still, listening. He had heard, he thought, nothing but the cicadas in the surrounding trees. And then he heard, coming fast, the sound of loud talking and the rapid hooftread of horses. He stepped into a patch of weeds and watched several riders go by on the road. They were boys and young men from the town who, having waited through the aftermath of the shooting, had now been carried by their excitement into pursuit of him. 'Boys,' he thought. He felt in no danger from them – he did not think of the pistol – and yet he feared them. He imagined himself hurrying on foot along the road, while the young riders picked and pecked at him.

The quiet returned, and he could feel, as if in the hair roots and pores of his skin, that Martha Elizabeth was coming near. He went back to the road again.

The walking and the water drying on his face cleared his mind, and now he knew himself as he had been and as he was and knew that he was changed beyond unchanging into something he did not love. Now that his anger had drained away, his body seemed to him not only to be a burden almost too heavy to carry but to be on the verge of caving in. He walked with one hand pressed to his belly where the collapse seemed already to have begun.

The best way between Port William and Hargrave was still the river. The road found its way as if by guess, bent this way and that by the whims of topography and the convenience of landowners. At intervals, it was interrupted by farm gates.

After a while, hearing several more horses coming behind him, he stepped out of the road and lay down in a small cane-brake. When they had passed, he returned to the road and went on. Always he was watchful of the houses he passed, but he stayed in the road. If he was to protect the one choice of which he was still master, he had to hurry.

And now, as he had not been able to do when he left it, he could see his farm. It shone in his mind as if inwardly lighted in the darkness that now surrounded both him and it. He could see it with the morning sun dew-bright on the woods and the sloping pastures, on the little croplands on the ridge and in the bottoms along the creek. He could see its cool shadows stretching out in the evening and the milk cows coming down the path to the barn. It was irrevocably behind him now, as if a great sword had fallen between him and it.

He was slow and small on the long road. The sun was slow overhead. The air was heavy and unmoving. He watched the steady stepping of his feet, the road going backward beneath them. He had to get out of the road only twice again: once for a family in a spring wagon coming up from Hargrave and once for another horse and rider coming down from Port William. Except for those, nothing moved in the still heat but himself. Except for the cicadas, the only sounds he heard were his own steady footfalls on the dry dust.

He seemed to see always not only the changing road beneath his feet but also that other world in which he had lived, now lighted in the dark behind him, and it came to him that on that day two lives had ended for a possibility that never had existed: for Abner Coulter's mounting up to a better place. And he felt the emptiness open wider in him and again heard himself groan. He wondered, so great was the pain of that emptiness, that he did not weep, but it exceeded weeping as it exceeded words. Beyond the scope of one man's grief, it cried out in the air around him, as if in that day's hot light the trees and the fields and the dust of the road all grieved. An inward pressure that had given his body its shape seemed to have been withdrawn, and he walked, holding himself, resisting step by step the urge to bend around the emptiness opening in his middle and let himself fall.

Where the valley began to widen toward the river's mouth, the road passed a large bottom planted in corn. Thad looked back, expecting that he would see Martha Elizabeth, and he did see her. She was maybe three-quarters of a mile behind him, small in the distance, and the heat rising off the field shimmered and shook between them, but he knew her. He walked faster, and he did not look back again. It seemed to him that she knew everything he knew, and loved him anyhow. She loved him, minute by minute, not only as he had been but as he had become. It was a wonderful and a fearful thing to him that he had caused such a love for himself to come into the world and then had failed it. He could not have bowed low enough before it and remained above ground. He could not bear to think of it. But he knew that she walked behind him – balanced across the distance, in the same hot light, the same darkness, the same crying air – ever at the same speed that he walked.

Finally he came to the cluster of houses at Ellville, at the end of the bridge, and went across into Hargrave. From the bridge to the courthouse, he went ever deeper into the Saturday crowd, but he did not alter his gait or look at anybody. If anybody looked at him, he did not know it. At the cross streets, he could see on the river a towboat pushing a line of barges slowly upstream, black smoke gushing from its stacks. The walks were full of people, and the streets were full of buggies and wagons. He crossed the courthouse yard where people sat on benches or stood talking in little groups under the shade trees. It seemed to him that he walked in a world from which he had departed.

When he went through the front door of the courthouse into the sudden cool darkness of the hallway, he could not see. Lights swam in his eyes in the dark, and he had to prop himself against the wall. The place smelled of old paper and tobacco and of human beings, washed and unwashed. When he could see again, he walked to a door under a sign that said 'Sheriff' and went in. It was a tall room lighted by two tall windows. There was a row of chairs for people to wait in, and several spittoons, placed at the presumed convenience of spitters, that had been as much missed as hit. No one was there but a large man in a broad-brimmed straw hat and a suit somewhat too small, who was standing behind a high desk, writing something. At first he did not look up. When he finally did look up, he stared at Thad for some time, as if not sufficiently convinced of what he saw.

'In a minute,' he said, and looked down again and finished what he was writing. There was a badge pinned lopsidedly to the pocket of his shirt, and he held an unlit cigar like another pen in his left hand. He said as he wrote, 'You look like most of you has been wore off.'

'Yes,' Thad said. 'I have killed a man.'

The sheriff laid the pen on the blotter and looked up. 'Who?'

Thad said, 'Ben Feltner, the best friend I ever had.' His eyes suddenly brimmed with tears, but they did not fall. He made no sound and he did not move.

'You're a Coulter, ain't you? From up about Port William?'

'Thad,' Thad said.

The sheriff would have preferred that Thad had remained a fugitive. He did not want a self-confessed murderer on his hands – especially not one fresh from a Saturday killing in Port William. He knew Ben Feltner, knew he was liked, and feared there would be a commotion. Port William, as far as he was concerned, was nothing but trouble, almost beyond the law's reach and certainly beyond its convenience – a source, as far as he was concerned, of never foreseeable bad news. He did not know what would come next, but he thought that something would, and he did not approve of it.

'I wish to hell,' he said, 'that everybody up there who is going to kill each other would just by God go ahead and do it.' He looked at Thad for some time in silence, as if giving him an opportunity to disappear.

'Well,' he said, finally, 'I reckon you just as well give me that pistol.'

He gestured toward Thad's sagging hip pocket, and Thad took out the pistol and gave it to him.

'Come on,' the sheriff said.

Thad followed him out a rear door into the small paved yard of the jail, where the sheriff rang for the jailer.

The sheriff had hardly got back into the office and taken up his work again when a new motion in the doorway alerted him. He looked up and saw a big red-faced girl standing just outside the door as if uncertain whether or not it was lawful to enter. She wore a sunbonnet, a faded blue dress that reached to her ankles, and an apron. Though she was obviously timid and unused to public places, she returned his look with perfect candor.

'Come in,' he said.

She crossed the threshold and again stopped.

'What can I do for you, miss?'

'I'm a-looking for Mr Thad Coulter from up to Port William, please, sir.'

'You his daughter?'

'Yes, sir.'

'Well, he's here. I got him locked up. He claims he killed a fellow.'

'He did,' the girl said. 'Is it allowed to see him?'

'Not now,' the sheriff said. 'You come back in the morning, miss. You can see him then.'

She stood looking at him another moment, as if to make sure that he had said what he meant, and then she said, 'Well, I thank you,' and went out.

An hour or so later, when he shut the office and started home to supper, she was sitting on the end of one of the benches under the shade trees, looking down at her hands in her lap.

'You see,' my grandmother said, 'there are two deaths in this – Mr Feltner's and Thad Coulter's. We know Mr Feltner's because we had to know it. It was ours. That we know Thad's is because of Martha Elizabeth. The Martha Elizabeth you know.'

I knew her, but it came strange to me now to think of her – to be asked to see her – as a girl. She was what I considered an old woman when I first remember her; she was perhaps eight or ten years younger than my grandmother, the red long gone from her hair. She was a woman always near to smiling, sometimes to laughter. Her face, it seemed, had been made to smile. It was a face that assented wholly to the being of whatever and whomever she looked at. She had gone with her father to the world's edge and had come back with this smile on her face.

Miss Martha Elizabeth, we younger ones called her. Everybody loved her.

When the sheriff came back from supper, she was still there on the bench, the Saturday night shoppers and talkers, standers and passers leaving a kind of island around her, as if unwilling to acknowledge the absolute submission they sensed in her. The sheriff knew as soon as he laid eyes on her this time that she was not going to go away. Perhaps he understood that she had no place to go that she could get to before it would be time to come back.

'Come on with me,' he said, and he did not sound like a sheriff now but only a man.

She got up and followed him through the hallway of the courthouse, past the locked doors of the offices, out again, and across the little iron-fenced courtyard in front of the jail. The sheriff unlocked a heavy sheet-iron door, opened it, and closed it behind them, and they were in a large room of stone, steel, and concrete, containing several cages, barred from floor to ceiling, the whole interior lighted by one kerosene lamp hanging in the corridor.

Among the bars gleaming dimly and the shadows of bars thrown back against concrete and stone, she saw her father sitting on the edge of a bunk that was only an iron shelf let down on chains from the wall, with a thin mattress laid on it. He had paid no attention when they entered. He sat still, staring at the wall, one hand pressed against his belly, the other holding to one of the chains that supported the bunk.

The sheriff opened the cell door and stood aside to let her in. 'I'll come back after a while,' he said.

The door closed and was locked behind her, and she stood still until Thad felt her presence and looked up. When he recognized her, he covered his face with both hands.

'He put his hands over his face like a man ashamed,' my grandmother said. 'But he was like a man, too, who had seen what he couldn't bear.'

She sat without speaking a moment, looking at me, for she had much to ask of me.

'Maybe Thad saw his guilt full and clear then. But what he saw that he couldn't bear was something else.'

And again she paused, looking at me. We sat facing each other on either side of the window; my grandfather lay in one of his lengthening sleeps nearby. The old house in that moment seemed filled with a quiet that extended not only out into the whole broad morning but endlessly both ways in time.

'People sometimes talk of God's love as if it's a pleasant thing. But it is terrible, in a way. Think of all it includes. It included Thad Coulter, drunk and mean and foolish, before he killed Mr Feltner, and it included him afterwards.'

She reached out then and touched the back of my right hand with her fingers; my hand still bears that touch, invisible and yet indelible as a tattoo.

'That's what Thad saw. He saw his guilt. He had killed his friend. He had done what he couldn't undo; he had destroyed what he couldn't make. But in the same moment he saw his guilt included in love that stood as near him as Martha Elizabeth and at that moment wore her flesh. It was surely weak and wrong of him to kill himself – to sit in judgment that way over himself. But surely God's love includes people who can't bear it.'

The sheriff took Martha Elizabeth home with him that night; his wife fed her and turned back the bed for her in the spare room. The next day she sat with her father in his cell.

'All that day,' my grandmother said, 'he would hardly take his hands from his face. Martha Elizabeth fed him what little he would eat and raised the cup to his lips for what little he would drink. And he ate and drank only because she asked him to, almost not at all. I don't know what they said. Maybe nothing.'

At bedtime again that night Martha Elizabeth went home with the sheriff. When they returned to the courthouse on Monday morning, Thad Coulter was dead by his own hand.

'It's a hard story to have to know,' my grandmother said. 'The mercy of it was Martha Elizabeth.'

She still had more to tell, but she paused again, and again she looked at me and touched my hand.

'If God loves the ones we can't,' she said, 'then finally maybe we can. All these years I've thought of him sitting in those shadows, with Martha Elizabeth standing beside him, and his work-sore old hands over his face.'

Once the body of Ben Feltner was laid on his bed, the men who had helped Jack to carry him home went quietly out through the kitchen and the back door, as they had come in, muttering or nodding their commiseration in response to Nancy's 'Thank you'. And Jack stayed. He stayed to be within sight or call of his sister when she needed him, and he stayed to keep his eye on Mat. Their struggle in front of Chatham's store, Jack knew, had changed them both. Because he did not yet know how or how much or if it was complete, it was not yet a change that he was willing, or that he dared, to turn his back on.

Someone was sent to take word to Rebecca Finley, Margaret's mother, and to ask her to come for Bess.

When Rebecca came, Margaret brought Bess down the stairs into the quiet that the women now did their best to disguise. But Bess, who did not know what was wrong and who tactfully allowed the pretense that nothing was, knew nevertheless that the habits of the house were now broken, and she had heard the quiet that she would never forget.

'Grandma Finley is here to take you home with her,' Margaret said, giving her voice the lilt of cheerfulness. 'You've been talking about going to stay with her, haven't you?'

And Bess said, dutifully supplying the smile she felt her mother wanted, 'Yes, mam.'

'We're going to bake some cookies just as soon as we get home,' Rebecca said. 'Do you want to bake a gingerbread boy?'

'Yes, mam,' Bess said.

She removed her hand from her mother's hand and placed it in her grandmother's. They went out the door.

The quiet returned. From then on, though there was much that had to be done and the house stayed full of kin and neighbors coming and going or staying to help, and though by midafternoon women were already bringing food, the house preserved a quiet against all sound. No voice was raised. No door was slammed. Everybody moved as if in consideration, not of each other, but of the quiet itself – as if the quiet denoted some fragile peacefulness in Ben's new sleep that must not be intruded upon.

Jack Beechum was party to that quiet. He made no sound. He said nothing, for his own silence had become wonderful to him and he could not bear to break it. Though Nancy, after the death of their mother, had given Jack much of his upbringing and had been perhaps more his mother than his sister, Ben had never presumed to be a father to him. From the time Jack was eight years old, Ben had been simply his friend – had encouraged, instructed, corrected, helped, and stood by him; had placed a kindly, humorous, forbearing expectation upon him that he could not shed or shirk and had at last lived up to. They had been companions. And yet, through the rest of that day, Jack had his mind more on Mat than on Ben.

Jack watched Mat as he would have watched a newborn colt weak on its legs that he had helped to stand, that might continue to stand or might not. All afternoon Jack did not sit down because Mat did not. Sometimes there were things to do, and they were busy. Space for the coffin had to be made in the living room. Furniture had to be moved. When the time came, the laden coffin had to be moved into place. But, busy or not, Mat was almost constantly moving, as if seeking his place in a world newly made that day, a world still shaking and doubtful underfoot. And Jack both moved with him and stayed apart from him, watching. When they spoke again, they would speak on different terms. In its quiet, the house seemed to be straining to accommodate Ben's absence, made undeniable by the presence of his body lying still under his folded hands.

Jack would come later to his own reckoning with that loss, the horror and the pity of it, and the grief, the awe and gratitude and love and sorrow and regret, when Ben, newly dead and renewing sorrow for others dead before, would wholly occupy his mind in the night, and could give no comfort, and would not leave. But now Jack stayed by Mat and helped as he could.

In the latter part of the afternoon came Della Budge, Miss Della, bearing an iced cake on a stand like a lighted lamp. As she left the kitchen and started for the front door, she laid her eyes on Jack, who was standing in the door between the living room and the hall. She was a large woman, far gone in years. It was a labor for her to walk. She advanced each foot ahead of the other with care, panting, her hand on her hip, rocking from side to side. She wore many clothes, for her blood was thin and she was easily chilled, and she carried a fan, for sometimes she got too warm. Her little dustcap struggled to stay on top of her head. A tiny pair of spectacles perched awry on her nose. She had a face like a shriveled apple, and the creases at the corners of her mouth were stained with snuff. Once, she had been Jack's teacher. For years they had waged a contest in which she had endeavored to teach him the begats from Abraham to Jesus and he had refused to learn them. He was one of her failures, but she maintained a proprietary interest in him nonetheless. She was the only one left alive who called him 'Jackie'.

As she came up to him he said, 'Hello, Miss Della.'

'Well, Jackie,' she said, lifting and canting her nose to bring her spectacles to bear upon him, 'poor Ben has met his time.'

'Yes, mam,' Jack said. 'One of them things.'

'When your time comes you must go, by the hand of man or the stroke of God.'

'Yes, mam,' Jack said. He was standing with his hands behind him, leaning back against the doorjamb.

'It'll come by surprise,' she said. 'It's a time appointed, but we'll not be notified.'

Jack said he knew it. He did know it.

'So we must always be ready,' she said. 'Pray without ceasing.'

'Yes, mam.'

'Well, God bless Ben Feltner. He was a good man. God rest his soul.'

Jack stepped ahead of her to help her out the door and down the porch steps.

'Why, thank you, Jackie,' she said as she set foot at last on the walk.

He stood and watched her going away, walking, it seemed to him, a tottering edge between eternity and time.

Toward evening Margaret laid the table, and the family and several of the neighbor women gathered in the kitchen. Only two or three men had come, and they were sitting in the living room by the coffin. The table was spread with the abundance of food that had been brought in. They were just preparing to sit down when the murmur of voices they had been hearing from the road down in front of the stores seemed to converge and to move in their direction. Those in the kitchen stood and listened a moment, and then Mat started for the front of the house. The others followed him through the hall and out onto the porch.

The sun was down, the light cool and directionless, so that the colors of the foliage and of the houses and storefronts of the town seemed to glow. Chattering swifts circled and swerved above the chimneys. Nothing else moved except the crowd that made its way at an almost formal pace into the yard. The people standing on the porch were as still as everything else, except for Jack Beechum who quietly made his way forward until he stood behind and a little to the left of Mat, who was standing at the top of the steps.

The crowd moved up near the porch and stopped. There was a moment of hesitation while it murmured and jostled inside itself.

'Be quiet, boys,' somebody said. 'Let Doc do the talking.'

They became still, and then Doctor Starns, who stood in the front rank, took a step forward.

'Mat,' he said, 'we're here as your daddy's friends. We've got word that Thad Coulter's locked up in the jail at Hargrave. We want you to know that we won't stand for the thing he did.'

Several voices said, 'No!' and 'Nosir!'

'We don't think we can stand for it, or that we ought to, or that we ought to wait on somebody else's opinion about it.'

Somebody said, 'That's right!'

'We think it's our business, and we propose to make it so.'

'That's right!' said several voices.

'It's only up to you to say the word, and we'll put justice beyond question.'

And in the now-silent crowd someone held up a coil of rope, a noose already tied.

The doctor gave a slight bow of his head to Mat and then to Nancy who now stood behind Mat and to his right. And again the crowd murmured and slightly stirred within itself.

For what seemed to Jack a long time, Mat did not speak or move. The crowd grew quiet again, and again they could hear the swifts chattering in the air. Jack's right hand ached to reach out to Mat. It seemed to him again that he felt the earth shaking under his feet, as Mat felt it. But though it shook and though they felt it, Mat now stood resolved and calm upon it. Looking at the back of his head, Jack could still see the boy in him, but the head was up. The voice, when it came, was steady:

'No, gentlemen. I appreciate it. We all do. But I ask you not to do that.'

And Jack, who had not sat down since morning, stepped back and sat down.

Nancy, under whose feet the earth was not shaking, if it ever had, stepped up beside her son and took his arm.

She said to the crowd, 'I know you are my husband's friends. I thank you. I, too, must ask you not to do as you propose. Mat has asked you; I have asked you; if Ben could, he would ask you. Let us make what peace is left for us to make.'

84

Mat said, 'Come and be with us. We have food, and you all are welcome.'

He had said, in all, six brief sentences. He was not a forward man. This, I think, was the only public speech of his life.

'I can see him yet,' my grandmother said, her eyes, full of sudden moisture, again turned to the window. 'I wish you could have seen him.'

And now, after so many years, perhaps I have. I have sought that moment out, or it has sought me, and I see him standing without prop in the deepening twilight, asking his father's friends to renounce the vengeance that a few hours before he himself had been furious to exact.

This is the man who will be my grandfather – the man who will be the man who was my grandfather. The tenses slur and slide under the pressure of collapsed time. For that moment on the porch is not a now that was but a now that is and will be, inhabiting all the history of Port William that followed and will follow. I know that in the days after his father's death – and after Thad Coulter, concurring in the verdict of his would-be jurors in Port William, hanged himself in the Hargrave jail and so released Martha Elizabeth from her watch – my grandfather renewed and carried on his friendship with the Coulters: with Thad's widow and daughters, with Dave Coulter and his family, and with another first cousin of Thad's, Marce Catlett, my grandfather on my father's side. And when my father asked leave of the Feltners to marry their daughter Bess, my mother, he was made welcome.

Mat Feltner dealt with Ben's murder by not talking about it and thus keeping it in the past. In his last years, I liked to get him to tell me about the violent old times of the town, the hard drinking and the fighting. And he would oblige me up to a point, enjoying the outrageous stories himself, I think. But always there would come a time in the midst of the telling when he would become silent, shake his head, lift one hand and let it fall; and I would know – I know better now than I did then – that he had remembered his father's death.

No Feltner or Coulter of the name is left now in Port William. But the Feltner line continues, joined to the Coulter line, in me, and I am here. I am blood kin to both sides of that moment when Ben Feltner turned to face Thad Coulter in the road and Thad pulled the trigger. The two families, sundered in the ruin of a friendship, were united again first in new friendship and then in marriage. My grandfather made a peace here that has joined many who would otherwise have been divided. I am the child of his forgiveness.

After Mat spoke the second time, inviting them in, the crowd loosened and came apart. Some straggled back down into the town; others, as Mat had asked, came into the house, where their wives already were.

But Jack did not stay with them. As soon as he knew he was free, his thoughts went to other things. His horse had stood a long time, saddled, without water or feed. The evening chores were not yet done. Ruth would be wondering what had happened. In the morning they would come back together, to be of use if they could. And there would be, for Jack as for the others, the long wearing of grief. But now he could stay no longer.

As soon as the porch was cleared, he retrieved his hat from the hall tree and walked quietly out across the yard under the maples and the descending night. So as not to be waylaid by talk, he walked rapidly in the middle of the road to where he had tied his horse. Lamps had now been lighted in the stores and the houses. As he approached, his horse nickered to him.

'I know it,' Jack said.

As soon as the horse felt his rider's weight in the stirrup, he started. Soon the lights and noises of the town were behind them, and there were only a few stars, a low red streak in the west, and the horse's eager footfalls on the road.

A Half-Pint of Old Darling
(1920)

Ptolemy Proudfoot and Miss Minnie did not often take a lively interest in politics. They were Democrats, like virtually everybody else in the vicinity of Cotman Ridge and Goforth. They had been born Democrats, had never been anything but Democrats, and had never thought of being anything but Democrats. To them, being Democrats was much the same sort of thing as being vertebrates; it was not a matter of lively interest. Their daily lives were full of matters that were in the most literal sense lively: gardens and crops and livestock, kitchen and smokehouse and cellar, shed and barn and pen, plantings and births and harvests, washing and ironing and cooking and canning and cleaning, feeding and milking, patching and mending. That their life was surrounded by great public issues they knew and considered, and yet found a little strange.

The year 1920, however, was one of unusually lively political interest, especially for Miss Minnie. In January of that year, the constitutional amendment forbidding 'the manufacture, sale, or transportation of intoxicating liquors' went into effect. And in August the women's suffrage amendment was ratified. Miss Minnie did not approve of drinking intoxicating liquors, which she believed often led to habitual drunkenness. And she certainly did believe that women ought to have the vote.

Tol, for his part, enjoyed a bottle of beer occasionally, and occasionally he had been known to enjoy a good drink of somebody else's whiskey – whether homemade or bottled in bond he did not particularly care, so long as it was good. He liked whiskey of a quality to cure a sore throat, not cause one. This was not something that Miss Minnie knew or that Tol had ever considered telling her. It was not something she had ever had any occasion – or, so far as he knew, any need – to know. Liquor also was something that he could easily go without. If the country chose not to drink, then he could comfortably endure the deprivation as long as the country could.

And so very little was said between them on the subject of the Prohibition amendment. Miss Minnie belonged to the Women's Christian Temperance Union, and supported the amendment, and that was all right with Tol, and that was that.

On the question of the suffrage amendment, Tol's conclusion was that if he had the vote, and if (as he believed) Miss Minnie was smarter than he was, then Miss Minnie should have the vote. Miss Minnie (who did not think she was smarter than Tol, and did not wish to be) said that though Tol had not accurately weighed all the evidence, his reasoning was perfect.

'The vote', said Tol, 'means that us onlookers and by-standers get to have a little bit of say-so.'

'And I want my little bit,' Miss Minnie said.

'So it's out with the whiskey and in with the women,' Tol said.

Miss Minnie let him have a smile then, for she loved his wit, but she said that by and large she thought that was the way it would have to be, for women hated liquor because of all they'd had to suffer from drunken men. She had seen some of her own students grow up to be worthless drunkards.

Tol said that she was right there, and he knew it. By and large, he was content to believe as she believed. She had been a schoolteacher and knew books, and he looked up to her.

*

To say that Tol looked up to Miss Minnie is to use a figure of speech, for Tol was an unusually big man and Miss Minnie an unusually small woman. And so at the moment when he was in spirit looking up to her, he was in the flesh beaming down upon her from beneath a swatch of hair that projected above his brows like a porch roof.

It was still dark on a morning in the middle of November. Tol had done his chores while Miss Minnie fixed breakfast; they had eaten and, having completed their conversation, had stood up from the table. Tol's hair, which he had wetted and combed when he washed his face, had reverted to its habit of sticking out this way and that. This condition had been aggravated by Tol's habit of scratching under his cap from time to time without taking it off. To an impartial observer Tol might have looked a little funny, as though he had put a pile of jackstraws on his head.

Miss Minnie, however, was not an impartial observer. To her he looked comfortable. To her he was shelter and warmth. When he smiled down at her that way, it was to her as though the sun itself had looked kindly at her through the foliage of a tall tree.

It was a Saturday morning. That day they were going to make one of their twice- or thrice-yearly trips to Hargrave, the county seat, ten miles down the river from Port William.

Tol said he had a few odds and ends to do at the barn before he harnessed Redbird. And Miss Minnie said that would be fine, for she had to finish up in the house and ought to be ready by the time he would be.

Tol said, well, he thought they needn't be in a big hurry, for it was a little nippy out, and maybe they should give it a chance to warm up. And Miss Minnie said, yes, that was fine.

And so in the slowly strengthening gray November daylight

Tol set things to rights around the barn, the way he liked to do on Saturday, and brought Redbird out of his stall and curried and brushed and harnessed him, and left him tied in the driveway of the barn. Tol pulled the buggy out of its shed then and went back to the house. He shaved at the washstand by the kitchen door and put on the fresh clothes that Miss Minnie had laid out for him.

Miss Minnie had the gift of neatness. Her house was neat, and she was neat herself. Even in her everyday dresses she always looked as if she were expecting company. This in addition to her fineness of mind and character made her, Tol thought, a person of quality. Tol loved the word *quality* much as he loved the words of horse anatomy such as *pastern, stifle,* and *hock.* He liked it when a buyer said to him of his crop or a load of lambs or steers, 'Well, Mr Proudfoot, I see you've come with quality again this year.' And when he thought about what a fine woman Miss Minnie was, with her neat ways and her book learning and her correct grammar, he enjoyed saying to himself, 'She's got quality.'

Tol was like Miss Minnie in his love of neatness, and his farm was neatly kept. His barn was as neat in its way as Miss Minnie's house. But Tol was not a neat person. He was both too big, I assume, and too forgetful of himself to look neat in his clothes. The only time Tol's clothes looked good was before he put them on. In putting them on, he forgot about them and began, without the slightest malice toward them, to subject them to various forms of abuse. When he had got them on that morning, Miss Minnie came in and went over them, straightening his shirtfront, buttoning his cuffs, tucking in his pocket handkerchief and the end of his belt. She pecked over his clothes with concentrated haste, like a banty hen pecking over a barn floor, as if Tol were not occupying them at all, Tol meanwhile ignoring her as he transferred his pocket stuff from his discarded pants and put on his cap and coat.

'Now you look all nice,' she said.

And Tol said, 'You look mighty nice, too, little lady.' That was his endearment, and she gave him a pat.

The sun had come up behind clouds, and from the looks of the sky it would be cloudy all day.

'Is it going to rain?' Miss Minnie said.

'I doubt it,' Tol said. 'May snow along about evening, from the looks of things and the feel of that wind.'

They went together to where the buggy stood. Tol brought Redbird from the barn and put him between the shafts, handed Miss Minnie up into the buggy, and got in himself, the buggy tilting somewhat to his side as his weight bore on the springs, so that it was natural for Miss Minnie to sit close to him. Sitting close to him was not something she ever minded, but on that morning it was particularly gratifying, for the wind, as Tol said, was 'a little blue around the edges'. They snugged the lap robe around them and drove out onto the road.

For a while they did not talk. Redbird was a young horse in those days, Tol having hitched him for the first time only that spring, and he was feeling good. The sharp air made him edgy. He was startled by the steam clouds of his breath, and he enjoyed the notion that he was in danger of being run over by the buggy rolling behind him.

'Cutting up like a new pair of scissors, ain't he?' Tol said. 'Whoa, my little Redbird! Whoa, my boy! Settle down, now!' Tol sang to the colt in a low, soothing voice. 'You'll be thinking different thoughts by dark.'

Redbird and his notions amused Tol. He gave him his head a little, letting him trot at some speed.

'He requires a steady hand, doesn't he?' Miss Minnie said, impressed as always by Tol's horsemanship.

'He's a little notional,' Tol said. 'He'll get over it.'

Redbird abandoned his notions about halfway up the first long hill, and settled down to a steady jog. Tol could relax then, and he and Miss Minnie resumed their never-ending conversation about the things they saw along the road and the things those sights reminded them of, and this morning, too, they talked more from time to time about politics.

What brought the subject up now, as at breakfast, was that in this year of unusual political interest Latham Gallagher was running for the office of state representative. 'The Gallagher boy', as Miss Minnie called him, had been sheriff and court clerk, and now he aspired to the seat of government in Frankfort. He was the son of an old friend of Miss Minnie's, and for that reason Miss Minnie thought him fine and handsome and an excellent orator. A month or so ago she and Tol had gone to hear him speak on the porch of the old hotel in Port William.

Tol thought that the Gallagher boy had already made far too much of some of his opportunities, and he did not like oratory made up of too many sentences beginning 'My fellow Kentuckians', but he kept his opinions to himself. The boy, after all, was a Democrat, which meant that there was at least one worse thing he could have been.

Now and again as they drove along, Tol and Miss Minnie would see one of the Gallagher boy's posters attached to a tree or a telephone pole. 'Gallagher for Representative', the posters said, 'A Fair Shake for the Little Man'.

'A Fair Shake for the Little Woman,' said Tol Proudfoot, nudging Miss Minnie beneath the lap robe, and she nudged him back.

They went through Port William and on down the river road

to Ellville and over the bridge into Hargrave, talking the whole way. It had been a busy fall; Tol had been out of the house from daylight to dark, and Miss Minnie had been equally preoccupied with her own work, preparing for winter. So it was pleasant to ride along behind the now-dutiful Redbird, in no particular hurry, and just visit, telling each other all they'd thought of and meant to say as soon as they found a chance.

When they got to Hargrave, they left Redbird at the livery stable where he could rest well and have some hay to eat and a ration of grain while they went about their errands. At first they did a little shopping together, and carried their purchases back and stored them in the buggy. And then they went to the Broadfield Hotel to eat dinner. This was a place Tol particularly favored because they did not bring the meals out on individual plates to little separate tables, but instead the patrons sat together at long tables, and the food was set before them on heaped platters and in large bowls, and pans of hot biscuits and cornbread were passing around almost continuously, and pitchers of sweet milk and buttermilk and pots of coffee were always in reach, and when a person's plate began to look clean, there would be waiters coming around with various kinds of pie, and all of it was good. It was a place where a man like Tol could eat all he wanted without calling too much attention to himself – cooking for him, Miss Minnie had been heard to say, was like cooking for a hotel – and where also he could have his fill of conversation. Tol loved to eat and he loved to talk. The hotel dining room appealed to him because while he ate there he could expect to be in the company of some people he knew and of some he did not know, and in the course of a meal he would extract from all of them a great deal of information about themselves, their families, and their businesses or farms – also their opinions about the national and local economies, the market prospects for tobacco, cattle, sheep, and hogs, and any other opinions they might care to express. The meal characteristically would take an hour and a half or two hours, for Tol stretched to the limit the leisure and the pleasure of it. It was one of the main reasons for their trip to Hargrave, as Miss Minnie knew, though Tol never said so. He ate and talked and laughed and complimented the cooks and urged more food on his fellow guests just as if he were at home.

When the meal was over and they had lingered, talking, at the table for long enough, Tol and Miss Minnie strolled out onto the hotel porch, from which they could see the broad Ohio River flowing past and the mouth of their own smaller river opening into it. The ferry that connected Hargrave with the nearby towns in Indiana pulled away from the dock while they watched.

And then Miss Minnie, who wanted to buy Tol's Christmas present, a little awkwardly presented the falsehood that she had 'a few little errands' and would meet him at the livery stable in an hour and a half. Her business would not require that long, but she knew that Tol, wherever he went, would get to talking and would be that long at least. Tol, who wished to do some private shopping of his own, agreed, and they parted.

Tol first returned to a dry goods store that he and Miss Minnie had visited together that morning. He had heard her say to a clerk of a certain bolt of cloth, intending perhaps that he should overhear, 'Now *that's* pretty.' He bought her enough of the cloth to make a dress. And then, because it took so little cloth to make a dress for Miss Minnie, he went to another store and bought her a pretty comb that caught his eye, and also – what he had never done before – he bought a bottle of perfume, which lasted for years and years because, as Miss Minnie said, it smelled so wonderful that she used it seldom and only the teensiest bit at a time. He stuck these things into various pockets to be smuggled home, talked with the clerk until another customer came in, and went back out to the street.

The thought struck him then that he might not get back to Hargrave before his ewes started to lamb, and he was out of whiskey. Tol always liked to keep a little whiskey on hand during lambing. Some sheepmen would say that if you had a weak lamb and a bottle of whiskey, it paid better to knock the lamb in the head and drink the whiskey yourself. But Tol believed that 'a drop or two', on a bitter night, would sometimes encourage a little heart to continue beating – as, despite his religion and Miss Minnie, he believed it had sometimes encouraged bigger ones to do.

And so, without giving the matter much thought, he went to the drugstore where he was used to buying the occasional half-pint that he needed. And then, as he entered the door, he thought, 'Prohibition!' And then he thought, 'Well, no harm in trying.'

So he went up to the druggist, whom he knew, who was leaning against a wall of shelves behind the counter in the back.

'I don't reckon you could let me have half a pint of whiskey,' Tol said to him in a low voice.

'Medicinal?' the druggist asked.

'Medicinal,' Tol said, nodding.

The druggist handed him a half-pint bottle, and Tol stuck it into his pocket and paid. It was a local brand known as Old Darling – a leftover, Tol supposed.

The druggist, also a conversationalist, said, 'Somebody a little under the weather?'

'No,' Tol said. 'Lambs. I like to have a little on hand when I'm lambing.'

There followed an exchange of some length in which Tol and the druggist told each other a number of things that both of them already knew.

When he was back at the livery stable, hitching Redbird to the buggy, Tol remembered the bottle and tossed it onto the floor of the buggy box under the seat, thinking not much about it one way or another.

Redbird, well rested and fed and now going in his favorite direction, required a good bit of attention at first. They were across the bridge and well out into the country again before he settled down. When he settled down, Tol settled down, too, and so did Miss Minnie. The interests and pleasures of the town were all behind them, the trip had fulfilled its purposes, and now they had ahead of them only the long drive home and their evening chores, which would seem a little strange after their day in town. Tol drove with his eye on Redbird and the road ahead, humming to himself in a grunty, tuneless way that meant, Miss Minnie knew, that he had gone way off among his thoughts and no longer knew she was there. 'Mr Proudfoot,' she had actually said to him once, 'when you are thinking you might as well be asleep.'

That made him laugh, for he enjoyed a good joke on himself. But it was true. Sometimes, in his thoughts, he departed from where he was. Tol and Miss Minnie had been married for twelve years. In that time they had found how secret their lives had been before. They had made many small discoveries that were sometimes exciting, sometimes not. One of the best had been Tol's discovery that Miss Minnie could whistle.

Though he had known a whistling woman or two in his time, he had always known also the proverb holding that

> *These will come to no good end:*
> *A whistling woman and a crowing hen,*

and he assumed that Miss Minnie, who had quality, would be the last woman on earth to whistle. Imagine his surprise, then, not long after they were married, when he was going by the house one morning and overheard Miss Minnie rattling the breakfast dishes and whistling 'Old Joe Clark' as prettily and effortlessly as a songbird.

That night after supper, when they were sitting together by the fire, he said to her, 'Go ahead. Whistle. I know you can do it. I heard you.'

So she whistled for him – 'Soldier's Joy' this time. It was a secret revelation. It made them so gleeful she could hardly control her pucker.

And now I am going to tell about the more famous revelation by which Miss Minnie learned Tol's method of reviving a weak lamb.

Tol had been humming and thinking only a little while when Miss Minnie needed to blow her nose. Her handkerchief was in her purse, which she had set behind her heels under the seat of the buggy. She fished under the lap robe with her hand to bring it up and so encountered the cold hard shape of Tol's half-pint bottle of Old Darling. It was a shape that, as an avid student of the problem of drunkenness, she knew very well. Thereupon a suspicion flew into her mind – as sudden and dark as a bat this suspicion was, and as hard to ignore in such close quarters.

She felt the bottle again to make sure, and then stealthily drew

98

it up to the light on the side opposite Tol, and looked at it. At the sight of it, she could have wept and cried out with anger and with bitter, bitter disappointment. The label carried the seductive name of Old Darling, and it declared shamelessly that the bottle contained whiskey, ninety proof. That the amber liquid inside the bottle was actually rather beautiful to the eye did not surprise her, for she knew that the devil made sin attractive.

She almost flung the bottle into the roadside weeds right there and then, but two thoughts prevented her. First, she imagined that if the bottle did not hit a rock and break, then some innocent boy or young man might come along and find it and be tempted to drink the whiskey, and that would not do. Second – and perhaps this thought was not even second, for her mind was working fast – she remembered that whiskey was an expensive product. When she thought, 'It would be a shame to waste it,' she meant of course the money that Tol had spent for the whiskey, not the whiskey itself.

But she did think, 'It would be a shame to waste it', and the thought put her in a quandary. For if she did not want to throw the whiskey away, neither did she want to put it back under the seat to be carried home and drunk by her wayward husband, from the mystery of whose being this bottle had emerged.

And now Miss Minnie's mind revolved in a curious metamorphosis from the great virtue of thriftiness to the much smaller virtue of romantic self-sacrifice. Her anger and disappointment at Tol as she now had discovered him to be only increased her love for him as she had thought him to be – and as he might, in fact, become, if only she could save him from his addiction to the evil drug that she at that moment held in her hand. For such a man as he *might* be, she felt, she would do anything. She had read much of loyalties given and sacrifices made by the wives of drinking men. In her love for Tol, she had at times already wished to be capable of some legendary fidelity or sacrifice to make her worthy of her happiness in him. And by how much now was this wish magnified by her thought of Tol fallen and redeemed! 'Oh,' she thought, 'I will do it! I will say to the world I did it without hesitation.' She shifted as she might have shifted if she had wanted to look at something interesting off to the right-hand side of the road.

She broke the paper seal and twisted out the cork. She put her nose carefully over the opening and sniffed the vile fumes. *'Awful!'* she thought. And the thought of its awfulness made her sacrifice more pleasing to her. She tilted the bottle and drew forth bravely half a mouthful and swallowed it.

It was fire itself in her throat. If she had looked quickly enough, she thought, she would have seen a short orange flame protruding from her nose. Though she sternly suppressed the impulse to cough, there was no refusing the tears that filled her eyes.

But then as the fiery swallow descended into her stomach, a most pleasing warmth, a warmth at once calming and invigorating, began to radiate from it. For a few minutes she bestowed upon this warmth the meditation that it seemed to require, and then she tried another swallow, a more wholehearted one. The effect this time was less harsh, because less surprising, and the radiance even warmer and more reassuring than before. She felt strangely ennobled by the third, as if the rewards of her sacrifice were already accruing to her. The radiance within her had begun to gleam also in a sort of nimbus around her. If the devil made sin attractive, then she would have to admit that he had done a splendid job with Old Darling.

She sat half turned away from Tol, and leaning back so that

she sat also a little behind him. He was still departed in his thoughts, no more aware of what she was doing than were the occupants of the occasional buggies and wagons that they met.

Miss Minnie sipped from time to time as they drove along, finding her sacrifice not nearly so difficult as she had expected. In fact, she was amazed at how quickly she was getting rid of the repulsive contents of the bottle. It occurred to her that perhaps she should drink more slowly, for soon there would be none left.

Suddenly she experienced a motion that recalled her to her school days when she had swung in swings and ridden on seesaws. But the likeness was only approximate, for Redbird, the buggy, the road, and indeed the whole landscape had just executed a motion not quite like any she had ever known.

'Whoo!' said Miss Minnie.

Tol had been humming along, figuring and refiguring how much he might get for his crop in view of the various speculations and surmises he had heard in town. When Miss Minnie said 'Whoo!' it was news to him. 'What?' he said.

'Do that again,' she said. 'Oh! Whoo!'

He said, 'What?'

'Old Darling,' she said. 'Whoo!'

'Mam?' Tol Proudfoot said.

And then he saw the bottle in her hand. For a moment he thought he was going to laugh, and then he thought he wasn't. 'Oh, Lordy!' he said. 'Oh, Lordy Lord! Oh, Lord!'

Now as they went around a curve in the road they met another couple in a buggy. Miss Minnie leaned forward and called out to them momentously the name of Gallagher. 'A vote for Gallagher,' she cried, 'is a vote for the little man!'

'Come up, Redbird,' said Tol Proudfoot.

But as luck would have it, speeding up only brought them more quickly face-to-face with the next buggy coming down the road.

'Gallagher!' cried Miss Minnie. 'A fair shake for the little man is a fair shake for the little woman!'

'Miss Minnie,' Tol said, 'I believe you've had about all you need of that.'

He held out his hand for the bottle, and was surprised to see, when she handed it to him, how little was left.

'Take it, then!' she said. 'Drunkard!'

'Drunkard?' he said, and then put out his hand again to steady her, for she was attempting to stand up, the better to point her finger at him. 'No, mam. I'm not no drunkard. You know better.'

'Then *what*,' Miss Minnie said, pointing to the incontrovertible evidence, 'were you doing with *that*?'

'Lambs,' Tol said.

'You get little lambs drunk,' Miss Minnie declared. 'Oh, my dear man, you are the limit.'

'For when they're born on the cold nights,' Tol said. 'Sometimes it'll help the weak ones live.'

'Ha!' said Miss Minnie.

Tol said no more. Miss Minnie spoke only to urge Gallagher upon the people they met – though, fortunately, they met only a few.

By the time they went through Port William, she had ceased to call out, but she was saying in a rather loud voice and to nobody in particular that though she was not sure, she was sure the Gallagher boy had never taken a drink in *his* life – and though she was not sure, she was sure that *he* at least understood that now that women had the vote, there would be no more liquor drinking in the land of the free and the home of the brave. Her voice quivered patriotically.

When they drove in beside the house at last, and Redbird gladly stopped in front of the buggy shed, Tol stepped down and turned to help Miss Minnie, who stood, somewhat grandly spurning his offer, and fell directly into his arms.

Tol carried her to the house, helped her to remove her hat and coat and to lie down on the sofa in the living room. He covered her with the afghan, built up the fire, and returned to the barn to do his chores.

The house was dark when he came back in. Miss Minnie was lying quietly on the sofa with her forearm resting across her brow. Tol tiptoed in and sat down.

After a little while, Miss Minnie said, 'Was it really just for the lambs?'

Tol said, 'Yessum.'

And then Miss Minnie's crying jag began. Regrets flew at her from all sides, and she wept and wept. Of all her sorrows the worst was for her suspicion of Tol. But she mourned also, for his sake and her own, the public display that she had made of herself. 'I surely am the degradedest woman who ever lived,' she said. 'I have shamed myself, and most of all you.'

Tol sat beside her for a long time in the dark, patting her with his big hand and saying, 'Naw, now. Naw, now. You didn't do no such of a thing.'

It was, as Miss Minnie would later say, a lovely time.

When at last she grew quiet and sleepy, Tol helped her to bed and waited beside her until her breath came in little snores. And then he went down to the kitchen and cooked himself a good big supper, for it had been a hard day.

★

This was, oddly, a tale that Miss Minnie enjoyed telling. 'It was my only binge,' she would say, giggling a little. And she liked especially to quote herself. 'I surely am the degradedest woman who ever lived.'

She said, 'Mr Proudfoot was horrified. But after it was over, he just had to rear back and laugh. Oh, he was a man of splendid qualities!'

Down in the Valley Where the
Green Grass Grows
(1930)

You would think a fellow whose paunch was bigger than his
ass would take the precaution of underdrawers. Or suspenders. Or bib overalls. Big Ellis didn't, of course. He never thought
of precautions until too late. After it was too late he could
always tell you what the right precaution would have been
if only he had thought of it. 'Burley,' he would say, 'I see the
point. I've got my sights dead on it.' But he saw it going away,
from behind. And so when he was a young man, and had
grown to his full girth, his pants as a rule were either half
on or he was holding them with one hand to keep them from
falling off.

Big was late getting married. Marriage was a precaution he
didn't think of until his mother died and left him alone to cook
and housekeep for himself. And then he really began to hear
the call of matrimony.

He was quite a dancer in his young days. You would think
at first it was the funniest thing you ever saw. The fiddle music
would carry him clean out of his head, and there he would be,
swinging his partner like she didn't weigh anything, with his
hair in his eyes, his shirt-tail half out, sweating like a horse, his
pants creeping down, and that one hand from time to time
jerking them back up. But if you paid attention to him, you
would soon see that he really was a dancer. He was a smooth
mover, a big man but light on his feet. His feet had ways of
going about their business as if he himself didn't know what
they were up to. They were answering the music, you see, and

not just the caller. He could really step it off. He could cut a shine.

He did all right in his socializing until he got his eye set on a girl, and then he would get shy and awkward and tongue-tied. He would figure then that he needed to get her cornered in some clever and mannerly way that would be beyond his abilities. And he would come up with some of the damnedest, longest-way-around schemes such as nobody ever thought of before and were always well worth knowing about. He edged up to a girl one time at the Fourth of July and said, 'I know a girl's about the prettiest thing ever I looked at,' and was struck dumb when she said, 'Who?' He wrote one a love letter in his outrageous pencil-writing and signed it 'A Friend'. He brought one a live big catfish and held it out to her like it was gold-plated, and never offered so much as to skin it. Those times, I have to say, he was not very serious. What he had in his mind then was sport. As you might call it.

When he began to shine up to Annie May Cordle with the honorable intention of marrying her if she would have him, he outdid himself for judgment. She was about as near the right match for him as he could have found. But he went about the business as perfectly hind-end-foremost as you would have expected. For a while he just hung around her every time he got a chance, looking as big-eyed and solemn as a dying calf. If she looked at him or said anything to him, he turned red and grinned with more teeth than a handsaw and hitched up his pants with both hands.

After he got his crop sold that winter, Big did what he usually would do. He took it in his head to trade off the team of mules he already had, maybe adding a few dollars to boot, for a better team. He always thought he got 'a good deal' on 'a better team', and that was why he never in his life owned a team that was better than passable. In fact he was too big-hearted and generous, especially if he'd had a drink or two, to be any account at all as a trader. Somebody always took his old team and his money, and he wound up with a team just a teensy bit better or worse than what he had before. And so of course he was always wanting to trade.

By springtime sure enough he had his new team, a rabbity pair of three-year-old red mules, not above fifteen hands. Dick and Buck. They sort of matched, and he was proud of them, though they were not hardly what you would call well broke.

The weather got warm. We needed rain, and then we got a showery day that was about what the doctor ordered and made us feel good. The next day it faired up. The ground being too wet to work and the day fine, I walked over to Big's to see what I could put him up to. He was a good one to wander about with on such a day. He was a good companion, always ready for whatever you needed him for. I thought we might drop down to the river and fish a while, maybe.

But when I got to his place he was hitching his new team to the sled. He was going to take a bunch of broken tools to the blacksmith shop in town to get them fixed. It was never any trouble at Big's to find broken tools, which wasn't because he worked all that hard. He just *used* things hard, or he used them for purposes they weren't meant for. He treated wood the same as steel. He had piled onto the sled a plow with a broken handle, a hoe with a broken handle, a grubbing hoe with no handle, a broken doubletree, and other such, too big a load to take in his old car.

'Why don't you use the wagon?' I said.

'Oh,' he said. 'I forgot. Here. Hold the lines a minute.'

He went into the wagon shed and came back rolling a wagon wheel with two broken spokes.

So there was nothing for it but the sled, which wasn't the best vehicle on a gravel road, and with no tongue, behind a team the least bit touchous. And especially that little Buck mule, if I had pegged him right, was just waiting for a good reason to demonstrate his speed. He was the reason Big asked me to hold the lines while he went to get the wagon wheel.

Big had left himself a place to stand in amongst the load. I made myself a place and turned up a five-gallon bucket to sit on. Big told the mules to come up, gave the lines a little flip, and we started off with pretty much of a jerk.

When we hit the gravel, which we would be on all the way to town, you could see that both mules became deeply concerned. They got into a little jiggling trot and backed their ears so as not to miss anything that might be gaining on them. And the runners did screech and batter something awful. But Big was stout enough to hold them and two more like them, if his old lines and bridles held together. Just looking at the back of him, I could see how pleased he was with his team, showing spirit the way they were. And they matched, you know. To some people, and Big was one, a bad team that matches is better than a good team that don't.

So we went stepping pretty lively into Port William. I unloaded the sled at the blacksmith shop while Big kept hold of the lines. And then we started back. There was no chance of loafing a while in town, for the mules couldn't be trusted to stand tied. One backfire from somebody's automobile and they might've disappeared off like two mosquitoes.

But when we got to the mouth of our lane, Big drove right on by. I saw then what he had on his mind. His real business for that morning wasn't to take a bunch of broken tools to town. He was going on out by the Cordles' place. If Annie May was where she could see, she was going to have the benefit of a look at that well-matched, high-spirited team of mules, and of old Big standing there holding the lines, calm as George Washington, everything under control.

The trouble was, by the time we were closing in on the Cordles', after the extra mile or so, the mules had lost their fine edge. They had worn down to a civilized manner of doing business. They were walking along, nodding their heads and letting their ears wag like a seasoned team. Looked like they both together didn't have an ounce of drama left in 'em, and the large impression Big was wanting to make had fallen by the wayside.

So without making a sudden motion I got on my knees and skimmed up a rock about the size of a pocket watch and settled back onto my bucket.

Big, among other things, was a lucky creature. For when we came in sight of the Cordles' house down in the pretty little swale where their farm was, there was Annie May, sure enough, looking sweet as a rose, right out on the front porch. She was churning, working the dasher up and down at a steady gait. She looked patient, gazing off at the sky. Maybe the butter was slow to come and she had been at it a while.

I was wanting to help Big all I could, of course. I waited until I was sure Annie May had seen us coming, until we could almost hear the dasher chugging in the churn, and then I shied that little rock almost under the Buck mule's tail where he felt it the most.

He lost no time in taking offense. He clamped his tail down and humped up in the back, which notified the Dick mule that the end of the world was at hand. They shot off both at once like their tails were afire.

I swear I had no idea I was going to need a handhold as quick as I did. Just as I was starting backwards off of my bucket,

I grabbed a double handful of Big's pants, and down they came.

He said very conversationally, 'Burley Coulter, damn your impudent hide.'

But he stood to his work. He had to, of course. He made the drive past the Cordles' as magnificent as you please, proudly and calmly in control of his spirited team that was plunging on the bits, with his pants down around his ankles and his shirt-tail flying out behind. As we went past, I glanced up at Annie May and, so help me Jesus, she was smiling and waving – a good-hearted, patient, forgiving, well-fleshed girl, just right for Big.

Well, old Big did keep his team in hand. He never let them out of a short lope. Pretty soon he stopped them and got his pants back up more or less where they belonged, and took the long way home so he wouldn't have to pass the Cordles' again. He never looked at me or said a word. He wasn't speaking.

But when we finally got back to his place and had put away the mules, which were a good deal better broke by then, I felt obliged to have a serious talk with him.

'Big,' I said, 'you're going to have to ask that woman to marry you, after you've done showed yourself to her the way you have.'

You couldn't beat him for good nature. He just grinned, clean back to his ears. He said, 'All right. I reckon I will.'

So he was speaking to me again. And afterwards he told me all about it. He was giggling, red in the face, and absolutely tickled almost to death.

He gave up all his clever notions about courting, and was forthright. When he saw Annie May in town next time, he said, 'Come here. I want to talk to you.'

She followed him out of earshot of the other people, and he said, 'Well, you've done had a look at my private life. Don't you reckon me and you ought to get married?'

She looked straight back at him and laughed. She laughed right into his face like the good old gal she was.

She said, 'I would like to know why *not*!'

The Solemn Boy
(1934)

Ptolemy Proudfoot's ninety-eight-acre farm lay along the Goforth Hill road between the Cotman Ridge road and Katy's Branch. It included some very good ridgeland, some wooded hillside above the creek, and, down between Katy's Branch and the Katy's Branch road, two acres or so of bottomland. This creek-bottom field, small and narrow and awkwardly placed, seemed hardly to belong to the farm at all, and yet it was the one piece of truly excellent land that Tol owned. He called it the Watch Fob. He kept it sowed in red clover and timothy or lespedeza and timothy, and every three or four years he would break it and plant it in corn.

Since the Watch Fob was so out of the way, whatever work Tol had to do there tended to be put off until last. And yet, such was the quality of the crops that came from that land, and such the pleasantness of the place, down among the trees beside the creek, that Tol always looked forward to working there. The little field was quiet and solitary. No house or other building was visible from it, and the road was not much traveled. When Tol worked there, he felt off to himself and satisfied. There were some fine big sycamores along the creek, and while Tol worked, he would now and then hear the cry of a shikepoke or a kingfisher. Life there was different from life up on the ridge.

Nineteen thirty-four was one of the years when Tol planted the Watch Fob in corn. And that was fortunate, for it was a dry year; the ridge fields produced less than usual, and the Watch

Fob made up a good part of the difference. Tol cut and shocked that field last, and then he shucked and cribbed the upland corn before he went back again to the creek bottom.

Perhaps Tol agreed with the sage of Proverbs who held that 'he that hasteth with his feet sinneth' – I don't know. It is a fact, anyhow, that Tol never hurried. He was not by nature an anxious or a fearful man. But I suspect that he was unhurried also by principle. Tol loved his little farm, and he loved farming. It would have seemed to him a kind of sacrilege to rush through his work without getting the good of it. He never went to the field without the company of a hound or two. At the time I am telling about, he had a large black-and-tan mostly hound named Pokerface. And when Tol went to work, he would often carry his rifle. If, while he was working, Pokerface treed a squirrel or a young groundhog, then the workday would be interrupted by a little hunting, and Miss Minnie would have wild meat on the table the next day. When Tol went down to the Watch Fob to cultivate his corn, he always took his fishing pole. While he worked with plow or hoe, he would have a baited hook in the water. And from time to time he would take a rest, sitting with his back against a tree in the deep shade, watching his cork. In this leisurely way, he did good work, and his work was timely. His crops were clean. His pastures were well grassed and were faithfully clipped every year. His lambs and his steers almost always topped the market. His harvested corn gleamed in the crib, as clean of shuck and silk as if Tol had prepared it for a crowd of knowledgeable spectators, though as like as not he would be the only one who ever saw it.

By the time Tol got around to shucking the corn down on the Watch Fob that fall, it was past Thanksgiving. People had begun to think of Christmas. Tol had put off the job for two or three days, saying to himself, 'I'll go tomorrow.' But when he woke up on the morning he had resolved to go, he wished that he never had planted the Watch Fob in corn in the first place. Tol was sixty-two years old in 1934. He had not been young for several years, as he liked to say. And that morning when he woke, he could hear the wind ripping past the eaves and corners of the little farmstead, and rattling the bare branches of the trees.

'I'm getting old,' he thought as he heaved his big self off the mattress and felt beneath the bedrail for his socks.

'I'm getting old' – he had said that a number of times in the last few years, each time with surprise and with sudden sympathy for his forebears who had got old before him.

But he got up and dressed in the dark, leaving Miss Minnie to lie abed until he built up the fires. Tol was a big man. When he dressed, as Miss Minnie's nephew Sam Hanks said, it was like upholstering a sofa. In sixty-two years Tol had never become good at it. In fact, putting on his clothes was an affair not in the direct line of his interests, and he did not pay it much attention. Later, while he sat with his coffee after breakfast and was thus within her reach, Miss Minnie would see that his shirt collar was turned down and that all his buttons had engaged the appropriate buttonholes.

Tol, anyhow, approximately dressed himself, went down the stairs, built up the fire in the living room, and lit a fire in the cooking range in the kitchen. He sat by the crackling firebox of the range, wearing his cap and coat now, and put on his shoes. And then he sat and thought a little while. Tol had always been a man who could sit and think if he had to. But until lately he had not usually done so the first thing in the morning. Now it seemed that his sixty-two years had brought him to a new place, in which some days it was easier to imagine staying in by the fire than going out to work. He had an ache or two and a twinge or two, and he knew without imagining that the wind was from the north and he knew how cold it was. Tol thought on these things for some time there by the warming stove, and he thought that of all his troubles thinking about them was the worst. After a while he heard Miss Minnie's quick footsteps on the floor upstairs. He picked up the milk buckets then and went to the barn.

A little later, having eaten a good breakfast and hitched his team to the wagon, Tol experienced a transformation that he had experienced many times before. He passed through all his thoughts and dreads about the day, emerging at last into the day itself, and he liked it.

The wind was still whistling down from the north over the hard-frozen ground. But his horses looked wonderful, as horses tend to do on such a morning, with every hair standing on end and their necks arched, wanting to trot with the wagon's weight pressing onto their britchings as they went down the hill, and their breath coming in clouds that streamed away on the wind. Tol's fingers grew numb in his gloves with holding them back.

They quieted down presently, and he drove on to the Watch Fob, sticking first one hand and then the other into his armpits to warm his fingers. And then he untied the first shock, slipped his shucking peg onto his right hand, and began tossing the clean yellow ears into the wagon. It was not yet full daylight. He settled into the work, so that presently he paid less attention to it, and his hands went about their business almost on their own. He looked around, enjoying the look of the little field. Even on so gray a day it was pretty. After he had cut and shocked the corn, he had disked the ground and sowed it in wheat, and now the shocks stood in their straight rows on a sort of lawn that was green, even though it was frozen. And it was pleasant to see the humanly ordered small clearing among the trees. Nearby the creek flowed under thin ice and then broke into the open and into sound as it went over a riffle and back again under ice. But the best thing of all was the quiet. Though he could hear the wind clashing and rattling in the trees around the rim of the valley, there was hardly a breeze down there in the Watch Fob. Surrounded by the wind's commotion, the quietness of the little cornfield gave it a sort of intimacy and a sort of expectancy. As his work warmed him, he unbuttoned his jacket. A while later he took it off.

A little past the middle of the morning, snowflakes began to fall. It was nothing at all like a snowstorm, but just a few flakes drifting down. Up on the ridgetops, Tol knew, the wind would be carrying the flakes almost straight across. 'Up there,' he thought, 'it ain't one of them snows that falls. It's one of them snows that just passes by.' But down where he was, the flakes sifted lackadaisically out of the sky as if they had the day off and no place in particular to go, becoming visible as they came down past the treetops and then pretty much disappearing when they lit. It would take hours of such snowing to make even a skift of whiteness on the ground. Pokerface, who in dog years was older than Tol, nevertheless took shelter under the wagon.

'Well, if *you* ain't something!' Tol said to him. 'Go tree a squirrel.'

Pokerface had a good sense of humor, but he did not appreciate sarcasm. He acknowledged the justice of Tol's criticism by beating his tail two or three times on the ground, but he did not come out.

There had been a time when a Proudfoot almost never

worked alone. The Proudfoots were a big family of big people whose farms were scattered about in the Katy's Branch valley and on Cotman Ridge. They liked to work together and to be together. Often, even when a Proudfoot was at work on a job he could not be helped with, another Proudfoot would be sitting nearby to watch and talk. The First World War killed some of them and scattered others. Since then, the old had died and the young had gone, until by now Tol was the only one left. Tol was the last of the Proudfoots, for he and Miss Minnie had no children. And now, though he swapped work with his neighbors when many hands were needed, he often worked alone, amused or saddened sometimes to remember various departed Proudfoots and the old stories, but at other times just present there in the place and the day and the work, more or less as his dog and his horses were. When he was remembering he would sometimes laugh or grunt or mutter at what he remembered, and then the old dog would look at him and the horses would tilt their ears back to ask what he meant. When he wasn't remembering, he talked to the horses and the dog.

'Me and you,' he said to Pokerface, 'we're a fine pair of half-wore-out old poots. What are we going to do when we get old?'

It amused him to see that Pokerface had no idea either.

For a while after Tol started that morning's work, it seemed to him that he would never cover the bottom of the wagon box. But after he quit paying so much attention he would be surprised, when he did look, at how the corn was accumulating. He laid the stalks down as he snapped off the ears, and then when he had finished all the stalks, he stood them back up in a shock and tied them. The shucked ears were piling up nearly to the top of the wagon box by the time Tol judged it was getting on toward eleven o'clock. By then his stomach had begun to form the conclusion that his throat had been cut, as Proudfoot stomachs had always tended to do at that time of day. And now he began to converse with himself about how long it would take to get back up the hill and water and feed his horses. He knew that Miss Minnie would begin to listen for him at about eleven-thirty, and he didn't want to get to the kitchen much later than that. He thought that he *could* go in with what corn he had, but then he thought he might shuck just a *little* more. He had conducted thousands of such conversations with himself, and he knew just how to do it. He urged himself on with one 'little more' after another until he filled the wagon properly to the brim, and in plenty of time, too.

The day was still cold. As soon as he quit work, he had to put his jacket back on and button it up. The thought of re-entering the wind made him hunch his shoulders and draw his neck down into his collar like a terrapin.

He climbed up onto the wagon seat and picked up the lines. 'Come here, boys,' he said to the team. And they turned and drew the creaking load out of the field.

If Tol had a favorite thing to do, it was driving a loaded wagon home from the field. As he drove out toward the road, he could not help glancing back at the wagon box brimming with corn. It was a kind of wonder to him now that he had handled every ear of the load. Behind him, the little field seemed to resume a deeper quietness as he was leaving it, the flakes of snow still drifting idly down upon it.

When they started up the hill the horses had to get tight in their collars. It was a long pull up to the first bend in the road. When they got there, Tol stopped on the outside of the bend and cramped the wheels to let the horses rest.

'Take a breath or two, boys,' he said.

'Come on, old Poke,' he said to the dog, who had fallen a little behind, and now came and sat down proprietarily beside the front wheel.

Where they were now they could feel the wind. The snowflakes flew by them purposefully, as if they knew of a better place farther on and had only a short time to get there.

Pretty soon the cold began to get inside Tol's clothes. He was ready to speak to the team again when he heard Pokerface growl. It was a quiet, confidential growl to notify Tol of the approach of something that Pokerface had not made up his mind about.

When Tol looked back the way Pokerface was looking, he saw a man and a small boy walking up the road. Tol saw immediately that he did not know them, and that they were poorly dressed for the weather. The man was wearing an old felt hat that left his ears in the cold and a thin, raggedy work jacket. The boy had on a big old blue toboggan that covered his ears and looked warm, but his coat was the kind that had once belonged to a suit, not much to it, the lapels pinned shut at the throat. The sleeves of the boy's coat and the legs of his pants were too short. The man walked behind the boy, perhaps to shelter him a little from the wind. They both had their hands in their pockets and their shoulders hunched up under their ears.

'Hush, Poker,' Tol said.

When the man and boy came up beside the wagon, the boy did not look up. The man glanced quickly up at Tol and looked away.

'Well,' Tol said cheerfully, for he was curious about those people and wanted to hear where they came from and where they were going, 'can I give you a lift the rest of the way up the hill?'

The man appeared inclined to go on past without looking at Tol again.

'Give the boy a little rest?' Tol said.

The man stopped and looked at the boy. Tol could tell that the man wanted to let the boy ride, but was afraid or embarrassed or proud, it was hard to tell which. Tol sat smiling down upon them, waiting.

'I reckon,' the man said.

Tol put down his hand and gave the boy a lift up onto the load of corn. The man climbed up behind him.

'We hate to put the burden on your team,' the man said.

Tol said, 'Well, it's all right. All they been doing is putting in the time. Get up, boys.'

'They're right good ones,' the man said.

Tol knew the man said that to be polite, but it was a pleasing compliment anyhow, for the man spoke as if he knew horses. Tol said, 'They do very well.'

And then he said, 'You all come far?' hoping the man would tell something about himself.

But the man didn't. He said, 'Tolable.'

Tol glanced back and saw that the man had positioned his son between his spread legs and had opened his own coat to shelter him within it. As soon as he had stopped walking, the boy had begun to shiver. And now Tol saw their shoes. The man had on a pair of street shoes with the heels almost worn off, the boy a pair of brogans, too big for him, that looked as stiff as iron.

'Poor,' Tol thought. Such men were scattered around the country everywhere, he knew – drifting about, wearing their hand-me-downs or grab-me-ups, looking for a little work or a little something to eat. Even in so out-of-the-way a place as Cotman Ridge Tol and Miss Minnie had given a meal or a little work to two or three. But till now they had seen no boy. The boy, Tol thought, was a different matter altogether.

Tol wanted to ask more questions, but the man held himself and the boy apart.

'That wind's right brisk this morning, ain't it?' Tol said.

'Tolable so,' the man said.

'I'm Tol Proudfoot,' Tol said.

The man only nodded, as if the fact were obvious.

After that, Tol could think of nothing more to say. But now he had the boy on his mind. The boy couldn't have been more than nine or ten years old – just a little, skinny, peaked boy, who might not have had much breakfast, by the look of him. And who might, Tol thought, not have much to look forward to in the way of dinner or supper either.

'That's my place up ahead yonder,' he said to the man. 'I imagine Miss Minnie's got a biscuit or two in the oven. Won't you come in and eat a bite with us?'

'Thank you, but we'll be on our way,' the man said.

Tol looked at the boy then; he couldn't help himself. 'Be nice to get that boy up beside the stove where he can get warm,' he said. 'And a bean or two and a hot biscuit in his belly wouldn't hurt him either, I don't expect.'

He saw the man swallow and look down at the boy. 'We'd be mightily obliged,' the man said.

So when they came to his driveway, Tol turned in, and when they came up beside the house he stopped.

'You'll find Miss Minnie in the kitchen,' Tol said. 'Just go around to the back porch and in that way. She'll be glad to see you. Get that boy up close to the stove, now. Get him warm.'

The man and boy got down and started around the back of

the house. Tol spoke to his team and drove on into the barn lot. He positioned the wagon in front of the corncrib, so he could scoop the load off after dinner, and then he unhitched the horses. He watered them, led them to their stalls, and fed them.

'Eat, boys, eat,' he said.

And then he started to the house. As he walked along he opened his hand, and the old dog put his head under it.

The man and boy evidently had done as he had told them, for they were not in sight. Tol already knew how Miss Minnie would have greeted them.

'Well, come on in!' she would have said, opening the door and seeing the little boy. 'Looks like we're having company for dinner! Come in here, honey, and get warm!'

He knew how the sight of that little shivering boy would have called the heart right out of her. Tol and Miss Minnie had married late, and time had gone by, and no child of their own had come. Now they were stricken in age, and it had long ceased to be with Miss Minnie after the manner of women.

He told the old dog to lie down on the porch, opened the kitchen door, and stepped inside. The room was warm, well lit from the two big windows in the opposite wall, and filled with the smells of things cooking. They had killed hogs only a week or so before, and the kitchen was full of the smell of frying sausage. Tol could hear it sizzling in the skillet. He stood just inside the door, unbuttoning his coat and looking around. The boy was sitting close to the stove, a little sleepy looking now in the warmth, some color coming into his face. The man was standing near the boy, looking out the window – feeling himself a stranger, poor fellow, and trying to pretend he was somewhere else.

Tol took off his outdoor clothes and hung them up. He nodded to Miss Minnie, who gave him a smile. She was rolling out the dough for an extra pan of biscuits. Aside from that, the preparations looked about as usual. Miss Minnie ordinarily cooked enough at dinner so that there would be leftovers to warm up or eat cold for supper. There would be plenty. The presence of the two strangers made Tol newly aware of the abundance, fragrance, and warmth of that kitchen.

'Cold out,' Miss Minnie said. 'This boy was nearly frozen.'

Tol saw that she had had no luck either in learning who their guests were. 'Yes,' he said. 'Pretty cold.'

He turned to the little washstand beside the door, dipped water from the bucket into the wash pan, warmed it with water from the teakettle on the stove. He washed his hands, splashed his face, groped for the towel.

As soon as Tol quit looking at his guests, they began to look at him. Only now that they saw him standing up could they have seen how big he was. He was broad and wide and tall. All his movements had about them an air of casualness or indifference as if he were not conscious of his whole strength. He wore his clothes with the same carelessness, evidently not having thought of them since he put them on. And though the little boy had not smiled, at least not where Tol or Miss Minnie could see him, he must at least have wanted to smile at the way Tol's stiff gray hair stuck out hither and yon after Tol combed it, as indifferent to the comb as if the comb had been merely fingers or a stick. But when Tol turned away from the washstand, the man looked back to the window and the boy looked down at his knee.

'It's ready,' Miss Minnie said to Tol, as she took a pan of biscuits from the oven and slid another in.

Tol went to the chair at the end of the table farthest from

the stove. He gestured to the two chairs on either side of the table. 'Make yourself at home, now,' he said to the man and the boy. 'Sit down, sit down.'

He sat down himself and the two guests sat down.

'We're mightily obliged,' the man said.

'Don't wait on me,' Miss Minnie said. 'I'll be there in just a minute.'

'My boy, reach for that sausage,' Tol said. 'Take two and pass 'em.

'Have biscuits,' he said to the man. 'Naw, that ain't enough. Take two or three. There's plenty of 'em.'

There was plenty of everything: a platter of sausage, and more already in the skillet on the stove; biscuits brown and light, and more in the oven; a big bowl of navy beans, and more in the kettle on the stove, a big bowl of applesauce and one of mashed potatoes. There was a pitcher of milk and one of buttermilk.

Tol heaped his plate, and saw to it that his guests heaped theirs. 'Eat till it's gone,' he said, 'and don't ask for nothing you don't see.'

Miss Minnie sat down presently, and they all ate. Now and again Tol and Miss Minnie glanced at each other, each wanting to be sure the other saw how their guests applied themselves to the food. For the man and the boy ate hungrily without looking up, as though to avoid acknowledging that others saw how hungry they were. And Tol thought, 'No breakfast'. In his concern for the little boy, he forgot his curiosity about where the two had come from and where they were going.

Miss Minnie helped the boy to more sausage and more beans, and she buttered two more biscuits and put them on his plate. Tol saw how her hand hovered above the boy's shoulder, wanting to touch him. He was a nice-looking little boy, but he never smiled. Tol passed the boy the potatoes and refilled his glass with milk.

'Why, he eats so much it makes him poor to carry it,' Tol said. 'That boy can put it away!'

The boy looked up, but he did not smile or say anything. Neither Tol nor Miss Minnie had heard one peep out of him. Tol passed everything to the man, who helped himself and did not look up.

'We surely are obliged,' he said.

Tol said, 'Why, I wish you would look. Every time that boy's elbow bends, his mouth flies open.'

But the boy did not smile. He was a solemn boy, far too solemn for his age.

'Well, we know somebody else whose mouth's connected to his elbow, don't we?' Miss Minnie said to the boy, who did not look up and did not smile. 'Honey, don't you want another biscuit?'

The men appeared to be finishing up now. She rose and brought to the table a pitcher of sorghum molasses, and she brought the second pan of biscuits, hot from the oven.

The two men buttered biscuits, and then, when the butter had melted, laid them open on their plates and covered them with molasses. And Miss Minnie did the same for the boy. She longed to see him smile, and so did Tol.

'Now, Miss Minnie,' Tol said, 'that boy will want to go easy on them biscuits from here on, for we ain't got but three or four hundred of 'em left.'

But the boy only ate his biscuits and molasses and did not look at anybody.

And now the meal was ending, and what were they going to do? Tol and Miss Minnie yearned toward that nice, skinny, really pretty little boy, and the old kitchen filled with their yearning, and maybe there was to be no answer. Maybe that man and this little boy would just get up in their silence and say, 'Much obliged,' and go away, and leave nothing of themselves at all.

'My boy,' Tol said – he had his glass half-full of buttermilk in his hand, and was holding it up. 'My boy, when you drink buttermilk, always remember to drink from the near side of the glass – like this.' Tol tilted his glass and took a sip from the near side. 'For drinking from the far side, as you'll find out, don't work anything like so well.' And then – and perhaps to his own surprise – he applied the far side of the glass to his lips, turned it up, and poured the rest of the buttermilk right down the front of his shirt. And then he looked at Miss Minnie with an expression of absolute astonishment.

For several seconds nobody made a sound. They all were looking at Tol, and Tol, with his hair asserting itself in all directions and buttermilk on his chin and his shirt and alarm and wonder in his eyes, was looking at Miss Minnie.

And then Miss Minnie said quietly, 'Mr Proudfoot, you *are* the limit.'

And then they heard the boy. At first it sounded like he had an obstruction in his throat that he worked at with a sort of strangling. And then he laughed.

He laughed with a free, strong laugh that seemed to open his throat as wide as a stovepipe. It was the laugh of a boy who was completely tickled. It transformed everything. Miss Minnie smiled. And then Tol laughed his big hollering laugh. And then Miss Minnie laughed. And then the boy's father laughed. The man and the boy looked up, they all looked full into one another's eyes, and they laughed.

They laughed until Miss Minnie had to wipe her eyes with the hem of her apron.

'Lord,' she said, getting up, 'what's next?' She went to get Tol a clean shirt.

'Let's have some more biscuits,' Tol said. And they all buttered more biscuits and passed the molasses again.

When Miss Minnie brought the clean shirt and handed it to him, Tol just held it in his hand, for he knew that if he stood up to change shirts the meal would end, and he was not ready for it to end yet. The new warmth and easiness of their laughter, the straight way they all had looked at one another, had made the table a lovely place to be. And he liked the boy even better than he had before.

Tol began to talk then. He talked about his place and when he had bought it. He told what kind of year it had been. He spoke of the Proudfoots and their various connections, and wondered if maybe his guests had heard of any of them.

No, the man said, he had never known a Proudfoot until that day. He went so far as to say he knew he had missed something.

Tol then told about marrying Miss Minnie, and said that things had looked up around there on that happy day, which caused Miss Minnie to blush. Miss Minnie had come from a line of folks by the name of Quinch. Had their guests, by any chance, ever run into any Quinches?

But the man said no, there were no Quinches where he came from.

Which brought Tol to the brink of asking the man point-blank where he came from and where he was going. But then the man retrieved his hat from under his chair, and so put an end to all further questions forever, leaving Tol and Miss Minnie to wonder for the rest of their lives.

The man stood up. 'We better be on our way,' he said. 'We're much obliged,' he said to Tol. 'It was mighty fine,' he said to Miss Minnie.

'But wait!' Miss Minnie said. Suddenly she was all in a flutter. 'Wait, wait!' she said. 'Don't go until I come back!'

She hurried away. All three of them stood now, saying nothing, for a kind of embarrassment had come over them. Now that the meal had ended, now that they had eaten and talked and laughed together for a moment, they saw how little there was that held them. They heard Miss Minnie's footsteps hurry into the front of the house and up the stairs. And then they heard only the wind and the fire crackling quietly in the stove. And then they heard her footsteps coming back.

When she came into the kitchen again, she was carrying over her left arm an old work jacket of Tol's, and holding open with both hands a winter coat of her own that she had kept for second best. She put it on the boy, who obediently put his arms into the sleeves, as if used to doing as a woman told him.

But when she offered the work jacket to the man, he shook his head. The jacket was much patched, worn and washed until it was nearly white.

'It's old, but it's warm,' Miss Minnie said.

'No, mam,' the man said. For himself, he had reached some unshakable limit of taking. 'I can't take the jacket, mam,' he said. 'But for the boy, I thank you.'

He started toward the door then. Miss Minnie hurriedly buttoned the boy into the coat. Tol made as if to help her by prodding the coat here and there with his fingers, feeling between the weather and the boy's skinny back and shoulders the reassuring intervention of so much cloth.

'It's not a fit exactly, but maybe it'll keep him warm,' Miss Minnie said as if only to herself. The coat hung nearly to the top of the boy's shoes. 'It's good and long,' she said.

Her hands darted about nervously, turning the collar up, rolling up the sleeves so that they did not dangle and yet covered the boy's hands. She tucked the boy into the coat as if she were putting him to bed. She snatched a paper bag from a shelf, dumped the remaining biscuits into it out of the pan, and at the last moment, before letting the boy go, shoved the sack into the right-hand pocket of the coat. 'There!' she said.

And then they lifted their hands and allowed the boy to go with his father out the door. They followed. They went with the man and boy around the back of the house to the driveway.

The man stopped and turned to them. He raised his hand. 'We're mightily obliged,' he said. He turned to Miss Minnie, 'We're mightily obliged, mam.'

'You might as well leave that boy with us,' Tol said. He was joking, and yet he meant it with his whole heart. 'We could use a boy like that.'

The man smiled. 'He's a good boy,' he said. 'I can't hardly get along without this boy.'

The two of them turned then and walked away. They went out to the road, through the wind and the gray afternoon and the flying snow, and out of sight.

Tol and Miss Minnie watched them go, and then they went back into the house. Tol put on the clean shirt and his jacket and cap and gloves. Miss Minnie began to clear the table. For the rest of that day, they did not look at each other.

Tol lived nine more years after that, and Miss Minnie twenty more. She was my grandmother's friend, and one day Grand-dad left Granny and me at the Proudfoot house to visit while he went someplace else. The war was still going on, and Tol had not been dead a year. I sat and listened as the two women talked of the time and of other times. When they spoke of the

Depression, Miss Minnie was reminded of the story of the solemn boy, and she told it again, stopping with Tol's words, 'We could use a boy like that.'

And I remember how she sat, looking down at her apron and smoothing it with her hands. 'Mr Proudfoot always wished we'd had some children,' she said. 'He never said so, but I know he did.'

Andy Catlett: Early Education
(1943)

In grades one and two I was a sweet, tractable child who caused no trouble. I was 'little Andy Catlett', the second of that name, the first being my uncle Andrew who had raised more than his share of hell and mowed a wide swath among the ladies. My own public reputation so far was clean as a whistle. But in grade three I learned of the damage that could be done to a strict disciplinary harmony by a small discord, and I was never the same afterwards.

In grade four, Miss Heartsease, abandoning her premature hope that I might be educable, brought stacks of *National Geographics* to keep me quiet. In one of them I found several pictures of a chemistry laboratory, and I fell into what I can only call an infatuation. I had no idea what was done in a chemistry laboratory. What captivated me was the intricate plumbing of glass pipes, some of them in coils; the vials, tubes, beakers, and retorts; the neat rows of bottled powders and fluids; the Bunsen burners. The thought of working in such a room with such equipment sent me into urgent fantasies. I would be a chemist when I grew up. I would be a chemist *before* I grew up. I entertained seriously the possibility of becoming a child prodigy. I could see a picture of myself in my white coat in my laboratory in *National Geographic,* pouring a fuming green liquid from one container into another.

My scientific bent led me in that same year to the discovery of afterimages. One of the bare lightbulbs in the ceiling of our classroom was of clear glass and much larger than the others.

Inside it was a filament in the shape of a horseshoe that glowed with a white incandescence. I learned that I could stare at that lightbulb for a while, and then, by blinking, send a flock of brightly colored horseshoes flying all over the room. But my experimental looking around and blinking proved too violent for Miss Heartsease, and she soon forced me back into my chemical fantasies.

I asked for a chemistry set for Christmas, and got one. But it was a disappointment. It was deficient in apparatus and drama, and too obviously intended to be 'educational'. I mixed up a concoction that smelled bad but was otherwise uninteresting, and gave up chemistry.

I went instead into the business of candle-making. Since it was not long after Christmas, candles were on my mind and the makings readily findable. I made a colorful collection of candle drippings and butt-ends. For good measure I added one whole candle that didn't match any of the others in the pantry, and I knew my mother wouldn't want it if it didn't match. I had read in a book about pioneer days that you could make a candle by dipping a string into melted tallow, and I knew from looking at lighted candles how to go about melting them.

And so I waited until I was at home by myself, to avoid disturbing others, before I started my candle-making business. It was in fact going to be a business, for I fully intended to sell my candles at a profit, and I thought I could count on my grandmothers to buy at least two apiece.

I put my drips and fragments into a small pot, cutting up the nonmatching whole one so it would fit, measured a piece of string to about the right length, and turned on the burner. How what happened next happened I can't say, for I soon found that I didn't have time just to stand around watching a pot, but it did happen that a fairly spectacular tall flame was standing on top of the stove. Pretty quickly it burnt up all my wax and went out, and I soon got the kitchen back to rights and no harm done. There was no sign of fire except for the faintest little cloudy smoke stain on the ceiling that you wouldn't see if you didn't look close. If my parents ever looked close they must have wondered, but they never asked me.

So I went out of the candle business with no profit, but also with no loss except for the burnt wax, which I no longer needed.

My parents were very much afraid that my brother, Henry, and I would not live to be grown. This fear, when it manifested itself, could be oppressive. But we were fortunate, Henry and I, in having a father who was often busy at his office and a mother whose attention was often required by our two younger sisters. This state of things bestowed upon us boys a latitude of freedom that we knew exactly what to do with.

As a result, a secondary fear haunted particularly our mother – namely that the behavior of her sons would deviate so far beyond the known human range that an apocalyptic embarrassment would fall upon the family. This too could be oppressive. When my mother said to me, 'I don't know what's going to become of you!' I could hear the squeak of the hinges of the jailhouse door. In her worst moments, I fear my mother too could hear those hinges, and she also could see in her mind's eye the raw opening of an early grave for a boy drowned or burned or run over by a car or kicked in the head by a mule.

To save us from ourselves – and herself from the anguish she knew she would feel at the shutting of that iron door or the opening of that grave, if she had not done all she could have done by way of prevention – at certain extremities of our self-education and of her tolerance, she resorted to the use of a switch. The switch would be one of the sprouts that grew up from the roots of our lilac bush, and it would be keen, lithe, and durable. Our mother's use of it was fiercely honest. She dispensed the 'good whipping' she had promised, no fun for the recipient, though the pain was soon over. What was not soon over was my sense of her own reluctance and regret, which stayed with me and made me sympathize with her as maybe nothing else could have done.

I sympathized with her; in my sympathy, as I can see now, I greatly loved her, and yet her punishments wrought no significant change in my behavior. Her influence over me at that time did not extend many feet beyond the end of her lilac switch, whereas my quest for knowledge extended limitlessly round about.

Probably because of my early gift for science, I was eager to learn in school. But I was not intellectually stimulated by the schoolbooks or the established curriculum. What I wanted to learn was the precise line between what my teachers would put up with and what they would not put up with. And to draw a line of this sort required much experimentation. My curiosity about the limits of, for instance, Miss Heartsease was extraordinarily keen. I probed the coastlines of her patience and sounded its estuaries like an early navigator mapping the New World. When school let out, I shifted my interest to other continents as handily as an astronaut.

It may have been in the fall of my year of Miss Heartsease that I applied myself to a critical textual examination, and ultimately to the scientific debunking, of *The Night Before Christmas*.

At that time my sisters' upstairs bedroom still had an open fireplace with a grate that, before our time, had been used for burning coal. I had never paid it much attention until one night after supper, when I was loitering in that room, enjoying maybe the strangeness of its feminine prettiness, one of my earliest quandaries attached itself to that fireplace as if by magnetic attraction. It was far yet from Christmas, still warm. And by then I'm sure I 'knew about Santa Claus'. But my quandary was a Christmas quandary of long standing, and it had to do specifically with Santa Claus.

I knew from my close observation of falling bodies, and from having been a number of times a falling body myself, perhaps as much as one needs to know about gravity. And so I saw no great problem in the alleged descent of chimneys on the part of Santa Claus. If the chimneys had been big enough, and if he had no more graceful way of doing so, he could have got down them by falling.

How he got back up them again was my question. I was going, you see, by the book. As a critic, from the beginning I held the text in great honor, and the text did not say that he came down the chimney, left the toys for the children, and let himself out by the door. The text said in plain English: 'up the chimney he rose'.

In those days I was a true pure scientist. If the subject of my inquiry had been the nature of gravity itself, I would not have minded whether the falling body had been an apple or a bomb, or upon what or whom it might have fallen. I was hard driven in my quest for truth.

And so, being alone, and having therefore full intellectual freedom, I stooped into the fireplace, inserted my head and shoulders into the chimney, and did a passable job of standing up. Such was my objectivity in regard to the chimney that I would not have been surprised if I had been able to go right up it.

But it was not a roomy chimney. I could not raise my arms

to feel for a handhold, and except for the grate there was no foothold. And so I absolutely knew something: if I couldn't get up it, Santa Claus couldn't get up it. I wasn't entirely objective at this point, for I was truly sorry. It would have been extraordinarily pleasant to go up the chimney and climb out onto the peak of the roof. From there I could have gone down onto the roof of the back porch, from there into the branches of our big old apple tree, and from there to the ground.

But I accepted disappointment, shrank out of the dark chimney, and stood up again in the lighted room. And that, I think, must have been the occasion upon which I discovered soot. Coal soot is exceedingly black and exceedingly light. I was covered with it, which I only found out by using one of the curtains to wipe what felt like cobweb out of my eyes. I was a living pencil, for on everything I touched I left a mark.

And then I saw that the soot, in addition to being on me, was coming off. It was drifting loose in chunks and flakes and floating to the floor, where it broke into pieces that fled away on tiny currents of the air, insidious little breezes which I also discovered at that time.

The Christmas quandary I had started with, despite its scientific interest and the seriousness with which I had taken it up, began to look like a pleasant sort of ignorance. I would gladly have gone back to it, except that it had now evolved into an insistently present problem for which there was no present solution. In fact, every attempt I made at a solution reliably worsened the problem. Even when I merely rubbed my head the better to study the situation, I loosened more soot. I saw a flake of soot levitate from the top of my head and land on a bedspread, white to match the curtains. When I took a swipe at it to knock it to the floor, I made a broad dark streak. It began to seem to me that I needed to be going.

I started to the door and only then saw that my mother was standing in it, having just arrived. We paused and looked each other over. I saw from her stance and demeanor that the situation was not as she would have preferred it to be.

I managed to dodge past her, maybe because she was dazed, not having as quick an eye for the truth as I did, or maybe she was reluctant to touch me. She hadn't even thought of anything to say.

Once I was safely past her, I ran to one of the windows at the back of the hall, 'threw up the sash' (as *The Night Before Christmas* says), and flung myself out onto the porch roof. Thereupon, displaying a presence of mind I had never given her credit for, my mother shut the window. I heard her lock it. I heard her go to the window on the other side of the hall and lock that one.

Laying low seemed to be called for, and like Brer Rabbit I laid low. For a long time I didn't make a sound, and I didn't hear a sound. I thought hard, and I didn't come to a satisfactory conclusion. I was safe as long as I stayed on the roof. My mother, I knew, would not climb onto the roof. But then there was a limit to how long I could stay there. There was no bed or blanket on the roof, and there would be no breakfast. I could go down by the apple tree, but where would I go then? I didn't know where everybody else was, but I knew my mother was at home. Sooner or later my father would come home, and that did not brighten my prospects.

The idea of running away from home in case of need had been ready-made in my mind for a good while, but to do that I would have to be on the ground. Once on the ground and safely gone, I would maybe think of a place to go, some place an orphan boy might find welcome and shelter. So I got up ever so quietly, and slowly so as not to make a sound I eased down the slope of the roof. I went so far as to step from the roof into the apple tree before I looked down and saw my mother.

She was sitting on the ground with her back against one of the tree's three trunks. She looked comfortable. A lengthy switch was lying across her lap beneath her folded hands.

She looked strange. I had never before seen her or anybody else look as she did then. It took a long time for my education to catch up with the vision of her I had then, for though she was a Christian woman she was sitting down there looking positively Buddhist. She was sitting perfectly still. She was not going to move in so much as I could imagine of the future. She was not looking left or right, let alone up into the tree where I was. But I knew she knew where I was. I felt illuminated as if by omniscience. She was at peace down there. She was using up all the peace there was. There was none at all up in the apple tree where I was.

Without making a sound I eased back out of the tree and onto the roof again. Though I knew she was not looking at me and was not going to look at me, I moved back out of her line of sight, where at least I was relieved of looking at her.

My mind was breaking new ground and was working hard. It was working so hard I could spare no energy for standing up. I sat down. For quite a while I thought methodically and strenuously. I saw that I did not have many options. I had, in truth, only three options: I could climb down that tree, which, with precise reason, I was afraid to do; or I could kick the glass out of one of the hall windows and go back into the house, which, on second thought, did not seem to be an option; or I could jump off the roof, and then, if able, run.

To avoid thinking again of the tree, I gave a lot of thought to jumping off the roof. If I did that successfully, with no damage to myself, the option of running away would be renewed. But if I jumped it would be a long way to the ground, and I would have a fair chance of breaking a leg. This was a possibility not entirely unattractive, for if I broke a leg my mother surely would feel sorry for me and forget to whip me. On the other hand, I might kill myself, in which case I would lose the benefit.

And so I was driven back by my thoughts to the first option of climbing down the tree. But I lingered on a while to give my mother a reasonable opportunity to depart, an opportunity which she did not receive with favor. When I got up and eased back again to look for her, there she was. She had not moved. She looked exactly as she had before.

I was really getting to know my mother. I am many years older now than she was then, and I can easily imagine how knowingly she was amused. But I could imagine then, for I *saw*, how perfectly she was determined. It was getting dark. It was time to bring this story to an end.

Making no longer an effort to be quiet, I stepped back into the tree, slid down, and stood in front of my mother. I felt as if I were presenting myself to a bolt of lightning. It was somewhat like that: swift, illuminating, and soon over.

Stand By Me
(1921–1944)

When Jarrat married Lettie in 1921 and bought the little place across the draw from our home place and started to paying for it, in that time that was already hard, years before the Depression, he had a life ahead of him, it seemed like, that was a lot different from the life he in fact was going to live. Jarrat was my brother, four years older than me, and I reckon I knew him as well as anybody did, which is not to say that what I knew was equal to what I didn't know.

But as long as Lettie lived, Jarrat was a happy man. As far as I could see, not that I was trying to see or in those days cared much, he and Lettie made a good couple. They were a pretty couple, I'll say that, before this world and its trouble had marked them. And they laid into the work together, going early and late, scraping and saving and paying on their debt.

Tom was born the next year after they married, Nathan two years later. And it seemed that Tom hadn't hardly begun to walk about on his own until Nathan was coming along in his tracks, just a step or two behind. They had pretty much the run of the world, Lettie and Jarrat being too busy for much in the way of parental supervision, at least between meals.

The hollow that lays between the two places, that most people call Coulter Branch, before long was crisscrossed with boy-paths that went back and forth like shoestrings between the boys' house on one ridge and the old house on the other where I lived with Mam and Pap. The boys lived at both houses, you might as well say. They'd drop down through the pasture and into the woods on one side, and down through the woods to the branch, and then up through the woods and the pasture on the other side, and they'd be in another place with a different house and kitchen and something different to eat. They had maybe half a dozen paths they'd worn across there, and all of them had names: the Dead Tree Path, I remember, and the Spring Path and the Rock Fence Path.

And then, right in the midst of things going on the way they ought to have gone on forever, Lettie got sick and began to waste away. It was as serious as it could be, we could see that. And then instead of belonging just to Jarrat to pay attention to, she began to belong to all of us. Dr Markman was doing all he could for her, and then Mam and the other women around were cooking things to take to her and helping with her housework, and us others were hoping or praying or whatever we did, trying to help her to live really just by wishing for her to. And then, without waiting for us to get ready, she died, and the boys all of a sudden, instead of belonging just to her and Jarrat, belonged to us all. Nathan was five years old, and Tom was seven.

And I was one of the ones that they belonged to. They belonged to me because I belonged to them. They thought so, and that made it so. The morning of their mother's funeral, to get them moved and out of the house before more sadness could take place, I put a team to the wagon and drove around the head of the hollow to get them. Mam had packed up their clothes and everything that was theirs. We loaded it all and them too onto the wagon, and I brought them home to the old house.

Jarrat wasn't going to be able to take care of them and farm too, and they didn't need to be over there in that loneliness with him. But Pap and Mam were getting on in years then. Pap, just by the nature of him, wasn't going to be a lot of help. And Mam, I could see, had her doubts.

Finally she just out with it. 'Burley, I can be a grandmother, but I don't know if I can be a mother again or not. You're going to have to help me.'

She had her doubts about that too. But it didn't prove too hard to bring about. I belonged to them because they needed me. From the time I brought them home with me, they stuck to me like burrs. A lot of the time we were a regular procession – me in front, and then Tom in my tracks just as close as he could get, and then Nathan in Tom's the same way. The year Lettie died I was thirty-four years old, still a young man in my thoughts and all, and I had places I needed to go by myself. But for a long time getting away from those boys was a job. I'd have to hide and slip away or bribe them to let me go or wait till they were asleep. When I wanted to hunt or fish the best way to be free of them was just to take them with me. By the time they got big enough to go on their own, we had traveled a many a mile together, day and night, after the hounds, and had spent a many an hour on the river.

The grass and weeds overgrew the paths across the hollow. The boys somehow knew better than to go over there where their mother was gone and their daddy was living by himself. It took them a while to go back there even with me.

Jarrat did a fair job of batching. He kept the house clean, and he didn't change anything. He sort of religiously kept everything the way Lettie had fixed it. But as time went on, things changed in spite of him. He got busy and forgot to water the potted plants, and they died. And then gradually the other little things that had made it a woman's house wore out or got lost or broke. Finally it took on the bare, accidental look of the house of a man who would rather be outdoors, and then only Jarrat's thoughts and memories were there to remind him of Lettie.

Or so I guess. As I say, there was a lot about Jarrat that nobody in this world was ever going to know. I was worrying about him, which I hadn't ever done before, and I was going to worry about him for the rest of his life. I began to feel a little guilty about him too. I had a lady friend, and by and by we began to come to an understanding. When I wanted company, I had friends. When I didn't want company, I had the woods and the creeks and the river. I had a good johnboat for fishing, and always a good hound or two or three.

Jarrat didn't have any of those things, not that he wanted them. In his dealings with other people he was strictly honest, I was always proud of him for that, and he was friendly enough. But he didn't deal with other people except when he had to. He was freer than you might have thought with acts of kindness when he knew somebody needed help. But he didn't want kindness for himself, though of course he needed it. He didn't want to be caught needing it.

After Lettie died, he wasn't the man he was before. He got like an old terrapin. He might come out of his shell now and again to say something beyond what the day's work required: 'Hello', maybe, or he would compliment the weather. But if you got too close, he'd draw in again. Only sometimes, when he thought he was by himself, you'd catch him standing still, gazing nowhere.

What I know for sure he had in his life were sorrow, stubbornness, silence, and work. Work was his consolation, surely, just because it was always there to do and because he was so good at it. He had, I reckon, a gift for it. He loved the problems and the difficulties. He never hesitated about what to do. He never mislaid a lick. And half of his gift, if that was what it was, was endurance. He was swift and tough. When you tied in with him for a day's work, you had better have your ass in gear. Work was a fever with him. Anybody loved it as much as he did didn't need to fish.

So when Tom and Nathan needed him the most, their daddy didn't have much to offer. He wanted them around, he would watch over them when they were with us at work, he would correct and caution them when they needed it, but how could he console them when he couldn't console himself?

They were just little old boys. They needed their mother, was who they needed. But they didn't have her, and so they needed me. Sometimes I'd find one or the other of them off somewhere by himself, all sorrowful and little and lost, and there'd be nothing to do but try to *mother* him, just pick him up and hold him tight and carry him around a while. Their daddy couldn't do it, and it was up to me.

I would make them laugh. It usually wasn't too hard. Nathan thought I was the funniest thing on record anyhow, and sometimes he would laugh at me even when I was serious. But I would sing,

> Turkey in the straw settin' on a log
> All pooched out like a big bullfrog.
> Poked him in the ass with a number nine wire
> And down he went like an old flat tire.

I would sing,

Stuck my toe in a woodpecker hole,
In a woodpecker hole, in a woodpecker hole.
Woodpecker he said, 'Damn your soul,
Take it out, take it out, take it out!'

I would sing one of them or some other one, and dance a few steps, raising a dust, and Nathan would get so tickled he couldn't stand up. Tom would try to hold his dignity, like an older brother, but he would be ready to bust. All you had to do was poke him in the short ribs, and down he would go too.

What raising they got, they got mainly from their grandma and me. It was ours to do if anybody was going to do it, and somehow we got them raised.

To spare Grandma, and when they were out of school, we kept the boys at work with us. That way they learned to work. They played at it, and while they were playing at it they were doing it. And they were helping too. We generally had a use for them, and so from that time on they knew we needed them, and they were proud to be helping us to make a living.

Jarrat nor Pap wouldn't have paid them anything. Jarrat said they were working for themselves, if they worked. And Pap, poking them in the ribs to see if they would argue, and they did, said they ate more than they were worth. But I paid them ten cents a day, adjusted to the time they actually worked. Sometimes they'd get three cents, sometimes seven. I'd figure up and pay off every Saturday. One time when I paid him all in pennies, Nathan said, 'Haven't you got any of them big white ones?'

They worked us too. They didn't have minds for nothing. Sometimes, if the notion hit them, they'd fartle around and pick at each other and get in the way until their daddy or grandpa would run them off. '*Get* the hell out of here! Go to the house!'

But they wouldn't go to the house. They'd slip away into the woods, or go to Port William or down to the river. And since they were careful to get back to the house by dinnertime or suppertime, nobody would ask where they'd been. Unless they got in trouble, which they sometimes did.

I worried about them. I'd say, 'Boys, go to the river if you have to, but don't go *in* it.' Or I'd say, 'Stay *out* of that damned river, now. We ain't got time to go to your funeral.'

But of course they did go in the river. They were swimming, I think, from frost to frost, just like I would have at their age. Just like I in fact *did* at their age.

Or they would wander over to Big Ellis and Annie May's, which was the one place they could be sure of being spoiled. Big would never be busy at any job he wouldn't be happy to quit if company came. Annie May always had cookies in a jar or a pie or cold biscuits and jam to feed them when they showed up, and so they showed up pretty often.

Annie May and Big weren't scared of much of anything except lightning. They could be careless and fearless when they ought to have been scared. They would drive to Hargrave in their old car, calm as dead people, while Big drove all over the road and looked in every direction but ahead. But let a thunderstorm come up and they'd quiver like gun-shy dogs. They'd get into the bed then, because they slept on a feather-tick and they believed lightning wouldn't strike a bird.

I went in over there one day just ahead of a big black storm, and there were Big and Annie May and Tom and Nathan all four piled up in the bed together, all four smoking cigarettes to calm their fear.

★

One day when we were in the woods we saw a big owl, and I pointed out how an owl can turn his head square around to look at you. I said if you came upon an owl sitting, for instance, on a tree stump, you could walk round and round him, and he would turn his head round and round to watch you, until finally he would twist his neck in two and his head would fall off. I said that was the way we killed owls all the time when I was a boy.

I told them just about any bird would let you catch him if you crept up and put a little salt on his tail.

'Why?'

'He just will.'

'But why will he?'

'You'll have to ask somebody smarter than me.'

I told them how when I was a boy, back in the olden times, you could hear the wangdoodles of a night, squalling and screeching and fighting way off in the woods.

'Do they still do that?'

'Naw, you don't hear 'em so much anymore.'

At first they believed everything I said, and then they didn't believe anything I said, and then they believed some of the things I said. That was the best of their education right there, and they got it from me.

When they were little, you could always see right through Nathan. He didn't have any more false faces than a glass of water. Tom you couldn't always tell about. Maybe because Nathan was coming along so close behind him, Tom needed to keep some things to himself. It did him good to think he knew some things you didn't know. He wanted to call his life his own. He wasn't dishonest. If you could get him to look straight at you, then you had him.

As long as they were little, there would be times when they would be needing their mother, and who would be in the gap but only me? One or the other or both of them would be sitting close to me in the evening while it was getting dark, snuggled up like chickens to the old hen, and I would be doing all I could, and falling short. They changed me. Before, I was oftentimes just on the loose, carefree as a dog fox, head as empty as a gourd. Afterwards, it seemed like my heart was bigger inside than outside.

We got them grown up to where they weren't needy little boys anymore. They were still boys. They were going to be boys a while yet, but they were feeling their strength. They were beginning to find in their selves what before they had needed from us. Tom was maybe a little slower at it than he might have been, Nathan a little faster; Nathan was coming behind and was in a hurry.

It was a wonderful thing to watch that Tom grow up. For a while there, after he was getting to be really useful, he was still an awkward, kind of weedy, mind-wandery boy who needed some watching. To him, young as he was, it must have seemed he stayed that way a long time. But before long, as it seemed to me, he had gathered his forces together, body and mind. He got to be some account on his own. He could see what needed to be done, and go ahead and do it. He got graceful, and he was a good-looking boy too.

And then, the year he was sixteen, a little edge crept up between him and his daddy. It wasn't very much in the open at first, wasn't admitted really, but there it was. I thought, 'Uh-oh,' for I hated to see it, and I knew there wasn't much to be done about it. Tom was feeling his strength, he was coming in to his own, and Jarrat that year was forty-seven years old.

When he looked at Tom he got the message – from where he was, the only way was down – and he didn't like it.

Well, one afternoon when we were well along in the tobacco cutting, Tom took it in his head he was going to try the old man. Jarrat was cutting in the lead, as he was used to doing, and Tom got into the next row and lit out after him. He stayed with him too, for a while. He put the pressure on. He made his dad quiet down and work for his keep.

But Tom had misestimated. The job was still above his breakfast. Jarrat wasn't young anymore, but he was hard and long-practiced. He kept his head and rattled Tom, and he beat him clean. And then he couldn't stop himself from drawing the fact to Tom's attention.

Tom went for him then, making fight. They were off a little way from the rest of us, and both of them thoroughly mad. Before we could get there and get them apart, Jarrat had just purely whipped the hell out of Tom. He ought to've quit before he did, but once he was mad he didn't have it in him to give an inch. It was awful. Ten minutes after it was over, even Jarrat knew it was awful, but then it was too late.

It was a day, one of several, I'm glad I won't have to live again. Tom was too much a boy yet to get in front where he wanted to be but too much a man to stay and be licked. He had to get out from under his daddy's feet and onto his own. And so he bundled his clothes and went away. Afterwards, because the old ones were so grieved, me too, Nathan too, the house was like a house where somebody had died.

Because he didn't need much and asked little, Tom found a place right away with an old couple by the name of Whitlow over on the other side of the county, far enough away to be separate from us. I knew he would do all right, and he did. He knew how to work; and the use of his head, that was already coming to him, came fast once he got out on his own. He began to make a name for himself: a good boy, a good hand.

When we had found out where he was, Nathan and I would catch a ride on a rainy day or a Sunday and go over to see him, or we'd see him occasionally in town. After he got his feet under him and was feeling sure of himself, he would come over on a Sunday afternoon now and again to see his grandma and grandpa. In all our minds, he had come into a life of his own that wasn't any longer part of ours. To the old ones, who had given up their ownership of him by then and their right to expect things from him, every one of those visits was a lovely gift, and they made over him and honored him as a guest.

He stayed at the Whitlows' through the crop year of 1940. Mr Whitlow died that summer. After the place was sold and Mrs Whitlow settled in town, Tom struck a deal with Ernest Russet from up about Sycamore. Ernest and Naomi Russet were good people, we had known them a long time, and they had a good farm. Going there was a step up in the world for Tom. He soon found favor with the Russets, which not everybody could have done, and before long, having no children of their own, they'd made practically a son of him.

After Tom had been with them a while, the Russets invited us to come for Sunday dinner. Jarrat wouldn't go, of course, but Nathan and I did. The Russets' preacher, Brother Milby, and his wife were there too, a spunky couple. I took a great liking to Mrs Milby. It was a good dinner and we had a good time. Ernest Russet was the right man for Tom, no mistake about that. He was a fine farmer. The right young man could learn plenty from him.

*

By the time he went to the Russets, Tom was probably as near to the right young man as the country had in it. He had got his growth and filled out, and confidence had come into his eyes. He was a joy to look at.

One Sunday afternoon after the weather was warm and the spring work well started, he paid us a visit. Grandpa had died the summer before, so now it was just Grandma and Nathan and me still at home, and it was a sadder place. But we were glad to see Tom and to be together; we sat out on the porch and talked a long time.

Tom got up finally as if to start his hitchhike back to the Russets', and so I wasn't quite ready when he said he thought he'd go over to see his dad.

That fell into me with sort of a jolt. I hadn't been invited, but I said, 'Well, I'll go with you.'

So we went. We crossed the hollow, and clattered up onto the back porch, and Tom knocked on the kitchen door. Jarrat must have been in the kitchen, for it wasn't but seconds until there he was, his left hand still on the door knob and a surprised look on his face. Myself, I wasn't surprised yet, but I was expecting to be. I could feel my hair trying to rise up under my hat. I took a glance at Tom's face, and he was grinning at Jarrat. My hair relaxed and laid down peacefully again when Tom stuck out his hand. It was a big hand he stuck out, bigger than mine, bigger than Jarrat's. Jarrat looked down at that hand like it was an unusual thing to see on the end of a man's arm. He looked up at Tom again and grinned back. And then he reached out and took Tom's hand and shook it.

So they made it all right. And so when the war broke out and Tom was called to the army and had to go, he could come and say freely a proper good-bye to his dad.

It wasn't long after Tom got drafted until Nathan turned eighteen, and damned if he didn't go volunteer. I was surprised, but I ought not to've been. Nathan probably could have got deferred, since his brother was already gone and farmers were needed at home, and I reckon I was counting on that. But he had reasons to go, too, that were plain enough.

Nathan and Jarrat never came to an actual fight. Nathan, I think, had Tom's example in mind, and he didn't want to follow it. He was quieter turned than Tom, less apt to give offense. But Jarrat was hard for his boys to get along with. He just naturally took up too much of the room they needed to grow in. He was the man in the lead, the man going away while everybody else was still coming. His way was the right way, which in fact it pret' near always was, but he didn't have the patience of a henhawk.

'Let's go!' he'd say. If you were at it with him and you hesitated a minute: 'Let's go! Let's go!'

When we were young and he would say that, I'd say back to him,

'Les Go's dead and his wife's a widder.

You be right good and you might get her.'

But nobody was going to say that back to him anymore, not me, much less Nathan.

After Jarrat's fight with Tom, I would now and again try to put in a word for Nathan. 'Why don't you let him alone? Give him a little head room. Give him time to be ready.'

And Jarrat would say, 'Be ready, hell! Let him be started.'

It didn't take much of that, I knew, to be a plenty. When Nathan came back from the war his own man, Jarrat did get out of his way, and they could work together, but for the time being Nathan needed to be gone. Of course he got a bellyful of bossing in the army, but it at least didn't come from his dad.

He also had a brotherly feeling that he ought to go where Tom had gone. Grandma was dead by then. There was nothing holding him. So I reckon he went because he thought he had to, but I didn't want him to. For one thing, it would leave us short-handed. For another, I would miss him. For another, I was afraid.

As it turned out, Nathan never saw Tom again. They kept Nathan on this side till nearly the end of the war, but they gave Tom some training and taught him to drive a bulldozer and shipped him straight on across the waters into the fight. He was killed the next year. I know a few little details of how it happened, but they don't matter.

It came about, anyhow, that in just a couple of years the old house was emptied of everybody but me. It took me a while to get used to being there by myself. When I would go in to fix my dinner or at night, there wouldn't be a sound. I could *hear* the quiet. And however quiet I tried to be, it seemed to me I rattled. I didn't like the quiet, for it made me sad, and so did the little noises I made in it. For a while I couldn't hardly bring myself to trap the mice, I so needed to have something stirring there besides me. All my life I've hunted and fished alone, even worked alone. I never minded being by myself outdoors. But to be alone in the house, a place you might say is used to talk and the sounds of somebody stirring about in it all day, that was lonesome. As I reckon Jarrat must have found out a long time ago and, like himself, just left himself alone to get used to it. I've been, all in all, a lucky man, for the time would be again when the old house would be full of people, but that was long a-coming. For a while there it was just Jarrat and me living alone together, he in his house on one side of the hollow, me in mine on the other. I could see his house from my house, and he could see mine from his. But we didn't meet in either house, his or mine. We met in a barn or a field, wherever the day's work was going to start. When quitting time came we went our ways separately home. Of course by living apart we were keeping two houses more or less alive, and maybe there was some good in that.

The difference between us was that I wasn't at home all the time. When the work would let up, or on Saturday evenings and Sundays, for I just flat refused to work late on Saturday or much at all on Sunday, I'd be off to what passed with me for social life or to the woods or the river. But Jarrat was at home every day. *Every* day. He never went as far as Port William except to buy something he needed.

If you work about every day with somebody you've worked with all your life, you'd be surprised how little you need to talk. Oh, we swapped work with various ones – Big Ellis, the Rowanberrys, and others – and that made for some sociable times along, and there would be good talk then. But when it was just Jarrat and me, we would sometimes work without talking a whole day, or maybe two together. And so when he got the government's letter about Tom, he didn't say but two words. We were working here at my place. After dinner, when he walked into the barn, carrying the letter in his hand, he said, 'Sit down.'

I sat down. He handed me the letter, and it felt heavy in my hands as a stone. After I read it – 'killed in action' – and handed it back, the whole damned English language just flew away in the air like a flock of blackbirds.

For a long time neither one of us moved. The daily sounds of the world went on, sparrows in the barn lot, somebody's bull way off, the wind in the eaves, but around us was this awful, awful silence that didn't have one word in it.

I looked at Jarrat finally. He was standing there blind as a statue. He had Tom's life all inside him now, as once it had been all inside Lettie. Now it was complete. Now it was finished.

And then, for the first and last time I said it to him, I said, 'Let's go.' The day's work was only half finished. Having nothing else we could do, we finished it.

What gets you is the knowledge, and it sometimes can fall on you in a clap, that the dead are gone absolutely from this world. As has been said around here over and over again, you are not going to see them here anymore, ever. Whatever was done or said before is done or said for good. Any questions you think of that you ought to've asked while you had a chance are never going to be answered. The dead know, and you don't.

And yet their absence puts them with you in a way they never were before. You even maybe know them better than you did before. They stay with you, and in a way you go with them. They don't live on *in* your heart, but your heart knows them. As your heart gets bigger on the inside, the world gets bigger on the outside. If the dead had been alive only in this world, you would forget them, looks like, as soon as they die. But you remember them, because they always were living in the other, bigger world while they lived in this little one, and this one and the other one are the same. You can't see this with your eyes looking straight ahead. It's with your side vision, so to speak, that you see it. The longer I live, and the better acquainted I am among the dead, the better I see it. I am telling what I know.

It's our separatedness and our grief that break the world in two. Back when Tom got killed and the word came, I had never thought of such things. That time would have been hard enough, even if I had thought of them. Because I hadn't, it was harder.

That night after supper I lit the lantern and walked over to Jarrat's and sat with him in the kitchen until bedtime. I wasn't invited. I was a volunteer, I reckon, like Nathan. If it had been just me and I needed company, which I did, I could have walked to town and sat with the talkers in the pool room or the barber shop. But except that I would go to sit with him, Jarrat would have sat there in his sorrow entirely by himself and stared at the wall or the floor. I anyhow denied him that.

I went back every night for a long time. There was nothing else to do. There wasn't a body to be spoken over and buried to bring people together, and to give Tom's life a proper conclusion in Port William. His body was never going to be in Port William again. It was buried in some passed-over battlefield in Italy, somewhere none of us had ever been and would never go. The word was passed around, of course. People were sorry, and they told us. The neighbor women brought food, as they do. But mainly there was just the grieving, and mainly nobody here to do it but Jarrat and me.

There was a woman lived here, just out the road, a good many years ago. She married a man quite a bit older – well, he was an old man, you might just as well say – and things went along and they had a little boy. In four or five years the old man died. After that, you can imagine, the little boy was all in all to his mother. He was her little man of the house, as she called him, and in fact he was the world to her. And then, when he wasn't but nine or ten years old, the boy took awfully sick one winter, and he died, and we buried him out there on the hill at Port William beside his old daddy.

We knew that the woman was grieved to death, as we say, and everybody did for her as they could. What we didn't know was that she really was grieving herself to death. It's maybe a little hard to believe that people can die of grief, but they do.

After she died, the place had to be sold. I went out there with Big Ellis and several others to set the place to rights and get the tools and the household stuff set out for the auction. When we got to the room that had been the little boy's, it was like opening a grave. It had been kept just the way it was when he died, except she had gathered up and put there everything she'd found that reminded her of him: all his play pretties, every broom handle he rode for a stick horse, every rock or feather or string she knew he had played with. I still remember the dread we felt just going into that room, let alone moving the things, or throwing them away. Some of them we had to throw away.

I understood her then. I understood her better after Tom was dead. When a young man your heart knows and loves is all of a sudden gone, never to come back, the whole place reminds you of him everywhere you look. You dread to touch anything for fear of changing it. You fear the time you know is bound to come, when the look of the place will be changed entirely, and if the dead came back they would hardly know it, or not recognize it at all.

Even so, this place is not a keepsake just to look at and remember. You can't stop just because you're carrying a load of grief and would like to stop, or don't care if you go on or not. Jarrat nor I either didn't stop. This world was still asking things of us that we had to give.

It was maybe the animals most of all that kept us going, the good animals we depended on, that depended on us: our work mules, the cattle, the sheep, the hogs, even the chickens. They were a help to us because they didn't know our grief but just quietly lived on, suffering what they suffered, enjoying what they enjoyed, day by day. We took care of them, we did what had to be done, we went on.

Making It Home
(1945)

He had crossed the wide ocean and many a river. Now not another river lay between him and home but only a few creeks that he knew by name. Arthur Rowanberry had come a long way, trusting somebody else to know where he was, and now he knew where he was himself. The great river, still raised somewhat from the flood of that spring and flowing swiftly, lay off across the fields to his left; to his right and farther away were the wooded slopes of the Kentucky side of the valley, and over it all, from the tops of the hills on one side to the tops of the hills on the other, stretched the gray sky. He was walking along the paved road that followed the river upstream to the county seat of Hargrave. On the higher ground to the right of the road stood fine brick farmhouses that had been built a hundred and more years ago from the earnings of the rich bottomland fields that lay around them. There had been a time when those houses had seemed as permanent to him as the land they stood on. But where he had been, they had the answer to such houses.

'We wouldn't let one of them stand long in our way,' he thought.

Art Rowanberry walked like the first man to discover upright posture – as if, having been a creature no taller than a sheep or a pig, he had suddenly risen to the height of six feet and looked around. He walked too like a man who had been taught to march, and he wore a uniform. But whatever was military in his walk was an overlay, like the uniform, for he had been a man long before he had been a soldier, and a farmer long before he had been a man. An observer might have sensed in his walk and in the way he carried himself a reconciliation to the forms and distances of the land such as comes only to those who have from childhood been accustomed to the land's work.

The noises of the town were a long way behind him. It was too early for the evening chores, and the farmsteads that he passed were quiet. Birds sang. From time to time he heard a farmer call out to his team. Once he had heard a tractor off somewhere in the fields and once a towboat out on the river, but those sounds had faded away. No car had passed him, though he walked a paved road. There was no sound near him but the sound of his own footsteps falling steadily on the pavement.

Once it had seemed to him that he walked only on the place where he was. But now, having gone and returned from so far, he knew that he was walking on the whole round world. He felt the great, empty distance that the world was turning in, far from the sun and the moon and the stars.

'Here,' he thought, 'is where we do what we are going to do – the only chance we got. And if somebody was to be looking down from up there, it would all look a lot littler to him than it does to us.'

He was talking carefully to himself in his thoughts, forming the words more deliberately than if he were saying them aloud, because he did not want to count his steps. He had a long way still to go, and he did not want to know how many steps it was going to take. Nor did he want to hear in his head the counted cadence of marching.

'I ain't marching,' he thought. 'I am going somewheres. I am going up the river toward Hargrave. And this side of

Hargrave, before the bridge, at Ellville, I will turn up the Kentucky River, and go ten miles, and turn up Sand Ripple below
Port William, and I will be at home.'

He carried a duffel bag that contained his overcoat, a change
of clothes, and a shaving kit. From time to time, he shifted the
bag from one shoulder to the other.

'I reckon I am done marching, have marched my last step,
and now I am walking. There is nobody in front of me and
nobody behind. I have come here without a by-your-leave to
anybody. Them that have known where I was, or was supposed to, for three years don't know where I am now. Nobody
that I know knows where I am now.'

He came from killing. He had felt the ground shaken by men
and what they did. Where he was coming from, they thought
about killing day after day, and feared it, and did it. And out of
the unending, unrelenting great noise and tumult of the killing went little deaths that belonged to people one by one.
Some had feared it and had died. Some had died without fearing it, lacking the time. They had fallen around him until he
was amazed that he stood – men who in a little while had
become his buddies, most of them younger than he, just boys.

The fighting had been like work, only a lot of people got
killed and a lot of things got destroyed. It was not work
that *made* much of anything. You and your people intended to
go your way, if you could. And you wanted to stop the other
people from going their way, if you could. And whatever inter-
fered you destroyed. You had a thing on your mind that you
wanted, or wanted to get to, and anything at all that stood in
your way, you had the right to destroy. If what was in the way
were women and little children, you would not even know it,
and it was all the same. When your power is in a big gun, you

don't have any small intentions. Whatever you want to hit, you want to make dust out of it. Farm buildings, houses, whole towns – things that people had made well and cared for a long time – you made nothing of.

'We blew them apart and scattered the pieces so they couldn't be put together again. And people, too. We blew them apart and scattered the pieces.'

He had seen tatters of human flesh hanging in the limbs of trees along with pieces of machines. He had seen bodies without heads, arms and legs without bodies, strewn around indifferently as chips. He had seen the bodies of men hanging upside down from a tank turret, lifeless as dolls.

Once, when they were firing their gun, the man beside him – Eckstrom – began to dance. And Art thought, 'This ain't no time to be dancing.' But old Eckstrom was dancing because he was shot in the head, was killed, his body trying on its own to keep standing.

And others had gone down, near enough to Art almost that he could have touched them as they fell: Jones, Bitmer, Hirsch, Walters, Corelli.

He had seen attackers coming on, climbing over the bodies of those who had fallen ahead of them. A man who, in one moment, had been a helper, a friend, in the next moment was only a low mound of something in the way, and you stepped over him or stepped on him and came ahead.

Once while they were manning their gun and under fire themselves, old Eckstrom got mad, and he said, 'I wish I had those sons of bitches lined up to where I could shoot every damned one of them.'

And Art said, 'Them fellers over there are doing about the same work we are, 'pears like to me.'

There were nights when the sky and all the earth appeared

to be on fire, and yet the ground was covered with snow and it was cold.

At Christmas he was among those trapped at Bastogne. He had expected to die, but he was spared as before though the ground shook and the town burned under a sky bright as day. They held their own, and others, fighting on the outside, broke through.

'We was mighty glad to see that day when it come,' he thought. 'That was a good day.'

The fighting went on, the great tearing apart. People and everything else were torn into pieces. Everything was only pieces put together that were ready to fly apart, and nothing was whole. You got to where you could not look at a man without knowing how little it would take to kill him. For a man was nothing but just a little morsel of soft flesh and brittle bone inside of some clothes. And you could not look at a house or a schoolhouse or a church without knowing how, rightly hit, it would just shake down into a pile of stones and ashes. There was nothing you could look at that was whole – man or beast or house or tree – that had the right to stay whole very long. There was nothing above the ground that was whole but you had the measure of it and could separate its pieces and bring it down. You moved always in a landscape of death, wreckage, cinders, and snow.

And then, having escaped so far, he was sitting by his gun one afternoon, eating a piece of chocolate and talking to an old redheaded, freckle-faced boy named McBride, and a shell hit right where they were. McBride just disappeared. And a fragment came to Art as if it were his own and had known him from the beginning of the world, and it burrowed into him.

From a man in the light on the outside of the world, he was

transformed in the twinkling of an eye into a man in the dark on the inside of himself, in pain, and he thought that he was dead. How long he was in that darkness he did not know. When he came out of it, he was in a place that was white and clean, a hospital, and he was in a long room with many beds. There was sunlight coming in the window.

A nurse who came by seemed glad to see him. 'Well, hello, bright eyes,' she said.

He said, 'Why, howdy.'

She said, 'I think the war is over for you, soldier.'

'Yes, mam,' he said. 'I reckon it is.'

She patted his shoulder. 'You almost got away from us, you know it?'

And he said, 'Yes, mam, I expect I did.'

The uniform he wore as he walked along the road between Jefferson and Hargrave was now too big for him. His shirt collar was loose on his neck, in spite of the neatly tied tie, and under his tightened belt the waistband of his pants gathered in pleats.

He stayed in hospitals while his life grew back around the wound, as a lightning-struck tree will sometimes heal over the scar, until finally they gave him his papers and let him go.

And now, though he walked strongly enough along the road, he was still newborn from his death, and inside himself he was tender and a little afraid.

The bus had brought him as far as the town of Jefferson on the north side of the river, letting him out in the middle of the afternoon in front of the hotel that served also as a bus station. From there, he could have taken another bus to Hargrave had he been willing to wait until the next morning. But now that he was in familiar country he did not have it in him to wait.

He had known a many a man who would have waited, but he was old for a soldier; though he was coming from as far as progress had reached, he belonged to an older time. It did not occur to him, any more than it would have occurred to his grandfather, to wait upon a machine for something he could furnish for himself. And so he thanked the kind lady at the hotel desk, shouldered his bag, and set out for home on foot.

The muddy Ohio flowed beneath the bridge and a flock of pigeons wheeled out and back between the bridge and the water, causing him to sway as he walked, so that to steady himself he had to look at the hills that rose over the rooftops beyond the bridge. He went down the long southward arc of the bridge, and for a little while he was among houses again, and then he was outside the town, walking past farmsteads and fields in unobstructed day. The sky was overcast, but the clouds were high.

'It ought to clear off before morning,' he thought. 'Maybe it'll be one of them fine spring days. Maybe it'll do to work, for I have got to get started.'

They would already have begun plowing, he thought – his father and his brother, Mart. Though they had begun the year without him, they would be expecting him. He could hear his father's voice saying, 'Any day now. Any day.'

But he was between lives. The war had been a life, such as it was, and now he was out of it. The other life, the one he had once had and would have again, was still ahead of him; he was not in it yet.

He was only free. He had not been out in the country or alone in a long time. Now that he had the open countryside around him again and was alone, he felt the expectations of other people fall away from him like a shed skin, and he came into himself.

'I am not under anybody's orders,' he thought. 'What I expect myself to do, I will do it. The government don't owe me, and I don't owe it. Except when I have something again that it wants, then I reckon I will owe it.'

It pleased him to think that the government owed him nothing, that he needed nothing from it, and he was on his own. But the government seemed to think that it owed him praise. It wanted to speak of what he and the others had done as heroic and glorious. Now that the war was coming to an end, the government wanted to speak of their glorious victories. The government was made up of people who thought about fighting, not of those who did it. The men sitting behind desks – they spent other men to buy ground, and then they ruined the ground they had and more men to get the ground beyond. If they were on the right side, they did it the same as them that were on the wrong side.

'They talk about victory as if they know all them dead boys was glad to die. The dead boys ain't never been asked how glad they was. If they had it to do again, might be they wouldn't do it, or might be they would. But they ain't been asked.'

Under the clouds, the country all around was quiet, except for birds singing in the trees, wherever there were trees, and now and then a human voice calling out to a team. He was glad to be alive.

He had been glad to be alive all the time he had been alive. When he was hit and thought he was dead, it had come to him how good it was to be alive even under the shelling, even when it was at its worst. And now he had lived through it all and was coming home. He was now a man who had seen far places and strange things, and he remembered them all. He had seen Kansas and Louisiana and Arizona. He had seen the ocean. He had seen the little farms and country towns of

France and Belgium and Luxembourg – pretty, before they were ruined. For one night, he was in Paris.

'That Paris, now. We was there one day and one night. There was wine everywheres, and these friendly girls who said, "Kees me." And I don't know what happened after about ten o'clock. I come to the next morning in this hotel room, sick and broke, with lipstick from one end to the other. I reckon I must have had a right good time.'

At first, before he was all the way in it, there was something he liked about the war, a reduction that in a way was pleasing. From a man used to doing and thinking for himself, he became a man who did what he was told.

'That laying around half a day, waiting for somebody else to think – that was something I had to *learn*.'

It was fairly restful. Even basic training tired him less than what he would ordinarily have done at that time of year. He gained weight.

And from a man with a farm and crops and stock to worry about, he became a man who worried only about himself and the little bunch of stuff he needed to sleep, dress, eat, and fight.

He furnished only himself. The army furnished what little else it took to make the difference between a man and a beast. More than anything else, he liked his mess kit. It was all the dishes a man really needed. And when you weren't cooking or eating with it, you could keep things in it – a little extra tobacco, maybe.

'When I get to Ellville,' he thought, 'I won't be but mighty little short of halfway. I know the miles and how they lay out end to end.'

It had been evening for a while now. On the farmsteads that he passed, people were busy with the chores. He could hear people calling their stock, dogs barking, children shouting and laughing. On one farm that he passed, a woman, a dog, and a small boy were bringing in the cows; in the driveway of the barn he could see a man unharnessing a team of mules. It was as familiar to him as his own breath, and because he was outside it still, he yearned toward it as a ghost might. As he passed by, the woman, perhaps because he was a soldier, raised her hand to him, and he raised his own in return.

After a while, he could see ahead of him the houses and trees of Ellville, and over the trees the superstructure of the bridge arching into Hargrave. All during his walk so far, he had been offering himself the possibility that he would walk on home before he would sleep. But now that he had come nearly halfway and Ellville was in sight, he knew he would not go farther that day. He was tired, and with his tiredness had come a sort of melancholy and a sort of aimlessness, as if, all his ties cut, he might go right on past his home river and on and on, anywhere at all in the world. The little cluster of buildings ahead of him now seemed only accidentally there, and he himself there only accidentally. He had arrived, as he had arrived again and again during the healing of his wound, at the apprehension of a pure emptiness, as if at the center of an explosion – as if, without changing at all, he and the town ahead of him and all the long way behind him had been taken up into a dream in which every creature and every thing sat, like that boy McBride, in the dead center of the possibility of its disappearance.

In the little town a lane turned off the highway and went out beyond the houses and across the river bottom for perhaps a quarter of a mile to a barn and, beyond the barn, to a small weatherboarded church. It was suppertime then; the road and the dooryards were deserted. Art entered the lane and went back past the gardens and the clutter of outbuildings that lay behind the houses. At the barn there was a cistern with a chain pump. He set down his bag and pumped and drank from his cupped left hand held under the spout.

'Looks like I ought to be hungry,' he thought. 'But I ain't.'

He was not hungry, and there was no longer anything much that he wanted to think. He was tired. He told himself to lift the bag again and put it on his shoulder. He told his feet to walk, and they carried him on to the church. The door was unlocked. He went in.

He shut the door behind him, not allowing the latch to click. The quiet inside the church was palpable; he came into it as into a different element, neither air nor water. He crossed the tiny vestibule where a bell rope dangled from a worn hole in the ceiling, went through another door that stood open, and sat down on the first bench to his left, leaving his duffel bag in the aisle, propped against the end of the bench. He let himself become still.

'I will eat a little,' he thought, "gainst I get hungry in the night.'

After a while he took a bar of candy from the bag and slowly ate it. The church windows were glazed with an amber-colored glass that you could not see through, and though it was still light outdoors, in the church it was dusk. When he finished the candy, he folded the wrapper soundlessly and put it in his pocket. Taking his overcoat from the bag to use as a blanket, he lay down on the bench. Many thoughts fled by him, none stopping. And then he slept.

He woke several times in the night, listening, and, hearing no threat out in the darkness anywhere, slept again. The last time he woke, roosters were crowing, and he sat up. He sat still a while in the dark, allowing the waking quiet of the place to come over him, and then he took another bar of candy from his bag and ate it and folded the wrapper and put it in his pocket as before. The night chill had seeped into the church; standing, he put on the overcoat. He picked up his bag and felt his way to the door.

It had cleared and the sky was full of stars. To the east, upriver, he could see a faint brightening ahead of the coming day. All around him the dark treetops were throbbing with birdsong, and from the banks of the two rivers at their joining, from everywhere there was water, the voices of spring peepers rose as if in clouds. Art stood still and looked around him and listened. It was going to be the fine spring day that he had imagined it might be.

He thought, 'If a fellow was to be dead now, and young, might be he would be missing this a long time.'

There was a privy in back of the church and he went to it. And then, on his way out of the lane, he stopped at the barn and drank again at the cistern.

Back among the houses, still dark and silent among their trees, he took the road that led up into the smaller of the two river valleys. There was no light yet from the dawn, but by the little light of the stars he could see well enough. All he needed now was the general shape of the place given by various shadows and loomings.

'I have hoofed it home from here a many a night,' he thought. 'Might be I could do it if I was blind. But I can see.'

He could see. And he walked along, feeling the joy of a man who sees, a joy that a man tends to forget in sufficient light. The quiet around him seemed wide as the whole country and deep as the sky, and the morning songs of the creatures and his own footsteps occurred distinctly and separately in it, making a kind of geography and a kind of story. As he walked the light slowly strengthened. As he more and more saw where he was, it seemed to him more and more that he was walking in his memory or that he had entered, awake, a dream that he had been dreaming for a long time.

He was hungry. The candy bar that he had eaten when he woke had hardly interrupted his hunger.

'My belly thinks my throat has been cut. It is laying right flat against my backbone.'

It was a joy to him to be so hungry. Hunger had not bothered him much for many weeks, had not mattered, but now it was as vivid to him as a landmark. It was a tree that put its roots into the ground and spread its branches out against the sky.

The east brightened. The sun lit the edges of a few clouds on the horizon and then rose above them. He was walking full in its light. It had not shone on him long before he had to take off the overcoat, and he folded and rolled it neatly and stuffed it into his bag. By then he had come a long way up the road.

Now that it was light, he could see the marks of the flood that had recently covered the valley floor. He could see drift logs and mats of cornstalks that the river had left on the low fields. In places where the river ran near the road, he could see the small clumps of leaves and grasses that the currents had affixed to the tree limbs. Out in one of the bottoms he saw two men with a team and wagon clearing the scattered debris from their fields. They had set fire to a large heap of drift logs, from which the pale smoke rose straight up. Above the level of the flood, the sun shone on the small, still-opening leaves of the water maples and on the short new grass of the hillside pastures.

As he went along, Art began to be troubled in his mind: how would he present himself to the ones at home? He had not shaved. Since before his long ride on the bus he had not bathed. He did not want to come in, after his three-year absence, like a man coming in from work, unshaven and with his clothes mussed and soiled. He must appear to them as what he had been since they saw him last, a soldier. And then he would be at the end of his soldiering. He did not know yet what he would be when he had ceased to be a soldier, but when he had thought so far his confusion left him.

He came to the mouth of a small tributary valley. Where the stream of that valley passed under the road, he went down the embankment, making his way, first through trees and then through a patch of dead horseweed stalks, to the creek. A little way upstream he came to a place of large flat rocks that had been swept clean by the creek and were now in the sun and dry. Opening the duffel bag, he carefully laid its contents out on the rocks. He took out his razor and brush and soap and a small mirror, and knelt beside the stream and soaped his face and shaved. The water was cold, but he had shaved with cold water before. When he had shaved, he took off his clothes and, standing in flowing water that instantly made his feet ache, he bathed, quaking, breathing between his teeth as he raised the cold water again and again in his cupped hands.

Standing on the rocks in the sun, he dried himself with the shirt he had been wearing. He put on his clean, too-large clothes, tied his tie, and combed his hair. And then warmth came to him. It came from inside himself and from the sun outside; he felt suddenly radiant in every vein and fiber of his body. He was clean and warm and rested and hungry. He was well.

He was in his own country now, and he did not see anything around him that he did not know.

'I have been a stranger and have seen strange things,' he thought. 'And now I am where it is not strange, and I am not a stranger.'

He was sitting on the rocks, resting after his bath. His bag, repacked, lay on the rock beside him and he propped his elbow on it.

'I am not a stranger, but I am changed. Now I know a mighty power that can pass over the earth and make it strange. There are people, where I have been, that won't know their places when they get back to them. Them that live to get back won't be where they were when they left.'

He became sleepy and he lay down on the rock and slept. He slept more deeply than he had in the night. He dreamed he was where he was, and a great, warm light fell upon that place, and there was light within it and within him.

When he returned to the road after his bath and his sleep, it was past the middle of the morning. His steps fell into their old rhythm on the blacktop.

'I know a mighty power,' he thought. 'A mighty power of death and fire. An anger beyond the power of any man, made big in machines equal to many men. And a little man who has passed through mighty death and fire and still lived, what is he going to think of himself when he is back again, walking the river road below Port William, that we would have blowed all to flinders as soon as look at it if it had got in our way?'

He walked, as before, the left side of the road, not meaning to ask for rides. But as on the afternoon before, there was little traffic. He had met two cars going down toward Hargrave and had been passed by only one coming up.

Where the road began to rise toward Port William up on the ridge, a lesser road branched off to the left and ran along the floor of the valley. As Art reached this intersection, he heard a truck engine backfiring, coming down the hill, and then the truck came into sight and he recognized it. It was an old green International driven, as he expected and soon saw, by a man wearing a trucker's cap and smoking a pipe. The truck was loaded with fat hogs, heading for the packing plant at Jefferson. As he went by, the old man waved to Art and Art waved back.

'Sam Hanks,' he thought. 'I have been gone over three years and have traveled a many a thousand miles over land and ocean, and in all that time and all them miles the first man I have seen that I have always known is Sam Hanks.'

He tried to think what person he had seen last when he was leaving, but he could not remember. He took the lesser road and, after perhaps a mile, turned into a road still narrower, only a pair of graveled wheel tracks. A little later, when the trees were fully leaved, this would be almost a burrow, tunneling along between the creek and the hillside under the trees, but now the leaves were small and the sun cast the shadows of the branches in a close network onto the gravel.

Soon he was walking below the high-water line. He could see it clearly marked on the slope to his right: a line above which the fallen leaves of the year before were still bright and below which they were darkened by their long steeping in the flood. The slope under the trees was strewn with drift, and here and there a drift log was lodged in the branches high above his head. In the shadow of the flood the spring was late, the buds of the trees just opening, the white flowers of twinleaf and bloodroot just beginning to bloom. It was almost as if he were walking under water, so abrupt and vivid was the difference above and below the line that marked the crest of the flood. But somewhere high in the sunlit branches a redbird sang over and over in a clear, pealing voice, 'Even so, even so.'

And there was nothing around him that Art did not know. He knew the place in all the successions of the year: from the little blooms that came in the earliest spring to the fallen red leaves of October, from the songs of the nesting birds to the anxious wintering of the little things that left their tracks in snow, from the first furrow to the last load of the harvest.

Where the creek turned away from the road the valley suddenly widened and opened. The road still held up on the hillside among the trees, permitting him to see, through the intervening branches, the broad field that lay across the bottom. He could see that plowing had been started; a long strip had been back-furrowed out across the field, from the foot of the slope below the road to the trees that lined the creek bank. And then he saw, going away from him, almost out to the end of the strip, two mule teams with two plowmen walking in the opening furrows. The plowmen's heads were bent to their work, their hands riding easy on the handles of the plows. Some distance behind the second plowman was a little boy, also walking in the furrow and carrying a tin can; from time to time he bent and picked something up from the freshly turned earth and dropped it into the can. Walking behind the boy was a large hound. The first plowman was Art's father, the second his brother Mart. The boy was Art's sister's son, Roy Lee, who had been two years old when Art left and was now five. The hound was probably Old Bawler, who made it a part of his business to be always at work. Roy Lee was collecting fishing worms, and Art looked at the creek and saw, in an open place at the top of the bank, as he expected, three willow poles stuck into the ground, their lines in the water.

The first of the teams reached the end of the plowland, and Art heard his father's voice clear and quiet: 'Gee, boys.' And then Mart's team finished their furrow, and Mart said, 'Gee, Sally.' They went across the headland and started back.

Art stood as if looking out of his absence at them, who did not know he was there, and he had to shake his head. He had to shake his head twice to persuade himself that he did not hear, from somewhere off in the distance, the heavy footsteps of artillery rounds striding toward them.

He pressed down the barbed wire at the side of the road, straddled over it, and went down through the trees, stopping at the foot of the slope. They came toward him along the edge of the plowland, cutting it two furrows wider. Soon he could hear the soft footfalls of the mules, the trace ends jingling, the creaking of the doubletrees. Present to himself, still absent to them, he watched them come.

At the end of the furrow his father called, 'Gee!' and leaned his plow over so that it could ride around the headland on the share and right handle. And then he saw Art. 'Well now!' he said, as if only to himself. 'Whoa!' he said to the mules. And again: 'Well now!' He came over to Art and put out his hand and Art gave him his.

Art saw that there were tears in his father's eyes, and he grinned and said, 'Howdy.'

Early Rowanberry stepped back and looked at his son and said again, 'Well now!'

Mart came around onto the headland then and stopped his team. He and Art shook hands, grinning at each other.

'You reckon your foot'll still fit in a furrow?'

Art nodded. 'I reckon it still will.'

'Well, here's somebody you don't hardly know,' Mart said, gesturing toward Roy Lee, 'and who don't know you at all, I'll bet. Do you know who this fellow is, Roy Lee?'

Roy Lee probably did not know, though he knew he had an uncle who was a soldier. He knew about soldiers – he knew they fought in a war far away – and here was a great, tall, fine soldier in a soldier suit with shining buttons, and the shoes on his feet were shining. Roy Lee felt something akin to awe and something akin to love and something akin to fear. He shook his head and looked down at his bare right foot.

Mart laughed. 'This here's your Uncle Art. You know about Uncle Art.' To Art he said, 'He's talked enough about you. He's been looking out the road to see if you was coming.'

Art looked up the creek and across it at the house and outbuildings and barn. He looked at the half-plowed field on the valley floor with the wooded hillsides around it and the blinding blue sky over it. He looked again and again at his father and his young nephew and his brother. They stood up in their lives around him now in such a way that he could not imagine their deaths.

Early Rowanberry looked at his son, now and then reaching out to grasp his shoulder or his arm, as if to feel through the cloth of the uniform the flesh and bone of the man inside. 'Well now!' he said again, and again, 'Well now!'

Art reached down and picked up a handful of earth from the furrow nearest him. 'You're plowing it just a little wet, ain't you?'

'Well, we've had a wet time,' Mart said. 'We felt like we had to go ahead. Maybe we'll get another hard frost. We could yet.'

Art said, 'Well, I reckon we might.'

And then he heard his father's voice riding up in his throat as he had never heard it, and he saw that his father had turned to the boy and was speaking to him:

'Honey, run yonder to the house. Tell your granny to set on another plate. For we have our own that was gone and has come again.'

Mike
(1939–1950)

After my parents were married in 1933, they lived for three years with my father's parents, Marce and Dorie Catlett, on the Catlett home place near Port William. My mother and my grandmother Catlett did not fit well into the same house. Because of that, and I suppose for the sake of convenience, my parents in 1936 moved themselves, my younger brother, Henry, and me to a small rental house in Hargrave, the county seat, where my father had his law practice.

And then in 1939, when I was five years old, my father bought us a house of our own. It was a stuccoed brick bungalow that had previously served as a 'funeral home'. It stood near the center of town and next door to a large garage. After we had moved in – there being six of us now, since the births of my two sisters – my parents improved the house by the addition of a basement to accommodate a furnace, and by the installation of radiators and modern bathroom and kitchen appliances.

My brother and I were thus provided with spectacles of work that fascinated us, and also with a long-term supply of large boxes and shipping crates. The crate that had contained the bathtub I remember as especially teeming with visions of what it might be reconstructed into. These visions evidently occasioned some strife between Henry and me. The man who installed our bathroom assured me many years later that he had seen me hit Henry on the head with a ball-peen hammer.

One day, while Henry and I were engaged in our unrealizable

dream of making something orderly and real out of the clutter in our backyard, a man suddenly came around the corner of the house carrying a dog. The dog was a nearly grown pup, an English setter, white with black ears and eye patches and a large black spot in front of his tail. The man, as we would later learn, was Mike Brightleaf.

Mr Brightleaf said, 'Andy and Henry, you boys look a here. This is a pup for your daddy.'

He set the big pup carefully down and gave him a pat. And then, with a fine self-assurance or a fine confidence in the pup or both, he said, 'Call him Mike.'

We called, 'Here, Mike!' and Mike came to us and the man left.

Mike, as we must have known even as young as we were, came from the greater world beyond Hargrave, the world of fields and woods that our father had never ceased to belong to and would belong to devotedly all his life. Mike was doomed like our father to town life, but was also like our father never to be reconciled to the town.

Along one side of our property our father built a long, narrow pen that we called 'the dog lot', and he supplied it with a nice, white-painted dog house. The fence was made of forty-seven-inch woven wire with two barbed wires at the top. These advantages did not impress Mike in the least. He did not wish to live in the nice dog house, and he would not do so unless chained to it. As for the tall fence, he would go up it as one would climb a ladder, gather himself at the top, and leap to freedom. Our father stretched a third strand of barbed wire inside the posts, making what would have been for a man a considerable obstacle, and Mike paid it no mind.

As a result, since our father apparently was reluctant to keep him tied, Mike had the run of the town. For want of anything better to do, he dedicated himself to being where we children were and going where we went. I have found two photographs of him, taken by our mother. In both, characteristically, he is with some of us children, accepting of hugs and pats, submissive, it seems, to his own kindness and our thoughtless affection, but with the look also of a creature dedicated to a higher purpose, aware of his lowly servitude.

One day our father found Henry and me trying to fit Mike with a harness we had contrived of an old mule bridle. We were going to hitch him to our wagon.

Our father said, 'Don't do that, boys. You'll cow him.'

I had never heard the word 'cow' used in that way before, and it affected me strongly. The word still denotes, to me, Mike's meek submission to indignity and my father's evident conviction that *nothing* should be cowed.

Mike intended to go everywhere we went and he usually did, but he understood his limits when he met them. One Sunday morning we children and our mother had started our walk to church. Mike was trailing quietly behind, hoping to be unnoticed, but our mother looked back and saw him. She said sympathetically, 'Mike, go home.' And Mike turned sadly around and went home.

He was well known in our town, for he was a good-looking dog and he moved with the style of his breeding and calling. But his most remarkable public performance was his singing to the fire whistle. Every day, back then, the fire whistle blew precisely at noon. The fire whistle was actually a siren whose sound built to an almost intolerable whoop and then diminished in a long wail. When that happened, Mike always threw up his head and howled, whether in pain or appreciation it was impossible to tell. One day he followed us to school, and then at noon into the little cafeteria beneath the gymnasium. I don't believe I knew he was there until the fire whistle let go and he began to howl. The sound, in that small and supposedly civil enclosure, was utterly barbarous and shocking. I felt some pressure to be embarrassed but I was also deeply pleased. Who else belonged to so rare an animal?

But Mike knew well that his deliverer was my father. He might spend a lot of time idling about in town or playing with children, but he was a dog with a high vocation, and he knew what it was. He knew too that my father fully shared it. Mike loved us all in the honorable and admirable way of a dog, but his love for my father was too dedicated to be adequately described as doglike. He regarded his partnership with my father as the business of his life, as it was also his overtopping joy.

My father was a man of passions. I don't think he did much of anything except passionately. When he was removed from his passions, as in some public or social situations, he would be quiet, remote, uncomfortable, and unhappy. I think he was sometimes constrained by a sense of the disproportion between the force of his thoughts and the demands of polite conversation. He loved serious talk and the sort of conversation that is incited by pleasure. He loved hilarity. But he had little to offer in the way of small talk, and he always seemed to me to be uncomfortable or embarrassed when it was required of him.

He was passionate about the law. He loved its argumentative logic, its principles and methods, its discriminating language. He was capable of working at it ardently for long hours. His sentences, written or spoken, whatever the circumstances, were concise, exact, grammatically correct, and powerful in their syntax. He did not speak without thinking, and he meant what he said.

He used such sentences when instructing and reprimanding us children. We were not always on his mind, I am sure, but when we were he applied himself to fatherhood as he did to everything else. When we were sick or troubled he could be as tender and sympathetic as our mother. At other times, disgruntled or fearing for us as his knowledge of the world prompted him to do, he could be peremptory, demanding, impatient, and in various ways intimidating. I was always trying to keep some secret from him, and he had an uncanny way of knowing your secrets. He had a way of knowing your thoughts, and this came from sympathy. It could only have come from sympathy, but it took me a long time to know that.

I have always been a slow thinker, and he was fast. He could add, subtract, and figure averages in his head with remarkable speed. He would count a flock of sheep like this: one, five, seven, twelve, sixteen, nineteen, twenty-four ... One day when he had done this and arrived promptly at the correct number, a hundred and fifty or so, he turned and looked at me for my number. I was still counting. 'Honey,' he said with instant exasperation, 'are you counting by *twos*?' That was exactly what I was doing, and in my slowness I had started over two or three times.

He was as passionate about farming as about the law. He could not voluntarily have quit farming any more than he could voluntarily have quit breathing. He spent great love and excitement in buying rundown farms, stopping the washes, restoring the pastures, renewing the fences, buildings, and other improvements. He performed this process of regeneration seven times in his life, eventually selling six of the farms, but he kept one, and in addition he kept and improved over many years the home place where he was born and raised. He hired out most of the work, of course, but he worked himself too, and he watched and instructed indefatigably. He would drive out to see to things in the morning before he went to the office, and again after he left the office in the afternoon. He took days off to devote to farming. He would be out looking at things, salting his cattle and sheep, walking or driving his car through the fields, every Sunday afternoon. In the days before tractors he would be on hand to take the lines when there were young mules to break. He did the dehorning, castrating, and other veterinary jobs. All the time he could spare from his law practice he gave to the farms. Because of his work for an agricultural cooperative, he would frequently have to make a trip to Washington or some other distant place. Sometimes, returning from one of those trips in the middle of the night, he would go to the home place or one of the other farms and drive through the fields before going home to bed.

Of farming, he told me, 'It's like a woman. It'll keep you awake at night.' He loved everything about it. He loved the look and feel and smell of the land and the shape of it underfoot. He loved the light on it and the weather over it. He loved the economics of it. As characteristic of him as anything else were pages of yellow legal pads covered with columns of numbers written in ink in his swift hand, where he figured the outgoes and the incomes of his farming, or drew the designs of farm buildings to be built or rebuilt.

When he went to the farms, he would often take Mike with him. He would hurry home from the office, change his clothes, and hurry out again. Going to his car, he would raise the trunk lid. 'Here, Mike! Get in!' And Mike would leap into the trunk and lie down. My father would close the trunk, leaving the latch unengaged so Mike would have air.

If there were farm jobs to be done, Mike would just go along, running free in the open country, hunting on his own. If it was hunting season, my father might bring along his shotgun in its tattered canvas case. The gun was a pump-action Remington twenty-gauge, for in those days my father had excellent eyes and he was a good shot.

In those days too the tall coarse grass known as fescue had not yet been introduced here. That grass and the coming of rotary mowing machines have made the good old bobwhite a rare bird in this country now. The improved pastures in Mike's time were in bluegrass, and a lot of fields would be weedy in the fall. There was plenty of good bird cover and as a result plenty of birds. My father would know where the coveys were, and he and Mike would go to seek them out.

And here they came into their glory, and here I need to imagine them and see them again in my mind's eye, now that I am getting old and have come to understand my father far better than I did when I was young. For right at the heart of his passions for his family, for the law, and for farming, all consequential passions with practical aims and ends, was this other passion for bird hunting with a good dog, which had no practical end but was the enactment of his great love of country, of life, of his own life, for their own sake.

When he stepped out in his eager long strides, with Mike let loose in front of him, he was walking free on the undivided and priceless world itself. And Mike went out from him in a motion fluid and swift and strong, less running than flying, and he would find the birds.

Once he had learned his trade, I think Mike was a nearly perfect dog, giving a satisfaction that was nearly complete. I never heard my father complain of him. He understood that little pump gun in my father's hands as if it were a book of instructions, and he did what he was supposed to do.

He was remarkable in another way. He would retrieve, and to reward him my father started feeding him the heads of the birds when he brought them back. Before long, Mike got the idea. From then on, he ate the head of the downed bird where he found it and brought back the headless carcass.

From time to time during my father's life as a bird hunter, which had its summit during Mike's life, he would go somewhere down south on a hunting trip, usually with one other hunter. I know about these trips only from a handful of stories, all of which had to do in one way or another with the prowess of my father's great dog.

In Hargrave we lived across the street from Dr Gib Holston who was the town's only professed atheist. He had the further distinctions of a glass eye and a reputation for violence. Once, in the days of his youth, a man had insulted him, and Dr Holston had killed the offender by shooting him from a train window. Most of our fellow citizens who used profanity might properly have been said to cuss, for they used it thoughtlessly as a sort of rhetoric of emphasis, but Dr Holston *cursed*, with blasphemy aforethought and with the intention of offending anyone inclined to be offended. He was a small man, not much above five feet tall, but strongly built and without fat to the end of his days. He thought of himself as outrageous, and so of course he was, and he enjoyed his bad reputation. He was a strange neighbor for my good mother, a woman of vigilant faith, who obliged him by finding him on all points as outrageous as he wished to be. She, with conscientious good manners, and my father, with a ceremoniousness always slightly tainted with satire, called him 'Dr Holston'. The rest of us called him 'Doc' or, when we wished to distinguish him from other doctors, 'Dr Gib'.

Doc, then, was one of my father's clients, which sometimes required them to make a little business trip together, and at least once they went together on a hunting trip. Why my father would have put up with him to that extent I am not sure. Perhaps, as a man of my grandparents' generation, Doc knew and remembered things that my father was interested in hearing; he always liked his older clients and enjoyed listening to them. But mostly, I believe, he put up with Doc because Doc amused him. It amused him that when they went somewhere together, Doc insisted on sitting by himself in the back seat of the car. It amused him to see in the rearview mirror that when Doc dozed off, sitting back there bolt upright by himself, his glass eye stayed open. Once, when my father advised him that a neighbor of ours, an aristocratic and haughty old lady, Mrs J. Robert La Vere, had been 'dropped' in a certain town that they visited, Doc said, 'God damn her, I wish she had dropped on through!' That amused my father as if it had been the gift of divine charity itself and he was therefore *obliged* to be fully amused. The one story that came of their hunting together is about my father's amusement.

They had come to their hunting place, uncased and loaded their guns, and turned Mike loose. The place was rich in birds and Mike soon began finding them, working beautifully in cooperation with my father, as he always did, and my father was shooting well as *he* always did. But this story begins with my father's growing awareness and worry that Doc was not shooting well.

There is a good possibility, in my opinion, that Doc by then was not capable of shooting well. His one eye could not have been very clear. I have been on hunts with him myself, and I never saw him hit anything. He had bought a twelve-gauge Browning automatic, which he pointed hither and yon without regard to the company. You had to watch him. I think he bought that gun because he couldn't see well enough to shoot well. It was an expensive gun, which counted with him, and that it was automatic impressed him inordinately. He had the primitive technological faith that such a weapon simply could not help compensating for his deficiency. He had paid a lot of money for this marvelous gun that would enact his mere wish to hit the birds as they rose. If you can't shoot well, you must shoot a lot. And so when he heard the birds rise, he merely pointed the gun in their direction and emptied it: Boomboom-boom! And of course he was missing.

And of course he was eventually furious. He vented his fury by stomping about and cursing roundly everything in sight. He called upon God, in whom he did not believe, to damn the innocent birds who were flying too fast and scattering too widely to be easily shot, and his expensive shotgun that was guilty only of missing what it had not been aimed at, and the cover that was too brushy, and the landscape that was too ridgy and broken, and the day that was too cloudy. My father, who instantly appreciated the absurdity of Doc's cosmic wrath, took the liberty of laughing. He then, being a reasonable man, recognized the tactlessness of his laughter, which doubled his amusement, and he laughed more. Doc thereupon included my father in his condemnation, and then, to perfect his vengeance, he included Mike who, off in the distance, was again beautifully quartering the ground. This so fulfilled my father with amusement that he was no longer able to stand. As we used to say here, his tickle-box had turned completely over. He subsided onto the ground and lay there on his back among the weeds, laughing, in danger, he said, of wetting his pants. He was pretty certain too that Doc was going to shoot him and he was duly afraid, which somehow amused him even more, and he could not stop laughing.

How they leveled that situation out and recovered from it, I don't know. But they did, and my father, to his further great amusement, survived.

In the general course of my father's life, I suppose Doc was a digression, an indulgence perhaps, certainly a fascination of a sort, and a source of stories. His friendship with Billy Finn was another matter. Between the two of them was a deep affection that lasted all their lives. On my father's side, I know, this affection was weighted by an abiding compassion. Billy Finn was a sweet man who sometimes drank to excess, and perhaps for sufficient reason. He had suffered much in his marriage to an unappeasable woman, 'Mizriz Fannie Frankle Finn' as my father enjoyed calling her behind her back. To the unhappy marriage of Mr and Mrs Finn had been added the death in battle, early in the Second World War, of their son, their only child. The shadow of shared grief, cast over the marriage, had made it maybe even more permanent than its vows. Mr Finn was bound to Mrs Finn by his pity for her suffering, so like his own, he suffering in addition, as she made sure, his inability to pity her enough. Life for Mr Finn, especially after the death of his son, was pretty much an uphill trudge. I think his friendship with my father was a necessary solace to him to the end of his life, near which he said to a member of the clergy visiting him in the nursing home: 'Hell, preacher? You can't tell me nothing about Hell. I've lived with a damned Frankle for *forty-nine years!*'

When my father would go away on one of his bird-hunting

trips, his companion almost invariably would be Mr Finn. Mr Finn loved bird dogs, and he always had one or two. The dogs always were guaranteed to be good ones, and nearly always they disappointed him. He was not a good hand with a dog, perhaps because he had experienced too much frustration and disappointment in other things. He was impatient with his dogs, fussed at them too much, frightened them, confused them, and hollered at them. He was a noisy hunter, his utterances tending to be both excessive and obsessive, and this added substantially to my father's fund of amusement and of stories, but also to his fund of sorrow, for Billy Finn was a sad man, and my father was never forgetful of that.

On one of their hunting trips down south, as a companion to Mike, Mr Finn took a lovely pointer bitch he called Gladys, a dog on the smallish side, delicately made, extremely sensitive and shy – precisely the wrong kind of dog for him.

When the dogs were released, Mike sniffed the wind and sprang into his work. Gladys, more aware of the strangeness of the new terrain than of its promise, hung back.

'Go on, Gladys!' Mr Finn said. But instead of ranging ahead with Mike, Gladys followed Mr Finn, intimidated still by the new country, embarrassed by her timidity, knowing what was expected of her, and already fearful of Mr Finn's judgment.

'Gladys!' he said. 'Go on!'

And then, raising his voice and pointing forward, he said, 'Damn you, Gladys, go on! *Go on!*'

That of course ended any possibility that Gladys was going to hunt, for after that she needed to be forgiven. She stuck even closer to Mr Finn, fawning whenever he looked at her, hoping for forgiveness. And of course, in his humiliation, it never occurred to him to forgive her.

They hunted through the morning, Mr Finn alternately

apologizing for Gladys and berating her. His embarrassment about his dog eventually caused my father to become embarrassed about *his* dog. For in spite of Mr Finn's relentless fuming and muttering, they were having a fairly successful hunt. Mike was soaring through the cover in grand style and coming to point with rigorous exactitude. And the better it was, the worse it was. The better Mike performed, the more disgrace piled upon poor Gladys, the more embarrassed Mr Finn became, and the more he fumed and muttered, the more my father was punished by the excellence of Mike.

'Oh, Lord, it was awful,' my father would say later, laughing at the memory of his anguished amusement and his failure to think of anything at all to say.

And it got worse.

Sometime early in the afternoon Mr Finn's suffering grew greater than he could bear. He turned upon Gladys, who was still following him, and said half crying, 'Gladys, damn you to Hell! I raised you from a pup, I've sheltered you, I've fed you, I've loved you like a child, and now you've let me down, you thankless bitch!' He then aimed a murderous kick at her, which she easily evaded and fled from him until she was out of sight.

My father would gladly have ended the day there and then if he could have thought of a painless or even a polite way to do it. But he could think of no way. They hunted on.

But now Mr Finn was the one who needed forgiveness, and Gladys did not return to forgive him. He began to suffer the torments of the guilty and unforgiven, of shame for himself and fear for his dog. He began to imagine all the bad things that might happen to her, unprotected as she was and in a strange country. She might remain lost forever. She might get caught in somebody's steel trap. Some lousy bastard might find her wandering and steal her. She would be hungry and cold.

My father, being guilty of nothing except the good work of his own dog, was somewhat calmer. He thought Gladys would not go far and would be all right, and he sought to reassure his friend. But Mr Finn could not be comforted. From his earlier mutterings of imprecation he changed now to mutterings of self-reproach and worry.

As evening came on, they completed their long circle back to the car, and Gladys still was nowhere in sight. Mr Finn had been calling her for the last mile or so. For a long time they waited while Mr Finn called and called, his voice sounding more pleading, anxious, and forlorn as the day darkened. They were tired and they were getting cold.

Nearby, there was a culvert that let a small stream pass under the road. The culvert was dry at that time of year, and it would be a shelter.

'Billy,' my father said, 'lay your coat in that culvert. It's not going to rain. She'll find it and sleep there. We'll come back in the morning and get her.'

The only available comfort was in that advice, and Mr Finn took it. He emptied his hunting coat, folded it to make a bed, and laid it in the culvert. They went back to their hotel to their suppers, their beds, and an unhappy night for Mr Finn.

The next day was Sunday. On their hunting trips, my father and Mr Finn scrupulously attended church on Sunday. That morning they shaved, put on their church-going clothes, ate breakfast, and then hurried out into the country where they had lost Gladys and Mr Finn had left his coat.

Aside from ordering his breakfast, Mr Finn had said not a word. But now as they drove through the bright morning that still was dark to him, he uttered a sort of prayer: 'Lord, I hope she made it back.'

My father, who was driving, reached across and patted him on the shoulder. 'She'll be there,' he said.

She was there. When they climbed the fence to look, she was lying in the culvert on Mr Finn's coat, a picture of repentance and faithfulness that stabbed him to the heart. He knelt on the concrete beside her. He petted her, praised her, thanked her, and called her his good and beautiful Gladys, for she was at that moment all the world to him. And then he gathered her up in his arms, went to the fence, and started to climb over. It was a tall fence, fairly new with a barbed wire at the top, a considerable challenge to any man climbing it in a suit, let alone a man climbing it in a suit and carrying a dog. He got one leg over and was bringing the other when he lost his balance and fell, one cuff of his pants catching on a barb. And so he hung, upside down, with Gladys frantic and struggling in his arms.

My father would tell that story suffering with laughter, and then he would look down and shake his head. It was sadder than it was funny, but it was certainly funny, and what was a mere man to do?

I loved to hear my father tell those stories and others like them, and I can still see the visions they made me see when I was a boy. But now I love better to try to imagine the days, for which there are no stories, when Mike and my father hunted by themselves at home. On those days they passed beyond the margins of my father's working life and his many worries. Though they might have been hunting on a farm that my father owned, they passed beyond the confines even of farming.

They entered into a kind of freedom and a kind of perfection. I am thinking now with wonder of the convergence, like two birds crossing as they rise, of a passionate man and a gifted, elated, hard-hunting dog, and this in a country deeply loved and known, from many of the heights of which the man could see on its hill in the distance the house where he was born. And it would be in the brisk, fine weather of the year's decline when every creature is glad to be alive.

My father would have been in his early forties then, young still in all his energy and ability, his body light with thought and implicit motion even when he stood at rest. He and Mike would pass through a whole afternoon or a whole day in the same excitement, the same eagerness for the hidden birds and for the country that lay ahead.

Thinking of him in those days, I can't help wishing that I had known him then as a contemporary and friend, rather than as his son. As his son, I was to see him clearly only in looking back. He was obscured to me by his anxious parenthood, his fears for me, and by my own uneasy responses.

And yet I remember standing with him one day, when I was maybe eight or nine years old, on the top of a ridge in a weedy field. We were on the back of the farm we called the Crayton place. Beyond us, Mike was working with the beautiful motion that came of speed and grace together. My father held his gun in the crook of his left arm, at ease. He was in the mood that made him most comfortable to be with, enjoying himself completely, and with his entire intention allowing me to see what he saw.

Mike came to point, a forefoot lifted, his body tense from the end of his nose to the tip of his tail with a transfiguring alertness. Without looking at me, without looking away from the dog, my father allowed his right hand to reach down and find my shoulder and lie there.

'It comes over him like a sickness,' he said.

Like lovesickness, I think he meant, and even then I some-how understood. He was talking about a love, paramount if not transcendent, by which Mike was altogether moved, which he felt in his bones and could not resist.

And now of course I know that he was speaking from sym-pathy. He was talking also about himself, about his love, not only for the birds yet hidden and still somewhere beyond the end of Mike's nose, but for the country itself, his life in it, and the great beauty that sustained it then and always.

It was lovesickness, recognized in the dog because he knew it more fully in himself, that held him still, his hand on my shoulder, in that moment before we started forward to walk up the birds.

Mike, I think, was my father's one superlative dog, and his noontime just happened to coincide with my father's. It did not last long. After Mike, there were other dogs, but my father did not exult in them as he had in Mike. And he had less time for them. Griefs and responsibilities came upon him. His life as a hunter gradually subsided, and in his later years I don't think he much wished for it or often remembered it.

It may be that those summit years made the measure of the later ones, revealing them as anticlimactic and more than a little sad. The years with Mike may have established a zenith of performance and companionship that he could not hope, and even did not wish, to see equaled.

Mike lived long enough to become Old Mike to us all. And then the day arrived when we came down to breakfast and our mother told us, 'I wouldn't go out there if I were you. Your daddy's burying his dog.' And we could see him with a spade down in the far end of the garden, digging the grave.

That was all I knew about the burial of Mike until one day, near the end of his own life, when my father told me a little more: 'I had almost covered him up, when it occurred to me that I hadn't said anything. I needed to say something. And so I uncovered his head. I said, "Blessings on you, Mike. We'll hunt the birds of Paradise."'

The Boundary
(1965)

He can hear Margaret at work in the kitchen. That she knows well what she is doing and takes comfort in it, one might tell from the sounds alone as her measured, quiet steps move about the room. It is all again as it has been during the going on twenty years that only the two of them have lived in the old house. Sitting in the split-hickory rocking chair on the back porch, Mat listens; he watches the smoke from his pipe drift up and out past the foliage of the plants in their hanging pots. He has finished his morning stint in the garden, and brought in a half-bushel of peas that he set down on the drain-board of the sink, telling Margaret, 'There you are, mam.' He heard with pleasure her approval, 'Oh! They're nice!' and then he came out onto the shady porch to rest.

Since winter he has not been well. Through the spring, while Nathan and Elton and the others went about the work of the fields, Mat, for the first time, confined himself to the house and barn lot and yard and garden, working a little and resting a little, finding it easier than he expected to leave the worry of the rest of it to Nathan. But slowed down as he is, he has managed to make a difference. He has made the barn his business, and it is cleaner and in better order than it has been for years. And the garden, so far, is nearly perfect, the best he can remember. By now, in the first week of June, in all its green rows abundance is straining against order. There is not a weed in it. Though he has worked every day, he has had to measure the work out in little stints, and between stints he has had to rest.

But rest, this morning, has not come to him. When he went out after breakfast he saw Nathan turning the cows and calves into the Shade Field, so called for the woods that grow there on the slope above the stream called Shade Branch. He did not worry about it then, or while he worked through his morning jobs. But when he came out onto the porch and sat down and lit his pipe, a thought that had been on its way toward him for several hours finally reached him. He does not know how good the line fence is down Shade Branch; he would bet that Nathan, who is still rushing to get his crops out, has not looked at it. The panic of a realized neglect came upon him. It has been years since he walked that fence himself, and he can see in his mind, as clearly as if he were there, perhaps five places where the winter spates of Shade Branch might have torn out the wire.

He sits, listening to Margaret, looking at pipe smoke, anxiously working his way down along that boundary in his mind.

'Mat,' Margaret says at the screen door, 'dinner's ready.'

'All right,' he says, though for perhaps a minute after that he does not move. And then he gets up, steps to the edge of the porch to knock out his pipe, and goes in.

When he has eaten, seeing him pick up his hat again from the chair by the door, Margaret says, 'You're not going to take your nap?'

'No,' he says, for he has decided to walk that length of the boundary line that runs down Shade Branch. And he has stepped beyond the feeling that he is going to do it because he should. He is going to do it because he wants to. 'I've got something yet I have to do.'

He means to go on out the door without looking back. But he knows that she is watching him, worried about him, and he goes back to her and gives her a hug. 'It's all right, my old girl,' he says. He stands with his arms around her, who seems to him to have changed almost while he has held her from girl to wife to mother to grandmother to great-grandmother. There in the old room where they have been together so long, ready again to leave it, he thinks, 'I am an old man now.'

'Don't worry,' he says. 'I'm feeling good.'

He does feel good, for an old man, and once outside, he puts the house behind him and his journey ahead of him. At the barn he takes from its nail in the old harness room a stout stockman's cane. He does not need a cane yet, and he is proud of it, but as a concession to Margaret he has decided to carry one today.

When he lets himself out through the lot gate and into the open, past the barn and the other buildings, he can see the country lying under the sun. Nearby, on his own ridges, the crops are young and growing, the pastures are lush, a field of hay has been raked into curving windrows. Inlets of the woods, in the perfect foliage of the early season, reach up the hollows between the ridges. Lower down, these various inlets join in the larger woods embayed in the little valley of Shade Branch. Beyond the ridges and hollows of the farm he can see the opening of the river valley, and beyond that the hills on the far side, blue in the distance.

He has it all before him, this place that has been his life, and how lightly and happily now he walks out again into it! It seems to him that he has cast off all restraint, left all encumbrances behind, taking only himself and his direction. He is feeling good. There has been plenty of rain, and the year is full of promise. The country *looks* promising. He thinks of the men he knows who are at work in it: the Coulter brothers and Nathan, Nathan's boy, Mattie, Elton Penn, and Mat's grandson, Bess's and Wheeler's boy, Andy Catlett. They are at Elton's now, he thinks, but by midafternoon they should be back here, baling the hay.

Carrying the cane over his shoulder, he crosses two fields, and then, letting himself through a third gate, turns right along the fencerow that will lead him down to Shade Branch. Soon he is walking steeply downward among the trunks of trees, and the shifting green sea of their foliage has closed over him.

He comes into the deeper shade of the older part of the woods where there is little browse and the cattle seldom come, and here he sits down at the root of an old white oak to rest. As many times before, he feels coming to him the freedom of the woods, where he has no work to do. He feels coming to him such rest as, bound to house and barn and garden for so long, he had forgot. In body, now, he is an old man, but mind and eye look out of his old body into the shifting leafy lights and shadows among the still trunks with a recognition that is without age, the return of an ageless joy. He needs the rest, for he has walked in his gladness at a faster pace than he is used to, and he is sweating. But he is in no hurry, and he sits and grows quiet among the sights and sounds of the place. The time of the most abundant blooming of the woods flowers is past now, but the tent villages of mayapple are still perfect, there are ferns and stonecrop, and near him he can see the candle-like white flowers of black cohosh. Below, but still out of sight, he can hear the water in Shade Branch passing down over the rocks in a hundred little rapids and falls. When he feels the sweat beginning to dry on his face he gets up, braces himself against the gray trunk of the oak until he is steady, and stands free. The descent beckons and he yields eagerly to it, going on down into the tireless chanting of the stream.

He reaches the edge of the stream at a point where the boundary, coming down the slope facing him, turns at a right angle and follows Shade Branch in its fall toward the creek known as Sand Ripple. Here the fence that Mat has been following crosses the branch over the top of a rock wall that was built in the notch of the stream long before Mat was born. The water coming down, slowed by the wall, has filled the notch above it with rock and silt, and then, in freshet, leaping over it, has scooped out a shallow pool below it, where water stands most of the year. All this, given the continuous little changes of growth and wear in the woods and the stream, is as it was when Mat first knew it: the wall gray and mossy, the water, only a spout now, pouring over the wall into the little pool, covering the face of it with concentric wrinkles sliding outward.

Here, seventy-five years ago, Mat came with a fencing crew: his father, Ben, his uncle, Jack Beechum, Joe Banion, a boy then, not much older than Mat, and Joe's grandfather, Smoke, who had been a slave. And Mat remembers Jack Beechum coming down through the woods, as Mat himself has just come, carrying on his shoulder two of the long light rams they used to tamp the dirt into postholes. As he approached the pool he took a ram in each hand, holding them high, made three long approaching strides, planted the rams in the middle of the pool, and vaulted over. Mat, delighted, said, 'Do it again!' And without breaking rhythm, Jack turned, made the three swinging strides, and did it again – *does* it again in Mat's memory, so clearly that Mat's presence there, so long after, fades away, and he hears their old laughter, and hears Joe Banion say, 'Mistah Jack, he might nigh a *bird*!'

Forty-some years later, coming down the same way to build that same fence again, Mat and Joe Banion and Virgil, Mat's son, grown then and full of the newness of his man's strength, Mat remembered what Jack had done and told Virgil; Virgil took the two rams, made the same three strides that Jack had made, vaulted the pool, and turned back and grinned. Mat and Joe Banion laughed again, and this time Joe looked at Mat and said only 'Damn.'

Now a voice in Mat's mind that he did not want to hear says, 'Gone. All of them are gone.' And they *are* gone. Mat is standing by the pool, and all the others are gone, and all that time has passed. And still the stream pours into the pool and the circles slide across its face.

He shrugs as a man would shake snow from his shoulders and steps away. He finds a good place to cross the branch, and picks his way carefully from rock to rock to the other side, using the cane for that and glad he brought it. Now he gives attention to the fence. Soon he comes upon signs – new wire spliced into the old, a staple newly driven into a sycamore – that tell him his fears were unfounded. Nathan has been here. For a while now Mat walks in the way he knows that Nathan went. Nathan is forty-one this year, a quiet, careful man, as attentive to Mat as Virgil might have been if Virgil had lived to return from the war. Usually, when Nathan has done such a piece of work as this, he will tell Mat so that Mat can have the satisfaction of knowing that the job is done. Sometimes, though, when he is hurried, he forgets, and Mat will think of the job and worry about it and finally go to see to it himself, almost always to find, as now, that Nathan has been there ahead of him and has done what needed to be done. Mat praises Nathan in his mind and calls him son. He has never called Nathan son aloud, to his face, for he does not wish to impose or intrude. But Nathan, who is not his son, has become his son, just as Hannah, Nathan's wife, Virgil's widow, who is not Mat's daughter, has become his daughter.

'I am blessed,' he thinks. He walks in the way Nathan walked down along the fence, between the fence and the stream, seeing Nathan in his mind as clearly as if he were following close behind him, watching. He can see Nathan with axe and hammer and pliers and pail of staples and wire stretcher and coil of wire, making his way down along the fence, stopping now to chop a windfall off the wire and retighten it, stopping again to staple the fence to a young sycamore that has grown up in the line opportunely to serve as a post. Mat can imagine every move Nathan made, and in his old body, a little tired now, needing to be coaxed and instructed in the passing of obstacles, he remembers the strength of the body of a man of forty-one, unregarding of its own effort.

Now, trusting the fence to Nathan, Mat's mind turns away from it. He allows himself to drift down the course of the stream, passing through it as the water passes, drawn by gravity, bemused by its little chutes and falls. He stops beside one tiny quiet backwater and watches a family of water striders conducting their daily business, their feet dimpling the surface. He eases the end of his cane into the pool, and makes a crawfish spurt suddenly backward beneath a rock.

A water thrush moves down along the rocks of the streambed ahead of him, teetering and singing. He stops and stands to watch while a large striped woodpecker works its way up the trunk of a big sycamore, putting its eye close to peer under the loose scales of the bark. And then the bird flies to its nesting hole in a hollow snag still nearer by to feed its young, paying Mat no mind. He has become still as a tree, and now a hawk suddenly stands on a limb close over his head. The hawk loosens his feathers and shrugs, looking around him with his fierce eyes. And it comes to Mat that once more, by stillness, he has passed across into the wild inward presence of the place.

'Wonders,' he thinks. 'Little wonders of a great wonder.' He feels the sweetness of time. If a man eighty-two years old has not seen enough, then nobody will ever see enough. Such a little piece of the world as he has before him now would be worth a man's long life, watching and listening. And then he could go two hundred feet and live again another life, listening and watching, and his eyes would never be satisfied with seeing, or his ears filled with hearing. Whatever he saw could be seen only by looking away from something else equally worth seeing. For a second he feels and then loses some urging of the delight in a mind that could see and comprehend it all, all at once. 'I could stay here a long time,' he thinks. 'I could stay here a long time.'

He is standing at the head of a larger pool, another made by the plunging of the water over a rock wall. This one he built himself, he and Virgil, in the terribly dry summer of 1930. By the latter part of that summer, because of the shortage of both rain and money, they had little enough to do, and they had water on their minds. Mat remembered this place, where a strong vein of water opened under the roots of a huge old sycamore and flowed only a few feet before it sank uselessly among the dry stones of the streambed. 'We'll make a pool,' he said. He and Virgil worked several days in the August of that year, building the wall and filling in behind it so that the stream, when it ran full again, would not tear out the stones. The work there in the depth of the woods took their minds off their parched fields and comforted them. It was a kind of work that Mat loved and taught Virgil to love, requiring only the simplest tools: a large sledgehammer, a small one, and two heavy crow-bars with which they moved the big, thick rocks that were in that place. Once their tools were there, they left them until the job was done. When they came down to work they brought only a jug of water from the cistern at the barn.

'We could drink out of the spring,' Virgil said.

'Of course we could,' Mat said. 'It's dog days now. Do you want to get sick?'

In a shady place near the creek, Virgil tilted a flagstone up against a small sycamore, wedging it between trunk and root, to make a place for the water jug. There was not much reason for that. It was a thing a boy would do, making a little domestic nook like that, so far off in the woods, but Mat shared his pleasure in it, and that was where they kept the jug.

When they finished the work and carried their tools away, they left the jug, forgot it, and did not go back to get it. Mat did not think of it again until, years later, he happened to notice the rock still leaning against the tree, which had grown over it, top and bottom, fastening the rock to itself by a kind of natural mortise. Looking under the rock, Mat found the earthen jug still there, though it had been broken by the force of the tree trunk growing against it. He left it as it was. By then Virgil was dead, and the stream, rushing over the wall they had made, had scooped out a sizable pool that had been a faithful water source in dry years.

Remembering, Mat goes to the place and looks and again finds the stone and finds the broken jug beneath it. He has never touched rock or jug, and he does not do so now. He stands, looking, thinking of his son, dead twenty years, a stranger to his daughter, now a grown woman, who never saw him, and he says aloud, 'Poor fellow!' He does not know he is weeping until he feels his tears cool on his face.

Deliberately, he turns away. Deliberately, he gives his mind back to the day and the stream. He goes on down beside the flowing water, loitering, listening to the changes in its voice as he walks along it. He silences his mind now and lets the stream speak for him, going on, descending with it, only to prolong his deep peaceable attention to that voice that speaks always only of where it is, remembering nothing, fearing and desiring nothing.

Farther down, the woods thinning somewhat, he can see ahead of him where the Shade Branch hollow opens into the Sand Ripple valley. He can see the crest of the wooded slope on the far side of the creek valley. He stops. For a minute or so his mind continues on beyond him, charmed by the juncture he has come to. He imagines the succession of them, openings on openings: Sand Ripple opening to the Kentucky River, the Kentucky to the Ohio, the Ohio to the Mississippi, the Mississippi to the Gulf of Mexico, the Gulf to the boundless sky. He walks in old memory out into the river, carrying a heavy rock in each hand, out and down, until the water closes over his head and then the light shudders above him and disappears, and he walks in the dark cold water, down the slant of the bottom, to the limit of breath, and then drops his weights and cleaves upward into light and air again.

He turns around and faces the way he has come. 'Well, old man!' he thinks. 'Now what are you going to do?' For he has come down a long way, and now, looking back, he feels the whole country tilted against him. He feels the weight of it and the hot light over it. He hears himself say aloud, 'Why, you've got to get back out of here.'

But he is tired. It has been a year since he has walked even so far as he has already come. He feels the heaviness of his body, a burden that, his hand tells him, he has begun to try to shift off his legs and onto the cane. He thinks of Margaret, who, he knows as well as he knows anything, already wonders where he is and is worrying about him. Fear and exasperation hold him for a moment, but he pushes them off; he forces himself to be patient with himself. 'Well,' he says, as if joking with Virgil, for Virgil has come back into his thoughts now as a small boy, 'going up ain't the same as coming down. It's going to be different.'

It would be possible to go on down, and he considers that. He could follow the branch on down to the Sand Ripple road where it passes through the Rowanberry place. That would be downhill, and if he could find Mart Rowanberry near the house, Mart would give him a ride home. But the creek road is little traveled these days; if he goes down there and Mart is up on the ridge at work, which he probably is, then Mat will be farther from home than he is now, and will have a long walk, at least as far as the blacktop, maybe farther. Of course, he could go down there and just wait until Mart comes to the house at quitting time. There is sense in that, and for a moment Mat stands balanced between ways. What finally decides him is that he is unsure what lies between him and the creek road. If he goes down much farther he will cross the line fence onto the Rowanberry place. He knows that he would be all right for a while, going on down along the branch, but once in the creek bottom he would have to make his way to the road through dense, undergrowthy thicket, made worse maybe by piles of drift left by the winter's high water. He might have trouble getting through there, he thinks, and the strangeness of that place seems to forbid him. It has begun to trouble him that no other soul on earth knows where he is. He does not want to go where he will not know where he is himself.

★

He chooses the difficult familiar way, and steps back into it, helping himself with the cane now. He does immediately feel the difference between coming down and going up, and he wanders this way and that across the line of his direction, searching for the easiest steps. Windfalls that he went around or stepped over thoughtlessly, coming down, now require him to stop and study and choose. He is tired. He moves by choice.

He and his father have come down the branch, looking for a heifer due to calve; they have found her and are going back. Mat is tired. He wants to be home, but he does not want to *go* home. He is hot and a scratch on his face stings with sweat. He would just as soon cry as not, and his father, walking way up ahead of him, has not even slowed down. Mat cries, 'Wait, Papa!' And his father does turn and wait, a man taller than he looks because of the breadth of his shoulders, whom Mat would never see in a hurry and rarely see at rest. He has turned, smiling in the heavy bush of his beard, looking much as he will always look in Mat's memory of him, for Mat was born too late to know him young and he would be dead before he was as old as Mat is now. 'Come on, Mat,' Ben says. 'Come on, my boy.' As Mat conies up to him, he reaches down with a big hand that Mat puts his hand into. 'It's all right. It ain't that far.' They go on up the branch then. When they come to a windfall across the branch, Ben says, 'This one we go under.' And when they come to another, he says, 'This one we go around.'

Mat, who came down late in the afternoon to fix the fence, has fixed it, and is hurrying back, past chore time, and he can hear Virgil behind him, calling to him, 'Wait, Daddy!' He brought Virgil against his better judgment, because Virgil would not be persuaded not to come. You need me,' he said. 'I do need you,' Mat said, won over. 'You're my right-hand man.

Come on.' But now, irritated with himself and with Virgil too, he knows that Virgil needs to be carried, but his hands are loaded with tools and he can't carry him. Or so he tells himself, and he walks on. He stretches the distance out between them until Virgil feels that he has been left alone in the darkening woods; he sits down on a rock and gives himself up to grief. Hearing him cry, Mat puts his tools down where he can find them in the morning, and goes back for Virgil. 'Well, it's all right, old boy,' he says, picking him up. 'It's all right. It's all right.'

He is all right, but he is sitting down on a tree trunk lying across the branch, and he has not been able to persuade himself to get up. He came up to the fallen tree, and, to his surprise, instead of stepping over it, he sat down on it. At first that seemed to him the proper thing to do. He needed to sit down. He was tired. But now a protest begins in his mind. He needs to be on his way. He ought to be home by now. He knows that Margaret has been listening for him. He knows that several times by now she has paused in her work and listened, and gone to the windows to look out. She is hulling the peas he brought her before dinner. If he were there, he would be helping her. He thinks of the two of them sitting in the kitchen, hulling peas, and talking. Such a sense of luxury has come into their talk, now that they are old and in no hurry. They talk of what they know in common and do not need to talk about, and so talk about only for pleasure.

They would talk about where everybody is today and what each one is doing. They would talk about the stock and the crops. They would talk about how nice the peas are this year, and how good the garden is.

He thought, once, that maybe they would not have a garden. There were reasons not to have one.

'We don't need a garden this year,' he said to Margaret, wanting to spare her the work that would be in it for her.

'Yes,' she said, wanting to spare him the loss of the garden, 'of course we do!'

'Margaret, we'll go to all that work, and can all that food, and neither one of us may live to eat it.'

She gave him her smile, then, the same smile she had always given him, that always seemed to him to have survived already the worst he could think of. She said, 'Somebody will.'

She pleased him, and the garden pleased him. After even so many years, he still needed to be bringing something to her.

His command to get up seems to prop itself against his body and stay there like a brace until finally, in its own good time and again to his surprise, his body obeys. He gets up, steps over the tree, and goes on. He keeps himself on his feet for some time now, herding himself along like a recalcitrant animal, searching for the easy steps, reconciling himself to the hard steps when there are no easy ones. He is sweating heavily. So deep in that cleft of the hill, the air is hot and close. He feels that he must stretch upward to breathe. It is as though his body has come to belong in a different element, and the mere air of that place now hardly sustains it.

He comes to the pool, the wall that he and Virgil made, and pauses there. 'Now you must drink,' he says. He goes to where the spring comes up among the roots of the sycamore. There is a smooth clear pool there, no bigger than his hat. He lies down to drink, and drinks, looking down into the tiny pool cupped among the roots, surrounded with stonecrop and moss. The loveliness of it holds him: the cool water in that pretty place in the shade, the great tree rising and spreading its white limbs overhead. 'I am blessed,' he thinks, 'I could stay here.' He rests where he lies, turned away from his drinking, more comfortable on the roots and rocks than he expected to be. Through the foliage he can see white clouds moving along as if mindful where they are going. A chipmunk comes in quick starts and stops across the rocks and crouches a long time not far from Mat's face, watching him, as if perhaps it would like a drink from the little pool that Mat just drank from. 'Come on,' Mat says to it. 'There ain't any harm in me.' He would like to sleep. There is a weariness beyond weariness in him that sleep would answer. He can remember a time when he could have let himself sleep in such a place, but he cannot do that now. 'Get up,' he says aloud. 'Get up, get up.'

But for a while yet he does not move. He and the chipmunk watch each other. Now and again their minds seem to wander apart, and then they look again and find each other still there. There is a sound of wings, like a sudden dash of rain, and the chipmunk tumbles off its rock and does not appear again. Mat laughs. 'You'd *better* hide.' And now he does get up.

He stands, his left hand propped against the trunk of the sycamore. Darkness draws across his vision and he sinks back down onto his knees, his right hand finding purchase in the cold cup of the spring. The darkness wraps closely around him for a time, and then withdraws, and he stands again. '*That* won't do,' he says to Virgil. 'We got to do better than that, boy.' And then he sees his father too standing with Virgil on the other side of the stream. They recognize him, even though he is so much older now than when they knew him – older than either of them ever lived to be. 'Well,' he says, 'looks like we got plenty of help.' He reaches down and lets his right hand feel its way to the cane, picks it up, and straightens again. '*Yessir.*'

The world clears, steadies, and levels itself again in the light. He looks around him at the place: the wall, the pool, the spring mossy and clear in the roots of the white tree. 'I am not going to come back here,' he thinks. 'I will never be in this place again.'

Instructing his steps, he leaves. He moves with the utmost care and the utmost patience. For some time he does not think of where he is going. He is merely going up along the stream, asking first for one step and then for the next, moving by little plans that he carefully makes, and by choice. When he pauses to catch his breath or consider his way, he can feel his heart beating; at each of its beats the world seems to dilate and spring away from him.

His father and Virgil are with him, moving along up the opposite side of the branch as he moves up his side. He cannot always see them, but he knows they are there. First he does not see them, and then he sees one or the other of them appear among the trees and stand looking at him. They do not speak, though now and again he speaks to them. And then Jack Beechum, Joe Banion, and old Smoke are with them. He sees them sometimes separately, sometimes together. The dead who were here with him before are here with him again. He is not afraid. 'I could stay here,' he thinks. But ahead of him there is a reason he should not do that, and he goes on.

He seems to be walking in and out of his mind. Or it is time, perhaps, that he is walking in and out of. Sometimes he is with the dead as they were, and he is as he was, and all of them together are walking upward through the woods toward home. Sometimes he is alone, an old man in a later time than any of the dead have known, going the one way that he alone is going, among all the ways he has gone before, among all the ways he has never gone and will never go.

He does not remember falling. He is lying on the rocks beside the branch, and there is such disorder and discomfort in the way he is lying as he could not have intended. And so he must have fallen. He wonders if he is going to get up. After a while he does at least sit up. He shifts around so that his back can rest against the trunk of a tree. His movements cause little lurches in the world, and he waits for it to be steady. 'Now you have got to stop and think,' he says. And then he says, 'Well, you have stopped. Now you had better think.'

He does begin to think, forcing his vision and his thoughts out away from him into the place around him, his mind making little articulations of recognition. The place and his memory of it begin to speak to one another. He has come back almost to the upper wall and pool, where he first came down to the branch. When he gets there he will have a choice to make between two hard ways to go.

But his mind, having thought of those choices, now leaves him, like an undisciplined pup, and goes to the house, and goes back in time to the house the way it was when he and Margaret were still young.

About this time in the afternoon, about this time in the year, having come to the house for something, he cannot remember what, he pushes open the kitchen door, leans his shoulder on the jamb, and looks at Margaret, who stands with her back to him, icing a cake.

'Now nobody's asked for my opinion,' he says, 'and nobody's likely to, but if anybody ever was to, I'd say *that* is a huggable woman.'

'Don't you come near me, Mat Feltner.'

'And a spirited woman.'

'If you so much as lay a hand on me, I'm going to hit you with this cake.'

'And a dangerous, mean woman.'

'Go back to work.'

'Who is, still and all, a huggable woman. Which is only my opinion. A smarter man might think different.'

She turns around, laughing, and comes to get her hug. 'I could never have married a smart man.'

'She didn't marry *too* smart a one,' he thinks. He is getting up, the effort requiring the attendance of his mind, and once he is standing he puts his mind back on his problem. That is not where it wants to be, but this time he makes it stay. If he leaves the branch and goes back up onto the ridge by the way he came down, that will require a long slanting climb up across the face of a steep slope. 'And it has got steeper since I came down it,' he thinks. If he goes on up Shade Branch, which would be the easiest, surest route, he will have, somehow, to get over or through the fence that crosses the branch above the wall. He does not believe that he can climb the fence. Where the fence crosses the stream it is of barbed wire, and in that place a stronger man might go through or under it. But he does not want to risk hooking his clothes on the barbs.

But now he thinks of a third possibility: the ravine that comes into Shade Branch just above him to his right hand. The dry, rocky streambed in the ravine would go up more gently than the slope, the rocks would afford him stairsteps of a sort for at least some of the way, and it would be the shortest way out of the woods. It would bring him out farther from home than the other ways, but he must not let that bother him. It is the most possible of the three ways, and the most important thing now, he knows, is to get up onto the open land of the ridge where he can be seen if somebody comes looking for him. Somebody will be looking for him, he hopes, for he has to admit that he is not going very fast, and once he starts up the ravine he will be going slower than ever.

For a while he kept up the belief, and then the hope, that he could make it home in a reasonable time and walk into the house as if nothing had happened.

'Where on earth have you been?' Margaret would ask.

He would go to the sink to wash up, and then he would say, drying his hands, 'Oh, I went to see about the line fence down the branch, but Nathan had already fixed it.'

He would sit down then to help her with the peas.

'Mat Feltner,' she would say, 'surely you didn't go away off down there.'

But it is too late now, for something *has* happened. He has been gone too long, and is going to be gone longer.

Margaret has got up from her work and gone to the windows and looked out, and gone to the door onto the back porch and spoken his name, and walked on out to the garden gate and then to the gate to the barn lot.

He can see her and hear her calling as plainly as if he were haunting her. 'Mat! Oh, Mat!'

He can hear her, and he makes his way on up the branch to the mouth of the ravine. He turns up the bed of the smaller stream. The climb is steeper here, the hard steps closer together. The ascent asks him now really to climb, and in places, where the rocks of the streambed bulge outward in a wall, he must help himself with his hands. He must stoop under and climb over the trunks of fallen trees. When he stops after each of these efforts the heavy beating of his heart keeps on. He can feel it shaking him, and darkness throbs in his eyes. His breaths come too far between and too small. Sometimes he has roots along the side of the ravine for a banister, and that helps. Sometimes the cane helps; sometimes, when he needs both hands, it is in the way. And always he is in the company of the dead.

*

Ahead of him the way is closed by the branchy top of a young maple, blown down in a storm, and he must climb up the side of the ravine to get around it. At the top of the climb, when the slope has gentled and he stops and his heart plunges on and his vision darkens, it seems to him that he is going to fall; he decides instead to sit down, and he does. Slowly he steadies again within himself. His heart slows and his vision brightens again. He tells himself again to get up. 'It ain't as far as it has been,' he says to Virgil. 'I'm going to be all right now. I'm going to make it.'

But now his will presses against his body, as if caught within it, in bewilderment. It will not move. There was a time when his body had strength enough in it to carry him running up such a place as this, with breath left over to shout. There was a time when it had barely enough strength in it to carry it this far. There is a time when his body is too heavy for his strength. He longs to lie down. To Jack Beechum, the young man, Jack Beechum, who is watching him now, he says, 'You and I were here once.'

The dead come near him, and he is among them. They come and go, appear and disappear, like feeding birds. They are there and gone. He is among them, and then he is alone. To one who is not going any farther, it is a pretty place, the leaves new and perfect, a bird singing out of sight among them somewhere over his head, and the softening light slanting in long beams from the west. 'I could stay here,' he thinks. It is the thought of going on that turns that steep place into an agony. His own stillness pacifies it and makes it lovely. He thinks of dying, secretly, by himself, in the woods. No one now knows where he is. Perhaps it would be possible to hide and die, and never be found. It would be a clean, clear way for that business to be done, and the thought, in his weariness, comforts him, for he has feared that he might die a nuisance to Margaret and the others. He might, perhaps, hide himself in a little cave or sink hole if one were nearby, here where the dead already are, and be one of them, and enter directly into the peaceableness of this place, and turn with it through the seasons, his body grown easy in its weight.

But there is no hiding place. He would be missed and hunted for and found. He would die a nuisance, for he could not hide from all the reasons that he would be missed and worried about and hunted for. He has an appointment that must be kept, and between him and it the climb rises on above him.

He has an accounting he must come to, and it is not with the dead, for Margaret has not sat down again, but is walking. She is walking from room to room and from window to window. She has not called Bess, because she does not want Bess to drive all the way up from Hargrave, perhaps for nothing. Though she has thought about it, she has not even called Hannah, who is nearer by. She does not want to alarm anybody. But she is alarmed. She walks from room to room and from window to window, pausing to look out, and walking again. She walks with her arms tightly folded, as she has walked all her life when she has been troubled, until Mat, watching her, has imagined that he thinks as she thinks and feels, as she feels, so moved by her at times that he has been startled to realize again his separateness from her.

He remembers the smile of assent that she gave him once: 'Why, Mat, I thought you did. And I love you.' Everything that has happened to him since has come from that – and leads to that, for it is not a moment that has ever stopped happening; he has gone toward it and aspired to it all his life, a time that he has not surpassed.

Now she is an old woman, walking in his mind in the rooms of their house. She has called no one and told no one. She is the only one who knows that she does not know where he is. The men are in the hayfield, and she is waiting for one of them or some of them to come to the barn. Or Wheeler might come by. It is the time of day when he sometimes does. She walks slowly from room to room, her arms folded tightly, and she watches the windows.

Mat, sitting in his heaviness among the trees, she does not know where, yearns for her as from beyond the grave. 'Don't worry,' he says. 'It's going to be all right.' He gets up.

And now an overmastering prayer that he did not think to pray rushes upon him out of the air and seizes him and grapples him to itself: an absolute offering of himself to his return. It is an offer, involuntary as his breath, voluntary as the new steps he has already taken up the hill, to give up his life in order to have it. The prayer does not move him beyond weariness and weakness, it moves him merely beyond all other thoughts.

He gives no more regard to death or to the dead. The dead do not appear again. Now he is walking in this world, walking in time, going home. A shadowless love moves him now, not his, but a love that he belongs to, as he belongs to the place and to the light over it. He is thinking of Margaret and of all that his plighting with her has led to. He is thinking of the membership of the fields that he has belonged to all his life, and will belong to while he breathes, and afterward. He is thinking of the living ones of that membership – at work today in the fields that the dead were at work in before them.

'I am blessed,' he thinks. 'I am blessed.'

He is crawling now, the cane lost and forgotten. He crawls

a little, and he rests a lot. The slope has gentled somewhat. The big woods has given way to thicket. He has turned away from the stream, taking the straightest way to the open slope that he can see not far above him. The cattle are up there grazing, the calves starting to play a little, now that the cool of the day is here.

When he comes out, clear of the trees, onto the grassed hillside, he seems again to have used up all his strength. 'Now,' he thinks, 'you have got to rest.' Once he has rested he will go on to the top of the ridge. Once he gets there, he can make it to the road. He crawls on up the slope a few feet to where a large walnut tree stands alone outside the woods, and sits against it so that he will have a prop for his back. He wipes his face, brushes at the dirt on his knees and then subsides. Not meaning to, he sleeps.

The sun is going down when he wakes, the air cold on his damp clothes. Except for opening his eyes, he does not move. His body is still as a stone.

Now he knows what woke him. It is the murmur of an automobile engine up on the ridge – Wheeler's automobile, by the sound of it. And when it comes into sight he sees that it is Wheeler's; Wheeler is driving and Elton Penn and Nathan are with him. They are not looking for him. They have not seen Margaret. Perhaps they did not bale the hay. Or they may have finished and got away early. But he knows that Wheeler found Nathan and Elton, wherever they were, after he shut his office and drove up from Hargrave, and they have been driving from field to field ever since, at Elton's place or at Nathan's or at Wheeler's, and now here. This is something they do, Mat knows, for he is often with them when they do it. Wheeler drives the car slowly, and they look and worry and admire and remember and plan. They have come to look at the cattle now, to see them on the new grass. They move among the cows and calves, looking and stopping. Now and then an arm reaches out of one of the car windows and points. For a long time they do not turn toward Mat. It is as though he is only part of the field, like the tree he is leaning against. He feels the strangeness of his stillness, but he does not move.

And then, still a considerable distance away, Wheeler turns the car straight toward the tree where Mat is sitting. He sees their heads go up when they see him, and he raises his right hand and gives them what, for all his eagerness, is only an ordinary little wave.

Wheeler accelerates, and the car comes tilting and rocking down the slope. Where the slope steepens, forcing the car to slow down, Mat sees Nathan leap out of it and come running toward him, Elton out too, then, while Wheeler is still maneuvering the car down the hill. Seeing that they are running to help him, Mat despises his stillness. He forces himself to his knees and then to his feet. He turns to face Nathan, who has almost reached him. He lets go of the tree and stands, and sees the ground rising against him like a blow. He feels himself caught strongly, steadied, and held. He hears himself say, 'Papa?'

That night, when Margaret finds him wandering in the darkened house, he does not know where he is.

That Distant Land
(1965)

For several days after the onset of his decline, my grand-father's mind seemed to leave him to go wandering, lost, in some foreign place. It was a dream he was in, we thought, that he could not escape. He was looking for the way home, and he could not find anyone who knew how to get there.

'No,' he would say. 'Port William. Port William is the name of the place.'

Or he would ask, 'Would you happen to know a nice lady by the name of Margaret Feltner? She lives in Port William. Now, which way would I take to get there?'

But it was not us he was asking. He was not looking at us and mistaking us for other people. He was not looking at us at all. He was talking to people he was meeting in his dream. From the way he spoke to them, they seemed to be nice people. They treated him politely and were kind, but they did not know any of the things that he knew, and they could not help him.

When his mind returned, it did so quietly. It had never been a mind that made a lot of commotion around itself. One morn-ing when my grandmother went in to wake him and he opened his eyes, they were looking again. He looked at my grand-mother and said, 'Margaret, I'll declare.' He looked around him at the bright room and out the window at the ridges and the woods, and said, 'You got a nice place here, ma'am.'

My grandmother, as joyful as if he had indeed been gone far away and had come home, said, 'Oh, Mat, are you all right?'

And he said, 'I seem to be a man who has been all right before, and I'm all right now.'

That was the middle of June, and having come back from wherever it had been, his mind stayed with him and with us, a peaceable, pleasant guest, until he died.

He did not get out of bed again. What troubled us, and then grieved us, and finally consoled us, was that he made no effort to get up. It appeared to us that he felt his time of struggle to be past, and that he agreed to its end. He who had lived by ceaseless effort now lived simply as his life was given to him, day by day. During the time his mind had wandered he ate little or nothing, and though his mind returned his appetite did not. He ate to please my grandmother, but he could not eat much. She would offer the food, he would eat the few bites that were enough, and she would take the plate away. None of us had the heart to go beyond her gentle offering. No one insisted. No one begged. He asked almost nothing of us, only to be there with us, and we asked only to be with him.

He lay in a room from which he could look out across the ridges toward the river valley And he did often lie there looking out. Now that he felt his own claims removed from it, the place seemed to have become more than ever interesting to him, and he watched it as the dark lifted from it and the sun rose and moved above it and set and the dark returned. Now and then he would speak of what he saw – the valley brimming with fog in the early morning, a hawk circling high over the ridges, somebody at work in one of the fields – and we would know that he watched with understanding and affection. But the character of his watching had changed. We all felt it. We had known him as a man who watched, but then his watching had been purposeful. He had watched as a man preparing for what he knew he must do, and what he wanted to do. Now it had become the watching, almost, of one who was absent.

The room was bright in the mornings, and in the afternoons dim and cool. It was always clean and orderly. My grandfather, who had no wants, made no clutter around him, and any clutter that the rest of us made did not last long. His room became the center of the house, where we came to rest. He would welcome us, raising his hand to us as we came in, listening to all that was said, now and again saying something himself.

Because, wherever we were, we kept him in our minds, he kept us together in the world as we knew he kept us in his mind Until the night of his death we were never all in the house at the same time, yet no day passed that he did not see most of us. In the morning, my mother, his only surviving child, or Hannah Coulter, who had been his daughter-in-law and was, in all but blood, his daughter, or Flora, my wife, or Sara, my brother Henry's wife, would come in to spend the day with my grandmother to keep her company and help with the work. And at evening my father or Henry or I or Nathan Coulter, who now farmed my grandfather's farm and was, in all but blood, his son, would come, turn about, to spend the night, to give whatever help would be needed.

And others who were not family came: Burley Coulter, Burley's brother Jarrat, Elton and Mary Penn, Arthur and Martin Rowanberry. They would happen by for a few minutes in the daytime, or come after supper and sit and talk an hour or two. We were a membership. We belonged together, and my grandfather's illness made us feel it.

But 'Illness', now that I have said it, seems the wrong word. It was not like other illnesses that I had seen – it was quieter and more peaceable. It was, it would be truer to say, a great weariness that had come upon him, like the lesser weariness that comes with the day's end – a weariness that had been earned, and was therefore accepted.

I had lived away, working in the city, for several years, and had returned home only that spring. I was thirty year old, I had a wife and children, and my return had given a sudden sharp clarity to my understanding of my home country. Every fold of the land, every grass blade and leaf of it gave me joy, for I saw how my own place in it had been prepared, along with its failures and its losses. Though I knew that I had returned to difficulties – not the least of which were the deaths that I could see coming – I was joyful.

The nights I spent, taking my turn, on the cot in a corner of my grandfather's room gave me a strong, sweet pleasure. At first, usually, visitors would be there, neighbors or family stopping by. Toward bedtime, they would go. I would sit on a while with my grandmother and grandfather, and we would talk. Or rather, if I could arrange it so, they would talk and I would listen. I loved to start them talking about old times – my mother's girlhood, their own young years, stories told them by their parents and grandparents, memories of memories. In their talk the history of Port William went back and back along one of its lineages until it ended in silence and conjecture, for Port William was older than its memories. That it had begun we knew because it had continued, but we did not know when or how it had begun.

It was usually easy enough to get them started, for they enjoyed the remembering, and they knew that I liked to hear. 'Grandad,' I would say, 'who was George Washington Coulter's mother?' Or: 'Granny, tell about Aunt Maude Wheeler hailing the steamboat.' And they would enter the endlessly varying pattern of remembering. A name would remind them of a story; one story would remind them of another. Sometimes my grandmother would get out a box of old photographs and we would sit close to the bed so that my grandfather could see them too, and then the memories and names moved and hovered over the transfixed old sights. The picture that most moved and troubled me was the only consciously photographed 'scene': a look down the one street of Port William at the time of my grandparents' childhood – 1890 or thereabouts. What so impressed me about it was that the town had then been both more prosperous and more the center of its own attention than I had ever known it to be. The business buildings all had upper stories, the church had a steeple, there was a row of trees, planted at regular intervals, along either side of the road. Now the steeple and most of the upper stories were gone – by wind or fire or decay – and many of the trees were gone. For a long time, in Port William, what had gone had not been replaced. Its own attention had turned away from itself toward what it could not be. And I understood how, in his dream, my grandfather had suffered his absence from the town; through much of his life it had grown increasingly absent from itself.

After a while, my grandmother would leave us. She would go to my grandfather's side and take his hand. 'Mat, is there anything you want before I go?'

'Ma'am,' he would say, 'I've got everything I want.' He would be teasing her a little, as he was always apt to do.

She would hesitate, wishing, I think, that he did want something. 'Well, good night. I'll see you in the morning.'

And he would pat her hand and say very agreeably, as if he were altogether willing for that to happen, if it should happen, 'All right.'

*

She would go and we would hear her stirring about in her room, preparing for bed. I would do everything necessary to make my grandfather comfortable for the night, help him to relieve himself, help him to turn onto his side, straighten the bedclothes, see that the flashlight was in reach in case he wanted to look at the clock, which he sometimes did. I was moved by his willingness to let me help him. We had always been collaborators. When I was little, he had been the one in the family who would help me with whatever I was trying to make. And now he accepted help as cheerfully as he had given it. We were partners yet.

I was still a young man, with a young man's prejudice in favor of young bodies. I would have been sorry but I would not have been surprised if I had found it unpleasant to have to handle him as I did – his old flesh slackened and dwindling on the bones – but I did not find it so. I touched him gratefully. I would put one knee on the bed and gather him in my arms and move him toward me and turn him. I liked to do it. The comfort I gave him I felt. He would say, 'Thanks, son.'

When he was settled, I would turn on the dim little bed-lamp by the cot and go to bed myself.

'Sleep tight,' I would tell him.

'Well,' he would say, amused, 'I will part of the time.'

I would read a while, letting the remembered dear stillness of the old house come around me, and then I would sleep.

My grandfather did only sleep part of the time. Mostly, when he was awake, he lay quietly with his thoughts, but sometimes he would have to call me, and I would get up to bring him a drink (he would want only two or three swallows), or help him to use the bedpan, or help him to turn over.

Once he woke me to recite me the Twenty-third Psalm. 'Andy,' he said. 'Andy. Listen.' He said the psalm to me. I lay listening to his old, slow voice coming through the dark to me, saying that he walked through the valley of the shadow of death and was not afraid. It stood my hair up. I had known that psalm all my life. I had heard it and said it a thousand times. But until then I had always felt that it came from a long way off, someplace I had not lived. Now, hearing him speak it, it seemed to me for the first time to utter itself in our tongue and to wear our dust. My grandfather slept again after that, but I did not.

Another night, again, I heard him call me. 'Andy. Listen.' His voice exultant then at having recovered the words, he recited:

> There entertain him all the saints above,
> In solemn troops and sweet societies
> That sing, and singing in their glory move,
> And wipe the tears forever from his eyes.

After he spoke them, the words stood above us in the dark and the quiet, sounding and luminous. And then they faded.

After a while I said, 'Who taught you that?'

'My mother. She was a great hand to improve your mind.'

And after a while, again, I asked, 'Do you know who wrote it?'

'No,' he said. 'But wasn't he a fine one!'

As the summer went along, he weakened, but so slowly we could hardly see it happening. There was never any sudden change. He remained quiet, mainly comfortable, and alert. We stayed in our routine of caring for him; it had become the ordinary way of things.

In the latter part of August we started into the tobacco cutting. For us, that is the great divider of the year. It ends the summer, and makes safe the season's growth. After it, our minds are lightened, and we look ahead to winter and the coming year. It is a sort of ritual of remembrance, too, when we speak of other years and remember our younger selves and the absent and the dead – all those we have, as we say, 'gone down the row with'.

We had a big crew that year – eight men working every day: Jarrat and Burley and Nathan Coulter, Arthur and Martin Rowanberry, Elton Penn, Danny Branch, and me. Hannah Coulter and Mary Penn and Lyda Branch kept us fed and helped with the hauling and housing. And Nathan and Hannah's and the Penns' children were with us until school started, and then they worked after school and on Saturdays. We worked back and forth among the various farms as the successive plantings became ready for harvest.

'What every tobacco cutting needs,' Art Rowanberry said 'is a bunch of eighteen-year-old boys wanting to show how fast they are.'

He was right, but we did not have them. We were not living in a time that was going to furnish many such boys for such work. Except for the children, we were all old enough to be resigned to the speed we could stand. And so, when we cut, we would be strung out along the field in a pattern that never varied from the first day to the last. First would be Elton and Nathan and Danny, all working along together. Elton, I think, would have proved the fastest if anybody had challenged him, but nobody did. Then came Mart Rowanberry, who was always ahead of me, though he was nearly twice my age, and then, some distance behind me, would come Art Rowanberry, and then Burley Coulter, and then, far back, Burley's brother Jarrat, whose judgment and justification of himself were unswerving: 'I'm old and wore out and not worth a damn. But every row I cut is a cut row.'

In my grandfather's absence Jarrat was the oldest of us, a long-enduring, solitary, mostly silent man, slowed by age and much hard work. His brushy eyes could stare upon you as if you had no more ability to stare back than a post. When he had something to say, his way was simply to begin to say it, no matter who else was talking or what else was happening, his slow, hard-edged voice boring in upon us like his stare – and the result, invariably, was that whatever was happening stopped, and whoever was talking listened.

I never caught up with Elton and Nathan and Danny, or came anywhere near it, but at least when the rows were straight I always had them in sight, and I loved to watch them. Though they kept an even, steady pace, it was not a slow one. They drove into the work, maintaining the same pressing rhythm from one end of the row to the other, and yet they worked well, as smoothly and precisely as dancers. To see them moving side by side against the standing crop, leaving it fallen, the field changed, behind them, was maybe like watching Homeric soldiers going into battle. It was momentous and beautiful, and touchingly, touchingly mortal. They were spending themselves as they worked, giving up their time; they would not return by the way they went.

The good crew men among us were Burley and Elton. When the sun was hot and the going hard, it would put heart into us to hear Burley singing out down the row some scrap of human sorrow that his flat, exuberant voice both expressed and mocked:

Allll *our sins and griefs to* bear – *oh!*

– that much only, raised abruptly out of the silence like the howl of some solitary dog. Or he would sing with a lovelorn quaver in his voice:

Darlin', fool yourself and love me one more time.

*

And when we were unloading the wagons in the barn, he would start his interminable tale about his life as a circus teamster. It was not meant to be believed, and yet in our misery we listened to his extravagant wonderful lies as if he had been Marco Polo returned from Cathay.

Elton had as much gab as Burley, when he wanted to, but he served us as the teller of the tale of our own work. He told and retold everything that happened that was funny. That we already knew what he was telling, that he was telling us what we ourselves had done, did not matter. He told it well, he told it the way we would tell it when we told it, and every time he told it he told it better. He told us, also, how much of our work we had got done, and how much we had left to do, and how we might form the tasks still ahead in order to do them. His head, of course, was not the only one involved, and not the only good one, but his was indeed a good one, and his use of it pleased him and comforted us. Though we had a lot of work still to do, we were going to be able to do it, and these were the ways we could get it done. The whole of it stayed in his mind. He shaped it for us and gave it a comeliness greater than its difficulty.

That we were together now kept us reminded of my grandfather, who had always been with us before. We often spoke of him, because we missed him, or because he belonged to our stories, and we could not tell them without speaking of him.

One morning, perhaps to acknowledge to herself that he would not wear them again, my grandmother gave me a pair of my grandfather's shoes.

It was a gift not easy to accept. I said, 'Thanks, Granny,' and put them under my arm.

'No,' she said. 'Put them on. See if they fit.'

They fit, and I started, embarrassedly, to take them off.

'No,' she said. 'Wear them.'

And so I wore them to the field.

'New shoes!' Burley said, recognizing them, and I saw tears start to his eyes.

'Yes,' I said.

Burley studied them, and then me. And then he smiled and put his arm around me, making the truth plain and bearable to us both: 'You can wear 'em, honey. But you can't fill 'em.'

It got to be September, and the fall feeling came into the air. The days would get as hot as ever, but now when the sun got low the chill would come. It was not going to frost for a while yet, but we could feel it coming. It was the time of year, Elton said, when a man begins to remember his long underwear.

We were cutting a patch at Elton's place where the rows were longer than any we had cut before, bending around the shoulder of a ridge and rising a little over it. They were rows to break a man's heart, for, shaped as they were, you could not see the end, and those of us who were strung out behind the leaders could not see each other. All that we could see ahead of us was the cloudless blue sky. Each row was a long, lonely journey that, somewhere in the middle, in our weariness, we believed would never end.

Once when I had cut my row and was walking back to start another, Art Rowanberry wiped the sweat from his nose on the cuff of his sleeve and called out cheerfully to me, 'Well, have you been across? Have you seen the other side?'

That became the ceremony of that day and the next. When one of us younger ones finished a row and came walking back, Art would ask us, 'Have you seen the other side?'

Burley would take it up then, mourning and mocking: 'Have

you reached the other shore, dear brother? Have you seen that distant land?' And he would sing,

Oh, pilgrim, have you seen that distant land?

On the evening of the second day we had the field nearly cut. There was just enough of the crop left standing to make an easy job of finishing up – something to look forward to. We had finished cutting for the day and were sitting in the rich, still light under a walnut tree at the edge of the field, resting a little, before loading the wagons. We would load them the last thing every evening, to unload the next morning while the dew was on.

We saw my father's car easing back along the fencerow, rocking a little over the rough spots in the ground. It was a gray car, all dusty, and scratched along the sides where he had driven it through the weeds and briars. He still had on his suit and tie.

'Ah, here he comes,' Burley said, for we were used to seeing him at that time of day, when he would leave his office at Hargrave and drive up to help us a little or to see how we had got along.

He drove up beside us and stopped, and killed the engine. But he did not look at us. He looked straight ahead as if he had not quit driving, his hands still on the wheel.

'Boys,' he said, 'Mr Feltner died this afternoon. About an hour ago.'

And then, after he seemed to have finished, he said as though to himself, 'And now that's over.'

I heard Burley clear his throat, but nobody said anything. We sat in the cooling light in my grandfather's new absence, letting it come upon us.

And then the silence shifted and became our own. Nobody spoke. Nobody yet knew what to say. We did not know what we were going to do. We were, I finally realized, waiting on Jarrat. It was Elton's farm, but Jarrat was now the oldest man, and we were waiting on him.

He must have felt it too, for he stood, and stood still, looking at us, and then turned away from us toward the wagons.

'Let's load 'em up.'

The Wild Birds
(1967)

'Where have they gone?' Wheeler thinks. But he knows. Gone to the cities, forever or for the day. Gone to the shopping center. Gone to the golf course. Gone to the grave.

He can remember Saturday afternoons when you could hardly find space in Hargrave to hitch a horse, and later ones when an automobile could not move through the crowd on Front Street as fast as a man could walk.

Wheeler is standing at his office window, whose lower pane announces Wheeler Catlett & Son, Attorneys-at-Law; he is looking out diagonally across the courthouse square and the roofs of the stores along Front Street at the shining reach of the Ohio, where a white towboat is shoving an island of coal barges against the current, its screws roiling the water in a long fan behind it. The barges are empty, coming up from the power plant at Jefferson, whose dark plume of smoke Wheeler can also see, stretching out eastward, upriver, under the gray sky.

Below him, the square and the streets around it are deserted. Even the loafers are gone from the courthouse where, the offices shut, they are barred from the weekday diversions of the public interest, and it is too cold to sit on the benches under the Social Security trees, now leafless, in the yard. The stores are shut also, for whatever shoppers may be at large are out at La Belle Riviere Shopping Plaza, which has lately overborne a farm in the bottomland back of town. Only a few automobiles stand widely dispersed around the square, nosed to the curbs,

Wheeler's own and half a dozen more, to suggest the presence, somewhere, of living human beings – others like himself, Wheeler supposes, here because here is where they have usually been on Saturday afternoon.

But he knows too that he is *signifying* something by being here, as if here is where he agreed to be when he took his law school diploma and came home, or as near home as he could get and still practice law, forty-one years ago. He is here as if to prove 'to all to whom these presents may come' his willingness to be here.

And yet if he is here by agreement, he is here also in fidelity to what is gone: the old-time Saturday to which the country people once deferred all their business, when his old clients, most of them now dead, would climb the stairs to his office as often as not for no business at all, but to sit and speak in deference to their mutual trust, reassuring both to them and to him. For along with the strictly business or legal clientele such as any lawyer anywhere might have had, Wheeler started out with a clientele that he may be said to have inherited – farmers mostly, friends of his father and his father-in-law, kinsmen, kinsmen's friends, with whom he thought of himself as a lawyer as little as they thought of themselves as clients. Between them and himself the technical connection was swallowed up in friendship, in mutual regard and loyalty. Such men, like as not, would not need a dime's worth of legal assistance between the settling of their parents' estates and the writing of their own wills, and not again after that. Wheeler served them as their defender against the law itself, before which they were ciphers, and so felt themselves – and he could do this only as their friend.

'What do I have to do about that, Wheeler?' they would ask, handing him a document or a letter.

And he would tell them. Or he would say, 'Leave it here. I'll see to it.'

'What I owe you, Wheeler?'

And he would name a figure sometimes to protect himself against the presumptuousness and long-windedness of some of them, or to protect the pride of others. Or he would say, 'Nothing', deeming the work already repaid by 'other good and valuable considerations'.

So Wheeler is here by prior agreement and pursuant history – survivor, so far, of all that the agreement has led to. The office has changed little over the years, less by far than the town and the country around it. It contains an embankment of file cabinets, a small safe, a large desk, Wheeler's swivel chair, and a few more chairs, some more comfortable than others. The top of the desk is covered with books and file folders neatly stacked. On the blotter in the center is a ruled yellow tablet on which Wheeler has been writing, the top page nearly covered with his impatient blue script. By way of decoration, there are only a few photographs of Wheeler's children and grandchildren. Though the room is dim, he has not turned on a light.

A more compliant, less idealistic man than Wheeler might have been happier here than he has been, for this has been a place necessarily where people have revealed their greed, arrogance, meanness, cowardice, and sometimes their inviolable stupidity. And yet, though he has known these things, Wheeler has not believed in them. In loyalty to his clients, or to their Maker, in whose image he has supposed them made, he has believed in their generosity, goodness, courage, and intelligence. Mere fact has never been enough for him. He has pled and reasoned, cajoled, bullied, and preached, pushing events always toward a better end than he knew they could reach, resisting always the disappointment that he knew he should expect, and when the disappointment has come, as it too often has, never settling for it in his own heart or looking upon it as a conclusion.

Wheeler has been sketching at a speech. In that restless hand of his, that fairly pounces on each word as it comes to him, he has refined his understanding of the points to be made and has worked out the connections. What he was struggling to make clear is the process by which unbridled economic forces draw life, wealth, and intelligence off the farms and out of the country towns and set them into conflict with their sources. Farm produce leaves the farm to nourish an economy that has thrived by the ruin of land. In this way, in the terms of Wheeler's speech, *price* wars against *value*.

'Thus,' he wrote, 'to increase the *price* of their industrial products, they depress the *value* of goods – a process not indefinitely extendable,' and his hand rose from the page and hovered over it, the pen aimed at the end of his sentence like a dart. The last phrase had something in it, maybe, but it would not do. At that failure, his mind abruptly refused the page. A fidelity older than his fidelity to word and page began to work on him. He picked up another pad on which he had drawn with a ruler the design of a shed to be built onto a feed barn. The new shed would require changes in the dimensions of the barn lot and in the positions of two gates, and those changes he had drawn out also. His mind, like a boy let out of school, returned to those things with relief, with elation. His thoughts leapt from his speech to its sources in place and memory, the generations of his kin and kind.

For the barn is the work of Wheeler's father, Marcellus, who built it to replace an older barn on the same spot. So methodical and clever a carpenter was Marcellus that he built the new barn while the old one stood, incorporating the old into the new, his mules never absent a night from their stalls, and he did virtually all the work alone. The building of the barn was one of the crests of the life of Marce Catlett, a pride and a comfort to him to the end of his days. Adding a new shed to it now is not something that Wheeler can afford to intend lightly or do badly.

Why at his age – when most of his generation are in retirement, and many are in the grave – he should be planning a new shed is a question he has entertained dutifully and answered perhaps a trifle belligerently: because he *wants* to.

But his mind had begun a movement that would not stop yet. His mind's movement, characteristically, was homeward. What he hungered for was the place itself. He saw that his afternoon's work in the office was over, and that was when he got up and went to the window, as if to set eyesight and mind free of the room. He would go soon. By going so early, he would have time to salt his cattle.

This sudden shift of his attention is so familiar to him as almost to have been expected, for in its fundamental structure, its loyalties and preoccupations, Wheeler's mind has changed as little in forty years as his office. If change happens, it happens; Wheeler can recognize a change when he sees one, but change is not on his program. Difference is. His business, indoors and out, has been the making of differences. And not the least of these has been this shift that he is about to make again from office to farm.

But for a moment longer he allows himself to be held at the window by the almost solemn stillness of the square and the business streets of the little town, considering again the increasing number of empty buildings, the empty spaces where buildings have been burned or torn down and not replaced, hating again the hopeless expenditure of its decay.

And now, directly across from his office door, a pickup truck eases in to the curb; two men and a woman get out. Wheeler recognizes his cousin, Burley Coulter, Burley's nephew Nathan, and Hannah, Nathan's wife. The three come together at the rear of the truck, the woman between the two men, and start across the street.

'What are *they* doing here?' Wheeler wonders. And then from their direction he understands that they have come to see him. He smiles, glad of it, and presently he hears their footsteps on the stairs.

The footsteps ascend slowly, for Burley is past seventy now and, though still vigorous, no longer nimble.

Wheeler goes through the outer office, where his secretary's typewriter sits hooded on its desk, and meets them in the dim hallway at the top of the stairs, reaching his hand to them as they come up.

'Hello, Hannah. Go right on in there in the office, honey. How're you, Nathan? Hello, Burley.'

'How you making it, Wheeler?' Burley says in his hearty way, as if speaking to him perhaps across a wide creek. 'I told them you'd be here.'

'You were right,' Wheeler says, glad to feel his presence justified by that expectation. It is as though he has been waiting for them. Burley's hand is hard and dry, its grip quick on his own. And then Wheeler lays his hand on the shoulder of the older man, pressing him toward the door, and follows him through into the greater light of the windowed rooms.

In his office he positions chairs for them in a close arc facing his chair. 'Sit down. I'm glad to see you.'

They take chairs and he returns to his own. He *is* glad to see them, and yet seeing them here, where they regard him with a certain unaccustomed deference, is awkward for him. He sees them often, Burley and Nathan especially, but rarely indoors, and today they have made a formal occasion of their visit by dressing up. Hannah is wearing a gray suit, and looks lovely in it, not to Wheeler's surprise, for she is still a beautiful woman, her beauty now less what she has than what she is. Nathan is wearing a plaid shirt, slacks, and a suede jacket. Burley, true to custom, has put on his newest work clothes, tan pants and shirt, starched and ironed to creases stiff as wire, the shirt buttoned at the throat but without a tie, a dark, coarse wool sweater, which he has now unbuttoned, and he holds on his lap, as delicately as if it is made of eggshell, his Sunday hat. Only the hat looks the worse for wear, but any hat of Burley's will look the worse for wear two hours after he has put it on; the delicacy of his hold on it now, Wheeler knows, is a formality that will not last, a sign of his uneasiness within his own sense of the place and the occasion. In his square-cut, blunt hand, so demanding or quieting upon hound or mule or the shoulder of another man, he holds the hat so that it touches without weight the creased cloth of his pants.

'Kind of dreary out, Wheeler,' he says.

'Yes. It is, Burley. Or it looks dreary since it clouded up. I haven't been out. I was *going* out, though, pretty soon.'

'Well, we won't keep you very long.'

But Wheeler didn't mean to be hinting, and to make up for it, though he knows they have come on business, he says, 'You're caught up in your work, I reckon.'

Nathan laughs and shakes his head. 'No.'

'None of us, these times, will live to be caught up,' Burley says. 'We finished gathering corn yesterday. Monday morning,

I reckon, we'll take a load of calves to the market. After that we'll be in the stripping room.'

But Burley is waiting, Wheeler sees, for permission to begin his business. 'Well,' he says, 'what have you got on your mind?'

'Wheeler,' Burley says, 'I want you to write my will.'

'You do?' Wheeler is surprised and embarrassed. One does not normally write a person's will point-blank in the presence of his heirs. For Burley to bequeath his farm to Nathan right under Nathan's nose strikes Wheeler as a public intimacy of a sort. He is amazed to hear himself ask, 'What for?'

'Well, Wheeler, I'm old enough to die, ain't I?'

Wheeler grins. 'You always have been.' He leans back in his chair as if to make the occasion more ordinary than he can feel it becoming. 'Well then, Nathan, you and Hannah should let Burley and me talk this over alone.'

'But Hannah and Nathan ain't in it, Wheeler. They ain't going to be in it.'

Wheeler sits up. He says, 'Oh,' though that is not what he meant to say. And then, deliberately, he says, 'Then who is in it?'

'Danny Branch.'

'Danny.' Though he was determined not to be, Wheeler is again surprised. The springs of his chair sing as he leans slowly back. For a long moment he and Burley sit and look at each other, Burley smiling, Wheeler frowning and staring as if Burley is surrounded by a mist.

'Danny? You're going to leave your daddy's place, Dave Coulter's place, old George Coulter's place, to Danny Branch?'

'That's right.'

'Why?'

'He's my boy, Wheeler. My son.'

'Who said he is?'

'Well, Wheeler, for one, I did. I just said it.'

'Do you have any proof?'

Burley has not perceptibly moved, but his thumb and middle finger, which at first pinched just the brim of his hat, have now worked their way to the base of the crown, the brim rolled in his hand. 'I ain't *looking* for proof, Wheeler. Don't want any. It's done too late for proof. If there's a mistake in this, it has been my life, or a whole lot of it.'

'Did Kate Helen say he was yours?'

Burley shakes his head, not going to answer that one. 'Now Wheeler, I know you know the talk that has said he was my boy, my son, ever since he was born.'

Wheeler does know it. He has known it all along. But it is irregular knowledge, irregularly known. He does not want to know it, or to admit that he knows it. 'Talk's talk,' he says. 'Talk will be talk. To hell with talk. What we're dealing with now is the future of a good farm and the family that belongs to it, or ought to.'

'Yes indeed.'

'I don't think you ought to take a step like this, Burley, until you know for sure.'

'I know all I want to know, more than I need to know.'

Wheeler says, '*Well . . .*', ready to say that *he*, anyhow, can think of several questions he would like to know the answers to, but Burley raises the hand with the hat in it and stops him.

'It finally don't have anything to do with anything, Wheeler, except just honesty. If he's my boy, I've got to treat him like he is.'

'But you do treat him like he is, and you have. You gave him half his upbringing, or three-quarters. Right up to Kate Helen's death you saw that he raised a crop and went to school and had what he needed. You've taken him to live with you, him and Lyda and their children, and you've . . .' Wheeler stops, realizing that he is saying nothing that all four of them do not already know.

'But now it's time to go beyond all that. Now I have to say that what belongs to me will belong to him, so he can belong to what I belong to. If he's my boy, I owe that to him free and clear.'

'Suppose he's not.'

'Suppose he is.'

Wheeler is slouched low in his chair now, in the attitude, nearly, of a man asleep, except that his fingers are splayed out stiffly where they hang over the ends of his chair arms, and his eyes are widened, set on Burley in a look that would scour off rust. It is not a look easily met.

But Burley is looking back at him, still smiling, confidently and just a little indulgently smiling, having thought beyond where they have got to so far.

'It's wayward, Wheeler. I knowed you'd say what you've said. Or anyhow think it. I know it seems wayward to you. But wayward is the way it is. And always has been. The way a place in this world is passed on in time is not regular or plain, Wheeler. It goes pretty close to accidental. But how else *could* it go? Neither a deed or a will, no writing at all, can tell you much about it. Even when it looks regular and plain, you know that somewhere it has been chancy, and just slipped by. All I see that I'm certain of is that it has got to be turned loose – loose is the way it is – to who knows what. I can say in a will, and I'm going to, that I leave it to Danny, but I don't know how it's going to him, if it will, or past him, or what it's coming to, or what will come to it. I'm just the one whose time has come to turn it loose.'

Now it seems that they are no longer looking at each other, but at a cloud between them, a difference, that they have never before come so close to making or admitting. Whatever there may have been of lawyer and client in this conversation is long gone now, and Wheeler feels and regrets that departure, for he knows that something dark and unwieldy has impinged upon them, that they will not get past except by going through.

It is Burley's word *wayward* that names the difference that they are going to have to reckon with. Wheeler's mind makes one final, despairing swerve toward the field where his cattle are grazing. For a moment he sees it as he knows it will look now in the wind of late November, in the gray light under the swift clouds. And then he lets it go.

Wayward – a word that Burley says easily. If the things of this world are wayward, then he will say so, and love them as they are. But as his friends all know, it is hard to be a friend of Wheeler's and settle for things as they are. You will be lucky if he will let you settle for the possible, the faults of which he can tell you. The wayward is possible, but there must be a better way than wayward. Wheeler can remember Burley's grandfather, George Washington Coulter. He wrote his father's, Dave Coulter's, will here in this very room. He does not remember not knowing Burley, whom he has accompanied as younger kinsman, onlooker, and friend through all his transformations, from the wildness of his young years, through his years of devotion in kinship and friendship, to his succession as presiding elder of a company of friends that includes Wheeler himself. It has a pattern clear enough, that life, and yet, as Wheeler has long known without exactly admitting, it is a clear pattern that includes the unclear, the wayward. The wayward and the dark.

Almost as suddenly as his mind abandons its vision of the

daylit field, Wheeler recalls Burley as a night hunter. Back in his own boyhood and young manhood, he used to go hunting with Burley, and so he knows the utter simplicity of Burley's entrances into the woods.

He gets out of his car at the yard gate and walks across the dark yard and back porch to the kitchen door, to find Burley waiting for him. '*Here* you are! I was about to go ahead.'

Burley is at the door, ready to go, his Smith and Wesson twenty-two in its shoulder holster, hat and coat already on. He pulls on his overshoes, takes his lantern from its nail and lights it, steps off the porch, calls the dogs, and walks down over the brow of the hill. Within two hundred steps they are enclosed in the woods along the river bluff, the damp of the night cold on their faces. Along that margin of steep wild ground between the ridges and the gentler slopes lower down, where the woods has stood unmolested from before memory, they walk in the swaying room of yellow lantern light, their huge tapering shadows leaping from tree to tree beside them. And soon, from off in the dark, beyond time, the voice of a hound opens.

It was another world they went to. Wheeler, as often as he went, always went as a stranger and a guest. Or so it seemed to him, as it seemed to him that Burley went always as a native, his entrance into the wild darkness always a homecoming.

One night when they have made a fire and sat down to wait while the dogs make sense of a cold trail, Burley goes to sleep, lying on his back on a pile of rocks, the driest bed available, and wakes an hour later, intently listening. 'Dinah's treed. Let's go.'

Sometimes Nathan would be with them or Nathan's brother, Tom, before he went to the war and was killed, or, rarely, Old Jack Beechum or, later, Elton Penn, and nearly always the brothers, Arthur and Martin Rowanberry.

On a moonless, starless night, late, in the quiet after a kill, the dogs lying on the leaves around them, they realize that they are lost. Intent upon a course flagged through the dark by the hounds' cries, they have neglected the landmarks. Now they stand around the lanterns under a beech in a little draw on a steep, wooded hillside, debating which way they may have come. Below them they can hear water running, but they cannot be sure in which branch.

'Naw,' Arthur Rowanberry says to his brother, 'we come by that little barn on the Merchant place and down through the locust thicket.'

'Yes, and *then* we went up the Stillhouse Run, that's what we all know, but how many hollers did we pass before we turned up this one?'

'Well, I don't know.'

That is what it keeps coming back to and they all laugh. The debate is being conducted partly for pleasure, for they are not *much* lost, but they are tired now and would rather not risk finding themselves by going in the wrong direction.

Finally Burley, who has said nothing, but has stood outside the light, looking and thinking, says, '*I* know where we are.'

And they all turn to him.

'Where?'

'Where?'

'Right here.'

Though Wheeler is now long past any yen he ever had to roam the woods at night, he knows that Burley is still a hunter, and, with Danny Branch and the Rowanberrys, still a breeder of hounds. At Burley's house at this moment, probably asleep in their stall in the barn, there is a blue-tick hound named Rock, another much older one named Sputnik, and a bitch by the name of Queen. And now Wheeler's son, Andy, is apt to be in the company of the hunters on the thawing or the rainy winter nights, and that is the way Wheeler has learned some of the things he knows.

He knows, he has always known, that as often as he has hunted with companions, Burley has hunted alone. The thought of Burley solitary in the woods at night has beguiled Wheeler's imagination and held it, more strongly perhaps than anything else outside the reach of his own life. For he knows – or from his own memory and from hearsay he is able to infer – that at those times Burley has passed over into a freedom that is old and, because it is strenuous and solitary, also rare. Those solitary hunts of his have always begun by chance or impulse. He may be out of the house already when they begin – on his way afoot to visit a neighbor after supper, maybe, followed by the dogs, who pick up a trail, and he is off. Or he will wake in the night, hearing his dogs treed away on the bluff below his house or in a thicketed slue hollow in the river bottom, and he will get up and go to them, leaving the warm bed, and so begin a route through the dark that may not bring him home again until the sun is up. Or the fever, as he calls it, will hit him while he is eating supper, and he will go, pausing only to strap on the pistol, light the lantern, and stick into the game pocket of his canvas hunting coat an apple or two, a handful of cold biscuits, perhaps a half-pint 'against the chill'. They start almost accidentally, these hunts, and they proceed according to the ways of coon and hound, or if the hunting is slow, according to the curiosity of a night traveler over his dark-estranged homeland. If he goes past their house, he may call to the Rowanberrys to join him or at least turn loose their dogs. In his young manhood, before responsibilities began to call him home, these solitary hunts might carry him away two days and nights, across long stretches of the country and back again, ignoring the roads except to cross them, not seen by a human eye, as though in the dark traverses of his own silence he walked again the country as it was before Finley and the Boones, at home in it time out of time.

He has been a man of two loves, not always compatible: of the dark woods, and of the daylit membership of kin and friends and households that has cohered in one of its lineages through nearly a century of living memory, and surely longer, around Ben Feltner, and then Jack Beechum, and then Mat Feltner, and then Burley's brother, Jarrat, and now around himself. So Wheeler has known him. But it has made him more complex than Wheeler knows, or knows yet, that double love. He has never learned anything until he has had to – as he willingly says, as perhaps is so – but he has had to learn a good deal.

For Wheeler, behind this neatly, somewhat uncomfortably dressed Burley Coulter here in his office, there stands another and yet another: the Burley of the barns and fields of all their lives and of his own loyally kept place and household, and then the Burley of the nighttime woods and the wayward ways through the dark.

In Wheeler's mind the symbol of Burley's readiness to take to the woods at nightfall is the tan canvas hunting coat – or, he must suppose, the succession of them, though he does not remember seeing Burley in a new one – that he has worn through all the winters that Wheeler has known him, on all occasions except funerals, tobacco or livestock sales, or trips to Hargrave on business, such as this. The coat, as Wheeler remembers it, is always so worn that it seems more a creature than an artifact, ripped, frazzled, crudely patched, short a button or two, black at the edges. As a farmer, Burley seems, or has come to seem, constant enough, and yet, even as such, to Wheeler he has something of the aspect of a visitor from the dark and the wild – human, friendly to humans, but apt to disappear into the woods.

If Burley has walked the marginal daylight of their world, crossing often between the open fields and the dark woods, faithful to the wayward routes that alone can join them, Wheeler's fidelity has been given to the human homesteads and neighborhoods and the known ways that preserve them. Through dark time and bad history, he has been keeper of the names that bear hope of light to the human clearings, and an orderly handing down. He is a preserver and defender of the dead, the more so, the more passionately so, as his acquaintance among the dead has increased, and as he has better understood the dangers to their living heirs. How, as a man of law, could he have been otherwise, or less? How, thinking of his own children and grandchildren, could he not insist on an orderly passage of these frail human parcels through time?

It is not as though he is unacquainted with the wayward. He has, God knows, spent his life trying to straighten it out. The wayward is a possible way – because, for lack of a better, it has had to be. But a better way is thinkable, is imaginable, and Wheeler, against all evidence and all odds, is an advocate of the better way. To plead the possibility of the merely possible, losing in the process all right to insist on the desirability of what would be better, is finally to lose even the possible – or so, in one way or another, Wheeler has argued time and again, and against opponents of larger repute than Burley Coulter. If he is set now to do battle with his friend, his purpose is not entirely self-defense, though it is that.

He does not forget – it has been a long time since he has been able to forget – that he is making his stand in the middle of a dying town in the midst of a wasting country, from which many have departed and much has been sent away, a land wasting and dying for want of the human names and knowledge that could give it life. It has been a comfort to Wheeler to think that the Coulter Place, past Burley's death, would live on under that name, belonging first to Nathan, whom Wheeler loves as he loves Burley, and then to one of Nathan's boys. That is what he longs for, that passing on of the land, in the clear, from love to love, and it is in grief for that loss that he is opposing Burley. But this grief has touched and waked up a larger one. How many times in the last twenty years has Wheeler risen to speak, to realize that the speech he has prepared is a defense of the dead and the absent, and he is pleading with strangers for a hope that, he is afraid, has no chance?

'It was wayward when it come to me,' Burley is saying. 'Looked like to me I was there, born there and not someplace else, just by accident. I never took to it by nature the way Jarrat did, the way Nathan here, I think, has. I just turned up here, take it or leave it. I might have gone somewhere else when I got mustered out in 1919, but I come back, and looked like I was in the habit of staying, so I stayed. I thought of leaving, but the times was hard and Pap needed me – or needed somebody better, to tell the truth – and I stayed. I stayed to help bring up Tom and Nathan after their mother died. And then Pap died and Mam was old, and I stayed on with her. And when she died I stayed on and done my part with Jarrat; the boys was gone then, and he needed me. And somehow or other along the way, I began to stay because I wanted to. I wanted to be with Jarrat, and Nathan and Hannah here, and Mat and you and the others. And somewhere or other I realized that being here was the life I had because I'd never had another one any place else, and never would have.

'And that was all right, and is, and is going to be. But it looks like a bunch of intentions made out of accidents. I think of a night now, Wheeler – I lie awake. I've thought this over and over, from one end to the other, and I can't see that the way it has been is in line with what anybody planned or the way anybody thought it ought to be.'

'But they did plan. They hoped. They started hoping and planning as soon as they got here – way back yonder.'

'It missed. Or they did. Partly, they were planning and hoping about what they'd just finished stealing from the ones who had it before, and were already quarreling over themselves. You know it. And partly they were wrong. How could they be right about what hadn't happened? And partly it was wayward.'

'But what if they *hadn't* planned and hoped – the ones that did anyhow – the good ones.'

'Then we wouldn't know how far it missed, or how far we did, or *what* we missed. I ain't disowning them old ones, Wheeler.'

'But now it's your time to plan and hope and carry it on. That we missed doesn't make any difference.'

'No. That time's gone for me now, and I've missed probably as bad as the worst of the others. Now it's my time to turn it loose. You're talking to an old man, Wheeler, damn it!'

'Well, you're talking to an old man too, damn it, but I've still got some plans and hopes! I still know what would be best for my place!'

'I know the same as you, Wheeler. I know what would be best for my place too – somebody to live on it and care about it and do the work. And I know what it would look like if somebody did. But I come here today to turn it loose. And I've got good reason to do it.'

'You've got a better reason than you've told me?'

Burley has been sitting upright on his chair as if it were a stool. Now he sags back, and for a moment sits staring at Wheeler without paying any particular attention to him, as if he doesn't notice or it doesn't matter that Wheeler is staring back at him. And then he says, 'Cleanse thou me from secret faults.'

'What?'

'Cleanse thou me from secret faults.' As always when he quotes Scripture, Burley is grinning, unwilling, as Wheeler knows, to be entirely serious about any part of it that he can understand, even though, once he has understood it, he may be entirely willing to act on it.

Recognizing the passage now, Wheeler grins too, and then laughs and says what otherwise he would not say, 'Well, Burley, mighty few of *your* faults have been secret.'

And that is pretty much a fact. Burley Coulter's faults have been public entertainment in the town and neighborhood of Port William ever since he was a boy, most of his transgressions having been committed flagrantly in the public eye, and those that were not, if they had any conceivable public interest, having been duly recounted to the public by Burley Coulter himself. His escapades have now, by retelling, worn themselves as deeply into that countryside as its backroads.

Wheeler himself has loved to tell the story of Burley's exit from the back door of Grover Gibbs's house, having paid his compliments to Beulah Gibbs, as Grover returned unexpectedly through the front door. Carrying his clothes in his arms through a night black as the inside of a gourd, Burley ran through the stock pond behind the barn, and then, heading downhill into the woods, got behind a big calf who was going slower than he was, whereupon, according to him, he cried, 'Calf, get out of the way! Let somebody run that knows how!'

*

'All that's past,' Wheeler says. 'Whatever was wrong in it can be forgiven in the regular way. When the psalmist said "thou", he didn't mean anybody in Port William or Hargrave. That account's not to be settled here.'

'But some of it is.' Burley's smile is now gone altogether. 'Listen, Wheeler. I didn't come to take up a lot of your time, but we've done got this started now. I'm not telling you what you need to know to be my lawyer. I'm telling you what you need to know to be my friend. If a lawyer was all I wanted, I reckon I wouldn't have to hire a friend.'

'You're not hiring a friend. You *have* one. Go on.'

'Well, Kate Helen was an accommodating woman, too accommodating some would say, but she was good to me, Wheeler. We had what passed with me then for some good times. When I look back at them now, they still pass with me for good, though they come up with more results than I expected. I ain't going to go back on them, or on her, though I'm sorry, Lord knows, for some of the results.'

There is a tenderness in Burley's voice now that Wheeler did not expect, that confesses more than he is yet prepared to understand, but it gives Kate Helen a standing, a presence, there in the room, one among them now, who will not lightly be dismissed. And Wheeler is carried back to a day in his own life when he passed along the lane in front of Kate Helen's house, and saw her sitting on the porch in a rocking chair, barefooted, a guitar forgotten on her lap, a red ribbon in her hair. He has never forgotten. And the Kate Helen who attends them now, in Wheeler's mind as perhaps in Burley's, is Kate Helen as she was then – a woman, as Burley used to say, who could take up a lot of room in a man's mind. In Wheeler's opposition to Burley there is no uncertainty as to what Burley saw when he looked at Kate Helen; Wheeler saw too, and he remembers. But now she has come back to him with something added to her: all that was said or implied in the gentleness with which Burley spoke of her. If she is with them now, Burley is now with them as her protector, and there are some things that Wheeler might have said about her that he is not going to say, and will never say again. He feels under his breastbone the first pain of a change.

But he turns to Nathan. 'Is this what you want? If it wasn't to be Danny Branch's, it would be yours – your children's.' He is holding out against what he sees he will have to give in to, still determinedly doubting what he knows he is going to have to believe, and his voice has the edge of challenge in it. He will not settle easily for the truth just because it happens to be the truth. He wants a truth he can like, and they are not surprised.

As his way is, Nathan has been sitting without moving, staring down at the toe of his shoe, as if he is shy perhaps, and now he makes only the small movement that brings his gaze up to meet Wheeler's. It is the look of a man utterly resolved to mean what he says, and Wheeler feels the force of it.

'I know what Uncle Burley wants, Wheeler, and it's all right. And I aim to stick to Danny.'

Burley passes his hand through the air, the hat still in it, but forgotten now; it is just along for the ride. 'I've not asked that of him, Wheeler. I don't ask anything. If Nathan sticks to Danny after I'm dead, that'll be fine, but my ghost won't trouble him if he don't.'

Wheeler turns to look at Hannah, knowing what to expect, but his eyes tax her nevertheless, making it difficult.

'Yes,' she says, nodding once and smiling at him, being as nice to him as she can be, though he can sense how much she is forbearing. 'It's what we all want. It's best.' And without looking away from Wheeler, she reaches for Burley's left hand,

and drawing it over into her lap holds it in both of her own. To Wheeler's surprise then, her eyes suddenly fill with tears.

And then his own do. He looks down at his hands. 'Well.'

'Wheeler,' Burley says, 'Nathan and Hannah are going to have enough land, and their children too –'

'What if they weren't?'

'– and Danny's a good boy, a good young man.'

'What if he wasn't?'

'There's no use in coming with them what-ifs, Wheeler. I ain't responsible for them. They dried up and blowed away long years ago. What if I had been a better man?

'If Nathan needed what I've got, I'd have to think of that. He don't. Besides what he has got on his own, he's his daddy's heir, and in the right way. You might say that he has come, as far as he has got anyhow, by the main road, the way you have, Wheeler, and has been regular. I haven't been regular. I've come by a kind of back path – through the woods, you might say, and along the bluffs. Whatever I've come to, I've mostly got there too late, and mostly by surprise.

'I don't say everybody *has* to be regular. Being out of regular may be all right – I liked it mostly. It may be in your nature. Maybe it's even useful in a way. But it finally gets to be a question of what you can recommend. I never recommended to Jarrat's boys or Danny or your boys that they ought to be careless with anything, or get limber-legged and lay out all night in a hayrick. Your way has been different from mine, but by my way I've come here where you are, and now I've got to know it and act like it. I know you can't make the irregular regular, but when you have rambled out of sight, you have got to come back into the clear and show yourself.'

'Wait now,' Wheeler says. 'I didn't –'

But Burley raises his hand and silences him. It is as if they recognize only now a change that has been established for some time: Burley has quietly, without gesture, assumed the role of the oldest man – the first time he has ever done this with Wheeler – and has begun to speak for Wheeler's sake as well as his own.

'I know how you think it ought to be, Wheeler. I think the same as you. I even thought once that the way things ought to be was pretty much the way they were. I thought things would go on here always the way they had been. The old ones would die when their time came, and the young ones would learn and come on. And the crops would be put out and got in, and the stock looked after, and things took care of. I thought, even, that the longer it went on the better it would get. People would learn; they would see what had been done wrong, and they would make it right.

'And then, about the end of the last world war, I reckon, I seen it go wayward. Probably it had been wayward all along. But it got more wayward then, and I seen it then. They began to go and not come back – or a lot more did than had before. And now look at how many are gone – the old ones dead and gone that won't ever be replaced, the mold they were made in done throwed away, and the young ones dead in wars or killed in damned automobiles, or gone off to college and made too smart ever to come back, or gone off to easy money and bright lights and ain't going to work in the sun ever again if they can help it. I see them come back here to funerals – people who belong here, or did once, looking down into coffins at people they don't have anything left in common with except a name. They come from another world. They might as well come from that outer space the governments are wanting to get to now.

'When I think of a night, Wheeler, my mind sometimes slants off into that outer space, and I'm sorry the ones that knowed about it ever brought it up – all them lonesome stars and things up there so far apart. And they tell about these little atoms and the other little pieces that things are made out of, all whirling and jiggling around and not touching, as if a man could reach his hand right through himself. I know they know those things to blow them up.

'I lay my hand on me and quiet me down. And I say to myself that all that separateness, outside and inside, that don't matter. It's not here and not there. Then I think of all the good people I've known, not as good as they could have been, much less ought to have been, none of them, but good for the good that was in them along with the rest – Mam and Pap and Old Jack, and Aunt Dorie and Uncle Marce, and Mat and Mrs Feltner, and Jarrat and Tom and Kate Helen, all of them dead, and you three here and the others still living. And I think of this country around here, not purely good either, but good enough for us, better than we deserve. And I think of what I've done here, all of it, all I'm glad I did, and all I wish had been done different or better, but wasn't.'

'You're saying you're sorry for what you've done wrong? And by what you're proposing to do now you hope to make it right?'

'No! God damn it, Wheeler – excuse me, Hannah – no! What is done is done forever. I know that. I'm saying that the ones who have been here have been the way they were, and the ones of us who are here now are the way we are, and to *know* that is the only chance we've got, dead and living, to be here together. I ain't saying we don't have to know what we ought to have been and ought to be, but we oughtn't to let that stand between us. That ain't the way we are. The way we are, we are members of each other. All of us. Everything. The difference ain't in who is a member and who is not, but in who knows it and who don't. What has been here, not what ought to have been, is what I have to claim. I have to be what I've been, and own up to it, no secret faults. Because before long I'm going to have to look the Old Marster in the face, and when He says, "Burley Coulter?" I hope to say "Yes, Sir. Such as I am, that's me." '

And now he leans forward and, the hat brim clenched in the outer three fingers of his right hand, hooks his forefinger into Wheeler's vest. He does not pull, but only holds, as gently as possible given the hand's forthrightness and the rigor in the crook of the old finger.

'And, Wheeler, one thing I am is the man who cared about Kate Helen Branch – all her life, you might say.'

'You loved her,' Wheeler says.

'That's right.'

'You were a husband to her – in all but name.'

'That's right.'

'And you're her widower – in all but name.'

'That's right.'

Burley unhooks his finger and leans back. He is smiling again.

And finally the direction of this meeting declares itself to Wheeler. What Burley is performing, asking him to assist in, too late but nonetheless necessarily, is a kind of wedding between himself and Kate Helen Branch. It is the secrecy of that all-but-marriage of his that has been his great fault, for its secrecy prevented its being taken seriously, perhaps even by himself, and denied it a proper standing in the world.

'And so that secret fault you've been talking about – that

didn't have anything to do with the things we've always known.'

'No.'

'It was secret love.'

'That's right. In a way I don't think I even knowed it myself, Wheeler. Anyhow, not for a long time. Not till too late.'

Wheeler is smiling too now, asking and listening, helping him along. 'Why didn't you clear all this up any sooner?'

'I've never learned anything until I had to, Wheeler. That's the kind of head I've got.'

'And you've been learning this a long time?'

'Years and years. Pret' near all my life I've been figuring out where I am and what I'm responsible for – and, as I said, pret' near always too slow and too late. Some things haven't got my attention until they knocked me in the head.'

'But you and Kate Helen were involved in this friendly connection for a long time. She must not have minded.'

'That had a lot to do with it. We *were* friends, and she *didn't* mind – or didn't seem to.'

Burley crosses his arms over his lap, going ahead now on his own.

'You know the little paper-sided house in Thad Spellman's thicket field that she and her mother moved into after her daddy died – there by the creek at the foot of the hill. I could get there from town you might say by gravity, and at first that was usually how I got there.

'This is how it went. I want you to know.

'On Saturday night I'd walk to Port William and loaf around in one place and another a few hours, visiting, maybe shoot a game or two of pool. And after while I'd get me a pint from Alice Whodat and stroll out across the ridge, drinking along the way, listening to the sounds and looking all around at whatever there was light enough to see – free as a bird, as they say, and, as far as I can remember, nothing on my mind at all. Sometimes if the night was warm and dry, I'd sit down somewhere and sing a while. None of the real things that have happened to me had happened then. My head might as well have been a cabbage, except I could eat and drink with it. And after while I'd tumble down through the woods and the bushes to Kate Helen's house.

'And maybe the first real thing that ever happened to me was that I started going down there because I *liked* to. I liked Kate Helen. I liked to sit and jaw with old Mrs Branch. Sometimes I would go there in broad daylight, just to visit, if you know what I mean, and we would sit and talk and laugh. Part of it, I guess, was what you said. Kate Helen didn't mind. Or up to a point she didn't, however far that was. She liked me and her mother did too. And they wasn't *at* me all the time – which for a while I thought was pretty low class of them, I will admit.

'They were poor, of course, which anybody could see, and so it come about that whenever I went there I would gather up a few groceries, things I knew they needed, and bring them along, or if we'd killed hogs I'd bring a middling or a sack or two of sausage. And I'd always try to save out a head or two for them. The old woman was a great one to make souse, and made the best, too, that ever I ate. And then I got so I'd help them make a garden. And then in the winter I took to getting up their firewood. They needed those things to be done, and I was the only soul they had to do them. I liked being of use to them better than anything.

'But oftentimes, I'd go there just to sit a while and visit. We'd talk, maybe pop some corn. Sometimes we'd play and sing a little.'

★

Wheeler might never have remembered it again. He had forgot that he remembered. But now in thought he comes again down through the steep fields along the side of the little creek valley. He is hunting, supposedly, his shotgun lying in the crook of his arm, and busily quartering the slope ahead of him is his good English setter by the name of Romney; but the weather is dry, they have found no birds, and, submitting to the charm of the warm, bright, still afternoon, he has ceased to pay attention to the dog. He has idled down along the fall of the valley, pausing to look, watching the little fields and the patches of woodland open ahead of him with the intense, pleased curiosity that idleness on such an afternoon can sometimes allow. And now, climbing over a rock fence at the edge of a strip of woodland into a pasture, he pauses again, and hears in the distance a few muted, dispersed notes that it takes him a minute or two to recognize as human singing.

The curve of the slope presently brings him around to where he can see the square of tin roof within the square of yard and garden within the close network of leafless thicket overgrowing Thad Spellman's abandoned field. And now the voices are carried clearly up to him, rising and braiding themselves together over the sweet pacing of a fiddle and guitar:

> *Oh, he taught me to love him and called me his flower,*
> *A blossom to cheer him through life's dreary hour,*
> *But now he has gone and left me alone,*
> *The wildflowers to weep, the wild birds to mourn.*

Wheeler knows who they are. Burley he has heard play before at a dance or two, a little embarrassedly 'filling a gap' in a band, and has even heard him sing, though only emblematic scraps of songs sung out raucously at work. Now he realizes that Burley is better at both than he thought, though in both playing and singing his manner is straightforward and declarative, almost a speaking in support of the melody, which is carried by Kate Helen. It is Kate Helen's voice that takes Wheeler by surprise – by a kind of shock, in fact; he expected nothing like it – for it is so pure, and so feelingly intelligent in its singing of the words.

They finish the song and laugh at the end of it and speak a little, words that he cannot hear, and begin another – and another and another. The dog finally comes back and lies down at Wheeler's feet, and still he stands and listens – until it comes to him that they play and sing so well because they believe that nobody is listening. He turns away then, embarrassed for himself, and makes his way back up the long hollow onto the upland and to his father's place again, the country remaining bemused around him in the hovering late warmth and light, and the two voices seeming to stay with him a long part of the way, as if they too hung and hovered in the air:

I'll dance and I'll sing and my heart shall be gay . . .

'My lord,' he thinks, 'that was forty years ago!'

It was forty years ago almost to the day, he thinks, and remembering the clarity of that voice lifted into the bright air that carried it away, he says, 'And Kate Helen never did say anything? Never did suggest maybe that you two ought to get married?'

'Fact is, she never did. And you'll wonder why, Wheeler, and I can't tell you. I could give you some guesses, I've thought about it enough. But as for knowing, I don't. I don't know, and won't ever.'

'She thought you were a lucky catch any way she could get

you,' Hannah says to him, patting his hand. It is something Wheeler can tell that she has said to him before. And then she says, more seriously, 'She thought you were better than she deserved. So did her mother, I'll bet.'

'Well, I wasn't. But whatever her reason was, not to know it is wrong. It's the very thing that's wrong.'

They pause at that failure, allowing it its being. And then Burley speaks on, describing his long odd-times domestic companionship with Kate Helen. He tells of Danny's birth: 'I purely did not think of that ahead of time, Wheeler. It was a plumb surprise. And yet it tickled me.' He tells of the death of old Mrs Branch; and of how, as Danny grew, time and usage grew on him and Kate Helen; how he depended on her and was dependable, took her and was taken for granted, liking the world too well as it was, 'laying aside wars and such', to think how it might be improved, usually, until after his chance to improve it had gone by; how in time she became sick and died; how at her death, seeing it all then, he would have liked to have been openly and formally her mourner, but, faithful to appearances, he had shown himself only an interested bystander, acting a great deal more like himself than he felt. Behind appearances, he paid the doctor, paid the hospital, paid the undertaker, bought a lot in the cemetery; he saw to everything – as Wheeler knew pretty well at the time, and attributed to guilt of conscience – as quietly as he has done for the others who have been his declared dependents.

Danny, grown by then, was still living with his mother at the time of her death.

'You just as well come on, now,' Burley said, 'and live with me.' For then he saw it the way it should have been – though he let Danny go on calling him 'Uncle Burley', as he acknowledges now to Wheeler, and is shaken once by a silent laugh.

'Well, now that Mammy's gone, I want to get married.'

'Well, bring the gal. I got a big house.'

As though he has now finally lived in his own life up to that time when Danny came to live with Burley, Wheeler admits him into his mind. Or, anyhow, Danny Branch now turns up in Wheeler's mind, admitted or not, put there by the words of his would-be lawful father, after the failure of all events so far to put him there, and his face now takes its place among the faces that belong there.

Danny, Wheeler would bet, is not as smart as Burley, but he does look like him in a way; he has Burley's way of looking at you and grinning and nodding his head once before saying what he has to say – a fact that Wheeler now allows to underwrite Burley's supposition and his intent. He allows Burley's argument to make sense – not all the sense there is, but enough.

And so with Wheeler's consent Danny comes into their membership and also is one there with them, Wheeler already supposing that Nathan will not be the only one who will stick to Danny, and looking forward to the possibility of his own usefulness to that young man.

As often, the defeat of his better judgment has left him only with a job to do, a job that he *can* do, and he feels a sudden infusion of good humor. If Danny is Burley's son and heir, and if that is less than might have been hoped, it is what they are left with, what they have, and Wheeler will be as glad as the rest of them to make the most of it.

He feels preparing in himself the friendship for Danny Branch that these three, after all, have come to ask him for – and which, all three know, probably better than Wheeler, will be a gift and a blessing to the younger man, and also undoubtedly something of a burden, for once Wheeler has Danny on his mind he will be full of advice for him that Danny will not easily ignore.

As soon as he has a chance, Wheeler thinks, he will stop by for a visit with Burley and Danny and Lyda and the little ones. He would like, for one thing, to see if there is any resemblance to Burley or the other Coulters showing up in Danny's children.

'*So,*' he says. 'You just want to leave everything to Danny. That won't take but a few words. I'll get it typed up first thing Monday morning, and you can come in and sign it.' He smiles at Hannah and Nathan. 'You all can come with him and be witnesses.'

He leans back in his chair, having, as he thinks, brought the meeting to an end. He is ready for them to go, ready to go himself. He allows the wind and the gray sky back into mind.

Burley is busy restoring the shape of his hat, as though he might be about to put it on, but he does not. He looks up at Wheeler again and studies him a moment before he speaks.

'Wheeler, do you know why we've been friends?'

'I've thought so,' Wheeler says. He has thought so because of that company of friends to which they both belong, which has been so largely the pleasure and meaning of both their lives. 'But why?'

'Because we ain't brothers.'

'What are you talking about?' Wheeler says.

But he is afraid he knows, and his discomfort is apparent to them all. Nathan and Hannah obviously feel it too, and are as surprised as he is.

'If we'd been brothers, you wouldn't have put up with me. Or anyhow you partly wouldn't have, because a lot of my doings haven't been your kind of doings. As it was, they could be tolerable or even funny to you because they wasn't done close enough to you to matter. You could laugh.'

Wheeler sits forward now, comfortless, straight up in his chair, openly bearing the difficulty he knows it is useless to hide. Though this has never occurred to him before, because nobody has said it to him before, he knows with a seizure of conviction that Burley is right. He knows they all know, and again under his breastbone he feels the pain of a change that he thought completed, but is not completed yet. A great cavity has opened at the heart of a friendship, a membership, that not only they here in the office and the others who are living but men and women now dead belong to, going far back, dear as life. Dearer. It is a cavity larger than all they know, a cavity that somebody – their silence so testifies – is going to have to step into, or all will be lost.

If things were going slower, if he had the presence of mind he had even a minute ago, Wheeler would pray for the strength to step into it, for the *knowledge* to step into it. As it is, he does not know how. He sits as if paralyzed in his loss, without a word to his name, as if suddenly pushed stark naked into a courtroom, history and attainment stripped from him, become as a little child.

But Burley is smiling, and not with the vengeful pleasure that Wheeler feared, but with understanding. He knows that what he has given Wheeler is pain, his to give, but Wheeler's own. He sees.

'Wheeler, if we're going to get this will made out, not to mention all else we've got to do while there's breath in us, I think you've got to forgive me as if I was a brother to you.' He laughs, asserting for the last time the seniority now indisputably his, and casting it aside. 'And I reckon I've got to forgive you for taking so long to do it.'

He has spoken out of that cavity, out of that dark abyss.

It is as if some deep dividing valley has been stepped across. There can be no further tarrying, no turning back. To Wheeler, it seems that all their lives have begun again – lives dead, living, yet to be. As if feeling himself simply carried forward by that change, for another moment yet he does not move.

And then he reaches out and grips Burley's shoulder, recognizing almost by surprise, with relief, the familiar flesh and bone. 'Burley, it's all right.'

And Burley lays his own hand on Wheeler's shoulder. 'Thank you, Wheeler. Shore it is.'

Wheeler's vision is obscured by a lens of quivering light. When it steadies and clears, his sight has changed. Now, it seems to him, he is looking through or past his idea of Burley, and can see him at last, the fine, clear, calm, generous, amused eyes looking back at him out of the old face.

And Hannah, smiling again too, though she has averted her eyes, is digging in her purse for her handkerchief. 'Well!' she says.

The office is crowded now with all that they have loved, the living remembered, the dead brought back to mind, and a gentle, forceless light seems to have come with them. There in the plain, penumbral old room, that light gathers the four of them into its shadowless embrace. For a time without speaking they sit together in it.

Wheeler stands looking down into the street over the top of the reversed painted legend: WHEELER CATLETT & SON, ATTORNEYS-AT-LAW. The day remains as it was, the intensity of the clouded light the same. Except that the towboat is gone now, the world seems hardly to have moved, the smoke from the power plant still tainting the sky.

In a little while Wheeler will leave the office and leave town. The room he stands in is driven out of his mind by the thought of the raw, free wind over the open fields. But he does not go yet. He thinks of the fields, how all we know of them lies over them, taking their shape, for a little while, like a fall of snow.

He watches Burley and Hannah and Nathan walk back to their truck, waiting for their departure to complete itself before he will begin his own.

The Requirement
(1970)

Well, you get older and you begin to lose people, kinfolks and friends. Or it *seems* to start when you're getting older. You wonder who was looking after such things when you were young. The people who died when I was young were about all old. Their deaths didn't interrupt me much, even when I missed them. Then it got to be people younger than me and people my own age that were leaving this world, and then it was different. I began to feel it changing me.

When people who mattered to me died I began to feel that something was required of me. Sometimes something would be required that I could do, and I did it. Sometimes when I didn't know what was required, I still felt the requirement. Whatever I did never felt like enough. Something I knew was large and great would have happened. I would be aware of the great world that is always nearby, ever at hand, even within you, as the good book says. It's something you would maybe just as soon not know about, but finally you learn about it because you have to.

That was the way it was when Big Ellis took sick in the fall of 1970. He was getting old and dwindling as everybody does, as I was myself. But then all of a sudden he wasn't dwindling anymore, but going down. First thing you know, he was staying mostly in bed. And then he had to have help to get out of bed.

Heart, the doctor said, and I suppose it was. But it wasn't just that, in my opinion. I think pretty well all of Big's working parts were giving out. He was seventy-six years old.

I'd walk over there through the fields every day, early or late, depending on the weather and the work. I was feeling that requirement, you see.

I would say, 'Big, is there anything you need? Is there anything you want me to do?' hoping there would be something.

And he would say, 'Burley, there ain't one thing I need in this world. But thank you.'

But he didn't mean yet that he was giving up on this world. I would sit by the bed, and he would bring up things we would do when he got well, and we would talk about them and make plans. And in fact he really didn't need anything. Annie May, who loved him better than some people thought he deserved, was still healthy then. As far as I could tell, she was taking perfect care of him.

We called Big 'Big' of course because he was big. He was stout too. His strength sometimes would surprise you, even as big as he was. He sort of made a rule of not putting out more effort than the least he could get away with. He wouldn't pull his britches up until they were absolutely falling off. But if he thought he needed to, or ought to, he could pick up a two-bushel sack of wheat and toss it onto a load like it wasn't more than a basketball. Once I saw him pick up an anvil by its horn with one hand and carry it to where he needed it and set it down gently as you would set down an egg.

Big was a year or so older than me, and for a while that made a difference and I had to give him the lead. But as we got older we got closer to the same age, and we ran together as equal partners. We didn't settle down when we were supposed to, we were having too good a time. For a long time we stayed unattached, unworried, and unweary. We shined up to the ladies together, and fished and hunted together, and were about as free as varmints ourselves. We ran a many a Saturday night right on into Sunday morning. I expect we set records around here for some of our achievements, which I don't enjoy talking about now as much as I once did. But some of the stories about Big himself I will always love to tell.

One time we heard about a dance they were giving at the schoolhouse in a little place named Shagbark over on the far side of the river. We went to it in one of Big's old cars that never got anywhere except by luck. But we did get there, after a stop in Hargrave to get a lady to sell us some liquor. It was good stuff, Canadian whiskey, the real article.

It was a good dance too, good musicianers. They had this fellow playing the piano. He had twelve fingers and he was making music with every one of them. I never saw such a thing before. I haven't since. And they had a better than average number of good-looking girls. We got to where we were just letting it happen, we didn't mind what. We didn't know a soul over there and nobody knew us. We didn't have a thing to worry about, and we were cutting up like a new pair of scissors. And then all at once it went kaflooey.

Big was wearing his suit. We'd had to buy our whiskey in half-pints, it was all the lady had, and he had stuck one of those into the inside pocket of his jacket. He got to dancing with this girl, a good-looking girl, a big girl, a fair match for him. She must have set a record for bracelets and things. She was wearing enough metal to draw lightning. She was jingling like a two-year-old mule in a chain harness. Big got to feeling fond of her, and he pulled her up close to him, to where she could feel that bottle. And that was what changed things. Maybe she wasn't too smart, maybe she was a little bit looney, as some girls are, but she thought that bottle was a handgun.

Well, John Dillinger was on the loose at that time, and nobody knew for sure where he was. That gave this event a sort of framework, you see. First thing you know, everybody was glancing toward us and whispering. We got the story later. That big girl hadn't much more than told what she thought Big had in his pocket before they figured out that he was John Dillinger and I was his driver.

Everybody began to leave. They weren't long about it. They made use of both doors and every window, all of them being wide open, for it was a hot night. It wasn't long until Big and I were the only ones left. We were puzzled until, as I say, we heard the story. And then we enjoyed it. Especially Big enjoyed it. For a good while after that if you wanted to make him giggle all you had to do was call him 'John'.

To know how funny it was you have to picture Big the way he looked that night, all rumpled up in his suit and sweating, hot too on the track of that big girl, smiling like sugar wouldn't melt in his mouth, his feet stepping and prancing all on their own for he had forgotten about them, and if you'd asked him to tell you right quick where he was, he wouldn't have known.

He was a wonderfully humored man. Things that would make most people mad just slid off of him. He would forgive anything at all that he could get the least bit of amusement out of. And any amusement he got he paid back with interest. He was full of things to say that didn't have anything to do with anything else. You'd be talking to him maybe about getting his hay up or fixing a fence, and he would say, 'You know, I wish I'd a been born rich in place of pretty.'

One time when we were hardly more than grown boys, I got sent word of a dance they were giving on Saturday night down at Goforth. Well, it was a girl who sent the word, and I sent word back I couldn't come. The reason was I didn't have any good shoes, though I didn't tell her. I didn't have shoes nor money either. It was a time when money was scarce.

But the day of the dance I happened to go by Big's house and there his good shoes were, shined, sitting out on the well top. Wasn't anybody around, so I just borrowed the shoes and went my way and wore them to the dance that night. They were too big of course, and sometimes I had to dance a while to get all the way into the toes. I must say I danced the shine off of them too and nicked them up here and there. I left them on the well top at Big's house just before daylight.

Since he hadn't had any shoes to wear to the dance, Big got a full night's sleep. Next morning he left the house with the milk bucket on his way to the barn just after daylight, and there his shoes were, right where he'd left them the day before, but now they were all scuffed up.

'Well, shoes!' Big said. 'I don't know where you been, but looks like you had a good time.'

One evening after supper I walked over to his place. I'd heard about a litter of hound pups, pretty nice it was said. If Big was interested, I thought we might go together and see them for ourselves. I was ready for a young dog, and I thought Big might be.

Nobody was home, and Big's car was gone. I imagined he'd taken his folks off to visit somebody. On my way to the house I'd looked in the barn and seen his work harness lying in two pretty much heaps on the barn floor. I couldn't think why, and the matter got my attention. Big's daddy, I knew, would never ever have left his harness in any such a mess. But old Mr Ellis was sick by then, and the place was coming under the influence of Big and his way of doing, which I didn't yet know as much about as I was going to.

When I saw nobody was at home, I stopped again at the barn, thinking to do Big a favor while I had it on my mind. I picked up his harness and straightened it out and hung it up on the pegs where I knew it belonged and went my way.

After breakfast the next morning, still wanting to talk about the pups, I went back again and found Big in the barn. He had one of the harnesses half on a mule and half on himself, his clothes in about as bad a shape as the harness. He was tramping and grabbling among the chains and straps, blowing at the sweat dripping off his nose, with the look of despair and anguish all over his face. Things he'd left in a heap made better sense to him than things put straight by me.

I could have laughed, but I didn't. I said, 'Well, old bud, do you reckon you're going to make it?'

Before then he hadn't known I was there. He gave me a purely threatening look. He said, 'I wish I had ahold of the son of a bitch that hung my harness up.'

However mad he was, I knew he wouldn't stay mad more than a few minutes. He *couldn't* was why.

I helped him harness his mules. I told him about the pups, and we agreed to go look at them that evening. I never laughed, nor as much as smiled. And not one word did I ever say about that harness.

You almost couldn't make him mad. But if you didn't watch yourself he could make you mad, just by being so much himself he couldn't imagine that anybody could be different. He didn't go in much for second opinions. He stayed single until his mother and daddy both were dead, and then he married

Annie May pretty soon, which maybe was predictable. He liked company. He didn't like to be by himself.

Being married to Big, after the long head start he'd had, was not dependably an uplifting experience. Though Annie May was a good deal younger than he was, she was made pretty much on his pattern, ample and cheerful. But she could be fittified. I've seen her mad enough at Big, it looked like, to kill him, and maybe he'd be off on another subject entirely and not even notice, which didn't help her patience. One time when she got mad and threw an apple at him – it would have hurt, she had a good arm – he just caught it and ate it. I didn't see that. It was told.

But she never stayed mad long. One time when I went over there she was just furious at him, mainly because he wouldn't bother to argue with her over whatever she was upset about in the first place. She was crying and hollering, 'I'm a-leaving you, Big! You've played hell this time! I'm a-leaving here just as soon as I get this kitchen cleaned up!' That was like her. You wouldn't have minded eating dinner off of her kitchen floor. And of course by the time she got the kitchen cleaned up she had forgiven him. I think she loved him *because* he was the way he was. They never had any children, and he was her boy.

Maybe because they didn't have children Big and Annie May let their little farm sag around them as they got older, the way a lot of such couples do. Big's daddy had the place in fair shape when he died, but he died early in the Depression, and so Big couldn't have made a fast start even if he had wanted to. He and Annie May lived well enough, but that was mainly Annie May's doing. She made a wonderful big garden every year, and kept a flock of chickens and some turkeys. They always had three or four milk cows, milked mainly by Annie May, and they sold the extra cream and fed the extra milk to their meat hogs. So they always had plenty to eat. Annie May was as fine a cook as ever I ate after. When they had company or a bunch of us were there working, she would put on a mighty feed. Both of them loved to eat, and they loved to see other people eat.

But Big never tried for much or did much for his place. He wasn't, to tell the truth, much of a farmer. When he went to help his neighbors he'd work as hard as anybody, but put him by himself on his own place, and getting by was good enough. He was a great one then for 'a lick and a promise' or 'good enough for who it's for'.

I don't know that he ever owned a new piece of equipment, except for a little red tractor that he bought after the war just to be shed of the bother of a team of mules. When he got the tractor he stubbed off the tongues of his old horse-drawn equipment and went puttering about even more slipshod than before. My brother, Jarrat, and I swapped work with him all our lives, you might as well say, but when we went to his place we always took our own equipment. Jarrat's main idea was to get work done, and he didn't have enough patience to enjoy Big the way I did. 'If he gets in my way with one of them cobbled-up rigs of his, damned if I won't run over him.' That was Jarrat's limit on Big, and Big did keep out of his way.

His final sickness was pretty much like the rest of his life. He didn't seem to be in a hurry to get well, or to die either. He didn't make much of it. The doctor had said a while back that he had a bad heart and gave him some pills. Big more or less believed the doctor, but he also let himself believe he would sooner or later get well. I don't think he felt like doing much of anything.

Annie May said, 'Big, for goodness sake, let's take you to a heart doctor or *something*. You can't just lie there. We can't just do nothing.'

'I ain't going anywhere,' he said. 'I'm just feeling a little dauncy is all.'

She knew better than to push him. Easy-going as he was, when he took a stand you couldn't shake him. He *could* just lie there. They *could* just do nothing.

If he had been suffering, if something had hurt him or he had been uncomfortable, maybe he would have done something. Maybe he would be living yet. But the only thing the matter was he was getting weaker. His strength was just slowly leaking out of him. He didn't have much appetite, and he was losing flesh. But he was comfortable enough. He wasn't complaining.

So nothing was what they did. That was the way Big had solved most of his problems. He would work hard to help his neighbors, because he liked them and liked to be with them and wanted them to get their problems solved. He would wear people out talking to them and fishing for their opinions on anything whatsoever. He would go to no limit of trouble to have a good time, and he'd had a lot of good times. But when it came to doing some actual work for himself, he often simplified it by not doing anything.

That was why, when Big took sick, the old Ellis place, as some of us still call it, was pretty well run down. There wasn't a chicken or a hog or a cow. Another neighbor, a young fellow, was growing the crop and making a little hay on the shares, but that was all. Social Security, I reckon, was taking up the slack.

I got used to making some time every day to go to see how Big was doing and to sit with him a while. What was harder to get used to was the place. The fences all gone down. The barns and other outbuildings all paintless, and the roofs leaking. The lots grown up in weeds and bushes so you couldn't open the doors that were shut, or shut the doors that had been left open. And every building was fairly stuffed with old farm tools, most of them going back to Big's daddy's time or before, for Big always figured they might come in handy.

What they did, it turned out, was come to be antiques. When the farm was sold to a Louisville businessman after Big died, and the tools and a lot of the household plunder were auctioned off, about everything was bought at a good price by antique collectors. After she was too old to use it, or even want it, Annie May had more money than she ever imagined.

Walking across the fields, the way I usually went when I went to see Big, I would have to appraise every time what had become of the place, a good little farm dwindled down almost to nothing. Nobody going out to milk anymore. Nobody going out to feed the chickens or the hogs. You really couldn't see that anybody still lived there until you got to the yard. The yard was still Annie May's territory – her last stand, you might say – and it was kept neat. The house itself, the cellar and smokehouse out back, they still showed care. And well off to the side, out of the way, the rusty dinner bell that hadn't been rung in years was still perched on its leaning pole. A man on a tractor couldn't hear it. The bell was going to turn out to be an antique too. At the sale two ladies bid for it until you'd have thought it was made out of gold.

The day that was going to be the day Big died I went over there first thing in the morning, as soon as we finished up at the barn and ate breakfast. It was a fine morning, cold and bright, the sky blue and endless right down to the horizon, and everything below shining with frost. We had finished with the hog-killing the day before, and I was bringing some fresh spareribs and tenderloin, thinking they might tempt Big to eat. Until then Big and Annie May both were talking like he was going to get well.

But that morning things had changed. I could feel it as soon as I stepped in through the kitchen door. Annie May was busy setting the kitchen to rights. She didn't try to keep me from seeing that she was crying. Two of her friends, neighbor women, had come to be with her and help her, as the women do when there's trouble. What had happened was they had figured out – Big first, I think, and then Annie May – that Big wasn't going to get well. The whole feeling of the house had changed. My old granny would have said the Angel of Death had passed over and marked the house. Call it superstition if you want to, but that was what it felt like.

'I brought some meat,' I said. 'Lyda thought maybe Big would like something fresh.'

'Well, God love her heart!' Annie May said, taking the packages from me, as if she was mourning over them.

And then she said, 'Go on in, Burley. He's awake.'

I went in. Big was lying in the clean bed in the clean room, looking no different really, but that feeling of being in a marked house was there too. The counterpane was white as snow, and white as it was his hands lying on it looked pale. They looked useless. When I came in, he raised a hand to me and gave me a grin as usual. But now he seemed to be grinning to apologize for the feeling that was in the room. He would always get uneasy when things got serious, let alone solemn. He disliked by nature the feeling that was there, but he didn't refuse it either.

He said, 'Well, Burley, it come over me that I ain't going to come out of this.'

I went over to the bed and gave his hand a shake. I took my

jacket off and sat down by him. His hand and his voice were weak, but they weren't noticeably weaker than the day before.

He said, 'I'm about to be long gone from here.'

'Oh, sho'ly not,' I said.

'It's so,' he said.

I said, 'If it's so, old bud, it'll make a mighty difference around here. We'll look for you and we'll miss you.'

He had been stronger than me all his life, and now he was weak. And I was sitting there by his bed, still strong. What could you do? What could you do that would be anyways near enough? I could feel the greatness of life and death; and the great world endless as the sky swelling out beyond this little one. And I began again to hear from that requirement that seems to come from the larger world. The requirement was telling me, '*Do* something for him. Do more than you've ever done. Do more than you *can* do.'

As if he had read my mind, he said, 'I appreciate you coming, Burley. You've stuck by me. I imagine I'll remember it as long as I live.' And then he giggled, for in fact it was a fine joke.

'Well, I wish I could do more. Ain't there anything at all you want?'

'Not a thing. Not a thing in this world.'

We talked then, or mostly I did, for a while, about things that were going on round about. And finally I had to leave. They were busy at home, and they'd be looking for me. Big had said he wasn't long for this world, but he looked about the same as yesterday. For all I knew, he might live a long time yet. When somebody tells you he's going to die, you can't say, 'Well, go ahead. I'll just sit here till you do.' I was going to be surprised when I got word that afternoon that old Big had sure enough left us.

'Well,' I said, 'I got to be getting on home.' And I stood up.

He raised his hand to stop me. 'Wait, Burley. There *is* something I want you to do.'

'Sure,' I said. 'Name it.'

'Go yonder to the press' – he used the old word – 'and open the door.'

I went to the closet and opened the door. It was where they kept their good clothes, Annie May's Sunday dresses, not many, and Big's suit, all put away there together.

'Ain't my pistol there, just inside?'

The pistol was in its shoulder holster, hanging on a nail in the door jamb. It was a .22 revolver, heavy-built and uncommonly accurate for a pistol. It was the only really good thing Big had ever owned, and he had taken care of it like a king's crown. He bought it new when times were good back there in the forties, and the bluing was still perfect except for a spot or two where the holster had worn it. I had always thought highly of it, and he knew I had.

'It's right here,' I said.

'I want you to take it. I'd like to know where it'll be after I'm gone.'

It flew into me then just how far toward the edge of things we'd come, two old men who'd been neighbors and friends since they were boys, and if I'd thought of anything to say I couldn't have said it. For a while I couldn't even turn around.

'Put it on,' Big said. 'Button your jacket over it. I don't want Annie May to see it when you leave.'

I did as he told me. I said, 'Thanks, Big.'

'Sure,' he said.

'Well,' I said, 'I'll be seeing you.'

He said, 'Yeah. See you later.'

★

So I had come to do something for Big, if I could, and instead Big had done something for me, and I was more in debt to the requirement than ever.

I went out through the kitchen, speaking a few pleasantries with the women, and let myself out. I sat down on the porch step to put my overshoes back on, and started home. And all the time the requirement was staying with me. 'Can't you, for God's sake, think of *something* to do?' When I got to about the middle of the barn lot, I just stopped. I stood there and looked all around.

Oh, it was a splendid morning, still frozen, not much changed at all. The ground was still shining white under the blue sky. I thought of a rhyme that Elton Penn was always saying in such weather: 'Clear as a bell, cold as hell, and smells like old cheese.' Maybe that was what put me in mind to do what I did.

When I looked back toward the house, the only thing between me and the sky was that old dinner bell leaning on its post like it was about to fall.

Big's pistol, when I pulled it out, felt heavy and familiar, comfortable. It was still warm from the house. There were five cartridges in the cylinder, leaving an empty chamber to rest the hammer on. I cocked it and used my left hand to steady my right. What I wanted was a grazing hit that would send the bullet flying out free into the air.

Even as the bullet glanced and whined away, the old bell summed up all the dongs it had ever rung. It filled the day and the whole sky and brought the worlds together, the little and the great. I knew that, lying in his bed in the house, Big heard it and was pleased. Standing in the lot, I heard it and I was pleased. It wasn't enough, but it was something. It was a grand sound. It was a good shot.

Dismemberment
(1974)

It was the still-living membership of his friends who, with Flora and their children and their place, pieced Andy together and made him finally well again after he lost his right hand to a harvesting machine in the fall of 1974. He would be obliged to think that he had given his hand, or abandoned it, for he had attempted to unclog the corn picker without stopping it, as he had known better than to do. But finally it would seem to him also that the machine had taken his hand, or accepted it, as the price of admission into the rapidly mechanizing world that as a child he had not foreseen and as a man did not like, but which he would have to live in, understanding it and resisting it the best he could, for the rest of his life.

He was forty then, too old to make easily a new start, though his life could be continued only by a new start. He had no other choice. Having no other choice finally was a sort of help, but he was slow in choosing. Between him and any possibility of choice lay his suffering and the selfishness of it: self-pity, aimless anger, aimless blaming, that made him dangerous to himself, cruel to others, and useless or a burden to everybody.

He would not get over the loss of his hand, as of course he was plentifully advised to do, simply because he was advised to do it, or simply even because he wanted and longed to do it. His life had been deformed. His hand was gone, his right hand that had been his principal connection to the world, and the absence of it could not be repaired. The only remedy was to re-form his life around his loss, as a tree grows live wood over its scars. From the memory and a sort of foreknowledge of wholeness, after he had grown sick enough finally of his grieving over himself, he chose to heal.

To replace his lost hand he had acquired what he named contemptuously to himself his 'prosthetic device', his 'hook', or his 'claw', and of which he never spoke aloud to anybody for a long time. He began in a sort of dusk of self-sorrow and fury to force his left hand to learn to do the tasks that his right hand once had done. He forced it by refusing to desist from doing, or to wait to do, anything that he had always done. He watched the left hand with pity and contempt as it fumbled at the buttons of his clothes, and as it wrote, printing, at first just his name, in letters that with all his will it could not contain between the lines of a child's tablet. With two fingers of his pathetic left hand he would hold the head of a nail against the poll of a hammer, and strike the nail into the wood, and then, attempting to drive the nail, would miss it or bend it, and he would repeat this until he cursed and wept, crying out with cries that seemed too big for his throat so that they hurt him and became themselves an affliction. He was so plagued and shamed by this that he would work alone only where he was sure he could not be overhead.

To drive a stake or a steel post, he would one-handedly swing the sledgehammer back and forth like a pendulum to gain loft and force, and then strike. At first, more often than not, he missed. This was made harder by the necessity of standing so that, missing, he did not hit his leg. For propping, steadying, and other crude uses, he could call upon the stump of his right forearm. To avoid impossible awkwardnesses, he shortened the handles of a broom, a rake, and a hoe. From the first there were some uses he could make of the prosthetic device. So long as he regarded it as merely a tool, as merely a hook or a claw or weak pliers, he used it readily and quietly enough. But when some need forced him to think of it as a substitute for his right hand, which now in its absence seemed to have been miraculous, he would be infuriated by the stiffness and numbness of it. Sooner or later – still, in his caution and shame, he would be working alone – he would be likely to snatch it off and fling it away, having then to suffer the humiliation of searching for it in tall grass or, once, in a pond. One day he beat it on the top of a fence post as if to force sentience and intelligence into it. And by that, for the first time since his injury, he finally was required to laugh at himself. He laughed until he wept, and laughed again. After that, he got better.

Soon enough, because spring had begun and need was upon him, he put his horses back to work. By wonderful good fortune, for often until then he would have been starting a young pair, he had a team that was work-wise and dependable. They were six-year-olds, Prince and Dan. Andy's son, Marcie, who loved the horses and was adept at using them, was in his twelfth year then and could have helped. But Andy could not ask for help. His disease at that time, exactly, was that he could not ask for help, not from either of his children, not from Flora, not from his friends, not from anybody. His mode then was force. He forced himself to do what he required of himself. He thus forced himself upon the world, and thus required of the world a right-of-way that the world of course declined to grant. He was forever trying to piece himself whole by mechanical contrivances and devices thought up in the night, which by day more often than not would fail, because of some unforeseen complication or some impossibility obvious in daylight. He worked at and with the stump of his arm as if it were inanimate, tying tools to it with cords, leather straps, rubber straps, or using it forthrightly as a blunt instrument.

In the unrelenting comedy of his predicament he had no

patience, and yet patience was exacted from him. He became patient then with a forced resignation that was the very flesh and blood of impatience. To put the harness on the horses was the first obstacle, and it was immense. Until it is on the horse, a set of work harness is heavy and it has no form. It can be hung up in fair order, but to take it from its pegs and carry it to the horse's back involves a considerable risk of disorder. Andy went about it, from long habit, as a two-handed job, only to discover immediately, and in the midst of a tangle of straps, that he had to invent, from nothing at all that he knew, the usefulness of the prosthetic device, which was at best a tool, with an aptitude for entangling itself in the tangle of straps.

When, in his seemingly endless fumbling, he had got the horses harnessed and hitched, he became at once their dependent. He could ask help from no human, but he had to have the help of his horses, and he asked them for it. Their great, their fundamental, virtue was that they would stop when he said, 'Whoa.' When he dropped a line or had too many thoughts to think at once, he called out, 'Whoa!' and they stopped. And they would stand in their exemplary patience and wait while he put his thoughts and himself in order, sometimes in the presence of an imminent danger that he had not seen in time. Or they would wait while he wound and rewound, tied and re-tied, the righthand line to what was left of his right forearm. A profound collaboration grew between him and the horses, like nothing he had known before. He thought finally that they sensed his need and helped him understandingly. One day he was surprised by the onset of a vast tenderness toward them, and he wept, praising and thanking them. After that, again, he knew he was better.

His neighbors too, knowing his need, came when they could be of use and helped him. They were the survivors, so far, of the crew of friends who had from the beginning come there to help: Art and Mart Rowanberry, Pascal Sowers and his son Tommy, Nathan Coulter, whose boys by then had grown up and left home, and Danny Branch, usually with one or two of his boys, none of the five of whom ever would stray far or long from the Port William neighborhood.

The first time they came, to help him with his first cutting of hay, their arrival afflicted Andy with an extreme embarrassment. He had not dared so far as to ask himself how he would save the hay after he had cut it. He cut it because the time had come to cut it. If he could not save it, he told himself in his self-pity and despair, he would let it rot where it lay.

He did not, he could not, ask his friends to help him. But they came. Before he could have asked, if he had been going to ask, they knew when he needed them, and they came. He asked himself accusingly if he had not after all depended on them to come, and he wavered upon the answer as on a cliff's edge.

They came bringing the tractor equipment they needed to rake and bale his hay. When they appeared, driving in after dinnertime on the right day, he was so abashed because of his debility and his dependence, because he had not asked them to come, because he now was different and the world was new and strange, he hardly knew how to greet them or where to stand.

But his friends were not embarrassed. There was work to do, and they merely set about doing it. When Andy hesitated or blundered, Nathan or Danny told him where to get and what to do as if the place and the hay were theirs. It was work. It was only work. In doing it, in requiring his help in doing it, they moved him to the margin of his difficulty and his self-absorption. They made him one with them, by no acknowledgment at all, by not crediting at all his own sense that he had ever not been one with them.

When the hay was baled and in the loft and they had come to rest finally at the shady end of the barn, Andy said, 'I don't know how to thank you. I don't know how I can ever repay you.' He sounded to himself as if he were rehearsing the speech to give later.

And then Nathan, who never wasted words, reached out and took hold of Andy's right forearm, that remnant of his own flesh that Andy himself could hardly bear to touch. Nathan gripped the hurt, the estranged, arm of his friend and kinsman as if it were the commonest, most familiar object around. He looked straight at Andy and gave a little laugh. He said, 'Help us.'

After that Andy again was one of them. He was better.

The great obstacle that remained was his estrangement of himself from Flora and their children. He knew that in relation to those who were dearest to him he had become crazy. He had become intricately, painfully, perhaps hopelessly crazy. He saw this clearly, he despised himself for it, and yet he could not prevail upon himself to become sane. He looked at Flora and Betty and Marcie as across a great distance. He saw them looking at him, worried about him, suffering his removal from them. He understood, he felt, their preciousness to him, and yet he could not right himself. He could not become or recover or resume himself, who had once so easily reached out and held them to himself. He could not endure the thought of their possible acceptance of him as he had become. It was as if their acceptance, their love for him, as a one-handed man, if he allowed it, would foreclose forever some remaining chance that his lost hand would return or grow back, or that he might awaken from himself as he had become to find himself as he had been. He was lost to himself, within himself.

And so in his craziness he drove them away, defending the

hardened carapace of his self, for fear that they would break in and find him there, hurt and terribly, terribly in need – of them.

For a while, for too long, selfishness made him large. He became so large in his own mind in his selfish suffering that he could not see the world or his place in it. He saw only himself, all else as secondary to himself. In his suffering he isolated himself, and then he suffered his loneliness, and then he blamed chiefly Flora for his loneliness and her inability to reach him through it, and then he lashed out at her in his anger at her failure, and then he pitied her for his anger and suffered the guilt of it, and then he was more than ever estranged from her by his guilt. Eventually, inevitably, he saw how his selfishness had belittled him, and he was ashamed, and was more than ever alone in his shame. But in his shame and his loneliness, though he could not yet know it, he was better.

At that time his writings on agriculture had begun to make him known in other places. He had begun to accept invitations to speak at meetings that he had to travel to. On one of those wanderings far from home, and almost suddenly, he became able again to see past himself, beyond and around himself.

Memories of times and places he had forgotten came back to him, reached him at last as if they had been on their way for a long time. He realized how fully and permanently mere glances, touches, passing words, from all his life far back into childhood, had taken place in his heart. Memories gathered to him then, memories of his own, memories of memories told and re-told by his elders. The wealth of an intimate history, belonging equally to him and to his ancestral place, welled up in him as from a deep spring, as if from some knowledge the dead had spoken to him in his sleep.

A darkness fell upon him. He saw a vision in a dream. It was much the same as Hannah Coulter's vision of Heaven, as she would come to tell him of it in her old age: 'Port William with all its loved ones come home alive.' In his dream he saw the past and the future of Port William, of what Burley Coulter had called its membership, struggling through time to belong together, all gathered into a presence of itself that was greater than itself. And he saw that this – in its utterly surprising greatness, utterly familiar – he had been given as a life. Within the abundance of the gift of it, he saw that he was small, almost nothing, almost lost, invisible to himself except as he had been visible to the others who have been with him. He had come into being out of the history and inheritance of love, love faltering and wayward and yet love, granted to him at birth, undeserved, but then called out of him by the membership of his life, apart from which he was nothing. His life was not his self. It was not his own.

He had become small enough at last to enter, to ask to enter, into Flora's and his children's forgiveness, which had been long prepared for him, as he knew, as he had known, if only he could ask. He came into their forgiveness as into the air and weather of life itself. Life-sized again, and welcome, he came back into his marriage to Flora and to their place, with relief amounting to joy.

He came back into the ordinariness of the workaday world and his workaday life, answering to needs that were lowly, unrelenting, and familiar. He came into patience such as he had never suspected that he was capable of. As he went about his daily work, his left hand slowly learned to serve as a right hand, the growth of its dexterity surprising him. His displeasure, at times his enmity, against his stump and his left hand slowly receded from him. They rejoined his body and his life. He became, containing his losses, healed, though never again would he be whole.

His left hand learned at first to print in the fashion maybe of a first-grade boy. And then, with much practice, it mastered a longhand script that was legible enough and swift enough, and that he came to recognize as his own. His left hand learned, as his right hand once had known, to offer itself first to whatever his work required. It became agile and subtle and strong. He became proud of it. In his thoughts he praised its accomplishments, as he might have praised an exceptionally biddable horse or dog.

The prosthetic device also he learned to use as undeliberately almost as if it were flesh of his flesh. But he maintained a discomfort, at once reflexive and principled, with this mechanical extension of himself, as he maintained much the same discomfort with the increasing and equally inescapable dependence of the life of the country and his neighborhood upon mechanical devices.

And so the absence of his right hand has remained with him as a reminder. His most real hand, in a way, is the missing one, signifying to him not only his continuing need for ways and devices to splice out his right arm, but also his and his country's dependence upon the structure of industrial commodities and technologies that imposed itself upon, and contradicted in every way, the sustaining structures of the natural world and its human memberships. And so he is continually reminded of his incompleteness within himself, within the terms and demands of his time and its history, but also within the constraints and limits of his kind, his native imperfection as a human being, his failure to be as attentive, responsible, grateful, loving, and happy as he ought to be.

He has spent most of his life in opposing violence, waste, and destruction – or trying to, his opposition always fragmented and made painful by his complicity in what he opposes. He seems to himself to be 'true', most authentically himself, only when he is sitting still, in one of the places in the woods or on a height of ground that invites him to come to rest, where he goes to sit, wait, and do nothing, oppose nothing, put words to no argument. He permits no commotion then by making none. By keeping still, by doing nothing, he allows the given world to be a gift.

Andy Catlett and Danny Branch are old now. They belong to the dwindling remnant who remember what the two of them have begun to call 'Old Port William', the town as it was in the time before V-J Day, 1945, after which it has belonged ever less to itself, ever more to the machines and fortunes of the Industrial World. Now of an age when Old Port William might have taken up the propriety of naming them 'Uncle Andrew' and 'Uncle Dan', they fear that they may be in fact the only two whose memories of that old time remain more vivid and influential than yesterday evening's television shows. They remember the company of Feltners, Coulters, Rowanberrys, Sowerses, Penns, Branches, and Catletts as they gathered in mutual need into their 'membership' during the war years and the years following.

Andy and Danny are the last of the time gone. Perhaps, as they each secretly pray, they may be among the first of a time yet to come, when Port William will be renewed, again settled and flourishing. They anyhow are links between history and possibility, as they keep the old stories alive by telling them to their children.

Sometimes, glad to have their help needed, they go to work with their children. Sometimes their children come to work with them, and they are glad to have help when they need it, as they increasingly do. But sometimes only the two old men work together, asking and needing no help but each other's, and this is their luxury and their leisure. When just the two of them are at work they are unbothered by any youthful need to hurry, or any younger person's idea of a better way. Their work is free then to be as slow, as finical, as perfectionistical as they want it to be.

And after so many years they know how to work together, the one-handed old man and the two-handed. They know as one what the next move needs to be. They are not swift, but they don't fumble. They don't waste time assling around, trying to make up their minds. They never make a mislick.

'Between us,' says Danny Branch, 'we've got three hands. Everybody needs at least three. Nobody ever needed more.'

Fidelity
(1977)

For Carol and John Berry, with love and thanks

Lyda had not slept, and she knew that Danny had not either. It was close to midnight. They had turned out the light two hours earlier, and since then they had lain side by side, not moving, not touching, disturbed beyond the power to think by the thought of the old man who was lying slack and still in the mechanical room, in the merciless light, with a tube in his nose and a tube needled into his arm and a tube draining his bladder into a plastic bag that hung beneath the bed. The old man had not answered to his name, 'Uncle Burley'. He did not, in fact, appear to belong to his name at all, for his eyes were shut, he breathed with the help of a machine, and an unearthly pallor shone on his forehead and temples. His hands did not move. From time to time, unable to look any longer at him or at the strange, resistant objects around him in the room, they looked at each other, and their eyes met in confusion, as if they had come to the wrong place.

They had gone after supper to the hospital in Louisville to enact again the strange rite of offering themselves where they could not be received. They were brought back as if by mere habit into the presence of a life that had once included them and now did not, for it was a life that, so far as they could see, no longer included even itself. And so they stood around the image on the bed and waited for whatever completion would let them go.

There were four of them: Nathan Coulter, Burley's nephew, who might as well have been his son; Danny Branch, his son in fact, who had until recent years passed more or less as his nephew and who called him 'Uncle Burley' like the others; and there were Nathan's wife, Hannah, and Lyda, Danny's wife, who might as well have been his daughters.

After a while, Hannah rested her purse on the bed, and opened it, and took out a handkerchief with which she touched the corners of her eyes. She put the handkerchief back into her purse and slowly shut the clasp, watching her hands with care as if she were sewing. And then she looked up at Nathan with a look that acknowledged everything, and Nathan turned and went out, and the others followed.

All through the latter part of the summer Burley had been, as he said himself, 'as no-account as a cut cat'. But he had stayed with them, helping as he could, through the tobacco harvest, and they were glad to have him with them, to listen to his stories, and to work around him when he got in their way. He had begun to lose the use of himself, his body only falteringly answerable to his will. He blamed it on arthritis. 'There's a whole family of them Ritis boys,' he would say, 'and that Arthur's the meanest one of the bunch.' But the problem was not arthritis. Burley was only saying what he knew that other old men had said before him; he was too inexperienced in illness himself to guess what might be wrong with him.

They had a fence to build before corn gathering, and they kept him with them at that. 'We'll need you to line the posts,' they told him. But by then they could not keep him awake. They would find him asleep wherever they left him, in his chair at home, or in the cab of a pickup, or hunched in his old hunting coat against a post or the trunk of a tree. One day, laying a hand on Burley's shoulder to wake him, Danny felt what his eyes had already told him but what he had forborne to know with his hand: that where muscle had once piled and rounded under the cloth, there was now little more than hide and bone.

'We've got to do something for him,' Danny said then, partly because Lyda had been saying it insistently to him.

Nathan stared straight at him as only Nathan could do. 'What?'

'Take him to the doctor, I reckon. He's going to die.'

'Damn right. He's eighty-two years old, and he's sick.'

They were getting ready to go in to dinner, facing each other across the bed of Danny's pickup where they had come to put their tools. Burley, who had not responded to the gentle shake that Danny had given him, was still asleep in the cab.

Nathan lifted over the side of the truck a bucket containing staples and pliers and a hammer, and then, as he would not ordinarily have done, he pitched in his axe. 'He's never been to a doctor since I've known him. He said he wouldn't go. You going to knock him in the head before you take him?'

'We'll just take him.'

Nathan stood a moment with his head down. When he looked up again, he said, 'Well.'

So they took him. They took him because they wanted to do more for him than they could do, and doctors exist, and they could think of nothing else. Nathan held out the longest, and he gave in only because he was uncertain.

'Are you – are we – just going to let him die like an old animal?' Hannah asked.

And Nathan, resistant and grouchy in his discomfort, said, 'An old animal is maybe what he wants to die like.'

'But don't we need to help him?'

'Yes. And we don't know what to do, and we're not going to know until after we've done it. Whatever it is. What better can we wish him than to die in his sleep out at work with us or under a tree somewhere?'

'Oh,' Hannah said, 'if only he already had!'

Nathan and Danny took him to the doctor in Nathan's pickup, Nathan's being more presentable and dependable than Danny's, which anyhow had their fencing tools in it. The doctor pronounced Burley 'a very sick man'; he wanted him admitted to the hospital. And so, the doctor having called ahead, with Burley asleep between them, Danny and Nathan took him on to Louisville, submitted to the long interrogation required for admission, saw him undressed and gowned and put to bed by a jolly nurse, and left him. As they were going out, he said, 'Boys, why don't you all wait for me yonder by the gate. I've got just this one last round to make, and then we'll all go in together.' They did not know from what field or what year he was talking.

Burley was too weak for surgery, the doctor told them the next day. It would be necessary to build up his strength. In the meantime tests would be performed. Danny and Lyda, Nathan and Hannah stood with the doctor in the corridor outside Burley's room. The doctor held his glasses in one hand and a clipboard in the other. 'We hope to have him on his feet again very soon,' he said.

And that day, when he was awake, Burley was plainly disoriented and talking out of his head – 'saying some things', as Nathan later told Wheeler Catlett, 'that he never thought of before and some that nobody ever thought of before'. He was no longer in his right mind, they thought, because he was no longer in his right place. When they could bring him home again, he would be himself.

Those who loved him came to see him: Hannah and Nathan, Lyda and Danny, Jack Penn, Andy and Flora Catlett, Arthur and Martin Rowanberry, Wheeler and his other son and law partner, Henry, and their wives. They sat or stood around Burley's bed, reconstructing their membership around him in that place that hummed, in the lapses of their talk, with the sound of many engines. Burley knew them all, was pleased to have them there with him, and appeared to understand where he was and what was happening. But in the course of his talk with them, he spoke also to their dead, whom he seemed to see standing with them. Or he would raise his hand and ask them to listen to the hounds that had been running day and night in the bottom on the other side of the river. Once he said, 'It's right outlandish what we've got started in this country, big political vats and tubs on every roost.'

And then, in the midst of the building of strength and the testing, Burley slipped away toward death. But the people of the hospital did not call it dying; they called it a coma. They spoke of curing him. They spoke of his recovery.

A coma, the doctor explained, was certainly not beyond expectation. It was not hopeless, he said. They must wait and see.

And they said little in reply, for what he knew was not what they knew, and his hope was not theirs.

'Well, then,' Nathan said to the doctor, 'we'll wait and see.'

Burley remained attached to the devices of breathing and feeding and voiding, and he did not wake up. The doctor stood before them again, explaining confidently and with many large words, that Mr Coulter soon would be well, that there were yet other measures that could be taken, that they should not give up hope, that there were places well-equipped to care for patients in Mr Coulter's condition, that they should not worry. And then he said that if he and his colleagues could not help Mr Coulter, they could at least make him comfortable. He spoke fluently from within the bright orderly enclosure of his explanation, like a man in a glass booth. And Nathan and Hannah, Danny and Lyda stood looking in at him from the larger, looser, darker order of their merely human love.

When they returned on yet another visit and found the old body still as it had been, a mere passive addition to the complicated machines that kept it minimally alive, they saw finally that in their attempt to help they had not helped but only complicated his disease beyond their power to help. And they thought with regret of the time when the thing that was wrong with him had been simply unknown, and there had been only it and him and them in the place they had known together. Loving him, wanting to help him, they had given him over to 'the best of modern medical care' – which meant, as they now saw, that they had abandoned him.

If Lyda was wakeful, then, it was because she, like the others, was shaken by the remorse of a kind of treason.

Lyda must have dozed finally, because she did not hear Danny get up. When she opened her eyes, the light was on, and he was standing at the foot of the bed, buttoning his shirt. The clock on the dresser said a quarter after twelve.

'What are you doing?'

'Go back to sleep, Lyda. I'm going to get him.'

She did not ask who. She said 'Good,' which made him look at her, but he did not say more.

And she did not ask. He suited her, and moreover she was used to him. He was the kind, and it was not a strange kind to her, who might leave the bed in the middle of the night if he heard his hounds treed somewhere and not come back for hours. Like Burley, Danny belonged half to the woods. Lyda knew this and it did not disturb her, for he also belonged to her, in the woods as at home.

He finished dressing, turned the light off, and went out. She heard him in Burley's room and then in the kitchen. She heard the scrape of the latchpin at the smokehouse door. He was being quiet; she would not have heard him if she had not listened. But then the hounds complained aloud when he shut them in a stall in the barn.

Presently he came back, and she seemed to feel rather than hear or see him as he moved into the doorway and stopped. 'I don't know how long I'll be gone. You and the kids'll have to do the chores and look after things.'

'All right.'

'I fastened up the dogs.'

'I heard you.'

'Well, don't let them out. And listen, Lyda. If somebody wants to know, I've said something about Indiana.'

She listened until she heard the old pickup start and go out the lane. And then she slept.

Danny's preparations were swift and scant but sufficient for several days. He stripped the bedclothes from Burley's bed, laid them out neatly on the kitchen floor, and then rolled them up around a slab of cured jowl from the smokehouse, a small iron skillet, and a partly emptied bag of cornmeal. He tied the bundle with baling twine, making a sling by which it could hang from his shoulder. From behind the back hall door he took his hunting coat with his flashlight in one pocket and his old long-barreled .22 pistol in the other. He removed the pistol and laid it on top of the dish cabinet.

His pickup truck was sitting in front of the barn, and the confined hounds wailed again at the sound of his footsteps.

'Hush!' he said, and they hushed.

He pitched his bundle onto the seat and unlatched and raised the hood. He had filled the tank with gas that afternoon but had not checked the oil and water. By both principle and necessity, he had never owned a new motor vehicle in his life. The present pickup was a third-hand Dodge, which Burley had liked to describe as 'a loose association of semiretired parts, like me'. But Danny was, in self-defense, a good mechanic, and he and the old truck and the box of tools that he always kept on the floorboard made a working unit that mostly worked.

The oil was all right. He poured a little water into the radiator, relatched the hood, set the bucket back on the well-top, and got into the truck. He started the engine, backed around in front of the corncrib, turned on the headlights, headed out the lane – and so committed himself to the succession of ever wider and faster roads that led to the seasonless, sunless, and moonless world where Burley lay in his bonds.

The old truck roaring in outlandish disproportion to its speed, he drove through Port William and down the long slant into the river bottoms where the headlights showed the ripening fields of corn. After a while he slowed and turned left onto the interstate, gaining speed again as he went down the ramp. The traffic on the great road was thinner than in the daytime but constant nevertheless. As he entered the flow of it, he accelerated until the vibrating needle of the speedometer stood at sixty miles an hour – twenty miles faster than he usually drove. If at the crescendo of this acceleration the truck had blown up, it would not altogether have surprised him. Nor would it altogether have displeased him. He hated the interstate and the reeking stream of traffic that poured along it day and night, and he liked the old truck only insofar as it was a salvage job and his own. 'If she blows,' he thought, 'I'll try to stop her crosswise of both lanes.'

But though she roared and groaned and panted and complained, she did not blow.

Danny's mother, Kate Helen Branch, had been the love of Burley Coulter's life. They were careless lovers, those two, and Danny came as a surprise – albeit a far greater surprise to Burley than to Kate Helen. Danny was born to his mother's name, a certified branch of the Branches, and he grew up in the care of his mother and his mother's mother in a small tin-roofed, paper-sided house on an abandoned corner of Thad Spellman's farm, not far from town by a shortcut up through the woods. As the sole child in that womanly household, Danny was more than amply mothered. And he did not go fatherless, for Burley was that household's faithful visitor, its pillar and provider. He took a hand in Danny's upbringing from the start, although, since the boy was nominally a Branch, Danny always knew his father as 'Uncle Burley'.

If Danny became a more domestic man than his father, that is because he loved the frugal, ample household run by his mother and grandmother and later by his mother and himself. He loved his mother's ability to pinch and mend and make things last. He was secretly proud of her small stitches in the patches of his clothes. They kept a big garden and a small flock of hens. They kept a pig in a pen to eat scraps and make meat, and they kept a Jersey cow that picked a living in the green months out of Thad Spellman's thickety pasture. The necessary corn for the pig and chickens and the corn and hay for the cow were provided by Burley and soon enough by Burley and Danny.

If Danny became a better farmer than his father that is because, through Burley, he came under the influence of Burley's brother, Jarrat, and of Jarrat's son, Nathan, and of Burley's and Nathan's friend, Mat Feltner, all of whom were farmers by calling and by devotion. From them he learned the ways that people lived by the soil and their care of it, by the bounty of crops and animals, and by the power of horses and mules.

But if Danny became more a man of the woods and the streams than nearly anybody else of his place and time, that was because of Burley himself. For Burley was by calling and by devotion a man of the woods and streams. When duty did not keep him in the fields, he would be hunting or fishing or roaming about in search of herbs or wild fruit, or merely roaming about to see what he could see; and from the time Danny was old enough to want to go along, Burley took him. He taught him to be quiet, to watch and not complain, to hunt, to trap, to fish and swim. He taught him the names of the trees and of all the wild plants of the woods. Danny's first providings on his own to his mother's household were of wild goods: fish and game, nuts and berries that grew by no human effort but furnished themselves to him in response only to his growing intimacy with the place. Such providing pleased him and made him proud. Soon he augmented it with wages and produce from the farmwork he did with Burley and the others.

The world that Danny was born into during the tobacco harvest of 1932 suited him well. That the nation was poor was hardly noticeable to him, whose people had never been rich except in the things that they continued to be rich in though they were poor. He loved his half-wooded native country of ridge and hillside and hollow and creek and river bottom. And he loved the horse-and mule-powered independent farming of that place and time.

When Danny had finished the eighth grade at the Port William school, he was growing a crop of his own and was nearly as big as he was going to get, a little taller and somewhat broader than his father. He was a trapper of mink and muskrat, a hunter and fisherman. He farmed for himself or for wages every day that he was out of school and in the mornings and evenings before and after school. If Burley had not continued to be Kate Helen's main provider, Danny could and would have been.

When he began to ride the bus to the high school at Hargrave, the coaches, gathering around him and feeling his arms and shoulders admiringly as if he had been a horse, invited him to go out for basketball. He gave them the smile, direct and a little merry, by which he reserved himself to himself, and said, 'I reckon I already got about all I can do.'

He quit school the day he was sixteen and never thought of it again. By then he was growing a bigger crop, and he owned a good team of mules, enough tools of his own to do his work, and two hounds. When he married Lyda two years later, he had, except for a farm of his own, everything he had thought of to want.

By then the old way of farming was coming to an end. But Danny never gave it up.

'Don't you reckon you ought to go ahead and get you a tractor, like everybody else?' Burley asked him.

And Danny looked up at him from the hoof of the mule he was at that moment shoeing and smiled his merry smile. 'I ain't a-going to pay a company', he said, 'to go and get what is already here.'

'Well,' Burley said, though he knew far better than the Hargrave basketball coach the meaning of that smile, 'tractors don't eat when they ain't working.'

Danny drove in a nail, bent over the point, and reached for another nail. He did not look up this time when he spoke, and it was the last he would say on the matter: 'They don't eat grass when they ain't working.'

That was as much as Burley had wanted to say. He liked mules better than tractors himself and had only gone along with the change to accommodate his brother, Jarrat, who, tireless himself, wanted something to work that did not get tired. Burley loved to be in the woods with the hounds at night, and Danny inherited that love early and fully. They hunted sometimes with their neighbors, Arthur and Martin Rowanberry, sometimes with Elton Penn, but as often as not there would be just the two of them – man and little boy, and then man and big boy, and at last two men – out together in the dark-mystified woods of the hollows and slopes and bottomlands, hunting sometimes all night, but enacting too their general approval of the weather and the world. Sometimes, when the hunting was slow, they would stop in a sheltered place and build a fire. Sometimes, while their fire burned and the stars or the clouds moved slowly over them, they lay down and slept.

There was another kind of hunting that Burley did alone. Danny did not know of this until after Kate Helen died, when he and Lyda got married and, at Burley's invitation, moved into the old weatherboarded log house on the Coulter home place where Burley had been living alone. There were times – though never when he was needed at work – when Burley just disappeared, and Danny and Lyda would know where he had gone only because the hounds would disappear at the same time. Little by little, Danny came to understand.

In love Burley had assumed many responsibilities. In love and responsibility, as everyone must, he had acquired his griefs and losses, guilts and sorrows. Sometimes, under the burden of these, he sought the freedom of solitude in the woods. He might be gone for two or three days or more, living off the land and whatever leftovers of biscuits or cornbread he might be carrying in his pockets, sleeping in barns or in the open by the side of a fire. If the dogs became baffled and gave up or went home, Burley went on, walking slowly hour after hour along the steep rims of the valleys where the trees were old. When he returned, he would be smiling, at ease and quiet, as if his mind just fit within his body.

'Don't quit,' Danny said to the truck, joking with it as he sometimes did with his children or his animals. 'It's going to be downhill all the way home.'

He was making an uproar, and uproar gathered around him as he came to the outskirts of the city. The trailer trucks, sleek automobiles, and other competent vehicles now pressing around him made him aware of the disproportion between his shuddering, smoking old pickup and the job he had put it to, and he began to grin. He came to his exit and roared down into the grid of lighted streets. He continued to drive aggressively. Though he had no plan to speak of, it yet seemed to him that what he had to do required him to keep up a good deal of momentum.

At the hospital, he drove to the emergency entrance, parked as close to the door as he could without being too much in the light, got out, and walked to the door as a man walks who knows exactly what he is doing and is already a little late. His cap, which usually sat well to the back of his head, he had now pulled forward until the bill was nearly parallel with his nose. Only when he was out of the truck and felt the air around him again, did he realize that it was making up to rain.

The emergency rooms and corridors were filled with the bloodied and the bewildered, for it was now the tail end of another Friday night of the Great American Spare-Time Civil War. Danny walked through the carnage like a man who was used to it.

Past a set of propped-open double doors, an empty gurney was standing against the corridor wall, its sheets neatly folded upon it. Without breaking stride, he took hold of it and went rapidly on down the corridor, pushing the gurney ahead of him. When he came to an elevator, he thumbed the 'up' button and waited.

When the doors opened, he saw that a small young nurse was already in the elevator, standing beside the control panel. He pushed the gurney carefully past her, nodding to her and smiling. He said, 'Four, please.'

She pushed the button. The doors closed. She looked at him, sighed, and shook her head. 'It's been a long night.'

'Well,' he said, 'it ain't as long as it has been.'

At the fourth floor the doors slid open. He pushed the gurney off the elevator.

'Good night,' the nurse said.

He said, 'Good night.'

He had to go by the fourth floor nurse's station, but there was only one nurse there and she was talking vehemently into the telephone. She did not look up.

The door of Burley's room was shut. Danny pushed the gurney in and reshut the door. Now he was frightened, and yet there was no caution in him; he did not give himself time to think or to hesitate. Burley was lying white and still in the pallid light. Danny took a pair of rubber gloves from the container affixed to the wall and put them on. Wetting a rag at the wash basin, he carefully washed the handle of the gurney. He then pushed the gurney up near the bed and removed the folded sheet from it. Leaning over the bed, he spoke in a low voice to

Burley. 'Listen. I'm going to take you home. Don't worry. It's me. It's Danny.'

Gently he withdrew the tube from Burley's nose. Gently he pulled away the adhesive tapes and took the needle out of Burley's arm. He took hold of the tube of the bladder catheter as if to pull it out also and then, thinking again, took out his pocketknife and cut the tube in two.

He gathered Burley into his arms and held him a moment, surprised by his lightness, and then gently he laid him onto the gurney. He unfolded the sheet and covered the sleeper entirely from head to foot. He opened the door, pushed the gurney through, and closed the door.

The nurse at the nurse's station was still on the phone. 'I told you no,' she was saying. 'N, O, period. You have just got to understand, when I say no, I *mean* no.'

Near the elevator two janitors were leaning against the wall, mops in hand, as stupefied, apparently, as the soldiers at the Tomb.

When the elevator arrived, the same nurse was on it. She gave him a smile of recognition. 'My goodness, I believe we must be on the same schedule tonight.'

'Yes, mam,' he said.

She hardly glanced at the still figure on the gurney. 'She's used to it,' he thought. But he was careful, nonetheless, to stand in such a way as to make it hard for her to see, if she looked, that this corpse was breathing.

'One?' she asked.

'Yes, mam,' he said. 'If you please.'

Once out of the elevator, he rolled the gurney rapidly down the corridor and through the place of emergency.

A man with a bandaged eye stood aside as Danny approached and went without stopping out through the automatic doors.

Fidelity

A slow rain had begun to fall, and now the pavement was shining.

The Coulter lane turned off the blacktop a mile or so beyond Port William. Danny drove past the lane, following the blacktop on down again into the Katy's Branch valley. Presently he turned left onto a gravel road, and after a mile or so turned left again into the lower end of the Coulter lane, passable now for not much more than a hundred yards. Where a deep gulley had been washed across the road, he stopped the truck. He was in a kind of burrow, deep under the trees in a narrow crease of the hill: Stepstone Hollow.

He switched off the engine and sat still, letting the quiet and the good darkness settle around him. He had been gone perhaps two hours and a half, and not for a minute during that time had he ceased to hurry. So resolutely had he kept up the momentum of his haste that his going and his coming back had been as much one motion as a leap. And now, that motion completed, he began to take his time. In the quiet he could hear Burley's breathing, slow and shallow but still regular. He heard, too, the slow rain falling on the woods and the trees dripping steadily onto the roof of the truck. 'Well,' he said quietly to Burley, 'here's someplace you've been before.'

The shallow breathing merely continued out of the dark where Burley, wrapped in his sheet, slumped against the door.

'Listen,' Danny said. 'We're in Stepstone Hollow. It's raining just a little drizzling rain, and the trees are dripping. That's what you hear. You can pret' near just listen and tell where you are. In a minute I'm going to take you up to the old barn. You don't have a thing to worry about anymore.'

He got out and stood a moment, accepting the dark and the rain. There was, in spite of the overcast, some brightness in the sky. He could see a little. He took his flashlight from the pocket of his coat and blinked it once. The bundle of bed-clothes and food that he had brought from the house lay with the coat on the seat beside Burley. Danny dragged the bundle out and suspended it from his right shoulder, shortening the string to make the load more manageable. Taking the flash-light, he then went around the truck and gently opened the door on the other side. He tucked the sheet snugly around Burley and then covered his head and chest with the coat.

'Now,' he said, 'I'm going to pick you up and carry you a ways.'

Keeping the flashlight in his right hand, he gathered Burley up into his arms, kneed the door shut, and started up the hol-low through the rain. He used the light to cross the gulley. Beyond there, he needed only to blink the light occasionally to show himself the lay of things. Though his burden was awk-ward and the wet and drooping foliage brushed him on both sides, he could walk without trouble. He made almost no sound and was grateful for the silence and slowness and effort after his loud passage out from the city. It occurred to him then that this was a season-changing rain. Tomorrow would be clear and cool, the first fall day.

It was a quarter of a mile or more up to the barn, and his arms were aching well before he got there, but having once taken this burden up, he dared not set it down. The barn, doorless and sag-ging, stood on a tiny shelf of bottomland beside the branch. It was built in the young manhood of Dave Coulter, Burley's father, to house the tobacco crops from the fields, now long abandoned and overgrown, on the north slopes above it. Aban-doned along with its fields, the barn had been used for many years only by groundhogs and other wild creatures and by Burley and Danny, who had sheltered there many a rainy day or night. Danny knew the place in the dark as well as if he could see it. On the old northward-facing slopes on one side of the branch was a thicket of forty-year-old trees: redbud, elm, box elder, walnut, locust, ash – the trees of the 'pioneer generation', returning the fields to the forest. On the south slope, where the soil was rockier and shallower, stood the uninterrupted forest of white and red oaks and chinquapins, hickories, ashes, and maples, many of them two or three hundred years old.

Needing the light now that they were in the cavern of the barn, Danny carried Burley the length of the driveway, stepping around a derelict wagon and then into a stripping room attached at one corner. This was a small shed that was tighter and better preserved than the barn. A bench ran the length of the north side under a row of windows. Danny propped Burley against the wall at the near end of the bench, which he then swept clean with an old burlap sack. He made a pallet of the bedclothes and laid Burley on it and covered him.

'Now,' he said, 'I've got to go back to the truck for some things. You're in the old barn on Stepstone, and you're all right. I won't be gone but a few minutes.'

He shone the light a moment on the still face. In its profound sleep, it wore a solemnity that Burley, in his waking life, would never have allowed. And yet it was, as it had not been in the hospital, unmistakably the face of the man who for eighty-two years had been Burley Coulter. Here, where it belonged, the face thus identified itself and assumed a power that kept Danny standing there, shining the light on it, and that made him say to himself with care, 'Now these are the last things. Now what happens will not happen again in his life.'

He hurried back along the road to the truck and removed an axe, a spade, and a heavy steel spud bar from among the fencing tools in the back. The rain continued, falling steadily as it had fallen since it began. He shouldered the bar and spade and, carrying the axe in his left hand, returned to the barn.

Burley had not moved. He breathed on, as steadily and forcelessly as the falling rain.

'You're in a good place,' Danny said. 'You've slept here before and you're all right. Now I've got to sleep a little myself. I'll be close by.'

He was tired at last. There were several sheets of old tin roofing stacked in the barn, and he took two of these, laying one on the floor just inside the open door nearest to the shed where Burley slept and propping the other as a shield from the draft that was pulling up the driveway. He lay down on his back and folded his arms on his chest. His clothes were damp, but with his hunting coat snug around him he was warm enough.

Though in his coming and going he had hardly made a sound, once he lay still the woods around the barn reassembled a quiet that was larger and older than his own. It was as though the woods had permitted itself to be distracted by him and his burden and his task, and now that he had ceased to move it went back to its ancient preoccupations. The rain went on with its steady patter on the barn roof and on the leafy woods.

Danny lay still and thought of all that had happened since nightfall and of what he might yet have ahead of him. For a while he continued to feel in all his nerves the swaying of the old truck as it sped along the curves of the highway. And then he ceased to think either of the past or of what was to come. The rain continued to fall. The flowing branch made a varying little song in his mind. His mind went slowly to and fro with a dark treetop in the wind. And then he slept.

Lyda had the telephone put in when they closed the school in Port William and began to haul even the littlest children all the way to the consolidated grade school at Hargrave. This required a bus ride of an hour and a half each way for the Branch children and took them much farther out of reach than they had ever been.

'They'll be gone from before daylight to after dark in the winter, who with we don't know, doing what we don't know,' Lyda said, 'and they've got to be able to call home if they need to.'

'All right,' Danny said. 'And there won't anybody call us up on it but the kids – is that right?'

When it rang at night, it just scared Lyda to death, even when the kids were home. If Danny was gone, she always started worrying about him when she heard the phone ring.

She hurried down to the kitchen in her nightgown. She made a swipe at the light switch beside the kitchen door, but missed and went ahead anyhow. There was no trouble in finding the telephone in the dark; it went right on ringing as if she weren't rushing to answer it.

'Hello?' she said.

'Hello. May I speak to Mr Daniel Branch, please?' It was a woman's voice, precise and correct.

'Danny's not here. I'm his wife. Can I help you?'

'Can you tell us how to get in touch with Mr Branch?'

'No. He said something about Indiana, but I don't know where.'

There was a pause, as though the voice at the other end were preparing itself.

'Mrs Branch, this is the hospital. I'm afraid I have some very disturbing news. Mr Coulter – Mr Burley Coulter – has disappeared.'

'Oh!' Lyda said. She was grinning and starting to cry, and there had been a tremor of relief in her voice that she trusted might have passed for dismay.

'Oh, my goodness!' she said finally.

'Let me assure you, Mrs Branch, that the entire hospital staff is deeply concerned about this. We have, of course, notified the police –'

'Oh!' Lyda said.

'– and all other necessary steps will be taken. Please have your husband contact us as soon as he returns.'

'I will,' Lyda said.

After she hung up, Lyda stood a moment, thinking in the dark. And then she turned on the light and called Henry Catlett, whose phone rang a long time before he answered. She was not sure yet that she needed a lawyer, but she could call Henry as a friend.

'Henry, it's Lyda. I'm sorry to get you up in the middle of the night.'

'It's all right,' Henry said.

'The hospital just called. Uncle Burley has disappeared.'

'Disappeared?'

'That's what the lady said.'

There was a pause.

'Where's Danny?'

'He's gone.'

'I see.'

There was another pause.

'Did he say where he was going?'

'He said something about Indiana, Henry. That's all he said.'

'He said that, and that's all?'

'About.'

'Did you tell that to the lady from the hospital?'

'Yes.'

'Did she want to know anything else?'

'No.'

'And you didn't tell her anything else?'

'No.'

'Did *she* say anything else?'

'She said the police had been notified.'

There was another pause.

'What time is it, Lyda?'

'Three o'clock. A little after.'

'And you and the kids will have the morning chores to do, and you'll have to get the kids fed and off to school.'

'That's right.'

'So you'll have to be there for a while. Maybe that's all right. But you'll have to expect a call or maybe a visit from the police, Lyda. When you talk to them, tell them exactly what you told the lady at the hospital. Tell the truth, but don't tell any more than you've already told. If they want to know more, tell them I'm your lawyer and they must talk to me.'

'I will.'

'Are you worried about Burley and Danny?'

'No.'

'Are you worried about talking to the police?'

'I'm scared, but I'm not worried.'

'All right. Let's try to sleep some more. Tomorrow might be a busy day.'

Danny woke up cold and hungry. He was lying on his back with his arms folded on his chest; he had slept perhaps two hours, and he had not moved. Nor had anything moved in the barn or in the wooded hollow around it, so far as he could tell, except the little stream of Stepstone, which continued to make the same steady song it had been making when he fell asleep. A few crickets sang. The air was still, and in openings of mist that had gathered in the hollow he could see the stars.

Though he was cold, for several minutes he did not move. He loved the stillness and was reluctant to break it. An owl trilled nearby and another answered some distance away. Danny turned onto his side to face the opening of the doorway, pillowed his head on his left forearm, and, taking off his cap, ran the fingers of his right hand slowly through his hair.

He yawned, stretched, and got up. Taking the flashlight, he went in to where Burley lay and shone the light on him. Nothing had changed. The old body breathed on with the same steady yet forceless and shallow breaths. Danny saw at once all he needed to see, and yet he remained for a few moments, shining the light. And he said again in his mind, 'These are the last things now. Everything that happens now happens for the last time in his life.' He reached out with his hand and took hold of Burley's shoulder and shook it gently, as if to wake him, but he did not wake.

'It'll soon be morning,' he said aloud. 'I'm hungry now. I need to make a fire and fix a little breakfast before the light comes. We can't send up any smoke after daylight. I'll be close by.'

He gathered dry scraps of wood from the barn floor, and then he pried loose a locust tierpole with the bark still on it and rapidly cut it into short lengths with the axe. Just outside the doorway, he made a small fire between two rocks on which he set his skillet. By the light of the flashlight he sliced a dozen thick slices from the jowl and started several of them frying. He crossed the creek to where a walled spring flowed out of the hillside. He found the rusted coffee can that he kept there, dipped it full and drank, and then dipped it full again. Carrying the filled can, he went back to his fire, where he knelt on one knee and attended to the skillet. The birds had begun to sing, and the sky was turning pale above the eastward trees.

When all the meat was fried, he set the skillet off the fire.

With water from the spring and grease from the fried meat, he moistened some cornmeal and made six hoecakes, each the size of the skillet. When he was finished with his cooking, he took the pair of surgical gloves from his pocket and stirred them in the fire until they were burned. He brought water from the creek then and put out the fire. He divided the food carefully and ate half. He ate slowly and with pleasure, watching the light come. Movement, fire, and now the food in his belly had taken the chill out of his flesh, but fall was in the air that morning, and he welcomed it. The day would be clear and fine. And more would come – brisk, bright, dark-shadowed days colored by the turning leaves, days that would call up the hunter feeling in him. He remembered Elton Penn walking into the woods under the stars of a bright frosty night, half singing, as his way was, 'Clear as a bell, cold as hell, and smells like old cheese.' Now Elton was three years dead.

As Danny watched, the light reddened and warmed in the sky. The last of the stars disappeared. Above him, on both sides of the hollow, the wet leaves of the treetops began to shine among the fading strands and shelves of mist. Eastward, the mist took a stain of pink from the rising sun and glowed. And Danny felt a happiness that he knew was not his at all, that did not exist because he felt it but because it was here and he had returned to it.

He carried his skillet to the creek, scoured it out with handfuls of fine gravel and left it on a rock to dry.

He picked his way through the young thicket growth closing around the barn and entered the stand of old trees that covered the south slope. There the great trees stood around him, the thready night mists caught in their branches, and every leaf was still. When the first white man in this place – the first Coulter or Catlett or Feltner or whoever it was – had passed through this crease of the hill, these trees were here, and the stillness in which they stood and grew had been here forever.

Timber cutters, in recent years, had had their eye on these trees and had approached Burley about 'harvesting' them. 'I reckon you had better talk to Danny here,' Burley said. And Danny smiled that completely friendly, totally impenetrable smile of his, and merely shook his head.

Now Danny was looking for a place well in among the big trees and yet not too far from the creek or too readily access-ible to the eye. His study took him a while, but finally he saw what he was looking for. Under a tall, straight chinquapin that was sound and not too old, a tree that would be standing a long time, there was a shallow trough in the ground, left per-haps by the uprooting of another tree a long time ago; the place was open and clear of undergrowth but hard to see because of a patch of thicket around a windfall. Danny stood and thought again to test his satisfaction, and was satisfied.

As he turned away he noticed, strung between two saplings, the dew-beaded orb of a large orange spider. He stopped to look at it and soon found the spider's home, a sort of tube fash-ioned of two leaves and so not easy to see, where the spider could withdraw to sleep or take shelter from the rain. It would not be long, Danny thought, before the spiders would have to go out of business for the winter. Soon there would be hard frosts, and the webs would be cumbered and torn by the fall-ing leaves.

Sunlight now filled the sky above the shadowy woods. He went back to the barn, preoccupied with his thoughts, and so he was startled, on entering the stripping room, by Burley's opened eyes, looking at him.

He stopped, for the force of his surprise was almost that of fright. And then he went over to the bench and laid his hand on Burley's. Burley's eyes were perfectly calm; he was smiling. Slowly, pausing to breathe between phrases, he said, 'I allowed you'd get here about the same time I did.'

'Well, you were right,' Danny said. 'We made it. Do you know where you are?'

Again, smiling, Burley spoke, his voice so halting and weak as to seem not uttered by bodily strength at all but by some pure presence of recollection and will: 'Right here.'

'You're right again,' Danny said, knowing that Burley did know where he was. 'Are you comfortable? Is there anything you want?'

This time Burley said only, 'Drink.' He turned his head a little and looked at the treetops beyond the window.

Danny said, 'I'll go to the spring.'

At the spring, he drank and then dipped up a drink for Burley. When he returned, Burley's eyes were closed again, and he looked more deeply sunk within himself than before. It was as though his ghost, like a circling hawk, had swung back into this world on a wide curve, to look once more out of his eyes at what he had always known and to speak with his voice, and then had swung out of it again, the curve widening. Danny stood still, holding the can of water. He could hear Burley's breaths coming slower than before, tentative and unsteady. Danny listened. He picked up Burley's wrist and held it. And then he shouldered his tools and went up into the woods and began to dig.

Henry Catlett tried hard to take his own advice, but one thought ran on to another and he could not sleep. There was too much he needed to know that he did not know. Within twenty minutes he saw that he was not going to sleep again.

He got up in the dark and, taking care not to disturb Sarah, who had gone back to sleep after the phone rang, went downstairs, turned on a light and called the hospital. After some trial and error, he was transferred to the supervisor who had talked to Lyda.

'This is Henry Catlett. I have a little law practice up the river at Hargrave. I hear you've mislaid one of your patients.'

The voice in the receiver became extremely businesslike: 'The patient would be – ?'

'Coulter. Burley Coulter.'

'Yes. Well, as you no doubt have heard, Mr Catlett, Mr Coulter was reported missing from his room at a little before two o'clock this morning. Such a thing has never happened here before, Mr Catlett. Let me assure you, sir, that we're doing everything possible on behalf of the victim and his family.'

'Of course,' Henry said. 'I can imagine. Well, I'm calling on behalf of the family. Have you any clues as to what happened?'

'Um. For that, I think I had better have you talk with the investigating officer who was here from the police. Let me find his number. Please hold one minute.'

She gave him a name and a number, which Henry proceeded to dial.

'Officer Bush,' he said, 'I'm Henry Catlett, a country lawyer of sorts up at Hargrave. I'm calling on behalf of the family of Mr Burley Coulter, who seems to have disappeared from his hospital room.'

'Yes, Mr Catlett.'

'I understand that you were the investigating officer. What did you find out?'

'Not much, I'm afraid, sir. Mr Coulter was definitely kidnapped. His attacker disconnected him from the life-support

320

system and wheeled him out, we assume, by way of the emergency entrance. We have one witness, a nurse, who may have seen the kidnapper. She described him as a huge man in a blue shirt; she didn't get a good look at his face. She saw him on an elevator, going up with an empty gurney and down with what she took to be a corpse. Aside from that, we have only the coincidental disappearance of the victim's next of kin, Danny Branch, who his wife says may have gone to Indiana.'

'Anything solid? Any fingerprints?'

'Nothing, Mr Catlett. The man smeared everything he touched, and he didn't touch more than he had to. He may have used a pair of surgical gloves from the room.'

'Would you let me know as soon as you have anything more to report?'

'Be glad to.'

Henry gave him his phone numbers at home and at the office, thanked him, and hung up. He turned the light off then, felt his way to his easy chair, and sat down in the dark to think.

He knew several things. For one, he knew that Danny Branch, though by no means a small man, would not be described by most people as 'huge'. So far as he could see at present, all they had to worry about was the blue shirt, and that might be plenty.

He sat thinking until the shapes of the trees outside the window emerged into the first daylight, and then he went back to the phone and called Lyda.

Lyda called Nathan after she had talked to Henry the second time. Nathan, as was his way, said 'Hello' and then simply listened. When she had told him of Burley's disappearance and of Danny's, Nathan said, 'All right. Do you need anything?'

'No. We'll be fine,' she said. 'But listen. Henry called back a while ago. He said the police didn't find any fingerprints at the hospital. The only witness they found was somebody who saw a man in a blue shirt. Henry wants you and Hannah and me to come to his office as soon as we get our chores done and all. When the police find us, he said, he'd just as soon they'd find us there. He said to tell you, and he'd call Jack and Andy and Flora and the Rowanberrys. He wants everybody who's closest to Burley to be there.'

'All right,' Nathan said. 'It'll be a little while.'

He hung up, and having told Lyda's message to Hannah, he put one of his shirts into a paper sack and went out. He had his chores to do, but he would do them later. He got into his pickup and drove out to the Coulter lane and turned, and turned again into the farm that had been his father's and was now his, divided by a steep, wooded hollow from Burley's place, where Danny and Lyda and their children had lived with Burley since Danny's mother's death. Beyond the two houses in the dawn light, he could see the morning cloud of fog shining in the river valley.

He pulled the truck in behind the house, got out, and started down the hill. Soon he was out of sight among the trees, and he went level along the slope around the point beyond Burley's house, turning gradually out of the river valley into the smaller valley of Katy's Branch. He went straight down the hill then to the creek road, turned into the lower end of the Coulter lane, and soon came to Danny's truck. He saw that Danny's axe and the digging tools were gone.

For several minutes he stood beside the truck, looking up the hollow toward the old barn. And then he took the switch key from where Danny always hid it under a loose flap of floor mat, started the truck and eased it backward along its incoming tracks until it stood on the gravel of the county road.

There were a few bald patches of fresh mud that he had had to drive over, and he walked back to these and tramped out the tire tracks, taking care to leave no shoe track of his own.

When he returned to the truck, he drove back down the creek road toward the river and before long turned right under a huge sycamore into another lane. He forded the branch, went up by a stone chimney standing solitary on a little bench where a house had burned, and then down again to the dis-used barn of that place, and drove in. As before, he erased the few tire tracks that he had left in the lane. He stepped across the Katy's Branch Road and again disappeared into the woods.

While he did all this he had never ceased to whistle a barely audible whisper of a song, passing his breath in and out over the tip of his tongue.

The detective came walking out to the barn as if he were not sure where to put his feet. He was wearing shiny shoes with perforated toes, a tallish man, softening in the middle. He looked a little like somebody Lyda might have seen before. His dark hair was combed straight over his forehead in bangs. He walked with his left hand in his pocket, the jacket of his blue suit held back on that side.

Lyda herself was wearing a pair of rubber boots, but in expectation of company she had put on her best everyday dress. She was carrying two five-gallon buckets of corn that, as the detective approached, she emptied over the fence to the sows.

'Good morning. Mrs Branch?' the detective said.

'Yes. Good morning.'

The children were in the barn, doing the milking and the other chores, and Lyda, as she greeted the detective, started walking back toward the house.

He was showing her a badge. 'Detective Kyle Bode of the

state police, Mrs Branch. I hope you'll be willing to answer a few questions.'

Lyda laughed, looking out over the white cloud of fog that lay in the river valley. 'I reckon I'll have to know what questions,' she said.

'Well, you're Mrs Danny Branch? And Danny Branch is Mr Burley Coulter's next of kin?'

'That's right.'

'And you're aware that Mr Coulter has disappeared from his hospital room?'

'Yes.'

'Is Mr Branch at home?'

'No.'

'Can you tell me where he went?'

'Well, he said something about Indiana.'

'You don't know where?'

'Well, he sometimes goes up there to the Amish. You know, we farm with horses, and Danny has to depend on the Amish for harness and other things.'

'Hmmm. Horses. Well,' the detective said. 'When did Mr Branch leave?'

'I couldn't say.'

'You don't know, or you don't remember?'

'I can't say that I do.'

Lyda had not ceased to walk, nor he to walk with her, and now, as they were approaching the yard gate, the detective stopped. 'Mrs Branch, I have the distinct feeling that you are playing a little game with me. I think your husband has Mr Coulter with him in Indiana – or wherever he is – and I think you know he does, and you're protecting him. Your husband, I would like to remind you, may be in very serious trouble with the law, and unless you cooperate you may be, too.'

Lyda looked straight at him. Her eyes were an intense, surprising blue, and sometimes when she looked suddenly at you they seemed to leave little flashes of blue light dancing in the air. And the detective saw her then: a big woman, good-looking for her age, which was maybe forty or forty-five, and possessed of great practical strength (he remembered her tossing the contents of those heavy buckets over the fence), but her eyes, now that he looked at her, were what impressed him most. They were eyes not at all in the habit of concealment, but they certainly were in the habit of withstanding. They withstood him. They made him feel like explaining that he was only doing his duty.

'Mister,' she said without any trace of fear that he could detect, 'it scares me to be talking to the police. I never talked to the police before in my life. If you want to know any more, you'll have to talk to Henry Catlett down at Hargrave.'

'Is Henry Catlett your lawyer?'

'Henry's our friend,' she said.

'Yes,' the detective said. 'I'll go see him. Thank you very much for your time.'

When Detective Bode walked away from Lyda, he already felt the mire of failure pulling at his feet. He had felt it before. Long ago, it seemed, he had studied to be a policeman because he wanted to become the kind of man who solved things. He had imagined himself becoming a man who – insightful, alert, and knowing – stepped into the midst of confusion and made clarity and order that people would be grateful for. So far, it had not turned out that way. He was thirty-two years old already, and he had been confused as much as most people. In spite of the law and the government and the police, it seemed, people went right on and did whatever they were going to do.

They had motives that were confusing, and they left evidence that was confusing. Sometimes they left no evidence. The science of crime solving was much clumsier than he had expected. Many criminals and many noncriminals were smarter than Kyle Bode – or, anyhow, smarter than Kyle Bode had been able to prove himself to be so far. He had begun to believe he might end up as some kind of paper shuffler, had even begun to think that might be a relief.

He had understood all too well, anyhow, the rather cynical grin with which his friend, Rich Ferris, had handed him this case. 'Here's one that'll make you famous.'

And what a case it was! Here was an old guy resting easy in the best medical facility money could buy. And what happened? This damned redneck, Danny Branch, who was his nephew or something, came and kidnapped him out of his hospital bed in the middle of the night. And took him off where? To Indiana? Not likely, Detective Bode thought. He would bet that Mr Burley Coulter, alive or dead, and his kidnapper, Mr Danny Branch, were somewhere just out of sight in these god-forsaken hills and hollows.

Kyle Bode objected to hills and hollows. He objected to them especially if they were overgrown with trees. That the government of the streets and highways persisted in having business in wooded hills and hollows in every kind of weather was no small part of his disillusionment.

And that big woman with her boots and her unimpressed blue eyes – it pleased him to believe that she was looking him straight in the eye and lying. In fact, he had wished a little that she would admire him, and he knew that she had not.

Traveling at a contemplative speed down the river road toward Hargrave, he glanced up at his image in the rearview mirror and patted down his hair.

Kyle Bode's father had originated in the broad bottomlands of a community called Nowhere, two counties west of Louisville. Under pressure from birth to 'get out of here and make something out of yourself', Kyle's father had come to Louisville and worked his way into a farm equipment dealership. Kyle was the dealer's third child and second son. He might have succeeded to the dealership – 'You boys can be partners,' their father had said – but the older brother possessed an invincible practicality and a head start, and besides Kyle did not want to spend his life dealing with farmers. He had higher aims, which made him dangerous to those he considered to be below him. Unlike his brother, Kyle was an idealist, with a little bit of an ambition to be a hero. Perhaps by the same token, he was also a man given to lethargy and to sudden onsets of violence by which he attempted to drive back whatever circumstances his lethargy had allowed to close in on him. Sagged and silent in his chair at a party or beer joint, he would suddenly thrust himself, with fists flying, at some spontaneously elected opponent. This did not happen often enough to damage him much, and it remained surprising to his friends.

Soon after graduation, he married his high school sweetheart. And then while he was beginning his career as a policeman, they, and especially he, began to dabble in some of the recreational sidelines of the countercultural revolution. He became sexually liberated. He suspected that his wife had experienced this liberation as well, but he did not catch her, and perhaps this was an ill omen for his police career. On the contrary, as it happened, she caught him in the very inflorescence of ecstasy on the floor of the carport of a house where they were attending a party. He was afraid for a while that she would divorce him, but when it became clear to him that she would not, he began to feel that she was limiting his development, and he divorced her in order to be free to be himself.

He cut quite a figure at parties after that. One festive night a young lady said, 'Kyle, do you know who you really look like?' And he said, 'No.' And she said, 'Ringo Starr.' That was when he began to comb down his bangs. Girls and young women were always saying to him after that, 'Do you know who you look like?' And he would say, 'No. Who?' as if he had no notion what they were talking about.

His second wife – whom he married when he made her pregnant, for he really was a conscientious young man who wanted to do the right thing – was proud of that resemblance, at first seriously and then jokingly, for a while. And then he ceased to remind her of anyone but himself, whereupon she divorced him.

He knew that she had not left him because she was dissatisfied with him but because she was not able to be satisfied for very long with anything. He disliked and feared this in her at the same time that he recognized it in himself. He, too, was dissatisfied; he could not see what he had because he was always looking around for something else that he thought he wanted. And so perhaps it was out of mutual dissatisfaction that their divorce had come, and now they were free. Perhaps even their little daughter was free, who was tied down no more than her parents were, for they sent her flying back and forth between them like a shuttlecock, and spoiled her in vying for her allegiance, and gave her more freedom of choice than she could have used well at twice her age. They were all free, he supposed. But finally he had had to ask if they were, any of them, better off than they had been and if they could hope to be better off than they were. For they were not satisfied. And by now he had to suppose, and to fear, that they were not going to be satisfied.

Surely there must be someplace to stop. In lieu of a more final place, though it was too early in the day to be thinking about it, he would take the lounge of the Outside Inn, the comers and goers shadowy between him and the neon, a filled and frosted glass in front of him, a slow broken-hearted song on the jukebox.

And maybe the mood would hit him to ask one of the women to dance. Angela, maybe, who admitted to being lonesome and liked to dance close. They would dance, they would move as one, and after a while he would let his right hand slide down, as if by accident, onto her hip.

But his car, as though mindful of his duty when he was not, had taken him into Hargrave. He stopped for the first light and then turned to drive around the courthouse square; he was looking for a place to eat breakfast. The futility of this day insinuated itself into his thoughts, as unignorable as if it crawled palpably on his skin. Here he was, looking for a comatose old geezer who (if Detective Bode mistook not) had been abducted by his next of kin, who, if the old geezer died, would be guilty of a crime that probably had not even been named yet. Maybe he was about to turn up something totally new in the annals of crime, though he would just as soon turn it up someplace else. In fact, he would just as soon somebody else turned it up. It ought, he told himself, to be easy enough to turn up, for it was clearly the work of an amateur. And yet this amateur, who had had the gall or stupidity or whatever it took to kidnap his victim right out of the middle of a busy hospital, had managed to be seen, and not clearly seen at that, by only one witness and had left no evidence. So Detective Bode was working from a coincidence, a good guess, and no evidence. His success, he supposed, depended on the improbable occurrence of a lucky moment in which he would be able to outsmart the self-styled 'country lawyer of sorts', Henry Catlett.

'Later for that,' Kyle Bode thought.

Among the dilapidating storefronts he found the place he thought he remembered, the Front Street Grill, and he parked and went in.

When Lyda called, Nathan and Hannah were just waking up. Before Nathan turned the light on by the bed, they could see the gray early daylight out the window. After Nathan went to the phone, Hannah lay still and listened, but from Nathan's brief responses she could not make out who had called.

She heard Nathan hang up the phone. He came back into the bedroom and told her carefully everything that Lyda had told him.

'But wait,' she said. 'What's happening? Where *is* Danny?'

'We'd better not help each other answer those questions, Hannah – not for a while, anyhow.'

He opened a drawer of the bureau and took out one of his shirts, a green one.

'Where are you going?'

He smiled at her. 'I'll be back before long.'

Though Nathan was a quiet man, he was not usually a secretive one. But she asked no more.

He went out. She heard him go through the kitchen and out the back door. She heard the pickup start and go out the drive-way. And then the sound of it was gone.

Usually, after Nathan got up, there would be a few minutes when she could stay in bed, sometimes rolling over into the warmth where he had slept before she got up to start break-fast. She loved that time. She would lie still, listening, as the night ended and the day began. She heard the first birdsongs of the morning. She heard Nathan leave the house, the milk bucket ringing a little as he took it down from its nail on the back porch. She heard the barn door slide open, and then Nathan's voice calling the cows, and then the cowbells coming up through the pale light. If she got up when the cows reached the barn, she could have breakfast ready by the time Nathan came back to the house.

But this morning, as soon as the truck was out of earshot, she got up. For there was much to think about, much to do and to be prepared for. Now that she was fully awake, she had, like the others, caught the drift of what was happening.

She took the milk bucket and went to the barn and milked and did the chores, the things that Nathan usually did, and then she went to open the henhouse and put out feed and water for the hens – her work. At the house, she strained the milk, set the table for breakfast, and got out the food. But Nathan was not back. She sat down by the kitchen window where she could see him when he came in. She kept her sewing basket there and the clothes that needed mending. But now, though she took a piece of sewing onto her lap, she did not work. She sat with her hands at rest, looking out the window as the mists of the hollows turned whiter under the growing light. She wanted to be thinking of Burley, but amongst all the knowing and unknowing of this strangely begun day she could not think of him. Who was most on her mind now was Nathan, and she wished him home.

It was home to her, this house, though once it had not been, nor had this neighborhood been. She had come to Port William thirty-six years ago. She had married Virgil Feltner as war spread across the world, and had lived with him for a little while in the household of his parents, before he was called into the service. When he left, because her mother was dead and replaced long ago by an unkind stepmother, Mat and Margaret Feltner had made her welcome. She stayed on with them, and they were mother and father to her. In the summer of 1944, Virgil came home on leave; he and Hannah were together a little while again, and when he went back to his unit she was with child.

The life that Hannah had begun to live came to an end when her young husband was killed, and for a while it seemed that she had no life except in the child that she had borne into the world of one death and of many. And then Nathan had called her out of that world into the living world again, and a new life had come to her; she and Nathan had made and shaped it, welcomed its additions and borne its losses, together. They moved to this place that Nathan had bought not long before they married. Run-down and thicket-grown as it was, its possibility had beckoned to him and then to her. They had moved into the old house, restored it while they lived in it and while they restored the farm; they had raised their children here. And they were son and daughter both to Margaret and Mat Feltner and to Nathan's father, whose oldest son, Tom, had also been killed in the war.

They had raised their children, sent them to college, seen them go away to work in cities, and, though wishing they might have stayed, wished them well. Their children had gone, and over the years, one by one, so had their elders. And each one of these departures had left them with more work to do and, as Hannah sometimes thought, less reason to do it.

They were in their fifties now, farming three farms simply because there was no one else to do the work. In addition to the Feltner Place and their own, they were also farming Nathan's home place, which he had inherited from his father. Like everybody else still farming, they were spread too thin, and help was hard to find. The Port William neighborhood had as many people, probably, as it had ever had, but it did not have them where it needed them. It had a good many of them now on little city lots carved out of farms, from which they commuted to city jobs. Nathan and Hannah were overburdened, too tired at the end of every day, and with no relief in sight. And yet they did not think of quitting. Nathan worked through his long days steadily and quietly. Some days Hannah worked with him; when she needed help, he helped her. They had two jersey cows for milk and butter; they raised and slaughtered their meat hogs; they kept a flock of hens; they raised a garden. And still, in spite of all, there were quietnesses that they came to, in which they rested and were together and were glad to be.

And though their loneliness had increased, they were not alone. Of the membership of kin and friends that had held them always, some had died and some had gone, but some remained. There were Lyda and Danny Branch and their children. There were Arthur and Martin Rowanberry. After Elton Penn's death, his son Jack had continued to farm their place, and Mary Penn was living in Hargrave, still a friend. There were the various Catletts, who, whatever else they were, were still farmers and still of the membership: Bess and Wheeler who were now old, Sarah and Henry and their children, Flora and Andy and theirs.

When she thought of their neighborhood, Hannah wondered whether or not to count the children. Like the old, the young were leaving. The old were dying without successors, and Hannah was aware how anxiously those who remained had begun to look into the eyes of the children. They were watching not just their own children now but anybody's children. For as the burden of keeping the land increased for the always fewer who remained, as the difference continued to increase between the price of what they had to sell and the cost of what they had to buy, they knew that they had less and less to offer the children, and fewer arguments to make.

They held on, she and those others, who might be the last. They held on, and they held out, and they were seeing, perhaps, a little more clearly what they had to hold out against. Every year, it seemed to her, they were living more from what they could do for themselves and each other and less from what they had to buy. Nathan's refusals to buy things, she had noticed, were becoming firmer as well as more frequent. 'No,' he would say, 'I guess we can get along without that.' 'No. Not at that price.' 'No. I reckon the old one will run a while longer.' And though he spoke these answers kindly enough, there was no doubting their finality. Nobody ever asked twice.

Maybe, she thought, this was Danny's influence. Danny was eight years younger than Nathan, and it was strange to think that Nathan could have been influenced by him, but maybe he had been. Danny never had belonged much to the modern world, and every year he appeared to belong to it less. Of them all, Danny most clearly saw that world as his enemy – as *their* enemy – and most forthrightly and cheerfully repudiated it. He reserved his allegiance to his friends and his place.

Danny was the right one for the rescue that Hannah did not doubt was being accomplished, though she did not know quite how. He had some grace about him that would permit him to accomplish it with joy. She smiled, for she knew, too, that Danny was a true son to Burley, not only in loyalty but in nature – that he had shared fully in that half of Burley's life that had belonged to the woods and the darkness. Nathan, she thought, had understood that side of Burley and been friendly to it without so much taking part in it. Nathan would wander out with Burley and Danny occasionally and would enjoy it, but he was more completely a farmer than they were, more content to be bound within the cycle of the farmer's year. You never felt, looking at him, that he had left something somewhere beyond the cleared fields that he would be bound to go back and get. He did not have that air that so often hung about Danny and Burley, suggesting that they might suddenly look back, grin and wave, and disappear among the trees. He was as solid, as frankly and fully present as the doorstep, a man given to work and to quiet – like, she thought, his father.

They were her study, those Coulter men. Figuring them out was her need, her way of loving them, and sometimes her amusement. The one who most troubled her had been Nathan's father, Jarrat – a driven, work-brittle, weather-hardened, lonely, and nearly wordless man, who went to his grave without completing his sorrow for his young wife who had died when their sons were small, whom he never mentioned and never forgot. His death had left in Hannah an unused and yearning tenderness.

Burley lived in a larger world than his brother, and not just because, as a hunter and a woods walker, he readily crossed boundaries that had confined Jarrat. Burley was a man freely in love with freedom and with pleasures, who watched the world with an amused, alert eye to see what it would do next, and if the world did not seem inclined to get on very soon to anything of interest, he gave it his help. Hannah's world had been made dearer to her by Burley's laughter, his sometimes love of talk (his own and other people's), and his delight in outrageous behavior (his own and other people's). She knew that Burley did not forget the dead, whom he mourned and missed. She knew he grieved that he had not married Kate Helen Branch, Danny's mother, and that he regretted his late acknowledgment of Danny as his son. But she knew, too, how little he had halted in grief and regret, how readily and cheerfully he had gone on, however burdened, to whatever had come next. And because he was never completely of her world, she had the measure of his generosity to her and the others. Though gifted for disappearance, he had never entirely disappeared but had been with them to the end.

Now the thought of him did return to her. As he had grown sicker and weaker, the thought of him had come more and more into her keeping, and she had received it with her love and her thanks as she had received her children when they were newborn.

She thought it strange and wonderful that she had been given these to love. She thought it a blessing that she had loved them to the limit of her grief at parting with them, and that grief had only deepened and clarified her love. Since her first grief had brought her fully to birth and wakefulness in this world, an unstinting compassion had moved in her, like a live stream flowing deep underground, by which she knew herself and others and the world. It was her truest self, that stream always astir inside her that was at once pity and love, knowledge and faith, forgiveness, grief, and joy. It made her fearful, and it made her unafraid.

Like the others, she had mourned her uselessness to Burley in his sickness. Like the others, she had been persuaded and had helped to persuade that they should get help for him. Like the others, once they had given him into the power of the doctors and into the hard light of that way and place in which he did not belong, she had wanted him back. And she had held him to her in her thoughts, loving the old, failed flesh and bone of him as never before, as if she could feel, in thought, in nerve, and through all intervening time and distance, the little helpless child that he had been and had become again. Knowing now that he was with Danny, hidden away, somewhere at home, joy shook her and the window blurred in her sight.

She heard, after a while, the tires of Nathan's truck on the gravel, and then the truck came into sight, stopped in its usual place, and Nathan got out. She watched him as he walked to the house, not so light-stepping as he used to be. She knew that as he walked, looking alertly around, he would be whistling over and over a barely audible little thread of a tune.

When he came in and she looked at him from the stove, where she had gone to start their breakfast, he smiled at her. 'Don't ask,' he said.

She said, 'I will only ask one question. Are you worried about Burley?'

'No,' he said, and he smiled at her again.

Henry hurried up the steps to the office, knowing that his father would already be there. Wheeler came to the office early, an hour maybe before Henry and the secretary, because, as Henry supposed, he liked to be there by himself. It was a place of haste and sometimes of turmoil, that office, where they worked at one problem knowing that another was waiting and sometimes that several others were waiting. Wheeler would come there in the quiet of the early morning to meet the day on his own terms. He would sit down at his desk covered with opened books, thick folders of papers and letters, ruled yellow pads covered with his impulsive blue script, and with one of those pads on his lap and a pen in his hand he would call the coming day to order in his mind.

He had been at work there for more than fifty years. In all that time the look of the place had changed more by accretion than by alteration. There were three rooms: Wheeler's office in the front, overlooking the courthouse square; Henry's in the back, overlooking an alley and some backyards; and, between the two, a waiting room full of bookcases and chairs where the secretary, Hilda Roe, had her desk.

Wheeler was sitting at his desk with his hat on, his back to the door. He was leaning back in his chair, his right ankle crossed over his left knee, and he was writing in fitful jabs on a yellow pad. Henry tapped on the facing of the door.

'Come in,' Wheeler said without looking up.

Henry came in.

'Sit down,' Wheeler said.

Henry did not sit down.

'What you got on your mind?' Wheeler asked.

'Burley Coulter disappeared from the hospital last night.'

Wheeler swiveled his chair around and gave Henry a look that it had taken Henry thirty years to meet with composure. 'Where's Danny Branch?'

Henry grinned. 'Danny's away from home. Lyda said he said something about Indiana.'

'You've talked to the police?'

'Yes. And a state police detective, Mr Kyle Bode, has already been to see Lyda.'

Wheeler wrote Kyle Bode's name on the yellow pad. 'What did you find out?'

'Somebody went into Burley's room sometime around two o'clock. Whoever it was disconnected him from the life machines, loaded him onto a gurney, and escaped with him "into the night", as they say. They found no fingerprints or other evidence. They have found one witness, a nurse, who saw "a huge man" wearing a blue shirt going up on an elevator with an empty gurney and then down with what she thought was a dead person.'

'We don't know anybody huge, do we?' Wheeler said. 'What about the blue shirt?'

'Don't know,' Henry said.

'Do you know this Detective Bode?'

'I had a little talk with him once, over in the courtroom.'

'You're expecting him?'

'Yes.'

Wheeler spread his hands palm-down on his lap, studied them a moment, and then looked up again. 'Well, what are you going to do?'

'Don't know,' Henry said. 'I guess I'll wait to find out. I've told Lyda and everybody else concerned to come here as soon as they can. And I think you ought to call Mother and Mary Penn and tell them to come. I don't want the police to talk to any more of them alone.'

This time it was Wheeler who grinned. He reached for the phone. 'All right, my boy.'

Working with the spade, Danny cut into the ground the long outline of the grave. It was hard digging, the gentle rain of the night not having penetrated very far, and there were tree roots and rocks. Danny soon settled into a rhythm in keeping with the length and difficulty of the job. He used the spud bar to loosen the dirt, cut the roots, and pry out the rocks. With the spade he piled the loosened dirt on one side of the grave; with his hands he laid the rocks out on the other side. He worked steadily, stopping only to return to the barn to verify that the sleeper there had not awakened. On each visit he stood by Burley only long enough to touch him and to say, 'You're all right. You don't have to worry about a thing.' Each time, he saw that Burley's breath came more shallow and more slow.

And finally, on one of these trips to the barn, he knew as he entered the doorway that the breaths had stopped, and he stopped, and then went soundlessly in where the body lay. It looked unaccountably small. Now of its long life in this place there remained only this small relic of flesh and bone. In the hospital, Burley's body had seemed to Danny to be off in another world; he had not been able to rid himself of the feeling that he was looking at it through a lens or a window. Here, the old body seemed to belong to this world absolutely, it was so accepting now of all that had come to it, even its death. Burley had died as he had slept – he had not moved. Danny leaned and picked up the still hands and laid them together.

He went back to his digging and worked on as before. As he accepted again the burden of the work and measured his thoughts to it, Burley returned to his mind, and he knew him again as he had been when his life was full. He saw again the stance and demeanor of the man, the amused eyes, the lips pressed together while speech waited upon thought, an almost inviolable patience in the set of the shoulders. It was as though Burley stood in full view nearby, at ease and well at home – as though Danny could see him, but only on the condition that he not look.

When Detective Bode climbed the stairs to the office of Wheeler Catlett & Son, the waiting room was deserted. Through the open door at the rear of the room, he could see Henry with his feet propped on his desk, reading the morning paper. Kyle Bode closed the waiting room door somewhat loudly.

Henry looked up. 'Come in,' he called. He got up to greet his visitor, who shook his hand and then produced a badge.

'Kyle Bode, state police.'

Henry gave him a warm and friendly smile. 'Sure,' he said. 'I remember you. Have a seat. What can I do for you?'

The detective sat down in the chair that Henry positioned for him. He had not smiled. He waited for Henry, too, to sit down. 'I'm here in connection with what I suppose would be called a kidnapping. A man named Burley Coulter, of Port William, was removed from his hospital room without authorization at about two o'clock this morning.'

'So I heard!' Henry said. 'Lyda Branch called me about it. I figured you fellows would have made history of this case by now. You mean you haven't?'

'Not yet,' Kyle Bode said. 'It's not all that clear-cut, probably due to the unprecedented nature of the crime.'

'You show me an unprecedented crime,' Henry said, falling in with the detective's philosophical tone. 'Kidnapping, you said?'

'It's a crime involving the new medical technology. I mean, some of this stuff is unheard of. We're living in the future right now. I figure this crime is partly motivated by anxiety about this new stuff. Like maybe the guy that did it is some kind of religious nut.'

Henry put his dark-rimmed reading glasses back on and made his face long and solemn, tilting his head back, as he was apt to do when amused in exalted circumstances. 'In the past, too,' he said.

'What?'

'If we're living in the future, then surely we're living in the past, too, and the dead and the unborn are right here in our midst. Wouldn't you say so?'

'I guess so,' Kyle Bode said.

'Well,' Henry said, 'do you have any clues as to the possible identity of the perpetrator of this crime?'

'Yes, as a matter of fact, we do. We have a good set of fingerprints.'

Kyle Bode spoke casually, looking at the fingernails of his right hand, which he held in his left. When he looked up to gauge the effect, not the Henry of their recent philosophical exchange but an altogether different Henry, one he had encountered before, was looking at him point-blank, the glasses off.

'Mr Bode,' Henry said, 'that was a lie you just told. As a matter of fact, you don't have any evidence. If we are going to get along, you had better assume that I know as much about this case as you do. Now, what do you want?'

Kyle Bode felt a sort of chill crawl up the back of his neck and over the top of his head, settling for an exquisite moment among the hair roots. He maintained his poise, however, and was pleased to note that he was returning Henry's look. And the right question came to him.

'I want to find the victim's nephew, Danny Branch. Do you know where he is?'

'Son,' Henry said. 'The victim's son. I only know what his wife told me.'

'What did she tell you?'

'She said he said something about Indiana.'

'We have an APB on him in Indiana.' Detective Bode said this with the air of one who leaves no stone unturned. 'But we really think – *I* think – the solution is to be found right here.'

But looking at Henry and remembering Lyda, he felt unmistakably the intimation that he and his purpose were not trusted. These people did not trust him, and they were not going to trust him. He felt his purpose unraveling in his failure to have their trust. In default of that trust, *every* stone must be turned. And it was a rocky country. He knew he had already failed – unless, by some fluke of luck, he could find somebody to outsmart. Or, maybe, unless this Danny Branch should appear wearing a blue shirt.

'Maybe you can tell me,' he said, 'if Danny Branch is Mr Coulter's heir.'

'Burley was – is – my father's client,' Henry said. 'You ought to ask him about that. Danny, I reckon, is my client.'

The detective made his tone more reasonable, presuming somewhat upon his and Henry's brotherhood in the law: 'Mr Catlett, I'd like to be assured of your cooperation in this case. After all, it will be in your client's best interest to keep this from going as far as it may go.'

'Can't help you,' Henry said.

'You mean that you, a lawyer, won't cooperate with the law of the state in the solution of a crime?'

'Well, you see, it's a matter of patriotism.'

'Patriotism? You can't mean that.'

'I mean patriotism – love for your country and your neighbors. There's a difference, Mr Bode, between the government and the country. I'm not going to cooperate with you in this case because I don't like what you represent in this case.'

'What I represent? What do you think I represent?'

'The organization of the world.'

'And what does that mean?' In spite of himself, and not very coolly, Detective Bode was lapsing into the tone of mere argument, perhaps of mere self-defense.

'It means,' Henry said, 'that you want whatever you know to serve power. You want knowledge to *be* power. And you'll make your ignorance count, too, if you can be deceitful and clever enough. You think everything has to be explained to your superiors and concealed from your inferiors. For instance, you just lied to me with a clear conscience, as a way of serving justice. What I stand for can't survive in the world you're helping to make, Mr Bode.' Henry was grinning, enjoying himself, and allowing the detective to see that he was.

'Are you some kind of anarchist?' the detective said. 'Just what the hell are you, anyway?'

'I'm a patriot, like I said. I'm a man who's not going to co-operate with you on this case. You're here to represent the right of the government and other large organizations to decide for us and come between us. The people you represent will come out here, without asking our opinion, and shut down a barber-shop or a little slaughterhouse because it's not sanitary enough for us, and then let other businesses – richer ones – poison the air and water.'

'What's *that* got to do with it?'

'Listen,' Henry said. 'I'm trying to explain something to you. I'm not the only one who won't cooperate with you in your search for Danny Branch. There are several of us here who aren't reconciled to the loss of *any* good thing.'

'I'm just doing my duty,' Kyle Bode said.

'And you're here now to tell us that a person who is sick and unconscious, or even a person who is conscious and well, is ultimately the property of the medical industry and the government. Aren't you?' Henry was still grinning.

'It wasn't authorized. He asked nobody's permission. He told nobody. He signed no papers. It was a crime. You can't let people just walk around and do what they want to like that. He didn't even settle the bill.'

'Some of us think people belong to each other and to God,' Henry said. 'Are you going to let a hospital keep a patient hostage until he settles his account? You were *against* kidnapping a while ago.'

Detective Bode was resting his brow in the palm of his hand. He was shaking his head. When it became clear that Henry was finished, the detective looked up. 'Mr Catlett, if I may, I would like to talk to your father.'

'Sure,' Henry said, getting up. 'You going to tell on me?'

And only then, finally, did Detective Bode smile.

Danny dug the grave down until he stood hip deep in it. And then he dug again until it was well past waist deep. And then, putting his hands on the ground beside it, he leapt out of it, and stood looking down into it, and thought. The grave was somewhat longer than Burley had been tall; it was widened at the middle to permit Danny to stand in it to lay the body down; it was deep enough.

Using the larger flagstones that he had taken from the grave and bringing more from the creek, Danny shaped a long, narrow box in the bottom of the grave. He was making such a grave as he knew the Indians of that place had made long before Port William was Port William. Digging to varying depths to seat the stones upright with their straightest edges aligned at the top, he worked his way from the head of the grave to the foot and back again, tamping each stone tightly into place. The day grew warmer, and Danny paused now and again to wipe the sweat from his face. The light beams that came through the heavy foliage shifted slowly from one opening to another, and slowly they became perpendicular. Again he went to the spring and drank, and returned to his work. The crickets sang steadily, and the creek made its constant little song over the rocks. Within those sounds and the larger quiet that included them, now and then a woodpecker drummed or called or a jay screamed or a squirrel barked. In the stillness a few leaves let go and floated down. And always Danny could smell the fresh, moist earth of the grave.

When he had finished placing the upright stones, he paved the floor of the grave, laying the broad slabs level and filling the openings that remained with smaller stones. He made good work of it, though it would be seen in all the time of the world only by him and only for a little while. He put the shape of the stone casket together as if the stones had made a casket once before and had been scattered, and now he had found them and pieced them together again.

He carried up more stones from the creek, the biggest he could handle. These would be the capstones, and he laid them in stacks at the head and foot of the grave. It was ready now. He went down to the barn and removed the blankets that covered Burley and withdrew the pillow from under his head. He folded the blankets into a pallet on the paved floor of the grave and placed the pillow at its head.

When he carried Burley to the grave, he went up by the gentlest, most open way so that there need be no haste or struggle or roughness, for now they had come to the last of the last things. A heavy pressure of finality swelled in his heart and throat as if he might have wept aloud, but as he walked he made no sound. He stepped into the grave and laid the body down. He composed it like a sleeper, laying the hands together as before. And the body seemed to accept again its stillness and its deep sleep, submissive to the motion of the world until the world's end. Danny brought up the rest of the bedclothes and laid them over Burley, covering, at last, his face.

As before, the thought returned to him that he was not acting only for himself. He thought of Lyda and Hannah and Nathan and the others, and he went down along the creek and then up across the thickety north slope on the other side, gathering flowers as he went. He picked spires of goldenrod, sprays of farewell-summer and of lavender, gold-centered asters; he picked yellow late sunflowers, the white-starred flower heads of snakeroot with their faint odor of warm honey, and finally, near the creek, the triple-lobed, deep blue flowers of lobelia.

Stepping into the grave again, he covered the shrouded body with these, their bright colors and their weedy scent warm from the sun, laying them down in shingle fashion so that the blossoms were always uppermost, until the grave seemed at last to contain a small garden in bloom. And then, having touched Burley for the last time, he laid across the upright sides of the coffin the broad covering stones, first one layer, and then another over the cracks in the first.

He lifted himself out of the grave and stood at the foot of it. He let the quiet reassemble itself around him, the quiet of the place now one with that of the old body sleeping in its grave. Into that great quiet he said aloud, 'Be with him, as he has been with us.' And then he began to fill the grave.

Henry rapped on his father's door and then pushed it open. Wheeler was still wearing his hat, but now he was holding the telephone receiver in his right hand. His right arm was extended at full length, propped on the arm of his chair. Both Henry and Kyle Bode could hear somebody insistently and plaintively explaining something through the phone. When the door opened, Wheeler looked around.

'Detective Bode would like to talk with you.'

Wheeler acknowledged Henry with a wave of his left hand. To Kyle Bode he said, 'Come in, sir,' and gestured toward an empty chair.

Kyle Bode came in and sat down.

Wheeler put the receiver to his mouth and ear and said, 'But I *know* what your problem is, Mr Hernshaw. You've told me several times . . .' The voice never stopped talking. Wheeler shifted the receiver to his left hand, clamping his palm over the mouthpiece, and, smiling, offered his right hand to the detective. 'I'm glad to know you, Mr Bode. I'll get done here in a minute.' He dangled the receiver out over his chair arm again while he and Kyle Bode listened to it, its tone of injury and wearied explanation as plain as if they could make out the words. And then they heard it say distinctly, 'So. Here is what I think.'

In the portentous pause that followed, Wheeler quickly raised the receiver and said into it with an almost gentle patience, 'But, Mr Hernshaw, as I have explained to you a number of times, what you think is of no account, because you are not going to get anybody else on the face of the earth to think it.'

Something was said then that Wheeler interrupted: 'No. A verbal agreement is *not* a contract if there were no witnesses and you are the only one who can remember it. Now you think about it. I can't talk to you anymore this morning because I've got a young fellow waiting to see me.'

He paused again, listening, and then said, 'Yessir. Thank you. It's always good to talk with you too.' He hung up.

'That was Walter Hernshaw,' he said to Kyle Bode. 'Like many of my friends, he has got old. I've had that very conversation with him the last four Saturdays. And I'll tell you something: if I sent him a bill for my time – which, of course, I won't, because he hasn't hired me, and because I won't be hired by him – he would be amazed. Because he thinks that if he conducts his business on Saturday by telephone, it's not work. Now what can I do for you?'

The detective cleared his throat. 'I assume you're aware, Mr Catlett, that Mr Burley Coulter was taken from his hospital room early this morning by some unauthorized person.'

'Yes,' Wheeler said. 'Henry told me, and I'm greatly concerned about it. Burley is a cousin of mine, you know.'

'No,' the detective said, feeling another downward swerve of anxiety. 'I didn't.'

'Yes,' Wheeler said, 'his father and my father were first cousins. They were the grandsons of Jonas T. Coulter, who was the son of the first Nathan Coulter, who was, I reckon, one of the first white people to come into this country. Well, have you people figured out how Burley was taken by this unauthorized person?'

'He just went in with a gurney,' Kyle Bode said, 'and loaded Mr Coulter onto it, and covered him up to look like a corpse, and took him away – right through the middle of a busy hospital. Can you believe the audacity of it?'

'Sure, I believe it,' Wheeler said. 'But I've seen a lot of audacity in my time. Do you know who did this? Do you have clear evidence?'

'As a matter of fact, we don't. But we have a good idea who did it.'

'Who?'

'Danny Branch – who is, I'm told, Mr Coulter's son?'

'That's right,' Wheeler said. 'And you're wondering why he doesn't have his father's name.' Wheeler then told why Danny went by the name of Branch, his mother's name, rather than Coulter, which was a long and somewhat complicated story to which the detective ceased to listen.

'Anyhow,' Kyle Bode said, 'Danny Branch seems also to have disappeared. I wonder, Mr Catlett, if you have any idea where he might have gone.'

'I only know what Henry says Danny's wife told him.'

'And what did she tell him?'

'He said she said he said something about Indiana.'

'The Indiana police are watching for him,' Kyle Bode said. 'But a much likelier possibility is that he's somewhere around here – and that his father, alive or dead, is with him.'

'You're assuming, I see, that Danny Branch is the guilty

349

party.' Wheeler smiled at the detective as he would perhaps have smiled at a grandson. 'And what are you going to charge him with – impersonating an undertaker?'

Kyle Bode did not smile back. 'Kidnapping, to start with. And, after that, if Mr Coulter dies, maybe manslaughter.'

'Well,' Wheeler said. 'That's serious.'

'Mr Catlett, is Danny Branch Mr Coulter's heir?' The detective was now leaning forward somewhat aggressively in his seat.

Wheeler smiled again, seeing (and, Kyle Bode thought, appreciating) the direction of the detective's thinking. 'Yes,' he said. 'He is.'

'That makes it more likely, doesn't it?' Kyle Bode was getting the feeling that Wheeler was talking to him at such length because he liked his company. He corrected that by wondering if Wheeler, elderly as he was, knew that he was talking to a detective. He corrected that by glancing at the writing pad that Wheeler had tossed onto his desk. On one blue line of the pad he saw, inscribed without a quiver, 'Det. Kyle Bode'.

'Now your logic is pretty good there, Mr Bode,' Wheeler said. 'You've got something there that you certainly will want to think about. A man sick and unconscious, dependent on life-prolonging machinery, surely is a pretty opportunity for the medical people. "For wheresoever the carcase is, there will the eagles be gathered together." You suspect Danny Branch of experiencing a coincidence of compassion and greed in this case. And of course that suspicion exactly mirrors the suspicion that attaches to the medical industry.'

'But they were keeping him alive,' Kyle Bode said. 'Isn't that something?'

'It's something,' Wheeler said. 'It's not enough. There are many degrees and kinds of being alive. And some are worse than death.'

'But they were doing their duty.'

'Oh, yes,' Wheeler said, 'they were doing their solemn duty, as defined by themselves. And they were getting luxuriously paid. They were being merciful and they were getting rich. Let us not forget that one of the subjects of our conversation is money – the money to be spent and made in the art of medical mercy. Once the machinery gets into it, then the money gets into it. Once the money is there, then come the damned managers and the damned insurers and (I am embarrassed to say) the damned lawyers, not to mention the damned doctors who were there for the money before anybody. Before long the patient is hostage to his own cure. The beneficiary is the chattel of his benefactors.

'And first thing you know, you've got some poor sufferer all trussed up in a hospital, tied and tubed and doped and pierced, who will never draw another breath for his own benefit and who may breathe on for years. It's a bad thing to get paid for, Mr Bode, especially if you're in the business of mercy and healing and the relief of suffering.

'So there certainly is room for greed and mercy of another kind. I don't doubt that Danny, assuming he is the guilty party, has considered the cost; he's an intelligent man. Even so, I venture to say to you that you're wrong about him, insofar as you suspect him of acting out of greed. I'll give you two reasons that you had better consider. In the first place, he loves Burley. In the second place, he's not alone, and he knows it. You're thinking of a world in which legatee stands all alone, facing legator who has now become a mere obstruction between legatee and legacy. But you have thought up the wrong world. There are several of us here who belong to Danny and to whom he belongs, and we'll stand by him, whatever happens. After money, you know, we are talking about the question of the ownership of people. To whom and to what does Burley Coulter belong? If, as you allege, Danny Branch has taken Burley Coulter out of the hospital, he has done it because Burley belongs to him.'

Wheeler was no longer making any attempt to speak to the point of Kyle Bode's visit, or if he was Kyle Bode no longer saw the point. And he had begun to hear, while Wheeler talked, the sounds of the gathering of several people in the adjoining room: the opening and shutting of the outer door, the scraping of feet and of chair legs, the murmur of conscientiously subdued voices.

Kyle Bode waved his hand at Wheeler and interrupted. 'But he can't just carry him off without the hospital staff's permission.'

'Why not?' Wheeler said. 'A fellow would need their permission, I reckon, to get in. If he needs their permission to get out, he's in jail. Would you grant a proprietary right, or even a guardianship, to a hospital that you would not grant to a man's own son? I would oppose that, whatever the law said.'

'Well, anyway,' Detective Bode said, 'all I know is that the law has been broken, and I am here to serve the law.'

'But, my dear boy, you don't eat or drink the law, or sit in the shade of it or warm yourself by it, or wear it, or have your being in it. The law exists only to serve.'

'Serve what?'

'Why, all the many things that are above it. Love.'

Danny stood in the grave as he filled it, tamping the dirt in. The day in its sounding brightness stood around him. He kept to the rhythm he had established at the beginning, stopping only one more time to go to the spring for a drink. Though he sweated at his work, the day was comfortable, the suggestion of autumn palpable in the air, and he made good time.

As he filled the grave and thus slowly rose out of it, he felt again that the living man, Burley Coulter, was near him, watching and visible, except where he looked. The intimation of Burley's presence was constantly with him, at once troubling and consoling; in its newness, it kept him close to tears.

When the grave was filled, he spread and leveled the surplus dirt. He gathered leaves and scattered them over the dirt and brushed over them lightly with a leafy branch. From twenty feet, only a practiced and expectant eye would have noticed the disturbance. After the dewfall or frost of one night, it would be harder to see. After the leaves fell, there would be no trace.

He carried his tools down to the barn, folded the pot and skillet and the piece of jowl and the cornmeal into his hunting coat, making a bundle that he could sling over his shoulder as before. Again using a leafy branch, he brushed out his tracks in the dust of the barn floor. He sprinkled dust and then water over the ashes of his fire. When his departure was fully prepared, he brought water from the spring and sat down and ate quickly the rest of the food he had prepared at breakfast.

By the time he left, the place had again resumed its quiet. He walked away without disturbing it.

The absence of his truck startled Danny when he got back to where he had left it, but he stood still only for a moment before he imagined what had happened. If the wrong people had found the truck, they would have come on up the branch and found him and Burley. The right person could only have been Nathan, who would have known where the key was hidden and who would have taken the truck to the nearest unlikely place where he could put it out of sight. And so Danny shouldered his tools and his bundle again and went to the road.

353

The road was not much traveled. Only one car passed, and Danny avoided it by stepping in among the tall horseweeds that grew between the roadside and the creek. When he came to the lane that branched off under the big sycamore, he turned without hesitation into it, knowing he was right when he got to the first muddy patch where Nathan had scuffed out the tire tracks. And yet he smiled when he stepped through the door of the old barn and saw his truck. He laid his tools in with the other fencing tools in the back, and then, opening the passenger door to toss in his bundle, he saw Nathan's green shirt lying on the seat. He smiled again and took off the blue shirt he was wearing and put the green one on. He thought of burning the blue shirt, but he did not want to burn it. It was a good shirt. A derelict washing machine was leaning against the wall of the barn just inside the upper doorway, and he tossed the shirt into it. He would come back for it in a few days.

When he got home and went into the kitchen, he found Lyda's note on the table.

'We are all at Henry's and Wheeler's office,' she had written. 'Henry says for you to come, too, if you get back.' And then she had crossed out the last phrase and added, 'I reckon you are back.'

Wheeler talked at ease, leaning back in his chair, his fingers laced over his vest, telling stories of the influence of the medical industry upon the local economy. He spoke with care, forming his sentences as if he were writing them down and looking at Kyle Bode all the time, with the apparent intent to instruct him.

'And so it has become possible,' Wheeler said, 'for one of our people to spend a long life accumulating a few thousand dollars by the hardest kind of work, only to have it entirely taken away by two or three hours in an operating room and a week or two in a hospital.'

Listening, the detective became more and more anxious to regain control at least of his own participation in whatever it was that was going on. But he was finding the conversation difficult to interrupt not only because of the peculiar force that Wheeler's look and words put into it but because he did not much want to interrupt it. There was a kind of charm in the old man's earnest wish that the young man should be instructed. And when the young man did from time to time break into the conversation, it was to ask a question relative only to the old man's talk – questions that the young man, to his consternation, actually wanted to know the old man's answers to.

Finally the conversation was interrupted by Wheeler himself. 'I believe we have some people here whom you'll want to see. They are Burley's close kin and close friends, the people who know him best. Come and meet them.'

Kyle Bode had not been able to see where he was going for some time, and now suddenly he did see, and he saw that *they* had seen where he was going all along and had got there ahead of him. His mind digressed into relief that he was assigned to this case alone, that none of his colleagues could see his confusion. Conscientiously – though surely not conscientiously enough – he had sought the order that the facts of the case would make. And not only had he failed so far to achieve that clear and explainable order but he had been tempted over and over again into the weakness of self-justification. Worse than that, he had been tempted over and over again to leave, with Wheeler, the small, clear world of the law and its explanations and to enter the larger, darker world not ordered by human reasons or subject to them, in which he sensed obscurely that something might live that he, too, might be glad to have alive.

Standing with his right arm outstretched and then with his hand spread hospitably on Kyle Bode's back, Wheeler gathered him toward the door, which he opened onto a room now full of people, all of whom fell silent and looked expectantly at the detective as though he might have been a long-awaited guest of honor.

Guided still by Wheeler's hand on his back, Kyle Bode turned toward the desk to the left of the stairway door, at which sat a smiling young woman who held a stenographer's pad and pencil on her lap.

'This is Detective Kyle Bode, ladies and gentlemen,' Wheeler said. 'Mr Bode, this is Hilda Roe, our secretary.'

Hilda extended her hand to Kyle Bode, who shook it cordially.

Wheeler pressed him on to the left. 'This is Sarah Catlett, Henry's wife.

'This is my wife, Bess.

'This is Mary Penn.

'This is Art Rowanberry.

'This is his brother, Mart.

'This is Jack Penn, Jack Beechum Penn.

'This is my son, Andy.

'This is Flora Catlett, Andy's wife.

'You know Henry.

'This is Lyda Branch, Danny's wife.

'This is Hannah Coulter.

'And this is Hannah's husband, Nathan.'

One by one, they silently held out their hands to Kyle Bode, who silently shook them.

He and Wheeler had come almost all the way around the room. There was a single chair against the wall to the left of the door to Wheeler's office. Wheeler offered this chair, with a gesture, to Kyle Bode, who thanked him and sat down. Wheeler then seated himself in the chair between Hilda Roe's desk and the stair door.

'Mr Bode,' Wheeler said. 'All of us here are relatives or friends of Burley Coulter.'

The secretary, Kyle Bode noticed, now began to write in shorthand on her pad. It was noon and past, and he had learned nothing that he could tell to any superior or any reporter who might ask.

'Nathan,' Wheeler went on, 'is Burley's nephew.'

'Nephew?' Kyle Bode said, turning to Nathan, who looked back at him with a look that was utterly direct and impenetrable.

'That's right.'

'I assume you know him well.'

'I've known him for fifty-three years.'

'You've been neighbors that long?'

'We've been neighbors all my life, except for a while back there in the forties when I was away.'

'You were in the service?'

'Yes.'

The detective coughed. 'Mr Coulter, my job, I guess, is to find your uncle. Do you know where he is? Or where Danny Branch is?'

The eyes that confronted him did not look down, nor did they change. And there was no apparent animosity in the reply: 'I couldn't rightly say I do.'

'Now them two was a pair,' Mart Rowanberry said, as though he were not interrupting but merely contributing to the conversation. 'There's been a many a time when nobody knew where them two was.'

'I see. And why was that?'

'They're hunters!' Art Rowanberry said, a little impatiently, in the tone of one explaining the obvious. 'They'd be off somewheres in the woods.'

'A many a time,' Mart said, 'he has called me out after bedtime to go with him, and I would get up and go. A many a time.'

'You are friends, then, you and Mr Coulter?'

'We been friends, you might as well say, all along. Course, now, he's older than I am. Fifteen years or so, wouldn't it be, Andy?'

The Catlett by the name of Andy nodded, and Lyda said, 'Yes.'

And then she said, 'You knew him all your life, and then finally he didn't know you, did he, Mart?'

'He didn't know you?' said Kyle Bode.

'Well, sir,' Mart said, 'I come up on him and Danny and Nathan while they was fencing. Burley was asleep, propped up against the end post. I shook him a little, and he looked up. He says, "Howdy, old bud." I seen he was bewildered. I says, "You don't know me, do you?" He says, "I know I ought to, but I don't." I says, "Well, if you was to hear old Bet open up on a track, who'd you say it was?" And he says, "Why, hello, Mart!" '

There was a moment then in which nobody spoke, as if everybody there was seeing what Mart had told.

Kyle Bode waited for that moment to pass, and then he said, 'This Bet you spoke of' – he knew he was a fool, but he wanted to know – 'was she a dog?' It was not his conversation he was in; he could hardly think by what right he was in it.

'She was a blue tick mostly,' Mart said. 'A light, sort of cloudy-colored dog, with black ears and a white tip to her tail. And a good one.' He paused, perhaps seeing the dog again. 'I bought her from Braymer Hardy over by Goforth. But I expect,' he said, smiling at Kyle Bode, 'that was before your time.' And then, as if conscious of having strayed from the subject, he said,

'But, now, Burley Coulter. They never come no finer than Burley Coulter.'

Another small silence followed, in which everybody assented to Mart's tribute.

'Burley Coulter,' Wheeler said, 'was born in 1895. He was the son of Dave and Zelma Coulter. He had one older brother, Jarrat, who died in the July of 1967.

'Burley attended the Goforth School as long as he could be kept there – not long enough for him to finish the eighth grade, which he thought might have taken him forever. His fame at Willow Hole was not for scholarship but for being able to fight as well on the bottom as on the top.'

Wheeler spoke at first to Kyle Bode. And then he looked down at his hands and thought a minute. When he spoke again, he spoke to and for them all.

'He was wild, Burley was, as a young fellow. For me, he had all the charm of an older boy who was fine looking and wild and friendly to a younger cousin. I loved him and would have followed him anywhere. Though he was wild, he didn't steal or lie or misrepresent himself.

'He never was a gambler. Once I said to him, "Burley, I know you've drunk and fought and laid out at night in the woods. How come you've never gambled?" And he said, "No son of a bitch is going to snap his fingers and pick up *my* money."

'His wildness was in his refusal, or his inability, to live within other people's expectations. He would be hunting sometimes when his daddy wanted him at work. He would dance all night and neglect to sober up before he came home.

'He was called into the army during the First World War. By then he was past twenty, long past being a boy, and he had his limits. He hit an officer for calling him a stupid, briarjumping Kentucky bastard. He might have suffered any one of those insults singly. But he felt that, given all together, they paid off any obligation he had to the officer, and he hit him. He hit him, as he said, "thoroughly". I asked him, "How thoroughly?" And he said, "Thoroughly enough." They locked him up a while for that.

'He was acting, by then, as a man of conscious principle. He didn't believe that anybody had the right, by birth or appointment, to lord it over anybody else.

'He broke his mother's heart, as she would sometimes say – as a young man of that kind is apt to do. But when she was old and only the two of them were left at home, he was devoted to her and took dutiful care of her, and she learned to depend on him.

'Though he never gave up his love of roaming about, he had become a different man from the one he started out to be. I'm not sure when that change began. Maybe it was when Nathan and Tom started following him around when they were little boys, after their mother died. And then, when Danny came along, Burley took his proper part in raising him. He took care of his mother until she died. He was a good and loyal partner to his brother. He was a true friend to all his friends.

'He was too late, as he thought and said, in acknowledging Danny as his son. But he did acknowledge him, and made him his heir, and brought him and Lyda home with him to live. And so at last he fully honored his marriage in all but name to Kate Helen.

'He was sometimes, but never much in a public way, a fiddler. And he was always a singer. His head was full of scraps and bits of songs that he sang out at work to say how he felt or to make himself feel better. Some of them, I think, he made up himself.

'From some morning a long time ago, I remember standing

beside a field where Burley was plowing with a team of mules
and hearing his voice all of a sudden lift up into the quiet:

> *Ain't going to be much longer, boys,*
> *Ain't going to be much longer.*
> *Soon it will be dinnertime*
> *And we will feed our hunger.*

'And he had another song he sometimes sang up in the
afternoon, when the day had got long and he was getting tired:

> *Look down that row;*
> *See how far we've got to go.*
> *It's a long time to sundown, boys,*
> *Long time to sundown.*

'What was best in him, maybe, was the pleasure he took in
pleasurable things. We'll not forget his laughter. He looked at
the world and found it good.

'"I've never learned anything until I had to," he often said, and
so confessed himself a man like other men. But he learned what
he had to, and he changed, and so he made himself exceptional.

'He was, I will say, a faithful man.'

It was a lonely gathering for Henry Catlett. He was riding as a
mere passenger in a vehicle that he ought to have been guiding –
that would not be guided if he did not guide it – and yet he had
no better idea than the others where it might be going.

So far, he thought, he had done pretty well. He had gathered
all parties to the case – except, of course, for the principals – here
under his eye for the time being. How long he would need to
keep them here or how long the various ones of them would

stay, he did not know. He knew that Lyda had left a note for Danny where he would see it when he came home, telling him to join them here. But when Danny might come home, Henry did not know. Nobody, anyhow, had said anything about eating dinner, though it was past noon. He was grateful for that.

Either he would be able to keep them there long enough, or he would not. Either Danny would show up, or he would not – wearing, or not wearing, that very regrettable blue shirt. At moments, as in a bad dream, he had wondered what it would portend if Danny showed up with fresh earth caked on his shoes. He wondered what concatenation of circumstances and lucky guesses might give Detective Bode some purchase on his case. It occurred to Henry to wish that Danny had given somebody a little notice of what he was going to do. But if Danny had been the kind of man to give such notice, he would not have done what he had done. It did not occur to Henry to regret that Danny had done what he had done.

As Wheeler spoke, his auditors sat looking at him, or down at their hands, or at the floor. From time to time, tears shone in the eyes of one or another of them. But no tear fell, no hand was lifted, no sound was uttered. And Henry was grateful to them all – grateful to his father, who was presuming on his seniority to keep them there; grateful to the others for their disciplined and decorous silence.

Out the corner of his eye, Henry could see his brother, Andy, slouched in his chair in the corner and watching also. Henry would have given a lot for a few minutes of talk with Andy. They would not need to say much.

Henry would have liked, too, to know what Lyda thought, and Hannah and Nathan. But all he could do was wait and watch.

And without looking directly at him, he watched Kyle Bode, partly with amusement. The detective's questions to Nathan and to Mart and now his attention to Wheeler so obviously exceeded his professional interest in the case that something like a grin occurred in Henry's mind, though his face remained solemn.

'He was, I will say, a faithful man,' Wheeler said.

And then Henry heard the street door open and footsteps start slowly up the stairs.

Wheeler heard them too, and stopped. Kyle Bode heard them; glancing around the room, he saw that all of them were listening. He saw that Lyda and Hannah were holding hands. Silence went over the whole room now and sealed them under it, as under a stone.

The footsteps rose slowly up the stairs, crossed the narrow hallway, hesitated a moment at the door. And then the knob turned, the door opened, and Danny Branch stepped into the room, wearing a shirt green as the woods, his well-oiled shoes as clean as his cap. He was smiling. To those seated around the book-lined old walls, he had the aspect and the brightness of one who had borne the dead to the grave, and filled the grave to the brim, and received the dead back into life again. The knuckles of Lyda's and Hannah's interlaced fingers were white; nobody made a sound.

And then Henry, whose mind seemed to him to have been racing a long time to arrive again there in the room, which now was changed, said quietly, 'Well, looks like you made it home from Indiana.'

And suddenly Kyle Bode was on his feet, shouting at Danny, as if from somewhere far outside that quiet room. 'Where *have* you been? What have you done with him? He's dead, isn't he, and you have buried him somewhere in these end-of-nowhere, godforsaken hills and hollows?'

'I had an account to settle with one of my creditors,' Danny said, still smiling, to Kyle Bode.

'Sit down, Mr Bode,' Henry said, still quietly. 'You don't have the right to ask him anything. For that, you have got to have evidence. And you haven't got a nickel's worth. You haven't got any.'

The room was all ashimmer now with its quiet. There was a strangely burdening weight in Kyle Bode that swayed him toward that room and what had happened in it. He saw his defeat, and he was not even sorry. He felt small and lost, somewhere beyond the law. He sat down.

'And so,' Wheeler said, 'peace to our neighbor, Burley Coulter. May God rest his soul.'

At Home
(1981)

And so, past the heavy gunnery, the bombs, the blood and fire of Bastogne and beyond, there was this: the creek valley opening below him as he rose step by step up the two-track road. Since the days and nights of combat, before the wound that set him free of the army and free very nearly of this world, he had borne in the back of his mind for going on forty years, as a sort of comment on everything else, the clamor of the big gun he had served, of the guns that accompanied his, of the guns that answered. Against that immense sounding, so long ago, so little receded, the small valley holds its plea, frail as a flower, and as undeniable.

The valley had widened below him now so that when he stopped and looked back the whole legend of it had come clear: the house backed against the near slope, the cellar and smoke-house, the barns on the near and far sides of the creek, the creek itself, Sand Ripple, twisting and shining between parallel rows of still-leafless trees on its way to the river, the inverted arc of the footbridge swung across at the edge of the woods upstream. The valley revealed itself now as a bowl, in the greatness of the country less than a cup, as familiar to him as the palm of his hand.

It was a small place, humble enough in all its aspects, except for an ordinary splendor that would possess it from time to time in every season. And it was, as some would have thought it, remote, tucked away in one of the folds of the much-folded landscape surrounding the town, also small and humble, of

Port William. A stranger driving along the river road would not have suspected the existence of such a place, would have noticed no doubt the stand of trees that hovered about the creek mouth, but probably not at all the narrow opening, near the Sand Ripple bridge, of the lane that followed the creek upstream through the woods to the abrupt fall of light onto the opened valley.

He was Arthur Rowanberry, known as Art, whose family, ever intent on taking its living from the place, which the place, mostly hillside, yielded to them reluctantly, had forgot the number of their generations on it.

He was walking up the hill road to the Orchard Ridge, as they still called it, though the last of its apple trees was long gone from living memory, where he would count the calving cows and put out their daily ration of hay. His brother Martin, Mart for short, had gone up in the early morning to see about them, driving the tractor while the ground was frozen so that the heavy machine would do no harm to the road. Otherwise, Mart too would have walked. Unlike their eventual successors, four different owners in twenty-five years, who would wear the road to a raw wound by driving on it in all weather, no Rowanberry ever drove a wheeled vehicle up the hill when the ground was soft.

By the calendar it was almost spring. The days were lengthening, a tinge of green was showing in the pastures, and the buds were fattening on the water maples. But on that day the season was halted by a cold spell. A steady, bitter wind was blowing from the north, hard against his back as he came up into it and turned the sharp bend in the road. He warmed his hands by shifting them, first one and then the other, from his stick to a pocket.

But he liked weather, anyhow most weather. He liked its freedom from walls, its way of overcoming all obstructions and filling the world. And he liked walking, which was another kind of freedom: no preparation, no expense, just get up onto your legs and go. What he had liked best in the army was the marching, the passing through country, with the others, nearly all younger than he, stepping in the same cadence all around. But a greater pleasure was in walking by himself. There was pleasure also in the company of old Preacher, the gray-muzzled hound who was walking for the time being at Art's heels. Preacher knew the way, even the errand, as well as Art did, and like Art he was too old for needless haste.

With Mart away, at Port William or Hargrave or somewhere, doing whatever it was he did on Saturday afternoon, Art began his walk plenty early, giving himself time. It was not that he needed time, so early in the day, for anything in particular. He needed time only to take his time, to have time for the day and the weather, to walk in his own time, unhurried, with no reason not to stop and look around, or to take a 'long cut' off the knapped stone of the road and into the woods. In his own time, time asked nothing of him except to live in it and to keep alert, to watch, to see what he could see, the day and its light coming to him unburdened.

He had never minded company. He had always liked to be in the field, in the barn, at a wood sawing or hog killing, with a crew of friends and kin. Even then, at the age of seventy-six, he would hurry to get in on a lift, to do his part. 'Many hands make light work,' he liked to say, for he knew it was true. But to be alone was a different happiness. At times it was almost a merriment, when he liked his thoughts.

Some thoughts that had gathered to him in his time gave him no pleasure. There was always something that had to be subtracted from pleasure, 'always something', as he would say now and again, 'to take the joy out of life'. But he had acquired also many thoughts that gave him joy.

His thoughts were placed and peopled, and they seemed to come to him on their own, without any effort of his to call them up. He would think of the present day and place, as now, as the prospect widened below him and he felt in his flesh and in the breadth of the country the full, free stroke of the wind across the ridges.

'We'll have to face it, coming down,' he said to Preacher. And then he stopped and looked about. As if to console the dog he said, 'Well, maybe it'll fair up tomorrow.'

Or it would happen that another time would open to him, sometimes from long ago, and he would see his grandmaw and grandpaw Rowanberry at the log house back on the ridge, and the old life they had lived there when he was a boy. He would see their going among the fields and along the roads, mostly afoot even when they went to town, and the network of paths that connected house and barn and corn crib and hog lot, well and cellar and smokehouse. The life they lived there he recognized, even in his childhood, as old beyond memory, little changed in so much time beyond their marking of the ground. Some of the marks they left were wounds in the steeper land, slow to heal, for hard times and the family's unrelenting will to endure had driven them to crop the slopes, and the rains had imposed their verdict. Art knew the stern requirement that his elders, remembered and forgotten, should survive if they could, as he knew the inexorable judgment of weather and time. He saw the fault, knew the wrong, yet placed no blame. They had paid to live as resignedly as they had expected to die. In his thoughts they went from day to day to day in their steady work, eating their large and frugal meals, going to bed precisely at darkfall, rising to work again long before daylight even in summer. Of the things they needed they grew and made much, purchased little.

Art had been the first grandchild, and the elder Rowanberrys, his father's parents, made much of him. As his younger brothers and sisters came along, and at the rare times when he could escape the chores that were assigned to him almost as soon as he could walk, then oftener as his grandparents grew older and had need of him, he liked to leave the house down in the creek valley and go up to stay days and nights at a time at the old house on the ridge.

It was a house of two tall rooms broadly square with a wide hallway between, a long upstairs room under the pitch of the roof, two rock chimneys at either end with wide fireplaces, and at the back a large lean-to kitchen, weatherboarded. The house was finely made, the logs hewed straight and square, the corners so perfectly mitered that you could not insert a knife blade into the joints. The rafters were straight poles, saplings, notched and pegged together at the peak with the same artistry as elsewhere. When he had stayed overnight, Art slept upstairs in the drafty, unceiled attic room illuminated in the daytime only by the light that leaked under the eaves. The wind too came under them. He had waked some mornings when blown-in snow had whitened the covers of the bed.

Of the old house in the time of its human life, before its abandonment after the deaths of his grandparents, he remembered everything. Of his grandparents, their life, and all they remembered and told him, he remembered much. Whether or not he thought their thoughts, he thought at least the thoughts that belonged to such a house and such a life.

And so when he went into the army in 1942, he passed from

a world as old and elemental nearly as it had ever been into a world as ruthlessly new as by then it had managed to become.

He was the oldest child, the eldest son. It was his duty, as it appeared to him, to go first to the war, and by doing so to save his younger brothers from the draft – though at this he was not entirely successful. Early in the new year following the attack on Pearl Harbor, he volunteered. He was thirty-seven that year, old for a common soldier, which the younger men, the boys, he served with never let him forget. Soon enough the younger ones were calling him 'Pappy', which he accepted, amused to know that he was old enough in fact to have been father to most of them, and recognizing with at least tolerance that to some of them the name alluded to his rural speech and demeanor, his origin, as they put it, 'at the end of nowhere'.

But they knew him soon enough as a man by a measure that few of them had met or would meet. The rigor of basic training he took in stride, finding it no harder and sometimes easier than the work he was accustomed to at home. He did not have to be taught to fire a rifle, or to fire it accurately. Nobody had to urge him to keep to the pace of a long march. Sleeping on the ground, he rested well. He never complained of the weather. When they were called upon to use an axe or a mattock or a spade, he was the exemplary man. Boys who had never so much as seen an axe would be astonished, watching him work. 'You can tell a chopper by his chips,' he said to them, and they stood around to admire him as he made the big chips fly. He might, as one of his officers told him, have been promoted as high as sergeant, but he submitted to authority without envying or desiring it.

When he got home from the war, still recovering from his wound, he knew his life was a gift, not so probable as he had once thought, and yet unquestionable as that of any tree, not to be hoarded or clutched at, not to be undervalued or too much prized, for there were many days now lost back in time when he could have died as easily and unremarkably as a fly. It was a life now simply to be lived, accepting hardships and pleasures, joys and griefs equally as they came.

His time in the war had been a different and a separate time, his life then a different life. The memory of it remained always with him, or always near, and yet that time lay behind him, intact and separate as an island in the sea, divided from the time before and the time after.

Returning home from the war, he returned to memory. He returned to the time of his own life that he felt to be continuous from long before his birth until long past his death. He came back to the old place and its constant reminding, awakening memories and memories of memories as he walked in and across the tracks of those who had preceded him. He knew then how his own comings and goings were woven into the invisible fabric of the land's history and its human life.

He was accompanied again, at work and in his thoughts forever after, by people he had always known: his brother, Mart, with whom he lived on in their parents' house, batching, after their parents were gone; his sister, Sudie, and her husband, Pascal Sowers, who were neighbors; the Coulter brothers, Jarrat and Burley; Jarrat's son Nathan and Nathan's wife, Hannah; and then Burley's son, Danny Branch, and Lyda, Danny's wife; and Elton Penn and his wife, Mary. They were a membership, as Burley liked to call it, a mere gathering, not held together by power and organization like the army, but by kinship, friendship, history, memory, kindness, and affection – who were apt to be working together, in various combinations, according to need, and even, always, according to pleasure.

And then, after Andy Catlett's homecoming and settlement near Port William in 1965, because of Andy's cousinship to the Coulters and his friendships from his boyhood with the Penns and the Rowanberrys, Andy and his family became members of the membership and took part in the work-swapping and the old, long knowing in common.

Between Art and Andy there grew, within the larger membership, a sort of kinship, founded upon Art's long memory and his knowledge of old ways, and upon their mutual affection for the Port William countryside in all of its times, seasons, and weathers. They would often be together, at work or at rest, Art talking, Andy listening and asking. Their best times were Sunday mornings or afternoons, when they would travel together on foot or horseback or with a team and wagon, moving at large, sometimes at random, wherever their interest took them. Or they would trace out the now-pathless way, around the hill and up a hollow supposed to be haunted, that the young Rowanberrys had walked to school. Or they would follow the sunken track, long disused, that led from the log house on the ridge down into the river valley where it met the road to town. Or they would pick out other disused ways connecting old landmarks. As they went along, Art's parents and grandparents and other old ones he remembered, or they remembered, would appear in his mind, and he would tell about them: how his grandpaw would tell you a big tale and you could hear him laugh a mile; how old man Will Keith, a saw-logger, who worked a big horse and a little one, would take hold of the little horse's singletree to help him on a hard pull; how Art's own father, Early Rowanberry, never rode uphill behind a team even when the wagon was empty. By then Art's distant travels were long past. On his and Andy's Sunday journeys, having no place far to go, they were never in a hurry. It was never too early or too late to stop and talk. And when Andy needed help, if Art knew it, he would be there. 'Do you need anything I got?'

After so many days, so many miles, so many remindings, so much remembering and telling, Andy understood how precisely placed and populated Art's mind was, how like it was to a sort of timeless crossroads where the living and the dead met and recognized one another and passed on their ways, and how rare it was, how singular and once-for-all. When Art would be gone at last from this world, Port William would have no such mind, would be known in no such way, ever again.

Andy Catlett, under the same mortal terms of once for all, has kept Art's mind alive in his own. Some of Art's memories Andy remembers. As he follows and crosses Art's old footings over the land, adding his own passages to the unseen web of the land's history, some of those old ones, who were summoned by reminding into Art's mind, still again and again will appear in Andy's.

And so it is into Andy's thought, into his imagining, that Art has come walking up the hill on that bitter March day thirty years ago. Andy now is an old man, remembering an old man, once his elder and his teacher, with whom he is finally of an age.

Art was wearing a winter jacket, which in its youth had closed with a zipper down the front, but which, the zipper failing, he had overhauled with a set of large buttons and buttonholes, strongly but not finely sewn.

There may have been a time, Andy thinks, when Art was skilled at such work. From his time in the army and before, he had been used to doing for himself whatever he needed done.

His hands, hard-used and now arthritic, had become awkward at needlework, and yet he had continued to mend his clothes, pleasing himself both by his thrift and by the durability of his work. When the legs of his coveralls were worn and torn past mending, he lopped off the bottom half, hemmed up the top half, and thus made a light jacket that lasted several more years. When he needed a rope, he braided a perfectly adequate one with salvaged baler twine. He thus maintained a greater intimacy between himself and the things he wore and used, was more all-of-a-piece, than anybody else Andy ever knew.

As he climbed the hill, still keeping to the graveled track, old Preacher still walking behind with his head and tail down, Art watched the creek valley close on his right as the river valley opened on his left. As the country widened around him he breathed larger breaths. And the higher he went, the flatter the horizon looked, in contrast to the alternation of hill and hollow in the view from the creek bottom. He reached a place where he could look out and down over the tops of the bare trees instead of through them. He stopped again then and took in the whole visible length of the larger valley, from the gray, still-winterish slope that closed it a couple of miles upstream to the low rampart, blue with distance, that lay across it down toward the mouth of the river.

He turned presently and went on, the wind pushing him. Soon the track leveled, and he and the old dog were walking along the crest of the ridge. He was walking – as Andy, on his walks with him, had from time to time realized – both through the place and through his consciousness of the presence and the past of it, his recognition of its marks and signs, as his movement through it altered the aspect of it.

He and time were moving at about the same pace. He was neither hurried by it nor hurrying to catch it, his thoughts coming whole as he thought them, with nothing left out or left over. If he seemed to be getting ahead of his thoughts, he stopped and waited.

He was passing a high point out to his left above the river valley. In a certain place out there were what he had known for many years to be the graves of people who lived and were forgotten long before the time they might have been called Indians. He knew what the graves were because, back before the war, on a similar height of ground above Willow Run, a professor from Lexington had come and carefully dug up some graves of the same kind. Art went to see them while they were open, with the remains of skeletons lying in them. That taught him what to look for, and he found these on his own place. The giveaway was flagstones edged up in the shape of a box, hard to see if you didn't know what you were looking for. He rarely spoke of them, and he showed them to nobody. He told Andy about them, indicating with a look and a nod about where they were, but he never showed him. He rarely went near them himself, so as to leave them undisturbed, to leave no track or mark to expose them to indifference or dishonor. Looking at those opened graves, as Andy knew, Art had felt both awe and shame: so long a sleep pried in upon, so old a secret finally told.

The place of the graves now was behind him. They passed from his thought. But he was presently reminded of them again because he was looking into the opening of the Katy's Branch valley where, somewhere in the old woods, all of Burley Coulter that could die lay in a grave formed on the pattern of those ancient ones. This was the sort of thing the elders of Port William were apt to know without knowing quite how they knew it. But Art, with the rest of the old membership, had been in Wheeler and Henry Catlett's law office down in Hargrave the day Danny Branch, Burley's son, returned from somewhere, nobody ever said where, after Burley's disappearance from a Louisville hospital where he had been lying unwakable, kept alive by machines. Though nobody told where Danny had been, in Port William, where people didn't have much that was 'their own business', everybody who cared to know knew. And Art knew Danny's mind, as he had known Burley's.

Old Preacher, who still had been walking behind Art, suddenly became young again, bawling and flinging gravel behind him as simultaneously a fox squirrel sprang from the grass, flying his tail like a flag, and just ahead of the dog leapt to the trunk of a fair-sized hickory at the edge of the woods. Art heard the scramble of claws on bark. He followed the dog down through the sloping pasture to the tree.

Preacher, who was a coon hound in fair standing, had a sideline of squirrel hunting that he liked to indulge, to keep in practice maybe for worthier game. He reared against the tree and covered the whole visible world with chop-mouth cries of extreme excitement and longing.

'That's a squirrel,' Art told him. 'It ain't a bear.'

He felt reflexively for the .22 pistol that he often carried with him on such trips, and then realized with a small pang of regret that the pistol was still hanging in its shoulder holster from its nail by the kitchen door. But he did anyhow carefully study the tree, and he found the squirrel lying very still along a branch high up. Preacher stood looking expectantly from the squirrel to Art and back again. His expression appeared to turn indignant when he understood that Art was not going to shoot the squirrel.

'Well, I'm sorry, old dog,' Art said. 'I know it ain't right to disappoint you.'

But all the same he was glad he had forgot the pistol. Though he would gladly have cooked and eaten the squirrel, he discovered, as he more often had done as he had grown older, that he did not want to kill it.

He said to the squirrel, 'I reckon you're having a lucky day.' And then he said, 'I reckon every day you've had so far has been lucky.'

Preacher, born again to the life of a hunting dog with important business in the woods, turned and trotted off downhill among the trees. And that was the last Art saw of him until he turned up again at suppertime.

During the little while of Preacher's excitement and then his indignation, that particular slope of the ridge seemed to exist only in reference to the episode of the squirrel. But then the sound of the wind settled back upon it as a kind of quiet. Art looked about and took notice of where he was.

The whole Rowanberry place lay in his mind, less like a map than like a book, its times stratified upon it like pages. He remembered the seasons, crops, and events of the years he had known, of which almost always he remembered the numbers. And the living pages of his memory, as if blown or thumbed open, showed past days as they were, as perhaps they are.

In 1937, in the summer after the big flood, they grew a crop of tobacco on the slope above the hickory where Preacher had treed the squirrel. The summer of 1936, as if to require in justice the terrible flood of the next January, had been terribly dry. The country had been dying of thirst day after day and week after week. All the hard-won product of the farm had amounted almost to nothing. By the spring of 1937, the Rowanberrys seemed to have made it through by luck, if luck was what they wanted to call it. That was the time when Art's father began telling people who asked how he was, 'Here by being careful.'

But in the late winter and early spring, as people then did, as they had to do, Early Rowanberry and his four sons – Art, Mart, Jink, and Stob – cut the trees from the slope where Art would be standing and remembering in the cold March wind forty-four years later. They dragged off the logs and poles, burnt the brush, plowed and worked the soil, piled the rocks, and in a wet spell in late May, set out by hand the tobacco crop that would have to do for both that year and the year before.

The growing season of 1937 gave them enough rain, and they made a good crop. Art, as if standing and looking in both present and past, saw it in all its stages, from the fragile, white-stemmed plants of the setting-out to the broad, gold-ripe leaves at harvest.

The four sons and their father had kept faith with it, doing the hard handwork of it, through the whole summer. An old man already as they saw him and in fact getting to be old, but never forgetting the hard year before and other hard ones before that, their father drove them into the work, setting a never-slackening pace in the tobacco patch and everywhere else. As if in self-defense, the sons cherished every drink of water, every bite of food, every hour of sleep in fact and in anticipation, and they made the most of everything that was funny.

Just one time, in the midst of a breathless afternoon in July, Jink, who was the hardest of them in his thoughts, cried out, 'God *damn,* old man, where the hell's the fire!' It would have been a cry of defiance if Early Rowanberry had been defiable. He might as well have been deaf. He went on. The three brothers went on. Jink himself went on. His outcry hung in the air behind them like the call of some utterly solitary animal.

And then it was getting on toward the noon of a day late in

August. By then half the crop had been cut and safely housed in the barns. They had been cutting all morning, going hard, all of them by then moved by the one urgent need to save from the weather, from the possible hailstorm always on their minds, the crop by so much effort finally made. Half an hour earlier Sudie, the brothers' one sister, had brought a cooked dinner in two cloth-covered baskets and had left it in the barn farther back on the ridge. They quit cutting when they saw her pass and began loading a sled with cut tobacco to take with them when they went to the barn to eat.

They were letting Stob, the youngest, be the teamster, driving the horses and the sled as the others loaded. The tobacco they were loading had been cut the morning before and was well wilted. They put on a big load. Their father said, 'All right, boys, let's go eat,' and Stob spoke to the team.

Standing on the hillside a little behind the sled, Art saw it all as he still would see it when he thought of it in all the years that followed. Stob was sixteen that summer, a well-grown big stout boy who hadn't yet thought everything he needed to think. When he started for the barn he ought to have got on the uphill side of the load. But he stayed on its downhill side, practically under it, walking beside it with the lines in his hands. Maybe all four of the others were ready to tell him, but they never got a chance. All of a sudden the uphill runner slid up onto the ridge of a row, the ground steepened a little under the downhill runner, and the load started over. Stob, who was then stronger than he was smart and too proud of his strength, didn't stop the horses and run out of the way as he should have done, but just threw his shoulder against the load as if to prop it and kept driving. He pretty soon found out how strong he actually was, for the load, the hundreds of pounds of it, pushed him to the ground and piled on top him. The old team stopped and stood unflustered as if what had happened had happened before. The four men were already hurrying.

They unburied Stob, and Art would remember with a kind of wonder how deliberately they went at it. They righted the sled and loaded it again as, carefully, not to mistreat the tobacco, but quickly enough, they delivered Stob back again to the daylight. When finally he rolled over and stood up, as if getting out of bed, he was wetter with sweat than before and red in the face and wild-eyed, his straw hat crushed on the ground and his hair more or less on end.

Art said, 'What was you thinking down under there?'

And Stob said, as if Art ought to have known, 'I was thinking the air was getting mighty *scarce* down under there!'

Even their father laughed. At every tobacco harvest after that, down through the years, they would tell the story. And they would laugh.

In the wind, in the gray, cold light, Art went back to the ridge-top and the road. His thoughts returned to his amusement at Preacher. He had given a good deal of study to the old dog's character, and the story of the squirrel would stay on his mind. He told Andy about it, and about other events of that journey, for it had been a good one, a few days later. 'I reckon he don't have much time for a man without a pistol.'

He went on back the ridge, the road passing in front of the old log house, now a ruin, the doors and windows gaping, the hearths long ago dug up by descendants of a family of slaves who had once belonged to Art's family. Those descendants, Rowanberrys themselves since freedom, believed that during the Civil War money and other valuables had been buried under a stone of one of the hearths. Art and Mart told them to dig away, perfectly assured that no Rowanberry had ever owned anything greatly worth either burying or digging up. As they expected, the digging was motivated entirely by superstition, but since then the hearthstones had remained overturned onto the puncheons of the floors. The chimneys too had begun to crumble. All of the old making that remained intact were the cellar and the well. For a long time two apple trees had lived on at the edge of what had been the garden, still bearing good early apples that Art and Mart came up to pick every year. But life finally had departed from the trees as it had from the house.

Art went on to the wire gap into the pasture where they wintered the cows and let himself through. Adjoining at one of its corners the tobacco barn where the hay was stored, the pasture was a field of perhaps twenty acres now permanently in grass. It was enclosed by the best fence remaining on the place, but even that fence was a patchwork, the wire stapled to trees that had grown up in the line, spliced and respliced, weak spots here and there reinforced by cut thorn bushes and even an old set of bedsprings.

The place was running down. Art and Mart were getting old, and the family had no younger member who wanted such a farm or even a better one. After so many years as the Rowanberry place, it was coming to the time when finally it would have to be sold. Mart perhaps already would have sold it, had the decision belonged to him alone. Art so far had pushed away even the thought. He needed his interest in the farm. 'A fellow needs *something* to be interested in.' He had pushed away the thought of selling, as Andy still supposes, because so far he *could* not think of it. He could not distinguish between the place and himself.

But the place, its life as a farm, continued only by force of old habit. The two brothers went on from day to day, from year to year, doing only as they always had done. They did nothing new, and as their strength declined they did less. They extended the longevity of fences and buildings by stopgaps, patching and mending, and by the thought, repeated over and over, 'I reckon it'll last as long as it needs to.'

Their earnings in any year were not great, but they spent far less than they earned. They grew most of their food, or gathered it from the woods and the river. They heated the house with wood they cut and split still as they always had. They were thrifty and careful. Mart kept a pretty good used car and went places for pleasure. Art stayed mostly at home and spent, by the standards of the time, almost nothing.

There were ten cows and, as of that morning, four calves. The cows were Nancy, Keeny, Yellowback, Baby Sitter, Droopy Horn, Brown Eyes, Doll, Beulah, Rose, and Troublemaker. They had their tails to the wind, grazing to not much purpose the short grass. The four calves were lying together, curled up against the chill.

Seeing only nine of the cows, Art set off to find the tenth. He crossed over the ridge to the south side. There, in a swale affording some shelter, he found Troublemaker, afterbirth still hanging, and her still-wet heifer calf uneasily standing.

'Well, look a-there what you've done!' Art said to the cow. 'Ain't you proud of yourself!'

He said to the calf, 'You're going to make it, looks like.'

He didn't go near them. The cow would be ruled entirely now by the instinct to protect her calf. Her long acquaintance with Art would not have mattered. Not to her. She wasn't named Troublemaker for nothing.

'Well,' he said to her, 'I'll leave it to you.' He turned around and went to the barn.

The timbers and poles that framed the barn had come from the nearby woods. The posts, girders, and top plates all had been squared by somebody – Grandpaw Rowanberry, Art thought – who had been a good hand with a broadaxe, for the work was well done. The barn, in its time, had been a fair example of good work with rough materials. Its posts rested on footers of native rock, and it had been roofed originally with shingles rived out of white oak blocks also from the woods of the place. The only milled lumber had been the poplar siding. Now the barn, like the pasture fence, had become as much a product of the last-ditch cunning of making-do as of the skills that first had built it.

From the hay rick, by now much diminished, Art carried five bales one at a time into the pasture, spacing them widely, cutting the strings with his knife, dividing and scattering the hay, so that even Doll, the timidest cow, would get her share.

Having scattered the hay, he stood a while watching, to feel the culmination of his trip and the satisfaction of hunger fed. Soon it would be warmer and the new grass would come. The time of surviving would be past, and the cows and calves would begin to thrive.

On out beyond the winter pasture, the upland narrowed and then widened again, becoming what they called the Silver Mine Ridge. A long time ago Uncle Jackson Jones, an old man nobody knew much about, had passed through the country, digging for buried money. A number of his excavations were in the Port William neighborhood. Andy Catlett and a few other old men still know where they are, shallowed by time to mere depressions in the woods. The largest was the one on the Rowanberry place. Art's father had worked on that one when he was a boy. Uncle Jackson hired several of the local boys to help him dig. They made a hole long and wide and deep enough to bury a small house or a large corn crib. They had to use a ladder to get to the bottom of it.

While they were digging, Early Rowanberry remembered, another stranger, 'a man with a needle', happened by. The 'needle', Andy thinks, must have been the arrow on some sort of dial, some instrument of geological divining. The man with the needle took readings round and about. He then told Uncle Jackson that if he would dig a second hole, only a short distance away, he would strike a vein of pure silver. But Uncle Jackson said no, he was after coined money and nothing else. The man with the needle departed and was never seen again. The diggers dug on. But the only silver yielded by their big hole was in the coins paid out by Uncle Jackson to his crew of boys.

Every evening when they climbed out of the hole they left their picks and spades, spud bars, grubbing hoes, and other tools at the bottom. One night a terrific rain fell, collapsing the sides of the hole and burying the tools, which put an end to Uncle Jackson's work at that place.

'After that,' Art said to Andy, 'it was anyhow a tool mine.'

But nobody ever went back to dig for the tools.

'Too much digging for a few tools. And, I reckon maybe, too few tools to dig with.'

When the wind, pressing through his clothes, at last laid its cold touch against his flesh, Art turned to face it, buttoned the top button of his jacket, and started back the way he had come. Behind him, the small herd of cows, filling and warming themselves with hay for the night, seemed to him for the time being to have been completed, and he was free to go.

He went back the way he had come, again taking his time, seeing everything now from its opposite side. It was as though he made the place dimensional and substantial by his walking both ways over it, granting it the same interest in going as he had in coming. To his mind it was old beyond knowing and yet new, timeless and yet momentary, so that watching it as once more it opened before him, old as he was, he was renewed.

As the road began its slant downward and homeward, he let himself into the fall of it gladly, for he was tired now, and it was easier going down than coming up.

'If gravity wants to pitch in and help,' he told Andy, 'I ain't going to be the one to say no.'

Going this way, he was looking directly into the long view of the river valley, and he watched it as his passage opened it and then closed it again. And he watched for Preacher, thinking the old dog too might have got tired and decided to head in, but he neither saw nor heard him.

As it turned out, it was better that Preacher had not returned. If he had, the next thing that happened would not have happened.

Art had come down nearly to the bend where the road turned at last directly toward the house. He was looking down, taking care with his steps over the steepening descent, thinking of something he was not going to be able to remember – 'of something else' – when a large buck with splendid horns stepped into the road not a dozen feet away. Art stood without moving, downwind as he promptly realized, while the buck walked calmly, looking neither left nor right, across the road and disappeared. That he did not hurry and yet instantly was out of sight made his appearance just barely believable.

'I don't know if he ever even seen me,' Art said to Andy. 'He must've been thinking about something else too. But I seen him. I didn't make him up.'

'If you'd been deer hunting he'd have known it,' Andy said. 'He wouldn't have come that close.'

'Probably not. But if I'd had my shotgun I could a played thunder with him.'

'I reckon,' Andy said.

Art, however, had not finished his thought. '*But* if I'd a shot him with a shotgun, he might've gone two miles before he died.'

And so, for the second time that day, Art was glad not to have had a weapon.

He was sorry, though, to have forgot what he had been thinking about before he saw the buck. Nor could he remember, supposing he had counted them, the number of branches of the buck's horns.

'Maybe I never counted,' he said to Andy. 'He had more hatrack than most people got hats.'

The river valley was out of sight behind him now, the creek valley lying fully open ahead of him. Though the light had weakened, he could still see the house, the barns and outbuildings, the swinging bridge over the creek, at the end of nowhere the center of everything, and the day coming to rest upon it.

He knew he would walk on the earth a while yet, and then he would yield back his body to be with the old ones who had come and gone before him, and of this he made no complaint.

Acknowledgments

The stories in this collection were originally published in the following:

'The Hurt Man' *The Hudson Review* vol. 56, no. 3 (autumn 2003)

'Fly Away, Breath' *The Threepenny Review* 113 (spring 2008)

'A Consent' *The Draft Horse Journal*, autumn 1990

'Pray Without Ceasing' *The Southern Review* vol. 28, no 4 (autumn 1992)

'A Half-Pint of Old Darling' *The Draft Horse Journal* vol. 30, no. 2 (summer 1993)

'Down in the Valley Where the Green Grass Grows' *Oxford American* 77 (summer 2012)

'The Solemn Boy' *The Draft Horse Journal*, summer 1994

'Andy Catlett: Early Education' *The Threepenny Review* 117 (spring 2009)

'Stand By Me' *The Atlantic*, August 2008

'Making It Home' Originally published as 'Homecoming' in *The Sewanee Review* vol. 100, no. 1 (winter 1992)

'Mike' *The Sewanee Review*, winter 2005

'The Boundary' and 'That Distant Land' *The Wild Birds* (San Francisco: North Point, 1986)

'The Wild Birds' *Mother Jones* magazine vol. 9, no. 11 (April 1984)

'The Requirement' *Harper's*, March 2007

'Dismemberment' *The Threepenny Review* 142 (summer 2015)

'Fidelity' *Fidelity* (New York: Pantheon 1992)

'At Home' *Orion* magazine

Acknowledgments

The stories have also been published in the following Counterpoint Press US editions:

That Distant Land: The Collected Stories (Berkeley: Counterpoint, 2004): 'The Hurt Man', 'A Consent', 'Pray Without Ceasing', 'A Half-Pint of Old Darling', 'The Solemn Boy', 'Making It Home', 'The Boundary', 'That Distant Land', 'The Wild Birds', 'Fidelity'.

A Place in Time: Twenty Stories of the Port William Membership (Berkeley: Counterpoint, 2012): 'Fly Away, Breath', 'Down in the Valley Where the Green Grass Grows', 'Andy Catlett: Early Education', 'Stand By Me', 'Mike', 'The Requirement', 'At Home'.

ALLEN LANE
an imprint of
PENGUIN BOOKS

Also Published

Malena and Beata Ernman, Svante and Greta Thunberg, *Our House is on Fire: Scenes of a Family and a Planet in Crisis*

Paolo Zellini, *The Mathematics of the Gods and the Algorithms of Men: A Cultural History*

Bari Weiss, *How to Fight Anti-Semitism*

Lucy Jones, *Losing Eden: Why Our Minds Need the Wild*

Brian Greene, *Until the End of Time: Mind, Matter, and Our Search for Meaning in an Evolving Universe*

Anastasia Nesvetailova and Ronen Palan, *Sabotage: The Business of Finance*

Albert Costa, *The Bilingual Brain: And What It Tells Us about the Science of Language*

Stanislas Dehaene, *How We Learn: The New Science of Education and the Brain*

Daniel Susskind, *A World Without Work: Technology, Automation and How We Should Respond*

John Tierney and Roy F. Baumeister, *The Power of Bad: And How to Overcome It*

Greta Thunberg, *No One Is Too Small to Make a Difference: Illustrated Edition*

Glenn Simpson and Peter Fritsch, *Crime in Progress: The Secret History of the Trump-Russia Investigation*

Abhijit V. Banerjee and Esther Duflo, *Good Economics for Hard Times: Better Answers to Our Biggest Problems*

Gaia Vince, *Transcendence: How Humans Evolved through Fire, Language, Beauty and Time*

Roderick Floud, *An Economic History of the English Garden*

Rana Foroohar, *Don't Be Evil: The Case Against Big Tech*

Ivan Krastev and Stephen Holmes, *The Light that Failed: A Reckoning*

Andrew Roberts, *Leadership in War: Lessons from Those Who Made History*

Alexander Watson, *The Fortress: The Great Siege of Przemysl*

Stuart Russell, *Human Compatible: AI and the Problem of Control*

Serhii Plokhy, *Forgotten Bastards of the Eastern Front: An Untold Story of World War II*

Dominic Sandbrook, *Who Dares Wins: Britain, 1979-1982*

Charles Moore, *Margaret Thatcher: The Authorized Biography, Volume Three: Herself Alone*

Thomas Penn, *The Brothers York: An English Tragedy*

David Abulafia, *The Boundless Sea: A Human History of the Oceans*

Anthony Aguirre, *Cosmological Koans: A Journey to the Heart of Physics*

Orlando Figes, *The Europeans: Three Lives and the Making of a Cosmopolitan Culture*

Naomi Klein, *On Fire: The Burning Case for a Green New Deal*

Anne Boyer, *The Undying: A Meditation on Modern Illness*

Benjamin Moser, *Sontag: Her Life*

Daniel Markovits, *The Meritocracy Trap*

Malcolm Gladwell, *Talking to Strangers: What We Should Know about the People We Don't Know*

Peter Hennessy, *Winds of Change: Britain in the Early Sixties*

John Sellars, *Lessons in Stoicism: What Ancient Philosophers Teach Us about How to Live*

Brendan Simms, *Hitler: Only the World Was Enough*

Hassan Damluji, *The Responsible Globalist: What Citizens of the World Can Learn from Nationalism*

Peter Gatrell, *The Unsettling of Europe: The Great Migration, 1945 to the Present*

Justin Marozzi, *Islamic Empires: Fifteen Cities that Define a Civilization*

Bruce Hood, *Possessed: Why We Want More Than We Need*

Susan Neiman, *Learning from the Germans: Confronting Race and the Memory of Evil*

Donald D. Hoffman, *The Case Against Reality: How Evolution Hid the Truth from Our Eyes*

Frank Close, *Trinity: The Treachery and Pursuit of the Most Dangerous Spy in History*

Richard M. Eaton, *India in the Persianate Age: 1000-1765*

Janet L. Nelson, *King and Emperor: A New Life of Charlemagne*

Philip Mansel, *King of the World: The Life of Louis XIV*

Donald Sassoon, *The Anxious Triumph: A Global History of Capitalism, 1860-1914*

Elliot Ackerman, *Places and Names: On War, Revolution and Returning*

Jonathan Aldred, *Licence to be Bad: How Economics Corrupted Us*

Johny Pitts, *Afropean: Notes from Black Europe*

Walt Odets, *Out of the Shadows: Reimagining Gay Men's Lives*

James Lovelock, *Novacene: The Coming Age of Hyperintelligence*

Mark B. Smith, *The Russia Anxiety: And How History Can Resolve It*